KU-414-147

1

NOVEMBER 1949

Peggy Ronoscki finished washing up the pile of dirty coffee cups, used plates and dishes, sighing as she glanced at the clock on the wall of the café kitchen. It was gone six-thirty at night and she'd been on her feet since six that morning. The work at the little seaside café, situated approximately midway on the coast between Lyme Bay and Torquay, which she ran with her husband, Able, was hard and relentless, especially when her hired help, Masie Bennett, didn't turn up to wash the dishes and she had to do them as well as the clearing up after the café closed at a quarter to six in the evening.

'Tired?' Peggy turned at the sound of her husband's voice and smiled. However, weary she felt, her spirits lifted when Able walked into the room. 'I told you not to do it all, Peggy. I would have helped you when I finished wiping the tables and counter.'

'You work hard enough as it is,' Peggy said, her eyes caressing him with the deep love she felt for this man. Able had been a serviceman in the American forces during the last war and he'd lost his left arm just below the elbow. After several attempts to wear the prosthetic arm the hospital had fitted, which rubbed his flesh and gave him pain, Able had given up and managed very well with one arm and his stump. She was always amazed at what he could do but tried to avoid asking him to do things that were difficult for him. 'It's that girl, Able. I think I'm going to have to find someone else.'

'Yes, you must, because I don't want you doing the work of three people,' Able said and moved towards her. His right arm went around her waist and he bent his head to kiss her on the lips. 'You should have been home with the twins two hours ago...'

'It's all right,' Peggy reassured him. 'It's their youth club night and Sandra took them there. I said I'd be back in time to fetch them and I'll drive you home first. Then I'll go around to the club and collect them. I've got nearly an hour before they'll be ready to leave...'

Sandra Brooks was their nearest neighbour to the cottage and had turned out to be a good friend for Peggy and the children since their move to the cottage in Devon. She really didn't know how she would have managed without her.

Peggy did her early-morning cooking at home, leaving her husband to transport it in tins to the café; Able opened up and she joined him after giving the twins their breakfast and dropping them at school. Sandra had quickly realised it was difficult for Peggy to fetch her children after school and had offered to fetch them with her own two if Peggy was delayed. The two women drank coffee in each other's houses and exchanged recipes, inviting one another to lunch or dinner whenever they had time, which wasn't often because they were all busy. Sandra worked a few hours as her husband's secretary when not looking after her children or cleaning house, but she still had more free time than Peggy.

'At least you don't have to cook for us when we get back,' Able said. 'The twins love coming here for their tea even though they often eat the same things as you make them at home...'

'That's kids,' Peggy said fondly, thinking of Fay and Freddie, two very different characters although born only minutes apart.

Now it was November 1949 and they were a few months away from their ninth birthdays, they were eagerly looking forward to Christmas, full of life and fun and often into mischief. Peggy's non-working life mostly consisted of taking her twins to various clubs and events to keep them occupied, but she adored her life. Working every day with Able in their busy café, some twenty-odd miles from the busy seaside town of Torquay, and leaving at about a quarter to four to meet the children and take them home for tea kept her busy and happy, though sometimes she felt the work was a little too much.

'They can choose what they want from the menu and you always let them have an extra slice of apple pie or pancake if they want...'

Sandra often brought her own sons into the café too and gave them their tea. Peggy either refused payment or charged half price if Sandra insisted on paying. It worked for both families and all four children thought it was great, clamouring for Able's pancakes and Peggy's delicious apple pie with cream.

'How can I refuse when I always have double helpings?' Able said with a wicked gleam in his eyes. 'I've always loved your pies, Peggy, especially the apple ones with cream or custard.'

'During the war you were lucky to get either cream or custard,' Peggy said and a shadow passed over her pretty face. Now into her late forties, she still looked youthful – Able told her she didn't seem a day older than when he'd first walked into the pub in Mulberry Lane and fallen head over heels for her. 'At least now we don't go short of most things... apart from sugar. That's still rationed and the Government don't hold out any hope of it coming off just yet, though it's better than it was...'

Harold Wilson had announced the end to clothes rationing to the nation earlier that year and only a few things were now in short supply. Britain was recovering slowly, though the national debt caused by the long war, when the country had been forced to borrow from the Americans to keep going, was crippling.

'You've found ways round it,' Able said, smiling easily. 'You always did, even in the war...'

'You and your friends helped,' Peggy replied fondly, because Able had brought her coffee from his base when it was impossible to buy any in London, also tinned fruit, salmon and sometimes sugar. He had a sweet tooth and liked a couple of spoonsful in his coffee.

'We tried to help in a lot of ways,' Able said and a shadow passed over his face, because a couple of customers had recently cast aspersions on the help given by the Americans, calling it too little too late in loud voices, which made him seethe, even though he swallowed his anger and wouldn't let himself be drawn on the subject. 'Though some folk don't seem to think so...'

Peggy knew more than most just how much help the American people had given them, because Able had been a General's aide much of the time and knew about all the secret deals they'd done to keep Britain going through her darkest hours. Some British people even tended to forget that they'd had help from Canada, Australia, New Zealand and many other commonwealth countries, but many more seemed to blame the Americans, though for what she wasn't sure. Except, that if questioned, they thought that if America had stood with Britain at the start, Hitler would never have dared to do half what he had; perhaps that was right... and yet the help given once committed was invaluable and decisive, bringing the tyrant to his knees.

'They were just ignorant people,' Peggy said now, because she knew Able had been hurt by the rudeness of those particular customers, who weren't regulars but merely touring the coast of Devon. She'd been glad they only visited once. 'You wouldn't get that back home in Mulberry Lane. Our customers were friends there and wouldn't dream of insulting you. We just have to ignore people who don't understand.'

'I know, hon,' Able said, his smile reappearing. 'We've had a good day – clearing three hundred pounds this week so far and we've still got Saturday to come...'

Saturday was one of their busiest days. Peggy had two women to help her in the kitchen with the cooking from six until ten in the morning, after which she went home to be with the twins. They usually played with Sandra's two boys in the garden until Peggy got home, when she took them to the local indoor swimming baths or, if it was too cold for that, they often went to the roller-skating park. It too was an indoor venue and both children were good at it, though Fay was best. She loved skating and wanted to progress to ice-skating, but there were no rinks close enough for Peggy to be able to take her daily and even once a month would be difficult, because they would have to travel into Torquay or Exeter.

Fay had sulked over it on her last birthday when Peggy bought her a new pair of roller skates with smart white leather boots.

'You know I wanted ice skates,' she'd told her mother with a pout.

'I can't manage to take you to an ice rink,' Peggy had replied. 'It would be too far to travel after school, Fay. You like roller-skating and you're good at it, so why change?'

'Because ice skating is in the Olympics and roller skating isn't.'

Peggy had been shocked. Surely Fay's ambition wasn't set on becoming a champion ice skater? For a while in the summer her daughter had been entranced by Gorgeous Gussie Moran and the shocking outfit she'd worn for Wimbledon. Created by Teddy Tinling, it had caused a bit of an uproar and so captured Fay's imagination. Her fascination had faded once the tennis was no longer on the newsreel at the pictures or in the papers.

This latest craze would probably fade as quickly, Peggy imagined. She would never have thought of such a thing when she was a girl. If she got to swim with the school or play netball in the playground, it was as much as she would ever have thought of doing – but Fay was undoubtedly talented and it made Peggy feel guilty that she couldn't spare the time to drive her daughter to the rink in Torquay several times a week.

'What about you, Freddie?' she'd asked Fay's twin. 'Do you want to learn to ice-skate too?'

'No, thank you, Mum,' Freddie had replied with a loving smile. He was so like Able and he made her heart sing every time he smiled. 'I like roller-skating but only for fun – I wouldn't mind some new football boots so I can play in the school team though; mine are nearly worn out...'

'I'd have bought them before if I'd known,' Peggy said, feeling regretful, because Freddie asked for so little. 'Will Christmas do or do you need them now?'

'My old ones will do for now...'

Freddie never demanded or whined if he didn't get his own way.

He'd been born minutes after his sister, but she was the most demanding of the two. Fay had a temper and if thwarted could be difficult, while Freddie had the sweetest nature and never caused his mother a moment's worry.

'I'll see if I can get them sooner,' Peggy said. 'It will mean a smaller present at Christmas, but I'll see you have them in a couple of weeks...' And she had. Fay had pulled a face, but Peggy bought her a pair of red button-up shoes and her smile reappeared.

Money was never really tight these days in the Ronoscki household, but Peggy tried not to spoil the children and she liked to save a bit. Although the café was always busy, it cost money for rent, because they'd never actually bought a place of their own, and it was expensive to keep up to date with all the new coffee machines and replacements they constantly needed.

'We have to keep a shine on the place,' Able had told her when she'd hesitated over buying new crockery to replace sets that were depleted by chips and cracks. 'If we give folk odd china, they will think we're run-down and stop coming. A lot of our customers are youngsters at the weekend and they want a jukebox in the corner. I'll need at least a couple of hundred dollars to get a decent one shipped over from the States, Peggy, and I can't raise that overnight...' Even though he'd lived in England for some years now, Able still thought in dollars rather than pounds and he kept both American holidays as well as British ones. The twins loved it because it meant more treats for them – Peggy might try not to spoil her twins, but Able gave them everything he could. It was surprising, because although he spoiled them, he only had to say no and even Fay stopped plaguing him.

Peggy had raised her eyebrows at him over the jukebox, because in the pub during the war she'd only had to ask one of her older customers to entertain them with a song and Alice would perform one of the old musical hall numbers that were still loved by Londoners. However, the youngsters wanted something different these days. Jitterbugging had begun in the war, brought over by the Americans and developing into the Lindy Hop and the new dances that were all the rage in the dance halls now. Able was on the ball with his ideas, but Peggy hoped he wouldn't raise the cash for that jukebox too soon. They would never have any peace once that was installed.

Weekday mornings they got older people in for lunch or coffee and teas in the afternoon and they knew most of the regulars by name, but in summer there were lots of tourists from the seaside resort of Torquay, who just came in for coffee and a bun or a snack. That was when they made most of their easy profits, a family-friendly café and that's what it was, bringing in mums, dads, kids and grandparents.

'Right, time to go,' Able said and tried the kitchen door, which led out to the small yard at the back. It was locked and secure. They also had a large store out there, where extra stocks of drinks and foodstuffs were kept, but it couldn't be accessed from outside, only from the kitchen. The arrangement served as extra security, because Able knew that thieves considered small businesses like theirs fair game. He sold a few cigarettes and sweets from behind the counter and that sort of thing was popular with sneak thieves, but they were less likely to come in through the front door under the glare of a street lamp. The security was one of the reasons they'd decided on the place. 'Come on, Peggy. Anything else will wait until the morning...'

Peggy's gaze travelled round the large and spotless kitchen, looking for something she might have missed. The rubbish had all been disposed of in the large bin that the council collected twice a week using a side gate. Peggy used the side door to access it and that had double iron bars across it, because Able considered it their weakest link. Yes, she had locked and bolted it. Everything was done and they could go.

'Yes, I know... I just hope Mavis turns up tomorrow...'

'If she doesn't, she's on a week's notice and we'll get someone else,' Able said. 'If we employed an extra waitress, she could help with the washing up if it gets left to you, Peggy...'

Able served most of the customers himself across the counter, with a little help from Peggy who did all the cooking. She started early in the morning, cooking her apple pies, sausage rolls and various pastries. Egg and chips or bacon or other hot snacks were cooked when ordered and sandwiches were made fresh on demand. They also did American-style pancakes with various fillings, which were extremely popular, and omelettes with a mixed salad. Peggy found anything with eggs was popular and thought it might be because for years it had been impossible to get fresh eggs, but now they had a plentiful supply straight from the farm near their home. So, the omelettes, salads, savoury tarts, ham sandwiches and Peggy's apple pie came top of the popularity stakes, closely followed by Able's pancakes, freshly made at the counter. On Saturday mornings, the youngsters queued up to watch him toss them expertly with one hand and he was regularly given a round of applause.

The electric mixer Able had bought was a boon to him for making the batter, which he did himself. Peggy removed the blades regularly, replacing them with spares, and washed them so that they were always fresh and clean. It was Mavis's job to do the washing up, but Peggy helped if she wasn't cooking and she didn't quite trust the girl to change the mixer blades often enough. If she was truthful, she didn't trust Mavis much at all, but the girl had been one of the first to apply and she'd been desperate to get the job, so Peggy had taken her on. She'd had cause to regret it a few times and knew Able was right; they would have to let her go.

April Jenkins was the part-time waitress they employed at their busiest times and to relieve Peggy for a couple of hours in the evening. She also came in for three hours over lunchtime during the week, when Peggy was busy cooking the simple meals that appealed to so many, because the food was always perfectly cooked. Sometimes, Peggy did casseroles, soups and fancier dishes, but they made their money out of the simple food every time. On Saturdays, April worked until four in the afternoon and they had a cook called Mabel who worked from ten to four; the café closing at four thirty. April was reliable and Peggy liked her, but it wasn't easy to find a girl who wanted to earn her living washing up endless dishes. Yes, there were plenty of people who would reply to any advert for staff, but they didn't do things the way Peggy liked. She sometimes thought back to the days when Rose Barton had worked for her at the pub in Mulberry Lane, and how much she'd been able to trust the girl, both in the kitchen and looking after the twins.

Peggy had had lots of friends to help her in the pub. Her first husband Laurie had served in the bar of the Pig & Whistle until the war, when he'd gone off to do something secret. It had been the beginning of the end of their marriage and she'd learned to live without him – but she'd always had friends: Maureen and Anne and Rose and Peggy's own daughter, Janet...

Thinking of her daughter, Peggy frowned. It was nearly a month since she'd seen her and Janet hadn't been feeling well then. She was recovering slowly after an unfortunate miscarriage. Her first child, Maggie, who was now eight years old and the son of her late husband Mike, was thriving, but Janet had lost her present husband's child, Harry, soon after his birth and it had devastated them both. Janet had come to stay with Peggy for three months earlier that year to get over it and Peggy had feared that her daughter was in danger of splitting from her husband, but then Janet had pulled herself together and gone home to Ryan.

Things hadn't been easy for the two of them; Peggy had read between the lines, seeing the signs of tension both in Ryan and Janet. Her daughter was doing her best, but the loss of yet another baby had knocked her sideways and, unfortunately, she'd tended to take it out on her husband. Ryan had been patient and kind, but men wouldn't put up with a short-tempered, irritable wife forever. Peggy had tried to give Janet advice, but she'd gone into herself and rejected all help.

'It's all right for you,' she'd said accusingly. 'You don't lose everyone you love...'

She was referring to the husband, Mike, she'd lost during the war. It had been a terrible time for Janet and Peggy had been so pleased to see her married to Ryan. She'd thought they had a good marriage, and at first Janet had been truly happy, but since the loss of her son and then the miscarriage, it seemed the couple was suffering.

Peggy would have to find time to pop and see Janet again soon. It was an hour-and-a-half drive and she didn't do it as often as she should – perhaps because Janet wasn't always welcoming. She'd made her own friends and preferred to spend time with them these days, shutting out her mother's concern for her – just as she had when Mike died. And there was also Pip, Peggy's son, and his family to think of.

Pip had taken over the lease of the pub when she'd left London, because he was unable to continue flying as a pilot and although he'd brought his family to her the previous summer, she hadn't been back to London in a while. Pip didn't help out in the pub much, because he'd become a designer and now worked for a large company, working mostly from his home and commuting when it was necessary to meet his employers and other members of the design team. His wife, Sheila, ran the Pig & Whistle with help from regular staff and friends, particularly Maureen, and that was in addition to them running the little tea shop in the afternoons, where she also sold cakes over the counter. Peggy thought poor Sheila must be as busy as she was and worried that she might be overdoing things, but whenever she telephoned, her daughter-in-law was always positive. It was Janet who worried her most...

Sighing, Peggy put her worries from her mind as she drove home. Next month it would be Christmas and she could ask Janet whether she wanted to bring her family here or preferred her, Able, and the twins to go there to her lovely house in the country.

2

MULBERRY LANE, LONDON

'Do you fancy going to the flicks this weekend?' Gordon Hart said, making his wife, Maureen, look at him in surprise.

'Why, what's on that you'd like to see?'

'I don't know – a thriller or something you fancy. I'd just like to take my wife out.'

Maureen smiled, pleased at his thoughtfulness. 'Yes, I think we could go – if Shirley doesn't have any plans to go out with her friends.'

Shirley seldom went out with her friends, unless it was a school function or, sometimes on a Friday night, she went to first-aid classes at night school. Shirley wanted to be a doctor, which involved hard work and meant she had her nose in a medical book most of the time, studying.

'Rose Barton would keep an eye on the kids if Shirley doesn't want to...'

'Yes, all right. I like a good mystery and I think there's a Hitchcock film on at the Regal...'

Maureen Hart looked at her husband thoughtfully. He was looking a bit tired and she worried about him, even though she knew that he was completely recovered from the serious leg wound he'd received during the war. Gordon still had a bit of a limp, but he swore it didn't pain him now. Maureen wasn't sure if he always told her the truth on that score, because he would never worry her if he could help it. She had her children to look after and life had blessed them. Besides, their daughter Shirley – Maureen's stepdaughter but loved as much as any of her own children – they had little Gordon and Matthew, called Matty by all his adoring family and spoiled silly by Shirley. Matty was now three and Gordy would be eight next year. Had her darling little Robin lived, he would have been nine in March 1950...

Robin had been the child of a man Maureen had had an affair with when she was nursing. He'd come and gone in her life a few times, but when she discovered he'd cheated on her with a young nurse while also sleeping with her, Maureen had broken with him. Rory had caused her trouble a few times, refusing to take no for an answer even after she married Gordon, but he was dead now. He had blamed her for Robin's death, claiming she'd neglected his son. It was so far from the truth, it was ridiculous, but he'd been convinced she'd done it to punish him.

Maureen blinked hard to keep the tears away. Losing a child you adored was so painful and after all these years she still hadn't quite got over it. Most of the time, she was able to push the memory of her darling son's death to the back of her mind, but then something would bring it back and the tears would hover – however, she mustn't give way to self-pity. She had three lovely children and she was usually too busy to dwell on the past.

The tea shop she ran with Sheila, Pip Ashley's wife, was booming and they could hardly keep up with the trade. Rose Barton helped out as much as she could, but she had two children and that limited her hours. Maureen hadn't seen much of Anne Ross for years now. She'd been a regular visitor to the pub Peggy used to run, helping behind the bar in her spare time until her husband came home after the war and she'd at last given birth to her much-wanted child. Anne was now teaching in Cambridgeshire with her family and kept in touch, sending cards and gifts at Christmas and the occasional letter or phone call, but she seldom visited; although, in her last phone call, Peggy had told Maureen that Anne and Kirk had been down to visit them in the summer. They'd stayed in the nearby resort of Torquay and visited Peggy at home and at the café. Anne had told Maureen how much she'd enjoyed visiting with Peggy when she rang, but she still hadn't made time to come up to London other than once for Christmas, though she kept promising she would one day soon.

'You're not worried about the business, are you?' Maureen asked because her husband still looked a bit down. He ran the grocers on the corner, which had belonged to her family and was now theirs; Maureen had transferred the deeds into their joint names, because she thought it was only fair. She'd changed the name to Harts, too. Gordon worked hard there and deserved to be her partner, but he bore all the responsibility himself, determined to make a success of it for her and their children and she understood why he was anxious. Back in September, the pound had been devalued and that had led to rises in the price of food – the fourpence-ha'penny loaf had been raised to sixpence and for a week or two some of their customers had cut back on their shopping.

'No, we're still doing well,' Gordon told her now. 'Our customers are loyal, Maureen. They might cut back on their shopping if they have to, but they don't stop coming...' He smiled at her. 'I suppose they still remember we treated them right in the war...' Some shop-keepers had inflated their prices when food was short, but Maureen had always kept her prices as low as she could.

Sighing, Maureen did something she'd promised Gordon she wouldn't and that was to let herself wish they could go back to the days when Peggy lived just around the corner at the Pig & Whistle and she could visit with her every day. Yes, Sheila was a good friend; yes, Maureen had a wonderful family, but she did miss Peggy. They phoned each other at least twice a week and sent cards, presents and letters, but it wasn't like being able to hug each other when things got you down.

Gordon had taken Maureen down to Devon for a visit every year since Peggy had departed to run her café in the country. The week had flown by each time and was never enough for Maureen. She knew that annoyed Gordon a bit, because he thought that she should be satisfied with all she had – and she knew he was right. They had a good business; it was a large general shop and sold everything from newspapers and magazines to knitting wools and, of course, all the foodstuffs families needed, as well as cigarettes and sweets. Gordon had recently applied for a licence to sell alcohol. Maureen had been unsure about that, because Sheila and Pip Ashley ran the pub, but Sheila had assured her that it wouldn't affect her business.

'We sell alcohol to be consumed on the premises,' she'd told Maureen. 'We also sell cigarettes – but that doesn't affect your trade. If Gordon sells some bottles of sherry and whisky, it won't bother us much, because we sell ours over the bar...'

'As long as you don't feel we're treading on your toes,' Maureen had said. 'I should hate to do that, Sheila...'

'You've got a really good shop there,' Sheila had assured her. 'People round here like it that you sell such a variety. It means they don't have to walk far or catch a bus to buy what they want – and it's a different business. You sell biscuits and some cakes in boxes and we sell them in the café on the plate or in a paper bag...'

'Yes, I know – that's what Gordon says...' Maureen had replied. She still hadn't felt quite easy about the alcohol, but she'd put it out of her mind now, because Pip had told her it meant nothing to him.

'I earn my living designing aeroplanes,' he'd told her with a contented look. 'I only keep the pub going because Sheila says we have to...' He shrugged. 'She says it would upset Mum if we let it go, because she let us take over the lease for nothing when she moved – and it wouldn't be popular with folk in Mulberry Lane if new people took over...'

'She's right,' Maureen had replied. 'Alice was saying the other day that she misses Peggy too much and I think a lot of other people would feel the same...'

'Sheila has asked Mum to come up for Christmas for the past three years, but she was too busy and then Janet was ill and she felt she had to be with her...' Pip had frowned. 'I think I'm going to insist they come this year...'

'Oh yes, please do,' Maureen had said and squeezed his arm. 'I never see enough of her. I know I was there in July, but it's nearly the end of November now and it seems ages since she came here...'

'A couple of years, I think. We were down there in August – but we find it difficult to get people to look after the pub... I know you manage the tea shop when we go for a holiday, Maureen, but we can't expect you to do the pub as well. Mum said they're going to close the café for three weeks over Christmas and the New Year this time – she says they both need a rest and I think she'll only get that if she comes here...'

'Pip, if you can pull that one off, I'll kiss you,' Maureen had said and he'd laughed.

'In that case, I'll make sure she comes,' he'd promised. 'I shall keep you to that – a kiss under the mistletoe...'

'Thanks,' Maureen had laughed. 'Seriously, do make her come to you. I'm sure she works far too hard down there...'

'I was quite serious,' he'd said and grinned. 'I'll get her here by hook or crook...'

Maureen had been thoughtful afterwards. When Pip had lost some of his sight in one eye and been told his career as a pilot was finished towards the end of the war, he'd felt his life was over and it had taken Sheila's illness during her pregnancy to bring him out of himself. For a while he'd kept his drawings to himself as if fearing his designs wouldn't be good enough, but then he'd finally shown them to someone and been given a job with De Havilland, starting out as a junior and progressing to become one of their senior men.

It was an important job, because although the war with Germany was over, the troubles abroad continued. Konrad Adenauer had won the German elections and the blockade was over so that food could be taken into cities that had been on the brink of starving, but in other countries there was still unrest – as in China with Shanghai falling in May to Mao Tse-tung's People's Liberation Army. Maureen knew nothing of politics in the Middle East, but she knew the unrest made for unease in the world and the fear of another terrible war. No one wanted that after the years of conflict with Germany. What with that and the hysteria in America over the communists, it didn't exactly inspire confidence in a lasting peace.

Maureen's thoughts returned to Pip. She knew that he was now earning enough not to bother with the takings of the pub and he seldom, if ever, worked behind the bar. Sheila ran it with a full-time barman, a couple of part-time girls, and Rose gave a hand when she could. Maureen didn't offer these days. She had her hands full with the tea shop, her children and husband.

Shirley, her stepdaughter, was a wonderful help, with both the younger children and housework. Maureen often thought what a good wife she would make, but Gordon's daughter by his first wife was set on becoming a doctor. At sixteen years of age, she was a lovely girl and almost ready to take her final exams before she went off to college at the end of the next year, when she would be nearly eighteen.

Maureen reflected that she would miss her daughter very much when she left for medical school. Shirley was the one who often looked after her half-brothers to give Maureen time for a little relaxation; they'd never needed to look for a babysitter if they wanted to go to the pictures or a special meal out, because Shirley was always at home studying. Her boyfriend was already away at medical school, close now to taking his third-year exams, and Shirley couldn't wait to join him. Richard Kent had been Shirley's special friend for years now – since the terrible time when Robin and Richard's little sister had both died from a severe case of chicken pox. Maureen wasn't sure whether they were committed to each other as more than friends and she didn't ask. Shirley wrote to him regularly and his letters came twice a week like clockwork. Shirley was always pleased to get them, but she'd never mentioned the words marriage or love and talked endlessly of when she went to medical school and became a GP.

'I'm going to look for a job near you, Mum,' she'd told Maureen. 'I want to be based in London and visit my family all the time – I might even be able to live with you and Dad and Gordy and darling Matty for a while...'

'One day you might get married,' Maureen had suggested.

Shirley had looked serious and then nodded. 'Yes, I might,' she'd agreed, 'but not for ages, Mum. I want to qualify and then I have to make it worthwhile – to pay everyone back for their faith in me...'

'Of course, you want to do your job, but it isn't always necessary to give up your job when you marry.'

Shirley had given her a considering glance. 'I know you've always managed it, Mum, but a lot of women don't – their husbands think they should be at home looking after the house and family...'

'Yes, I know,' Maureen had agreed. 'But if a man loves you, he'll see that you need to do what you want. Marriage, children and a husband are something we all want if we're honest – but why shouldn't we work as well? We've proved we can do it. Life has moved on since the turn of the century and women are a necessary part of the workplace these days. We'd have gone under in the war in Britain, if the women hadn't rolled up their sleeves and done their bit.'

'I know you think so,' Shirley had agreed, 'but not everyone does. I hear what some folk say about you working – and I think sometimes Dad thinks it too...'

'Your father has never mentioned it to me...' Maureen had frowned. She hadn't consulted her husband when she took a half-share in Sheila's business in the café. She hadn't thought he would mind. After all, it brought extra money in and didn't interfere with Maureen's care of her home and children. She took Gordy to school and then went to help Sheila with the cooking, her youngest son playing in the playpen Peggy's twins had once used. Sheila only had one child, because the doctors had advised her not to have more for her health's sake. Her son was at junior school, collected and delivered by Rose Barton when she took her two to school. After that, Maureen took Matty home with her and did her own housework before preparing a light lunch for Gordon and the children. In the afternoons, she did two hours in the café serving delicious cakes and cups of tea and was home in time to prepare their evening meal. Shirley brought Gordy home from school and gave him his tea; ironing was often done in the evenings.

It was a full day, but Maureen made certain she took holidays, usually when one of the kids had something special on. Quite a few of the local kids went to the same school and played in the lanes afterwards. Maureen never worried if Gordy was a bit late in for his tea, because she knew he had lots of friends to play with. Sheila's son was only a year or so younger and Rose's daughter was not much different and so they teamed up with others from the lanes and there was a youth club they went to sometimes for an hour or so, and the school held sports and games on Saturday mornings. Maureen always managed to have Saturday afternoon off and she took her children to various sporting events or to a matinee at the pictures if the film was suitable, and sometimes in the summer on a trip to Southend. They went with her when she visited Peggy, of course, but that was a long journey and they'd visited Southend in their father's car on several Sundays the previous summer. They loved playing the slot machines on the pier, building sandcastles on the beach and eating fish and chips from a newspaper packet.

Shirley liked visiting museums and Gordon had taken her to visit some that stayed open on Sundays. Maureen never bothered with such visits, staying home to look after her other children or cook a delicious roast for when Shirley and Gordon got back.

Gordon had settled down to read the evening paper and listen to music on the wireless so Maureen decided she would write to Peggy that evening and ask her if she was coming to visit Sheila and Pip at Christmas. It would be lovely if Peggy had several days at the pub over the festive season – almost like old times...

She did her usual chores that evening, noting that Shirley was looking a little quiet, but not feeling concerned enough to ask her what was wrong. Her daughter usually came to her with any problems, so this was probably just a school thing.

Sighing, she drew her pad of lined notepaper to her and used the special fountain pen Gordon had bought her on her birthday.

'You're always writing letters,' he'd told her. 'You might as well have a good pen...'

Maureen thought carefully before she began. Peggy always had lots of excuses for putting her daughter first, but it was a bit unfair. Sheila and Pip could do with a family visit and Peggy needed a little prodding in that direction...

Finishing her letter, she saw it was nearly time for their evening cocoa. Shirley normally offered to make it if Maureen was busy, but she seemed absorbed in the latest letter to be delivered from Eastbourne, which was near where Richard was doing his final two years of study...

* * *

Shirley frowned over the letter she had received. Richard was coming home for five days at Christmas and said he hoped to see her then but had a lot of work to do for his exams.

It seems ages since I saw you, Shirley. I miss talking to you and letters aren't quite the same, are they? Still, I've got an idea for the long summer holiday – if you can get your father to agree. I've been planning it for a while, but I'll tell you at Christmas...

Shirley felt a bit let down. She'd thought they would have at least two weeks together at Christmas and she'd lined up several trips to museums and also some good films she'd thought Richard would like. It was too cold to wander the streets at this time of the year and sitting in cafés wasn't her idea of fun, though it was one way to keep warm and be together.

They couldn't go to Richard's home often; his mother didn't like Shirley much, because, for some reason, she'd blamed her when Richard's sister died of chicken pox. Mrs Kent thought her little girl had caught it from him being in contact with Robin – and she hated it that her son had chosen to be a doctor and not go to work straight out of school. However, Richard's father had encouraged him and provided him with some of the money he needed, though he was working part-time in a bar to fund his life at medical school. Unlike Mrs Kent, Shirley's mother would have let them have the front room to sit and talk by a fire, but her father had a habit of walking in on them and asking a lot of questions. So, they visited art galleries and museums and went to the pictures, where they could sit and hold hands in the warm.

Shirley smiled as she finished her latest letter. Richard was full of what he was doing, of the friends he'd made and of the way some of them got drunk at night and played lots of pranks on each other. Shirley thought his life sounded like fun, even though he always ended his letter by saying how much he wished she was there with him at his school and hoping she would pass her exams and go to the same place, though by the time she got there he would probably be close to taking his finals and moving on.

A sigh left her because when she arrived at the school, Richard would probably be working full-time as a junior doctor in a hospital and there was no telling where that would be. He might have to go anywhere to get a post – perhaps back to London, while she was in Eastbourne. It was a pity he was nearly four years older. If she'd been that bit closer in age, they could have done their training together... Although Richard had always behaved as if she were nearer his age, looking out for her when she was in senior school until he'd left for college.

Shirley was thoughtful. Their relationship was based on friendship and caring. Shirley had comforted him when his mother blamed him for bringing home the disease that killed his sister, the same illness she'd lost her darling brother Robin to. Shirley had believed she was responsible for Robin's death until Richard told her about his own loss. Her beloved gran had tried to tell her it wasn't her fault and that Robin had caught the disease from one of the neighbour's children, but Shirley had seen her mother's grief and blamed herself. They'd all been helpless to save their families and that was one of the reasons why Shirley wanted so badly to become a doctor – so that perhaps she could save children and stop their loved ones feeling the way she and Mum had...

Shirley remembered that time as filled with grief – first Robin and then, a few months later, Gran. She hated people dying and longed to make them well again. Being a doctor was important to her and Richard understood that – he knew they couldn't be more than friends until they'd both passed their exams and she sometimes wondered if that was asking too much of him. He was, after all, that bit older and must meet lots of pretty girls at medical school and in the bar where he worked some nights.

Richard had mentioned a girl named Katie. She also worked in the bar, serving drinks. Her boyfriend was in the Army and, according to Richard, his new friend was hoping to become engaged at Christmas.

Katie says Ricky asked her before he left for Cyprus. She's hoping he'll be home for Christmas and give her a ring – and then she'll be off to the sun and a new life with him. It sounds wonderful doesn't it... maybe I should've been in the Army...

Now what did that mean? Shirley wondered. Was he thinking that if he was in the Army and able to offer married quarters in Cyprus, Katie might have been interested in him? Was he interested in her as more than a friend?

Shirley felt a shard of jealousy pierce her like a piece of broken glass. She'd never given a thought to Richard's girlfriends before, if he'd had any, she'd never asked him, and was content to just be friends – but now she couldn't help feeling jealous and a bit angry too. Richard was hers – wasn't he?

It was only friendship for now, because she was not quite seventeen and too young to be courting, but they were so close in thought and laughter and the unspoken understanding between them was that one day it would be more... she'd always anticipated that and she believed he had too.

3

Leaving the doctor's surgery, Rose Barton bent to pick up her toddler. Just under two years old, Jackie was tiny compared to his elder sister, but despite his size he looked like his father and grandfather. Tom and Jack Barton were alike in many ways – honest, hardworking, direct men who lived by the rules and didn't fear calling a spade a spade. Tom didn't often see Jack these days as his father lived abroad much of the time and only visited, mostly around Christmas or in the summer, with the woman he'd met and married at the end of the war. Jack seemed satisfied with his life as a regular in the Army, because it was a better job than he'd found in civilian life and took him and his wife abroad. Tom was fond of him and always pleased when he came back to the lane for a while; Rose loved him too, because he'd been kind to her when she needed help after Jimmy died. She'd been carrying Jimmy's baby and feeling lost and lonely, but Jack, Peggy and Maureen had all stood by her, seeing her through the period of her life when she hadn't cared what happened to her.

Jackie had messed himself again and Rose's nose wrinkled. He had what Tom called the runs at the moment and it meant Rose was forever washing his clothes. For some reason, Jackie had a bit of a weak tummy, where her elder child was as tough as they come. Her daughter was Jimmy's child, of course. Tom didn't make any difference between the children, but Rose couldn't bring herself to love her daughter Jenny as much as she ought. That was strange, because she'd loved Jimmy very much, but, in a roundabout way, she blamed Jenny for Jimmy letting her down, though it could never have been her fault. Rose tried not to discriminate between the two but couldn't help herself. Nor could she help being angry with Jimmy, even though he'd died a hero and been awarded a medal posthumously. If he'd truly cared for her, he would never have volunteered for that suicide mission...

Sighing, Rose made an effort to banish the memory to the tiny corner of her subconscious where it usually dwelled. She shouldn't let herself think about what might have been. Tom was a wonderful husband and she loved him – really, she did. Yet, at the back of her mind, Rose knew there was a tiny niggle of doubt. Had she not just given birth to her daughter when Tom returned from the Army and asked her to wed him might she have refused? He'd made the idea sound so attractive and she'd always liked Tom. Sometimes, when they made love, she knew that he was kinder and more generous in every way than Jimmy had ever been, but then, when she was least expecting it, the doubts crept back in.

What would her life have been like had Jimmy returned a hero? What if she hadn't got pregnant just before he was killed and she'd been free to just walk away and make a new life? Had she settled for marriage with Tom simply because he was there, loved her and wanted to look after both her and the child?

Rose wasn't sure and she hated herself for her doubts. Tom worked all hours to make a good living and he was undoubtedly a good provider. There were times when she was sure she loved him and had done the right thing, and others when she wished Jimmy would come striding down the lane to claim her.

It was so ridiculous to long for something that could never happen! Too many years had passed for the news of his death to have been a mistake. It had happened during that terrible war and some men had returned long after they were reported dead, but Jimmy was never going to be one of them. Besides, Rose knew she was lucky to have a good man. Plenty of women had terrible husbands and lived wretched lives. So why couldn't she be content?

'Rose...' Hearing Maureen calling to her from the end of the street, Rose waited, turning to greet her as she came hurrying up. Maureen and her husband owned the grocer's shop on the corner and since the end of the war it had become busier and busier, because a lot of people made it their local these days. 'How are you?'

'I'm fine,' Rose said cheerfully, hiding her inner doubts and anxiety. 'Except, poor Jackie has the runs. I've just fetched some medicine for him, so hopefully it will clear up now...'

'I expect it will,' Maureen said reassuringly. 'Children go through phases when they're little. Upset tummies and sickness can be awful for a few days and then over in an instant, at least I've found it so. Did you take him to the doctor?'

'Yes, but I saw a nurse. She prescribed something, so I went to the chemist on my way home.' She showed Maureen the milky white liquid in the thick glass bottle and Maureen nodded.

'Yes, that's a soothing mixture and I give my children a spoonful if it's just an upset tummy and a bit of looseness, but if Jackie gets hot or a rash develops take him straight to the doctor, Rose. It's always best...'

Rose nodded her agreement. 'Yes, I shall,' she said. 'I've let Sheila know I'm not available for a couple of days. I've had extra washing and I need to be around for Jackie. Tom works hard and he doesn't need to cope with a crying child when he gets home.'

'No, I agree.' Maureen smiled ruefully. 'We can only do what we can, Rose. Children are up and down at the best of times, but we wouldn't be without them.'

'No, I suppose not,' Rose said and smothered a sigh. 'I'm thinking of taking Jackie to a nursery school for a couple of hours in the mornings next year. I suppose I shall have more time to myself then. At the moment he follows me about the house and wants to help all the time, but he gets in the way...'

'Bless him.' Maureen laughed. 'Gordy was just the same until he started school and then he was suddenly independent and more interested in his dad than me...'

'Jenny adores Tom, she always has,' Rose replied. 'He has been wonderful with her, Maureen. He couldn't have been better if...' She bit back the words, though she had no need to because Maureen knew the truth about Jenny's birth. However, they hadn't told Jenny, though Rose agonised over the decision to withhold the truth because she knew that it was likely someone could discover their secret, and another child might tell Jenny that Tom wasn't her real daddy. Rose had asked him if he wanted her told the truth, but Tom was dead against it.

'She is my daughter in every way but one,' he'd said and there was a hurt look in his eyes that made Rose feel like hell. 'If it happens, Rose, I'll just tell her whoever said it is jealous and that I am her daddy.'

Rose had let him have his way. She was grateful for the manner in which he showered love on her and the children and would never willingly hurt him.

'Are you coming to the church bazaar on Friday afternoon?' Maureen asked, interrupting her thoughts. 'I gave them some of Gran's old things when they came collecting – if I don't see anything else, I'll buy her glass dressing table pots back again...'

'Oh, I love the church sales,' Rose said. 'I've found lots of bargains there. Last time, I bought a set of silver spoons for a shilling!' She made a wry face. 'Not sure I can go, though – unless Jackie is better...'

'I'm sure he will be,' Maureen said, then: 'those spoons were a bargain; I love a bit of silver to use for special occasions. I know it needs cleaning, but Gordon bought me a beautiful tea set for our wedding anniversary and I enjoy keeping it bright and clean.'

'Have you used it?'

'Yes, on Sundays, and when I have guests...' Maureen hesitated. 'Speaking of which, I've written to Peggy asking her if she can come up to town this Christmas. I know how busy she is, but it would be lovely to see her here – and she has so many friends who ask after her.'

'All the time,' Rose agreed. 'I like Peggy. She was good to me when I first arrived in London. If she hadn't given me a job, I might not be here now.'

They chatted for a few minutes and then Maureen walked off in the direction of the pub.

Rose took Jackie home to the small terrace house they rented across the road from Tom's office and workshop. She went straight upstairs to change her son, because a dirty nappy could cause a sore bottom and she was a good mother, even if she had a few failings as a wife.

Rose thought about her marriage. She couldn't grumble really, because she was better off than many wives in the lanes. Tom always gave her money for whatever she needed for the housekeeping and the children, and Rose was able to spend the few pounds she earned with her part-time work on whatever she wanted. He also spent time and money on making their home nice. At first, they'd lived over the office, but then he'd decided they needed a house and when one had come up for rent, he'd applied and taken it on.

'I suppose I might just manage to buy a house,' he'd told Rose when they moved into their rented property. He'd decorated and spruced it up for her and she was content enough living there. 'I want to wait a bit, though, because if anything happened to affect trade, I might not be able to afford to repay the loan...'

'This is fine for me, Tom,' Rose had assured him. She'd been feeling content that day and she did like her house. Tom had made it really smart for them and she appreciated what he did. Even though at times the doubts came to her mind, she had to be grateful for what she had now.

It took her a few minutes to clean Jackie up, dress him in fresh things and give him some of the medicine. He cried until she'd finished and then laughed up at her from his playpen. He looked better lying on his blanket playing with a toy car and Rose knew that once he was over the upset tummy, he would soon be out of nappies altogether, running everywhere and getting into mischief. He'd taken a little longer to train to the potty than Jenny, but until he got the runs he had nearly been there. Rose was pretty sure it was just a case of an upset tummy and not something worse. He was already looking better after just one dose of his medicine. The nurse had told her he might. So, it wasn't the measles or chicken pox and she could stop worrying, just as the nurse had told her.

'Sometimes you need a few doses to settle them down, but others are soon over the worst,' she'd said. Rose hadn't believed her, but now she saw that she'd known what she was talking about.

Perhaps she would be able to go to the church sale on Friday after all.

* * *

Tom entered the house at a quarter to six and heard the sound of Jenny crying. In the background was the hit comedy radio show from Richard Murdoch and Kenneth Horne, *Much Binding in the Marsh*, but the child's crying drowned out the sound of the witty jokes. Rose must be trying to get Jenny to bed, and if he knew his Jenny, she wouldn't go quietly, not if her daddy hadn't been home to kiss her and wish her sweet dreams. Nearly five years old and with a will of her own, she wasn't an easy child to control and sometimes got over-tired at her preparatory school, but he adored her whatever she did.

As he went into the kitchen, Tom saw Jenny was in one of her tantrums. She was stamping her feet and pulling at her mother's skirts as Rose attempted to wash her face and hands with a wet flannel.

'No! Don't want to go,' Jenny screamed and then caught sight of Tom. Giving a shriek of delight, she avoided her mother's clutches and rushed at him, clinging to his legs and sobbing. 'Daddy...'

'Yes, Daddy is home,' Tom said and bent down to sweep her up in his arms. He smiled and kissed her wet cheeks and, as if by magic, the tears stopped and she flung her arms about his neck, her wet jam-sticky mouth kissing his face. 'What is wrong with my little princess?' His eyes moved to Rose over her head and she shook hers at him.

'I was just trying to get her to bed,' Rose said. 'She didn't want her face washed and she wouldn't let me undress her...'

'Shall Daddy take you up and then Mummy can undress you?'

Jenny's head went up and down in agreement and peace was restored. Tom laughed and tickled her, delighting in the sound of her laughter as she was carried up to her bedroom and tossed high in the air before being caught safely in his strong arms.

'She'll be sick,' Rose warned, but Tom ignored the warning. Rose always thought he was too playful with his children, but they loved to be tossed and caught and he would never let them fall; never do anything that would harm them, because he adored them both, equally. His little prince and princess! Tom was determined that if hard work could do it, he would build them a kingdom – or at least make enough money so that his family would have all the things that he wanted to give them. All the things he and his brother had never had...

For a moment he recalled his younger brother's tragic death on a bomb site in the early days of the war and a shadow passed across his heart, but it soon was forgotten as Jenny planted a sticky kiss on his cheek.

Jenny allowed her mother to undress her and gave her a kiss on the cheek. Tom wasn't sure she would have done it if he hadn't directed it, but she obeyed willingly enough.

When he'd told her one of her favourite fairy stories about a beautiful princess in a tower being rescued by a prince, she slipped into a peaceful sleep and Tom left her lying there, looking every bit the perfect angel – which he knew she often wasn't. Jenny played her mother up and Rose got cross and then Jenny started crying and screaming. He paused to look at her for a moment before going back downstairs.

Rose was making a pot of tea when he reached the kitchen. She looked a bit drained and he wondered if Jackie had been worse, but when he asked, she smiled and looked happier.

'No, he's much better, sleeping like a log,' she said. 'The medicine they gave me has worked wonders. That's the beauty of the Health Service – a few years back we'd probably have gone to the chemist and bought the wrong thing. We're so lucky it's all free now.'

'I'd pay for a doctor anyway,' Tom told her.

Rose nodded, but her lovely smile was missing. 'Yes, that is one good thing this Government has done, but I wish they would end sugar rationing.'

'You and millions of others,' Tom quipped, laughing. 'I know it gets tedious, but we're all much better off than we were in the war.' He smiled at the memory of his brief but heroic time in the war.

'I know.' Rose laughed suddenly. 'Take no notice of me, Tom. I think I must be tired. I've been on the go with Jackie and anxious...'

'I know,' Tom murmured, moving towards her and taking her into his arms. He kissed her hair, inhaling the wonderful scent of her. His love for Rose just seemed to get stronger. 'I wish I could wave a magic wand and give you all the things you deserve, Rose. One day we'll have a lovely new house in the suburbs and go on long holidays to the sea. We'll have all of it, you'll see...'

'Oh, Tom,' Rose cried and hugged him. 'I do love you – and it's not because of the house or holidays at the sea. You give me so much already. I love you because you're kind and generous.'

Tom held her closer, his lips moving against her neck. His love had never wavered, but he sometimes wondered if he'd pushed Rose into marriage. She wasn't always happy, he knew. Sometimes he thought it was just tiredness. She helped him with his accounts, worked a few hours for Sheila in the tea shop and the previous week she'd done a two-hour stint in the bar one evening and that was on top of caring for their children. He would have forbidden her to work, except that he knew she enjoyed it. It was a way for her to meet friends and earn some pocket money and Tom wasn't selfish enough to insist she stayed home and looked after him and the children the whole time.

'If you're tired, Rose, you don't need to work so often...' he suggested mildly.

'I know. I've told Sheila I shan't be in for a couple of days, but I love my work, Tom. I talk to people I know and if I stayed home all day, I should get bored.'

'Yes, I understand. Besides, Alice likes the couple of shillings you give her for babysitting and I know she can do with it.'

Their friend and neighbour had had to give up taking in lodgers because it had got too much for her. She was well over seventy now and showing her age. Tom was very fond of Alice, who had given him a bed in her home when he'd needed it and he worried that she was struggling to manage. He would have given her money, but he knew she would refuse, so he took her some fish and chips once a week and bought her a bit of shopping from Maureen's now and then. She always wanted to pay him, but he pretended to be in a hurry and somehow it was forgotten. If Peggy had been here, she would have taken food over to Alice several times a week, but Sheila didn't realise and Tom couldn't tell her to do it, but he knew that Maureen took Alice a casserole sometimes so perhaps she would be all right.

'You know I love you,' he told Rose. 'Why don't you treat yourself to a new dress or some good shoes, love?' He took a five-pound note from his pocket. 'I got paid for a job today – here take this and spend it on yourself.'

'I don't need the money, Tom,' Rose said, hesitating to accept.

'No, but you work hard and I want you to have it,' he said. 'I shall expect to see something nice, so don't spend it all on the children...'

'I won't,' Rose promised and hugged him. 'Thanks, Tom. You spoil me. I've got lamb chops for supper – is that all right?'

'One of my favourites,' he said, 'and if that is your mint sauce I can smell, I'm in heaven...'

4

'Oh – well, if Ryan is taking you all on holiday to Scotland for Christmas then I can't push you to come to us,' Peggy said, trying hard not to let her disappointment show in her voice. 'It sounds lovely – have a wonderful time, all of you...'

'I know you wanted us to come to you, Mum,' Janet said contritely, 'but we do need this holiday – you know how hard it has been for us these past months.'

'Yes, I do,' Peggy replied, her voice dropping to a sympathetic murmur. 'I'm sorry for what happened to you, love, but you're still young enough to have another baby.'

'No, Mum, I've made up my mind,' Janet said and the hardness in her tone made her mother wince. 'I've told Ryan I'm not prepared to go through that again. It isn't just that it makes me feel so ill for weeks afterwards, I can't stand any more pain and disappointment. I just want a quiet, peaceful life...'

'I understand perfectly. After all, you've got Maggie. I know Ryan thinks the world of her and he loves you, Janet.'

'Does he?' Janet's voice carried uncertainty and Peggy wished that she was with her daughter. Janet needed a hug, and perhaps a little shake, but you couldn't do that over the phone. 'He was the one who pushed for another baby after we lost Harry. He so much wants a son and I can't give that to him...' She caught back a sob. 'I feel so useless and worthless.'

Peggy could hear the tears in her voice and the pain caught at her chest. 'Shall I drive down this Sunday?'

'No, don't,' Janet said hastily. 'Ryan has invited some of his work friends to lunch and if you came, he'd know I'd been crying down the phone to you. He thinks I should tell him if I have a problem, not come running to you...'

'That's a bit unfair of him,' Peggy retorted, a note of anger in her own voice. 'You should be able to talk to your mother and your friends.'

'Ryan hates me discussing our problems with other people. He says it is private and I shouldn't need to tell anyone else.'

'It sounds to me as if your husband needs a good talkin' to,' Peggy's reprimand came out more sharply than she intended. 'I'll put him straight if you like?'

'No!' Janet sounded wary. 'He would be furious with me for going behind his back, Mum.'

'Is he becoming a bully?'

'No – it isn't like that,' Janet said. 'I can't explain, Mum – he's so good with Maggie and he gives me everything but... he doesn't think I should tell anyone our business. He says it should stay between him and me.'

'I agree to a certain extent.' Peggy nodded to herself. 'Some things are private, but others – well, it helps to talk to your friends. I talk to Maureen on the phone for hours and I always feel better for it. I wouldn't talk about private things, like bedroom stuff, but everything else... you need to let off steam, Janet love. You know I wouldn't do anything you didn't want – but perhaps Ryan doesn't understand how you feel?'

'I don't know. I shouldn't have said anything, but sometimes I get so miserable.'

'Oh, Janet. I thought you were so sure when you married him?'

'I was – but it's losing our son and trying for another baby and feeling so ill all the time...' She was silent for a moment and then it came out in a rush, 'I think there may be someone else...'

'You think Ryan is seeing another woman? Surely he wouldn't?' Peggy was astounded. Ryan had always seemed so desperately in love with Janet. 'What makes you suspect him?'

'He comes home late from work night after night and since I told him I didn't want another child he refuses to make love, just says he's too tired...' She caught back a sob. 'And I found a hankie in his pocket with red lipstick. It's not my colour. I wear a peach shade or a pale pink.'

'There could be a lot of reasons for that, Janet,' Peggy said reasonably. 'He might have lent it to a girl in his office if she had grit in her eye or if she was crying.'

'Yes, I know,' Janet agreed, a note of uncertainty in her voice now. 'It's lots of little things, Mum – the way he looks at me sometimes; you must remember what it was like when you and dad split up?'

'Yes, I do.'

Peggy remembered, nodding to herself. She'd noticed the little signs for a long time before she understood that she and Laurie were drifting apart. It had been painful, hurtful – but then she'd met Able and the world had changed for Peggy. Even when he'd been missing and she'd thought him dead, his love had remained in her heart.

'I hoped it would never happen to you,' Peggy said now. 'Don't let go too soon, love. It might be just a passing phase. I'm not sure Laurie would ever have been unfaithful to me if the war hadn't happened. We should probably have drifted along in the same old way.'

'Is that all there is in life?'

'You sound bitter, Janet. You shouldn't let yourself be bitter, love.'

'Don't you think I've had cause?'

Peggy knew her daughter was remembering the way she'd lost her first husband Mike. He'd come back to her after being missing at sea during the war but suffering from loss of memory and just as they had a chance of happiness and he'd seemed to be remembering, he'd suffered a reversal and died from the brain injury caused by the shrapnel lodged in his head.

'Yes, Janet, you have – but you've also got a second chance. You have a lovely home and a comfortable life; that's more than many have, love.'

'Money and comfort are nothing without love,' Janet said and put the receiver down sharply the other end.

Peggy stood with it in her hand for a moment before replacing hers. She wondered whether to ring her daughter back, but knowing Janet, she wouldn't answer. Janet had always been temperamental and stubborn. She would get over whatever was eating at her and Peggy would telephone her – perhaps that evening.

'I'm leaving for the café,' Able said, coming out into the hall. 'You should put your feet up as much as the twins will allow, Peggy.'

'That's zero.' Peggy sent him a loving glance, thanking her lucky stars that her man had come back to her after the war and was unfailingly considerate and loyal. 'We're going skating, a drink and a bun at the café and then Christmas shopping. The twins want to find presents for their friends, Aunty Sheila and Uncle Pip and their cousins – and you! They've already got something for Janet, Maggie and Ryan. Freddie made an ornament in pottery class and Fay made a leather bookmark for Ryan, but they want to buy some presents too.' Peggy spoke of her children and her grandchildren as being cousins because the uncle-nephew relationship was too complicated for the children.

'Oh good.' Able grinned wickedly. 'I'm up for some brandy and cigars – or a new tie...'

'You will get what they choose,' Peggy reprimanded with mock severity and then laughed. 'Freddie bought you that rubber duck for the bath when he was five, do you remember?'

'Remember? I play with it every morning in the bath,' he murmured, eyes twinkling. 'Have you got enough money for all you want, hon?'

'I'm fine thanks,' Peggy said. 'Have a good day, love. You've got the stuff I cooked last night to take with you?' She'd baked at home to save going in, and her part-time cook would do the simple meals for once. Able had insisted that she have a well-earned day off.

'Six apple pies, two large cherry Bakewell tarts and three dozen sausage rolls.' Able ticked them off on his fingers. 'You'll have to start on the mince pies next week, Peggy. I've already been asked when our Christmas menu starts and we'll put a few decorations up next week.'

'People are so impatient for it to come,' she said with a laugh. 'We've got another three weeks to go. Janet and Maggie won't be coming to us for Christmas...'

'Is she unwell again?' Able looked concerned.

Peggy shook her head. 'Ryan is taking her on holiday to Scotland. They're going up several days before Christmas, taking the car to London, so they can call on Sheila and Pip, sleeping there overnight and travelling the rest of the way by train. Janet says the train is a sleeper so they'll have a comfortable journey and will be staying until the day after Boxing Day.'

'Good for him,' Able said. 'It will do them all good – we could go somewhere if you wanted, Peggy. We're taking a longer break this year, so we could afford to go away for a while.'

'I like a family Christmas.'

'Well, why don't we visit Pip and Sheila?' Able asked. 'It's a while since you've been up to London, hon. You could see all your friends. Ask if it is all right – and we'll take a big hamper of food up with us as well as the presents.'

Peggy moved towards him in a rush of emotion, putting her arms about him to give him the hug her talk with Janet had left her needing. 'They threw away the mould after they made you, Able.' Her throat was tight and she sounded a bit hoarse. 'You'd better go, love.'

'Yes, mustn't be late. They will be queuing up to get in...' He grinned and kissed her softly on the lips. 'I'll see you this evening – ring Pip, don't wait to write. I'd enjoy seeing the pub and everyone in the lanes again.'

'I will telephone, later,' Peggy promised, turning as she heard a shout from the back parlour. 'I'd better see what they're up to before total war breaks out.'

As he opened the front door, they heard the sound of planes in the air. The new fast planes were breaking speed limits and when they did so overhead the noise could be deafening. Able put his hands to his ears and made a face until they passed. Only after the planes had disappeared could they hear the noise their children were making.

Able laughed as they heard the squabble going on in the back room. Fay and Freddie were very close but they quarrelled often and sometimes hair got pulled and shins kicked. Fay had always been the most quarrelsome, perhaps because her hearing had been slightly damaged when she was very small, but Peggy knew that her younger daughter was the dominant twin. For a long time, Freddie hadn't retaliated, but these days he had a way of quietening his sister with a look. He was now the stronger of the two and she'd once seen him hold Fay captive by the wrists. She'd struggled but couldn't break free, even though he didn't hurt her, and Fay had understood that he could if he chose. Since then, she'd ceased to plague him so much and they got on well most of the time, but every now and then it could be chaos between them.

'I'll leave it to you to settle,' Able said and went off with a smile and a wave.

Peggy turned as the sound of the fight increased in intensity.

'It's mine!' Fay screamed as Peggy walked into the room and pulled at something Freddie was holding.

'I made it, it's mine,' Freddie replied, stubbornly holding on to what his sister was trying to wrench from his hands. It suddenly ripped and Fay retreated triumphantly with the largest piece of what appeared to be a calendar. 'You've ruined it,' Freddie looked at his twin accusingly. 'I spent hours making it and you've torn it in half...'

'You should have let me see...' Fay said but looked a bit shamed as Peggy gave her a hard stare.

'Give it to me...' Fay handed over the torn cardboard and Peggy saw it was a calendar decorated with drawings of girls ice-skating on their own or with a partner. Her gaze moved to Freddie. 'Were you making this as a gift for your sister?'

Freddie nodded. 'I didn't want her to see – it was a surprise...'

Fay suddenly realised what she'd done and her big blue eyes filled with tears. 'I'm sorry. I didn't know it was for me. I just wanted to see...'

'You've spoiled it now and it took me ages to make,' Freddie said. 'I copied the pictures from a book and was making it for you for Christmas...'

Now the tears were dripping off the end of Fay's nose. Peggy handed her a tissue to wipe her face and picked up the piece of the calendar that Freddie had thrown down in disgust. She looked at it for a moment and nodded.

'We can fix this with some glue. It isn't ruined, Freddie. If I put a strip of blank paper along here and glue both pieces to it, the jagged edges will disappear and you can draw some more figures or some holly on the blank paper. It will look pretty.'

Freddie looked, saw what needed to be done, and hesitated. 'What's the point if Fay is going to tear it again?'

His twin sidled up to him, her small hand on his arm, her look pleading. 'I'm sorry for what I did, Freddie. Please mend it and make it nice for me – I love it.'

He looked at her for a moment and then smiled. Freddie's smile was the mirror image of his father's and made Peggy's heart catch with love. 'All right,' he said. 'Now I shall have to think of something else as a surprise – but you're not to peek or try to steal whatever I make, Fay.'

'I won't. I promise.' Her face was earnest, trusting, as she looked up at him. 'You're the bestest brother in the world and I shouldn't have teased you.'

'Right, put this away for later and let's get off,' Peggy said firmly. 'Get your coats on while I just pop next door to Sandra and ask her if there's anything she needs while we're out shopping. I know she has visitors this morning so she'll be busy...'

'Yes, Mum,' the twins chorused, looking like the angels they most definitely were not.

Peggy popped her coat on and went out of the back door and up her neighbour's garden path. It was strange how forlorn most gardens looked at this time of year, trees bereft of their leaves and the roses straggling unless they'd been pruned in the autumn, which Sandra's hadn't for some reason.

Sandra saw her coming and opened the back door with a big smile. 'Have you time for coffee?'

'I haven't come to hinder you,' Peggy told her. 'We're off to the skating rink and then Christmas shopping after a snack in the café. I just wondered if there was anything, I could fetch you from town...'

'No thank you, Peggy. I shopped yesterday,' Sandra said and wrinkled her brow. 'Oh, yes, there was one thing – I could do with some sugar. I have some coupons somewhere...'

'It's all right. I'll bring you a bag and you can pay me back another day,' Peggy offered. 'You know we get a bit extra because of the café and I always scrounge some for us if I can, so I can manage for a few days.'

'Don't let me forget then,' Sandra replied. 'I've been a bit here and there recently. What with John's work at the office going on for hours after it should and me trying to catch up with Mum and Dad's problems...'

Peggy nodded sympathetically. Sandra was coping with her work, a home, children and a busy husband, as well as a father who had been diagnosed with early-onset brain syndrome, another name for senility, or the curse that often came with old age, and a mother who was increasingly fragile due to a weak heart. She spent hours helping them when her husband and children were out, which left her busy all the time at home. It was mentally hard, as well as physically, and her husband couldn't help because he was struggling to keep his business on an even keel. Even so, Sandra was a good friend and picked the twins up from school when asked, delivering them either to the café or taking them to their club when she knew Peggy was working late. In return, Peggy cooked for the elderly couple, taking

Sandra's parents casseroles and apple pies and offering to do whatever she could to help.

'What's a pound of sugar between friends?' Peggy said, but she knew Sandra would return it anyway when she was ready. 'I'll see you later then – I hope you enjoy your visitors.'

'I shall – Millicent is my sister-in-law, but you haven't met her. We lost touch for a while, because they've been overseas. Richie is still in the Army; he's a career soldier and has recently been promoted to Major. They're back in England for a couple of years now, so I hope to see more of them and their children – they have two boys, six and seven.'

'A bit younger than yours then,' Peggy said. 'I'd better go or the twins will be in trouble again. I'll call round later.'

Waving goodbye to her friend, Peggy returned to the house, collected her twins and popped them in the little Morris car that Able had bought for her when she had passed her test a few years back. It was nearly new then and she had it serviced regularly so it kept going and was fine as a runabout for the children and Peggy. Able wanted to buy her a new one, but he had many calls on his purse so Peggy didn't push for a new car. She was content enough with the one she had, even if she had spotted a bit of rust on the rear bumper.

As she was about to drive away, the postman arrived and Peggy took the letters from him. She saw from the handwriting that one of them was a bill and there were two postmarked London – one from Pip and one from Maureen. Smiling, Peggy popped them in her coat pocket. She would read them while the twins were enjoying themselves on the rink. They were both pretty good so she didn't need to watch the whole time and she would enjoy her letters from her eldest son and her friend.

5

Maureen replaced the phone receiver and went into the kitchen, where Gordon was sitting with the evening newspaper and a cup of tea. He looked up and smiled at her, indicating the pot.

'I've not long made it – would you like a cup?' he asked.

She nodded and sat down next to Shirley, who had her nose in a medical book. 'Still working, love?'

'I want to learn all I can before I go to med school,' Shirley said. 'You know I'm going to specialise in children's medicine, Mum. I'll need to pass lots of exams and so I'd rather read this than fashion magazines.'

'You used to enjoy reading history and all sorts...' Maureen was slightly wistful, because sometimes Shirley seemed a little too serious.

'I still do when I have time,' Shirley replied and smiled. 'Don't worry. It's important to me to become a doctor, Mum.'

'I know.' Maureen leaned towards her and kissed her hair. She smiled as Gordon put a cup of tea in front of her. 'Lovely. Well, it was good news. Peggy has agreed to come up for Christmas. She says they will stay with Pip for twelve days or so; she is coming up the day before Christmas Eve, so that's on the Friday – and it means we'll see lots of her. I shall have her to lunch and them all to dinner and it will be so nice.'

'We guessed as much,' Gordon said, smiling indulgently at her. 'You sounded so animated and full of it on the phone. I'm glad Peggy is coming to stay. It will make Christmas even more fun for you.'

'Mum loves Christmas anyway,' Shirley said and closed her book. 'How soon can we get the tree and put the paper chains up, Dad?'

'Not until a week before the day,' Gordon said. 'It will drop its spines all over if we have it too soon – besides, Christmas shouldn't go on forever. When I was a lad, my grandfather refused to decorate until Christmas Eve. He said it was a celebration of Christ's birth and nothing more. I think he only agreed to some greenery because my grandmother would have hit him with her rolling pin if he hadn't...'

Shirley shook her head at him. 'That's so old-fashioned, Dad,' she chided. 'Some of my friends are already starting to put them up and the junior classes are making decorations at school. They will decorate the hall next week. We've all got to take a little present in that the school can give to a children's home.'

'I'll find you some bits and pieces,' Maureen said. 'Are second-hand toys and good clothes acceptable?'

'Yes. My teacher says there are so many children who have nothing that we should all find something to give away at Christmas, as well as sending money to the poor of other countries. We're going to wrap our gifts up in pretty tissue or brown paper decorated with gold stars we've cut out – and any decorations we make will come down on the last school day and go to the children's home. That's why we have our parties and celebrations early.'

'That's a school, so it's understandable,' her father said. 'It's more fun if we leave it a bit later, Shirley. I like all the last-minute rush of getting presents and wrapping them – but I'll give you five shillings for the school's Christmas fund.'

'Thanks, Dad!' Shirley hugged her father.

'That doesn't mean you can have your tree early or presents...'

'Mum started her shopping weeks ago,' Shirley said and laughed as Maureen shot her a suspicious look. 'No, I haven't been peeking,

Mum, but I know when you start hiding things under the tea towel when I come in and acting furtively.'

'I don't!'

'You do,' Gordon and Shirley chorused together with a laugh. 'You get that secretive look in your eyes...' Gordon added with a wink at his daughter. 'And you made the Christmas puddings weeks ago.'

'That's different; they're better if they mature a little – and as for the presents, I hide them because I like surprises,' Maureen said. 'Christmas presents should be a surprise, unless it has to fit and then sometimes you can't keep it a secret.'

'That's a hint,' Gordon said. 'We haven't got something to wear this year, Shirley.'

Father and daughter laughed as Maureen put on her 'wait and see' face. 'You two do not deserve any presents,' she claimed with mock severity. 'I'm going up to check on little Gordy, because he had a bit of a cough earlier – so you can whisper and laugh about me to your hearts' content.' The usual winter coughs and colds had been circulating in the lanes, but apart from a slight cough her family were well, thank goodness!

'You are my heart's content,' Gordon said and caught her about the waist, giving her a little squeeze as she passed.

'I shall deal with you later,' she threatened and departed to make sure her beloved son was sleeping peacefully. Maureen knew she did not need to check on him but having lost one son to a childhood illness she was even more careful of her other children. Whooping cough, measles, influenza, any of them could kill if they were severe enough.

Maureen looked down at her sleeping child with love and then passed on to little Matty. Both were peaceful, their faces slightly flushed with sleep but not in the least hot to the touch. She smiled and turned to return to her kitchen, where a small pile of ironing awaited her if she felt like tackling it.

Her thoughts went to Peggy and the news about Janet. It seemed that things weren't quite right there again. Poor Janet had had a rough time of it, one way and another. She'd lost her home in the war when a German bomber crashed into it but, far worse, she'd lost her first husband. After she remarried, they'd all thought she was happy, but the loss of her baby son soon after his birth had changed things. Since then, she'd suffered miscarriages and that pulled you down, as Maureen knew only too well.

Gordon had decided that, after Matty was born, three children was enough. 'I want you well and strong,' he'd told his wife. 'We've got a perfect family. From now on, I'll take charge.' He had and, though it wasn't always satisfactory, they'd managed and Maureen hadn't quickened again. She sometimes thought she wouldn't, even if her husband wasn't so meticulous in looking after her. There were other methods of contraception, of course, and Maureen had considered being fitted with a cap. She thought that might be better for both of them but hadn't got around to talking to her doctor about it yet, though maybe she would next time she went to the surgery.

Shirley was writing a letter and looking rather serious when Maureen got back to the kitchen. She looked up and frowned as she saw her reach for the ironing basket.

'Can I do that for you, Mum?'

'No, it's all right, love. You get on with your letter.' Maureen didn't need to ask if she was writing to Richard. Shirley only ever wrote to one person – unless it was something to do with her hopes for medical school. She had written two letters asking medical schools about their requirements and received nice letters in return. It wasn't so long ago that the authorities had thought women should be nurses and leave the real medicine to men, but now more and more of them were realising that women could play a big role in the hospital as well as the practice. Many women were embarrassed to talk to male doctors about personal problems and were turning to the female doctor whenever possible. It was because Maureen had heard rumours of a clinic with a female doctor that she was considering having a cap fitted to take the responsibility from Gordon.

She glanced at her husband quietly reading his paper at the table and smiled. How lucky she was to be married to such a good, gentle man.

'Richard isn't coming home for long this Christmas,' Shirley said with a sigh. 'He has to work most of the time...'

'I think that is quite usual for medical students,' Maureen responded sympathetically. She knew how much her daughter looked forward to Richard's visits. It was a pity that they weren't a little closer in age. It hadn't mattered that there was nearly four years difference when he'd walked her home from school. He was like her big brother, protecting her, but now he was way ahead at medical school, leaving Shirley languishing at home wishing she could be there with him.

'I think I'll go up and read in bed,' Shirley said after a moment or so. 'I'll read my library book, Mum. It's a Greek legend and I'm enjoying it...'

'I don't mind what you do as long as you're all right,' Maureen said and kissed her. 'Shall I bring you some cocoa up when I make it in an hour?'

'Yes please. I shan't be asleep, but my reading lamp is better than the light here.'

'I know – that's why your dad bought it for you.' It had a head that could be angled to put the light where it was needed and was very modern and stylish – a little too modern for Maureen's taste, Gordon liked all the new things that were coming in these days and often suggested buying labour-saving devices for Maureen, though she wasn't as keen.

Maureen smiled and kissed her again as she passed, then took the flatiron that had been warming on the range and held it close to her face so that she could gauge the heat. She had two that Gran had given her years before so that one heated while the other was being used and then, once it had cooled too much, she exchanged it for the second.

'You should let me buy you an electric iron,' Gordon said. 'One of my customers was telling me that she swears by hers. It steams as well as irons apparently – or that's what I think she meant.'

'I don't fancy those,' Maureen said. 'I'll stick to these for the time being. Gran gave them to me years ago and I've always got on with them well.'

'Time moves on,' Gordon said but didn't push his theory. As he'd told Maureen, things were changing and there were all sorts of useful tools coming along. He would see if he could find anything to make Maureen's work easier. She would never ask or even think of looking for something to help her, but she'd liked the carpet sweeper he'd bought her. It was light and you just pushed it over carpets or floors and it picked up the bits rather than using a broom. It was easy to empty the little pan underneath and she had refused to have one of those Hoover things. She thought they were noisy and could blow dust out and she didn't want one. So, her considerate husband had found the sweeper instead and she loved it.

'What are you thinking?' Maureen asked as she looked up from ironing a shirt and saw Gordon looking at her. 'I always know when you're planning something...'

'I was just thinking about the shop, Maureen. I've been offered several new stock items recently and I'm wondering if we should expand into things for the kitchen and home...'

'What kind of things?' She stood with iron paused mid-air, awaiting his answer.

'Oh, just bits and pieces,' he said. 'We don't have anyone near us selling kitchen stuff, so we wouldn't be treading on anyone's toes.'

'It sounds a good idea,' Maureen decided and returned to her ironing. 'What made you think of it?'

'Something I saw in *The Grocer* magazine,' Gordon replied. 'In America, they have these big shops that sell all kinds of things – they call them convenience stores or something like that.'

Maureen nodded. 'It would save so much time if you could buy useful things like mixing bowls, kettles and stuff without walking miles to find them,' she agreed. 'Yes, go ahead and do it, love. I like it.'

'I thought you might,' he said. 'I'm also considering whether we should expand out into part of what used to be Mrs Tandy's yard. She didn't ever use the full potential of her premises. Tom could build it out a bit and I could line it with shelves myself...'

And fill them with stock that won't perish,' Maureen said. 'In the ,ar, I sold handmade toys and it surprised me that people just snapped them up. No one cared they were being sold in a food shop.'

Gordon nodded his agreement. 'They were so desperate for something to buy in those days that things went off the shelf immediately. I look forward to seeing our shop filled with all kinds of things.'

Maureen smiled as she put her iron back in the grate to cool down. 'I've done all I need to do. I'm going to make the cocoa now, love.'

'Good, I'll be glad of an early night.' Gordon stood and put his arms about her. 'Especially if you feel like a bit of a cuddle.'

Maureen laughed naughtily and kissed him on the lips. 'You never know your luck if you play your cards right,' she said and then went to pour the milk into the saucepan and put it on the range to heat. 'Lock up, Gordon, and I'll bring the drinks up in a few minutes...'

6

Sheila answered the phone when Peggy rang. She thought it was a call from the brewery and her smile lit up her face when she heard her mother-in-law's voice and was told she wanted a chat about the coming visit.

'Oh, Mum, it's lovely to talk to you,' she said excitedly as Peggy told her they would come up the day before Christmas Eve and stay for ten days afterwards. 'Pip asked you to come but he wasn't sure you would; he will be so pleased and so am I – we don't see half enough of you and your grandson often asks why you don't live nearer so he can visit like other kids do...'

'I know,' Peggy said, sounding sorrowful. 'We're much nearer to Janet and I get to see Maggie more than my grandson, but Janet doesn't always want us to go down. Part of the reason I moved was to be nearer to her, but it hasn't worked out that way...'

'Pip often says you shouldn't have left London. There isn't a day goes by we don't have some of your customers asking after you. They all say no one cooks like you do, Peggy, and they swear you were a lifeline in the war – when everyone else was serving rubbish, you still managed to serve up tasty food, even though you couldn't get more rations than anyone else.'

'I did get a bit extra though, sometimes,' Peggy said. 'Friends brought me fresh vegetables from their allotments and Able got me stuff from the American base. He probably shouldn't have done it, but he did... besides, lots of people bought black-market stuff. I didn't very often, because it was trouble if you got caught, but what was given to me felt different.'

'Your extras weren't stolen,' Sheila remarked. 'I know my parents bought some whisky under the counter once and lived in fear the inspectors would come around and arrest them, so they never did it again.'

'I did buy a turkey that I was told was reared as a pet one year.' Peggy laughed at the memory. 'I'm sure it was nicked from a farm or the farmer decided to hide a few birds from the Government inspectors – but since we were going to eat the evidence, I didn't worry too much.'

'We all had to do things like that sometimes,' Sheila replied, giggling. 'I bought some nylons from a girl who'd got them from American friends. You couldn't buy stockings here for love nor money.'

'I know,' Peggy sighed, making Sheila wonder what was on her mind. 'So how are you all then, love?'

'We're all pretty good,' Sheila said. 'Pip has a new commission to work on, so he has been away for three days discussing it, but he's back this evening. He will be over the moon to know you're coming for twelve days at Christmas.'

'Is there anything Christopher particularly wants?' Peggy asked. 'I've bought him a little surprise so far, but you'll know what he really wants?'

'Pip has told me to get him a bike and I'm also giving him book tokens, because he loves reading – but I do know he wants a guitar. Pip wouldn't buy it because he doesn't believe Chris will keep the lessons up; he thinks he's too young to learn something like that, but I believe he could because he's very musical. If he hears a new song on the radio, he whistles the tune straight away. You could buy the guitar for him if you want – but it is expensive and will cost five pounds...'

'Yes, I shall buy it,' Peggy said instantly. 'Maggie gets lots of little things from me, but I don't get to spoil Chris enough. Is there any particular model he likes?'

'Yes – they've got one in a shop here and I've seen him looking at it, but I don't know the make...'

'Can you reserve it for me and I'll send you the money by postal order?'

'Yes, of course,' Sheila said. 'I was wondering if I should get it as well as the bike, but if you buy the guitar, I'll pay for his lessons...'

'That's settled then,' Peggy said. 'I've done most of my shopping now and we're popping down to Janet's this Sunday. I'm taking her Christmas presents because they're off to Scotland for two weeks over Christmas.'

'How lovely for them,' Sheila said. 'Janet wrote me a letter and said she would call in on us when they stopped overnight in London with gifts for us – she said it will be surprises for the children and book tokens for Pip, as usual...' She laughed. 'I'll be giving them a huge parcel of bits and pieces I've bought. I was going to send it, but now I can give it to them while they're here.'

'Postage is so expensive if you send anything heavy,' Peggy said. 'I don't like giving them tokens, but if we lived in London as you do, that's what I'd do...'

'Pip always says I should send tokens because it is easier, but I love buying, so I pay the postage other years and grit my teeth...'

Peggy laughed, sharing the joke. 'Well, I have to get the terrible twins to bed, Sheila love, but I'm really looking forward to seeing you all again soon.'

'I know you're enjoying life down there, Mum, but we do all miss you...' Sheila said. 'Look forward to seeing you all. Give the family my love...' She replaced the receiver quickly because otherwise she might get too emotional and cry. It wasn't that Sheila was miserable. She knew Pip loved her and his son and she adored him. Her parents lived too far away for her to visit more than a few times a year and her mother never came to London these days.

'I don't have time, Sheila,' she'd said when she'd last asked her to pop up, if only for a couple of days. 'Your father is always busy and I can't desert him – besides, I hate London. I came up once and disliked it very much. You're welcome to visit us and bring your family, but don't expect me to visit.'

It sometimes seemed to Sheila that her mother resented the fact that she'd married and moved away. She'd believed that her daughter would always be there, helping out in the house and pub and running errands for her mother and she hadn't forgiven her for putting her husband first and moving to London.

Sighing, Sheila moved away from the phone and went into the big old-fashioned kitchen. It had hardly changed since Peggy left, except for a new scrubbed pine table that was easy to keep clean, a bigger gas oven, and the solid marble slabs she used for making pastry. Peggy had taken hers with her to the country.

Sheila used both the range and the new gas oven, because she needed the capacity to keep up the production of cakes and tarts for the shop and savouries for the pub. She and Maureen worked solidly for four hours in the morning, cooking batches of cakes and making soups, sausage rolls, fresh bread rolls and sandwiches for the pub. They now served soup and crusty bread with butter, sandwiches, salads and a savoury tart made with cheese or bacon and egg or sometimes sweet mincemeat twists that could be eaten cold or hot. The menu was popular with girls from the factories and working men, as well as travelling salesmen, some of whom had been visiting since before the war, but some of the older customers said it wasn't a patch on Peggy's food, but Sheila tried her best to please and she'd had the best teacher in Peggy.

The main change to the kitchen was the larger double sink. It held all the plates and baking tins soaking until the woman Sheila employed for washing up came in at twelve o'clock and then she gave them all a good scrub and returned them to the dresser shelves sparkling clean.

Nellie – the lady who had helped Peggy for years – had finally retired the previous year, taking retirement down by the seaside with her daughter, husband and two grandchildren in a nice big boarding house. Before Nellie went off to the sea, she recommended a friend of hers called Doris Giles. Dot was in her forties, filled with energy and mother to three strapping sons who all worked in the jam factory. She had two jobs, scrubbing floors at a prestigious office block and then washing up for Sheila.

'My man says I don't need to do the scrubbin',' she'd told Sheila recently. 'He earns enough to keep us and the lads bring home their wages, bless 'em. He reckons I ought ter ask yer if yer could give me an extra hour or two in the pub and forget the scrubbin'.'

'Oh, Dot, I'd love to give you extra hours,' Sheila had said, smiling at her. 'You're a worker and if you'd like to serve in the bar at night for an hour or two, you're welcome – or you can just wash up, help us cook or pretty much whatever you choose…'

'Well, I never,' Dot had said, looking delighted. 'I never thought of serving in the bar…' She'd looked at Sheila in wonder. 'I could do wivout the scrubbin' ter tell yer the truth, so I'll ask me old man and see what he says…'

'You do that,' Sheila had encouraged, feeling pleased. She could manage as she was, but Dot was reliable and if she wanted an extra few hours it would take the pressure from Sheila's shoulders. Rose Barton came in sometimes and Maureen helped as much as she could, but they all had busy lives and it helped to have reliable domestic help. Pip could be pushed into serving in the bar occasionally, but he didn't really enjoy it and preferred to retire to his study and get on with his real work. He wasn't cut out for the life of a publican and would no doubt wish to be flying planes. His success at drawing them didn't make up for what he'd lost when his eyesight was affected by war wounds, and though he'd been able to take up a small light aircraft from a private airfield a few times and fly it with a co-pilot to help him land, it wasn't enough for him.

In September 1920, de Havilland had taken on modest premises at Stag Lane Aerodrome in north London, close to where the defunct Airco company had been before they went bust. With the help of a man named George Holt Thomas, de Havilland had set up his company on a modest capital of £50,000, provided by various friends and associates. After making small profits for the first few years, the company went public in 1928. Initially, they'd concentrated on making single and two-seat biplanes until they introduced the Gipsy and Tiger Moth. These aircraft set many speed records and were flown by de Havilland himself and Amy Johnson, who flew solo from England to Australia in a Gipsy Moth in 1930. In later years, the company had expanded to a factory in Lostock near Manchester, to produce propellers for the RAF, and had continued to grow, playing an important part during the war.

It was not until two years after the war that Pip had approached the firm to ask if they were interested in a design for a propeller that he'd been working on. Although the design had not been accepted, he'd been offered a job to join the design team and travelled to meetings in various parts of the country, but, of late, Sheila understood that he was working with a team at the Hatfield Aerodrome. It was closer to London and meant that he didn't have such long journeys or need to stay away as long as when he travelled up north for his work. However, most of his actual work was done at home in his study, where he drew endlessly and made his ideas into models out of wood to show his employers.

Sheila often felt lonely when Pip was away working and wished she had more children to keep her company. She shook her head. It didn't do to dwell on what wasn't perfect in her life. She'd always wanted more children despite the warnings from the hospital that it could cause the loss of her life. She'd risked leaving off the vaginal cap she'd had fitted in the hope that she might become pregnant, without consulting her husband's wishes. She knew she ought not to have done it, but it hardly mattered. Even though Pip regularly made love to her and they were content in most ways she hadn't become pregnant again. Perhaps the doctors were right when they told her that she couldn't have more children.

Poor Peggy had only the two grandchildren to spoil, though, of course, she'd had the twins late in life and they were of a similar age to their cousins. At nearly six, Chris was actually just over three years younger than the twins, but extremely clever and bright for his age, and Maggie was a couple of years older than Freddie and Fay.

A little smile touched Sheila's lips. In her mind, there was no doubt that her son was exceptionally talented and advanced, almost a child genius in her opinion, although that could be a fond mother's imagination. Pip maintained that he was too young to learn the guitar seriously and would be better having toys to play with, but Sheila knew that her son, although possessed of a delightful smile and laugh, was a serious boy who liked to study. He read well, which was hardly surprising since his father had taught him as soon as he could hold a book, but he was extremely quick at picking things up and his teachers told Sheila that he was talented musically.

'He plays the triangle and the drums during school music lessons,' Mrs Andrews, the headmistress, had told her when she attended a school open day. 'In tune, I might add.' She'd paused and smiled oddly before proceeding, 'However, we had someone here to play guitar for us when we had our summer concert and Chris was fascinated. He wanted to touch it and he picked out a tune immediately. Most of the children just strummed it, but your son played a tune he'd heard. I think he should have guitar lessons.'

'Could I pay for lessons?' Sheila had inquired.

'Yes, the young man who played for us at the concert does private tuition when he isn't giving concerts – his name is Tony Cantrell and he is a very good tutor. He offered to give lessons at the school, but the headmaster says we cannot afford to pay for his time. I believe Chris would benefit from the experience.'

'Thank you for telling me,' Sheila had replied. 'I'll speak to his father.'

She had done so immediately, but Pip hadn't been interested. Sometimes, Sheila thought his mind was immersed in his work and that he seemed to forget about her and have little time to spare for his family. She knew he loved her; he just didn't get around to showing it often.

'I want Chris to concentrate on maths and English, and perhaps French and German languages,' Pip had said when she told him of his son's love of music. 'If he has those behind him, he will have a good career at his fingertips, Sheila. He might even become a commercial pilot.'

'Supposing he'd prefer to play music?'

'He can do that in his spare time when he's older,' Pip had told her. 'Besides, he's far too young to learn music seriously. Let him play games until he's ready to leave preparatory school, Sheila. Time enough then for him to develop his own interests...'

Sheila had got a book from the library about a child genius who began playing the piano at the age of five, and the more she read, the more she believed that her son should have the chance to start music lessons now. Some of the famous musicians like Mozart and others had begun very young. So why not her Chris?

Sheila was glad Peggy had asked what Chris wanted for Christmas. Pip might have got cross if she'd bought the guitar herself, but if it came from Peggy, he wouldn't say a word. Peggy had a way of calming him down and making him see sense, and that was another reason she was glad her mother-in-law was coming for Christmas. If she had her way, she would love to see Peggy back in the lanes permanently. She could always pick up the phone and ring her, but Maureen was right, it just wasn't the same as living close by.

'Mum... can I read in bed tonight?' Chris tugged at her skirt and she looked down at her son, smiling as she saw he had the library books she'd fetched for him. There was one on Roman history with lots of pictures of soldiers and ancient Rome and another album about football, because Chris liked sport as much as the next schoolboy and often spent an hour before supper kicking a ball in the lane with his friends.

'Yes, of course you can, darling,' she said. 'I'll bring you some cocoa up soon – and don't forget to clean your teeth and wash your ears...'

'Aw, Mum,' Chris said, wriggling uncomfortably. 'My ears are clean. I had a bath on Sunday and I wash every day...'

'Yes, a lick and a promise,' she said, but she was laughing because she made sure he had a bath every Sunday and after games. Small boys got very muddy after playing football at school. 'I shall inspect them to make sure.' She sent him off to bed with the threat and laughed inwardly at the face he pulled.

Sheila continued laughing as she put the milk on for his cocoa. Pip was still in his study working and would be for the next couple of hours. Sheila decided to go into the bar after she'd taken her son his bedtime drink. She may as well help out for a while as sit here on her own. She enjoyed the customers' gossip and hearing them talk about their lives and the changes since the war. Pip found it boring, but she didn't.

So, she would take cocoa to her son and ask her husband if he wanted one and then she'd pop into the bar and pull a few pints, even though her barman could manage perfectly well with the help of young Pamela Makepeace, who was still at typing college but did a shift on Friday nights.

7

Rose had left her youngest son with Alice for the morning. Her elderly neighbour wasn't as spry as she had been during the war years, but Jackie was very good for her. Alice talked to him and told him stories and he would happily munch a piece of her home-made flapjack and listen, as good as gold, until his mother returned.

'Are you sure you don't mind?' Rose had asked Alice as she sat Jackie in the high chair in Alice's warm kitchen. 'He isn't too much trouble for you?'

'It's the best part of my week when you go shoppin' and leave this little love with me,' Alice had declared, her now very wrinkled face lighting with pure pleasure. 'Take all the time you want, love, me and this little 'un will be fine.'

Rose had thanked her and left quickly. Jackie was gurgling with laughter and hardly noticed her go. He'd got over his tummy trouble and was back to his normal sunny self. Alice was his unofficial grandmother, because neither Tom nor Rose had a mother and so Alice was always ready to stand in. Rose had worried whether it was fair to put so much on her, but Tom told her that Alice would live until she was at least a hundred and do her own housework until the day she died.

'Alice is as tough as old boots,' he'd declared stoutly. 'She's one of the old breed of Londoners, Rose. They sailed through the war and they might not like the way things are changing in the East End these days, with all the new building and regulations, but it would take more than our Jackie to upset Alice.

So, Rose went off happily to do her weekly food shop. Besides, the normal groceries, which she ordered from Maureen's shop and would be delivered, Rose wanted fruit and vegetables from the market. You could get a better variety and at Christmas some of the stalls had special big sweet oranges and tangerines, nuts and extras for the children. Also, it was easier to buy the Christmas gifts for her family without having to lug Jackie around.

Jenny's gift was almost complete. Rose had bought her a lovely dress for best in a sky blue with a neat little collar of white and a nipped-in waist and flared skirt. It was a little girl's version of the Dior sensation that had hit the high streets the previous year. As soon as Christian Dior's New Look had appeared in the national papers, every workshop in London had started to make their own version. Rose was wearing a dark blue dress with a full skirt and a coat that had a shaped waist over it. She'd bought them for a good price in the dress shop she favoured and Tom said her clothes looked every bit as smart as those the high-fashion models wore.

Of course, Jenny had wanted a dress like her mother's, so Rose had bought material and had it made. She'd bought white leather button-up shoes to go with it and Tom had purchased an imitation pearl necklace and bracelet for his daughter as his special gift and he'd made her a special surprise as well.

Jackie would have a new pair of short trousers and a bright red jumper, because he loved the colour red. However, his main present was an electric train set. Rose suspected that his father was looking forward to setting it up for him and teaching him how it worked. Tom hadn't been given much in the way of toys when he was small; times were harder then, and his parents had known more of a struggle. So that was perhaps why he insisted that his children had toys. Jenny preferred costume jewellery and clothes or a colouring book and pencils and she would find all those things in her pillowcase, because Rose's friends all gave the children little things to open on Christmas Day.

Rose wanted to buy several little bits and pieces too. It was fun wrapping them with Tom last thing on Christmas Eve and the children often loved a toy that cost two shillings as much as their main gifts.

Rose walked briskly towards the covered market where she liked to shop. Between her lane and the official market, several unlicensed stalls often set up in little alleys or at the side of the road, especially at Christmas, and she bought some nuts from one young lad selling them on his dad's stall.

'I like the look of those walnuts,' she said to the cheeky youngster. He must have been fifteen or so but was small for his age and had an infectious grin. 'They're almost like wet walnuts and I love those.'

'Them give yer the runs, them do,' the lad chortled.

'Mind your manners, Nobby,' his father said and winked at Rose. 'Sorry, missus, my lad don't mean nuthin' wrong. He's just full of it 'cos I've let him help me on the barrow.'

'He hardly looks old enough to have left school,' Rose answered. He seemed friendly enough, though she didn't care for men winking at her in a familiar way,

'Don't rub it in,' his father groaned. 'Had the school inspector after me blood, so I carry 'is birth certificate now. Face like an innocent cherub this one, but he were fifteen last October and nuthin' would do but he left school and come to help me. Wants his own barrow this one does and as soon as 'e can push it, I'll set 'im up.'

'Lucky Nobby,' Rose said and smiled at the man. He seemed all right and was clearly a generous father. 'My husband started off doing odd jobs even younger than your son and now he has his own business.'

'Yeah, I thought I knew yer,' the man said and rubbed his grubby hand on his trousers before offering it to her. Rose shook his hand. 'You're Tom Barton's missus. He's done some jobs fer me. I'm Jim Broad and I've got two lads. My youngest is just ten years, but he's more like his Ma. Robbie wants ter be an engine driver on the trains. He's the brains of the family now that my Lisa's gorn…'

'Your wife died?' Rose said, feeling a wave of sympathy.

'Nah, cleared orf and left me when I got back after the war.' Jim made a wry face. 'She'd found herself a Yank she liked and he come back for her in nineteen forty-six, so she told me she was orf and left me with two boys ter bring up. It was a bit of luck fer me that me ma 'elped out, otherwise we'd have been up the creek – but yer've got a good gran, ain't yer, Nobby?' His son's grin told its own story.

'That was rotten luck,' Rose said. 'I must get off. I have a lot of shopping to do this morning…'

'Yeah, it's nearly Christmas,' Jim said and grinned. 'Best time of the year for us – enjoy those walnuts, Rose Barton.' Something in his eyes made her flush and look away.

'We shall, thank you,' Rose said and hurried away. She felt a bit hot under the collar, because the look in Jim Broad's eyes was a little familiar. He'd looked her up and down and liked what he saw and it had sent little warning tingles down Rose's spine. She didn't like men being too forward; it always made her uneasy.

'Don't be stupid, Rose Barton…' She scolded herself as she reached the market and began to look around for the things she needed. The man was just being friendly that was all – and she liked his son. He had a cheeky smile and was keen to do well, which reminded her of Tom. Her husband was a worker and she thought perhaps Nobby would be too, given the chance. His father was just an East End trader and many of them were a bit on the cheeky side if you didn't watch them, but Rose didn't think she'd said or done anything to encourage him, so there was no reason for the icy tingle at her nape. Anyway, she was unlikely to see the man again. He probably didn't have a licence to be where he was; a lot of men set up stalls illegally at Christmas just for the extra trade. Something that upset the regular traders in the market, because they thought the intruders pinched their customers, which was true, of course.

Rose shook her head. She had Christmas shopping to buy and, so far, she hadn't bought Tom a gift. Rose bought him smart shirts and ties for his birthday and Christmas, but this year she'd saved hard, because she wanted to buy him a surprise gift. Tom liked to watch his children play in the street and, when he had time, would join in a game of football with the other kids; quite a few of the men did if they were around. He'd remarked once or twice that it would be nice to have photographs of the children playing. All they had were a couple of studio pictures that looked too poised. So Rose was going to buy Tom a cine camera and a couple of rolls of film this year, something she was sure he would enjoy far more than another new shirt.

Tom had bought them a television earlier that year. He'd read that the BBC was going to produce many more films in future and would be taking over a film studio to make its programmes. Tom enjoyed a good film and took Rose to the cinema once a week if they could find a babysitter for the children.

'Once the BBC get cracking, we'll have something interesting to watch on the telly most nights,' he'd told her excitedly when a friend of his had installed it for them, but so far Rose couldn't see where the small black and white screen with flickering pictures came anywhere near the lovely technicolour of the cinema. However, Tom was very into film and photographs and she thought he would love a camera that took moving pictures of the kids. A home movie camera was something that folk in the lanes would never have been able to aspire to before the war, but since then most of them had prospered a little. Tom was making decent money and was generous with his housekeeping. Rose kept all the money she earned and she'd been saving hard for Tom's present all year.

She'd seen the one she wanted three weeks previously and reserved it and that morning she was going to pay for it, having withdrawn the money from her Post Office account. She felt excited as the man wrapped the box in brown paper and she tucked it under the children's bits and pieces in her large shopping bag. It was a surprise for under the Christmas tree and it gave Rose a warm feeling inside that she'd done something nice for Tom.

The barrow she'd bought her nuts from on the way home had

gone when she passed the place it had pitched. She thought they'd probably sold out for the day and gone to fetch the third member of the family from school. It was probably a good thing, she thought, saving her from more intimate glances from the owner, and decided she would take a different route to the market the following week.

* * *

Tom entered the house to the smell of a delicious casserole. Rose was a much better cook now than she'd been when they had first married. Alice had taught her some of it and Sheila and Maureen had given her recipes too and time had done the rest. He was hungry and looked forward to a good hearty meal at the end of the day.

'You're home then.' Rose came out of the kitchen, wearing a pretty blue apron covered with forget-me-nots over her dress. 'It's almost ready to serve, Tom. I'm just cooking some vegetables and I didn't want them on too soon.'

'Are the children in bed?' Tom asked.

'Yes, Jenny wanted to read and she promised Jackie she would play with him for a while so they both went up without an argument this evening.'

'Good, that means we have time to ourselves...' Tom put his arms about her and kissed her. 'I may smell of sweat, so perhaps I should go and wash before we eat...'

'You smell good,' Rose told him. 'The way a man should – I like it, Tom.'

'Good.' His kiss was passionate and possessive. 'I love you so much, Rose.' He hesitated then, 'One of my customers called into the yard to see me half an hour ago. He has a job for me, repairing some windows and painting the outside of his house. Apparently, you bought some nuts from his son this morning?'

'I bought some lovely walnuts,' Rose agreed.

Tom saw the flush in her cheeks and frowned. He hadn't much liked the way Jim Broad had brought her name into what should have been business. Tom was aware that Rose was a beautiful, sensual woman. He'd known that from the beginning, when she'd still thought of him as a boy. It was inevitable that other men would see it too and want her, but Rose was his! A mild-tempered man, Tom had wanted to punch the bugger in the face.

He bit back words of reproach that he knew Rose did not deserve. She couldn't help it if other men wanted her and she'd never given him cause to think she might stray. He suspected that she remembered Jimmy, the brave soldier who had given his life to destroy German V2 weapons destined to maim and kill thousands of British people. However, she never flinched from him in bed and their loving was satisfying and good. Tom was too level-headed to force a quarrel on the woman he adored just because he'd seen lust in another man's eyes. He'd rather put his fist in the so-and-so's mouth!

Forcing his jealousy to the backwaters of his mind, Tom smiled. 'Did you get everything you wanted for the kids?'

'Yes, lots of little bits and pieces, like we said,' Rose replied and looked pleased. 'I've done my shopping now, apart from the turkey and the trimmings.'

'I ordered the turkey and that will be delivered,' Tom told her. He had a good customer with contacts in the country and they delivered a lovely farm fresh turkey to the door every year.

'It's wonderful what we can buy again now,' Rose said. Most of the strict rationing had disappeared during the years since the war, though sweets were still rationed. 'I've saved our sweet rations for months and so we'll have plenty for Christmas.'

'I'm partial to a mint humbug now and then or a pear drop,' Tom murmured, 'but the kids can have most of mine, Rose. Get some nice chocolates for yourself, though.'

'I like a big box to hand round,' Rose said. 'Peggy is coming up for Christmas and I've asked if they will all come to tea on Boxing Day – you don't mind, do you?'

'Of course, I don't,' Tom said and grinned. 'I love Peggy and Able and the terrible twins...'

'You shouldn't call them that, Tom. I'm sure they're all grown up and not terrible at all now.'

'Peggy still calls them that,' Tom said, unrepentant. 'That girl is a handful – she could teach our Jenny a few tricks, and that's sayin' something. Freddie was always a loving little boy, but I dare say he stands up for himself these days.'

'Well, we'll see soon enough,' Rose said and giggled at his expression. 'I'd better dish the dinner up – and then we could have an early night if you like?'

'I was thinking...' he said, looking at her in a way that made her heart catch. 'I can't afford it yet – but perhaps next year when Jackie is a bit older, we might go for a holiday abroad – France or Jersey or somewhere...'

'Oh, Tom, I don't know,' Rose looked at him doubtfully. 'Think of all the folk that got killed in plane crashes last month – the paper said a hundred and forty-two...'

'It sounds a lot,' Tom agreed, 'but thousands travel safely all the time. I reckon it would be fun going somewhere like that...'

'Yes, it might,' she agreed and looked at him in wonder. 'I'd never thought of it, Tom. If we could afford a holiday – why don't we go down to Cornwall? Have a little cottage near the beach for the kids?' She looked thoughtful. 'Wouldn't you rather save any spare money for your house than squander it on a foreign holiday?'

'Would you rather do that?' He smiled at her and kissed her. 'Yes, I think you're right – but you always are, my beautiful, sensible, gorgeous wife.'

Tom smiled contentedly as he followed her into the kitchen and admired the sway of her hips. No wonder other men lusted after his wife, but she was all his – and she loved him. He was a fool to be jealous because there was no need.

8

Sheila suddenly felt sick as she got out of bed and ran to the bathroom, bending over the toilet as the thin acrid vomit rose in her throat. She didn't bring up much and frowned as she rinsed her mouth with cold water. She hoped she wasn't going down with a winter bug; there were a few about in the lanes and people brought them into the bar. She couldn't have flu for Christmas, not with Peggy and her family coming. All the arrangements were made, the food ordered and the cupboards stacked with goodies, some purchased but the majority made specially for Christmas. She'd even persuaded Pip to put some greenery up in the bar, decked with silver strands and a small bunch of mistletoe in the middle of the room, where eager young lads could kiss the girls and claim it was tradition. Sheila refused to give into infections. She rarely had them, even though the children and Pip went down with colds every year, she always kept going.

Anyway, she felt better now and she didn't have a temperature. Perhaps she'd eaten something that disagreed with her, though she'd thrown all the leftovers from the bar into the bin. Sheila didn't believe in keeping food at the end of the day because it really wasn't sensible. If it hadn't been bought and eaten, it went out, though her mother said it was a waste, and on the rare occasions a sausage twist was left, Pip would eat it and never showed any ill effects.

'You're too fussy,' he'd told her. 'Mum never wasted anything.'

'There was never anything left of her cooking by closing time...'

'No, Mum is a great cook,' Pip had said. 'You're good, Sheila, but I must admit Mum is the best...'

Sheila had pulled a face but didn't let him see. She agreed with him about Peggy's cooking, but it would be nice if Pip praised hers once in a while. He ate it and didn't complain but seldom told her it was really tasty even after she tried to please him with things he particularly liked. Pip said things as he saw them, never pulling his punches. He always had and she loved him so she didn't complain, but it did hurt a little to have her cooking compared unfavourably with his mother's.

Sheila's food sold well in the pub and the tea shop was always busy. They seldom had anything go to waste from there and only ever occasionally the odd sausage twist or savoury from the bar, so most people obviously thought her cooking adequate. Adequate – but not like Peggy's. Sheila acknowledged ruefully that Pip wasn't the only one to extol his mother's cooking.

Anyway, her sickness couldn't be something she'd eaten, Sheila thought as she dressed for work; she was always scrupulous in the kitchen and hadn't eaten anything heavy or greasy that she could recall. She switched on the wireless when she entered the kitchen and heard the sound of Christmas carols, which made her smile. *Away in a manger, no crib for a bed...* She hummed to the tune. There was nothing like a choir singing carols to make you feel it was nearly Christmas. Nearer the time, they would get groups of singers coming into the pub, collecting for various charities. Sheila always gave them a pound for their collecting tin and if she knew them well, she sometimes offered a sip of port too, to keep the cold out when they left.

She always wore a thin cotton dress and a wraparound apron for cooking, because the range made it warm in the kitchen. Both she had Maureen had chosen the same white aprons. They had to be properly dressed, just as her kitchen had to be spotless, because from time to time food inspectors called to check. Peggy hadn't had to put up with any of that, but the new regulations were probably needed, Sheila thought, because some cafés were not as particular as they might be. Sheila's kitchen had passed with flying colours.

'I wish everywhere I went was as clean as this,' the last inspector had told her. 'If I asked you to give a lecture on keeping food stations clean – would you do it, Mrs Ashley?'

'I'm not much of a one for public speaking,' Sheila had told the woman, who came and poked her nose into every cupboard and drawer. 'I would have thought it was a case of keeping things clean – as simple as that...'

'Your big sinks are ideal,' the woman had said, 'and you have sections for different things, so there's less chance of cross-contamination. I shall give you top marks again and I congratulate you on your cleanliness.'

Sheila had glowed with the praise. She and Maureen scrubbed all the work surfaces before they started each morning, and the floor was done every night. Every spill was immediately mopped up and disinfectant was used behind the gas cooker and round the dresser to make sure there was no dirt anywhere. Sometimes, Pip scolded her, telling her she was too fussy, but Sheila was particular. Perhaps in the war you could get way with lower standards but not now.

Going outside to the shed in the yard, she fetched a bowl of potatoes she wanted to use later in the day for the hotpot she was planning. The sickness had eased a bit now but she still felt slightly queasy.

Pip was eating toast and honey for his breakfast when she got down to the kitchen. He'd made some for their son and Chris was tucking into thick slices of toast oozing with butter and honey.

'Didn't you fancy bacon this morning?' Sheila asked her husband.

'No, we just wanted toast, didn't we, Chris?' Pip said, looking at his son with affection. 'Chris has a football match at school this afternoon and he doesn't want greasy food inside him. He's asked for a ham sandwich and an apple for his lunch, can he have that?'

'Yes, of course,' Sheila agreed and went to take the large home-cooked ham from the larder, cut some slices and make her son's packed lunch. She put the sandwiches into a biscuit tin she'd saved for the purpose and added an apple and a slice of Victoria sponge cake without asking.

'Thanks, Mum,' Chris smiled at her and slipped the tin into his smart leather satchel; a present from his father when he'd started school. 'I'm ready, Dad.'

'Right, we're off,' Pip said, turning to her to kiss her cheek. He walked his son to school every day, leaving her free to get on with her work. 'I shan't be back for lunch today, love. I have a meeting in the city with an engineer and I'll get a sandwich out. I'll be back in time to collect Chris after his match, if I can't get there in time to watch it all – so wait for me, son. I shan't let you down.' He aimed a peck at Sheila's cheek. 'Why don't you ask Alice to look after Chris one night and I'll take you to see that film – what was it about, red shoes or something?'

'Maureen says it's wonderful,' Sheila replied. 'Moira Shearer is in it and Robert Helpmann. The music is award-winning and everyone is raving about it...'

'We'll go then,' Pip said and put a hand on his son's shoulder. 'Don't forget, son. I shan't forget to pick you up after you football...'

'You never do, Dad,' Chris said and smiled at his father. He gave his mother a quick hug round her waist and the two of them left together.

Sheila was aware of a queasy tummy as she made herself a slice of toast, spread it thinly with butter and a tiny spot of honey. She normally liked her toast the way her family did, but not this morning. It would be just too bad if she felt like this when Peggy and the others came – cooking Christmas lunch would be a chore if she was ill, but surely she would be over it by then?

Forcing herself to eat her toast, she gulped her coffee down and then started scrubbing the surfaces. She had half of them done by the time Maureen arrived.

'You should have waited for me,' Maureen said and rolled her sleeves up.

'Pip has taken Chris to school and I thought I'd get on,' Sheila said. 'We're icing those last Christmas cakes today as well as the usual bake, so I wanted an early start...' She sighed. 'I felt a bit sick earlier on, but it seems to have gone. I was a bit worried I was getting a bug...'

'There are a few around,' Maureen said. 'Gordon said half his customers were snuffling yesterday, but so far we've kept clear.'

'We have too, which is why I was annoyed at myself. I can't have the flu with Peggy coming for Christmas.'

'If the worst happens, send her to me,' Maureen said. 'You know I'd help you out, Sheila love.'

'Yes...' Sheila started to weigh some flour for the scones she was making. 'It was just that first thing I vomited and then gradually felt better...' Maureen was looking at her, eyebrows raised. 'What?'

'You don't think you're pregnant?' she asked in the way that only close friends can.

Sheila shook her head firmly. 'Couldn't be. I had my monthlies three weeks ago.'

'Doesn't always mean anything,' Maureen said. 'Was it a normal one – or lighter than usual?'

Sheila stared. 'How did you know? It hasn't been normal for a couple of months now. I thought I must be a bit anaemic and was going to visit the doctor if it happened again, especially as I'd felt a little tired.'

'See what happens this month and then go to the doctor,' Maureen advised. 'When I was nursing, I did a stint in midwifery and you'd be surprised how many women told me that same tale.'

'You think I might be pregnant?' Sheila's eyes widened and she felt the sting of tears, her throat tight with emotion, and the words came tumbling out, words she hadn't been able to say to her busy husband. 'Oh, Maureen, I want that so much. I've longed for it, hoped it would happen, but I never thought it would – the doctors were pretty certain I couldn't have another child...'

'Didn't they say you shouldn't?' Maureen asked and suddenly looked anxious. 'What does Pip say? He was so worried when you had to stay in hospital all those weeks before Chris was born. Have you considered that you might be made ill by pregnancy?'

'I know I had a rough time,' Sheila said. 'I wanted another child and I stopped using what the doctors gave me two years ago, but nothing happened and I thought that was it, it would never happen.'

'What if it has?' Maureen asked. 'You needn't worry about the shop. I'll keep it going. We can ask Rose to do more hours and I'll find someone who can help with the cake making on a temporary basis... but I'm thinking of *you*. Pip said he didn't care about more children as long as he had you and Chris...'

'Yes, I know,' Sheila sobered. 'I didn't tell him what I'd done. He might not be pleased at first, but he loves Chris so much, he will love another child – and I'd like a little girl.'

'Pip loves you, Sheila,' Maureen said, looking at her anxiously. 'You will have to tell him if the doctor confirms it. He has a right to know...'

'Yes, of course he does,' Sheila agreed. 'I shall tell him as soon as I know anything.'

She knew Maureen was right and a little chill touched her spine. Pip was a loving husband, but he wouldn't be pleased she'd made the decision to leave her cap out without telling him. In fact, he might be angry with her, but if he was, it would be worry for her that made him cross and he would forgive her when he thought about it. After all, it was her body and she had a perfect right to risk it for another child if she chose. It might not even be happening anyway, although now that Maureen had pointed it out, Sheila suspected the truth. She'd noticed a few things, but the false periods had hidden it from her.

She felt a mixture of emotions swirl through her: fear and excitement and a longing for it to be true. If she could bear another healthy child, it would be a wonderful gift and she was so thrilled that there was a chance.

9

Maureen saw the two letters lying on the mat when she got in after finishing her morning's work in Sheila's spotless kitchen. Setting down her son Matty on the sofa, she bent down to pick them up, hardly glancing at them as she shrugged off her coat and put on her apron.

She wasn't helping in the café that afternoon, because Rose and Pamela were in the tea shop. It meant she could get on with her housework and finish her own Christmas preparations. Her puddings were made and everyone had had a go at stirring, putting in the silver sixpence and making a wish. Also, the big, rich fruit cake was in the tin and she'd added brandy to it twice, keeping it moist and making it even more tasty. She would do the almond paste today and then ice it two days before Christmas.

She'd missed these lovely cakes during the war and even now you had to save the ingredients, like dried fruit and brown sugar, as you went along, to be sure of having all you needed for the cake at Christmas. Maureen wasn't entitled to more sugar than her customers, even though she owned the grocers at the end of the road. Dried fruit was available in limited quantities these days, but she bought some each month if she could and kept most of it for

Christmas. Sometimes she made a light fruit cake for the weekend, but Gordon liked a plain cake with cherries in it and she made that most of the time, as well as coconut pyramids, which were simply condensed milk, a little sugar and desiccated coconut with a cherry on top.

She picked up the kettle to make a welcome cup of tea for herself, placing the letters on the kitchen table. Now that she had time to look, she saw that both envelopes were addressed to Shirley but in different handwriting. She knew Richard's, because they came regularly, but the other had a boldness to it and the lettering wasn't neat. Maureen didn't think it was an official letter, an answer to Shirley's inquiries about medical school. However, she wasn't tempted to open it, even though her curiosity was aroused. It wasn't in her nature to pry into Shirley's things, though she would read it with interest if her daughter chose to show it to her.

She made the tea, sat down to drink it and then began to prepare for an afternoon of cooking, setting to with a will and fetching out her precious hoard of special ingredients. First, she would get her cakes and puddings underway and then she was going to write her Christmas cards this afternoon, though she wouldn't send them until a week before, unless they were out of London. Some of her parcels were packed and hidden, but she still had more gifts to buy and she would make the first batch of mince pies later, too. They would all be gone by the weekend and she would make several batches before Christmas, no doubt.

She finished her ironing, polished the front room and fed Matty with a small ham sandwich and a tiny piece of cake. He had a drink of orange juice and Maureen had a sandwich and a cup of tea as she wrote out some of her Christmas cards and then checked on her cake. She'd done nothing but bake all day, she thought and was beginning to feel a bit tired, because they'd worked hard to get all the cakes ready to be sold over the counter too.

The tea shop opened at one-thirty and closed at five in the afternoon. During that time, tea and cake was served to customers who wanted to sit down and chat over a pot of tea and the shelves were cleared each day because the cakes sold out to folk who called in to purchase them and it was unusual to have more than the occasional sponge left at the end of the day.

Maureen enjoyed working with Sheila. She also enjoyed serving in the tea shop, but only did that twice a week, leaving herself plenty of time to look after her home and family.

Gordy was at school and at three o'clock she took Matty in his pushchair and went around to the school to collect him. On the two afternoons she worked in the shop, Rose or Sheila fetched him. They all had children at the same school so helped each other out and it all worked well.

This afternoon, Maureen was fetching Jenny and Gordy from school, but Sheila had told her that Chris was being fetched by his father because of the football match. It was very cold and she hoped it wouldn't snow just yet and spoil their afternoon. Pip would hopefully be there to see the second half of the match and take his son home. He had meetings with his firm from time to time, but he often worked in his study above the pub and Sheila said he sometimes sat up long into the night if he was concentrating on a project. He seemed content enough, though Maureen knew he still hankered over his ambition to be a pilot.

'I thought if he got a few hours' private flying with a co-pilot it might help,' Sheila had confided once. 'I'm not sure it makes things better; he just wants it more when he gets home. He says it doesn't matter and he's content, but I know he longs to do the things he can't do any more...'

'He's lucky compared to some,' Maureen had told her. 'So many young men died and others were left crippled. Pip's eyes enable him to do most things...'

'Except fly commercial aeroplanes...' Sheila had said regretfully. 'I know – and I'm sure he does too, but it doesn't stop him wanting what he can't have...'

Maureen had nodded. She'd known enough pain and disappointment of her own to understand, but, in her experience, you just got on with things. Pip had always been a bit spoiled. Peggy could straighten him out, but he only saw his mother a few times a year. It was a pity she wasn't around more to make him see how much he had in life.

10

Shirley picked up her letters when she came in from school, dumping her battered old satchel in the hall. She saw Richard's letter and felt pleased. He never missed writing to her and she loved getting his letters and writing to him; it made the distance between them easier to bear.

Richard's letter was filled with news about his exams, the hospital patients he saw as a medical student and his friends. They were having a big end-of-term Christmas party at college and it was fancy dress. He was going as Richard the Lionheart and Katie was going as his queen. Shirley frowned over it a little, because this same friend had been mentioned several times lately, a little too much for Shirley's liking. Richard was her special friend, even if they weren't in love, and she didn't like him being too friendly with another girl – but, of course, she couldn't rule Richard's life. He'd never promised to love or marry her.

Brushing away the unwanted tears that stung her eyes, Shirley told herself not to be foolish. Richard was honest. He would tell her if he had a proper girlfriend, but, according to his letters, Katie was just one of the friends he went drinking with some nights.

Putting his letter to one side, Shirley slit the second open and then stared at it in horror. It was written in big letters in red and the message was spiteful.

RICHARD IS SHAGGING A GIRL IN HIS CLASS AT MEDIC SCHOOL. YOU OUGHT TO KNOW HE ISN'T THE SHINING KNIGHT YOU THINK HE IS. WHY DON'T YOU TELL HIM TO GET LOST?

For a moment, Shirley stared at it in shock. How could anyone write such vicious filth to her? What had she done to make someone dislike her this much?

Shirley had friends at school, but because she travelled to the grammar school most of them lived further out and she only saw them at school or on special outings planned by the teachers. Here in the lanes, she knew girls, who passed the time of day and stopped to chat about the new dress they'd bought or a film they'd seen, but most thought her a swot because she was always studying or reading her medical journals and never asked her to visit their homes or go the pictures. Was that enough to make one of them send her a letter like this? She couldn't believe she'd done anything to make anyone hate her this much.

She'd been asked out a few times by local lads but usually refused. The once or twice she had accepted an invitation to meet someone at the church hall for the monthly social, which her mother also attended, and included dancing, she'd found them on a different level to her. She didn't think anyone local had written the letter. No, it had come from away.

Shirley reviewed the friends she had in the lanes. She was quite friendly with Carol, the daughter of a woman who worked in her parents' shop and they went to a matinee at the cinema together sometimes on Saturday, or shopping to buy a new dress if they had saved enough money, but otherwise she spent most of her time at home, studying or playing with her young brothers. If she thought about it honestly, Shirley realised she'd felt herself committed to Richard and hadn't wanted to go out seriously with anyone else.

She'd thought of him as her special friend – but had she been fooling herself?

Shirley wrinkled her brow and thought seriously about her feelings for Richard. She'd always seen him as being very close and assumed they would become closer as the years passed, possibly working together and – had she thought of marriage? – she wasn't sure. Was she in love with him – and was Richard in love with her? He'd never said anything to make her think so, but his smile and the way he looked at her made her feel special – but perhaps he smiled at Katie the same way?

A shaft of jealousy struck her and she realised she minded if he smiled at other girls the way he smiled at her, which was ridiculous. He wasn't hers; she didn't own him. So why had someone sent her this horrid letter?

Shirley looked at it in disgust. The wording was crude and common and her father would be furious if he saw it. He would probably tell her she was to stop writing to Richard and Mum would tell her it was someone with a nasty mind who was jealous.

She felt the prick of tears but brushed them away. She wasn't a pushover and she wouldn't let this coward make her quarrel with Richard or think badly of him. The letter had been sent to make her miserable and she refused to let it come between her and the friend she'd loved so many years. Yes, she did love Richard, she accepted that – but loving a friend was not being in love, was it? Shirley didn't really know what being in love meant. She had a vague idea that girls went all giggly and silly over boys they were in love with, but she didn't feel like that, so perhaps she wasn't. She sighed, because this letter was forcing her to think about stuff she wasn't truly ready for...

For years it had just been friendship between them, but during his last visit she'd been aware of new feelings stirring inside her and she'd thought he felt the same – but how could she expect him to remain faithful to her when there were other more available women? He probably still thought of Shirley as his childhood friend, a little girl he'd walked home from school and comforted when her baby brother died.

That wicked letter! The writer hadn't even had the guts to sign it!

Angry now, Shirley tore the offending letter into little pieces. Richard was her friend and she trusted him. If he had a girlfriend he loved, he would tell her when he came home – and she would wish him good fortune. She would never let him, or anyone, see that she was feeling hurt or let down.

She put the torn letter into the kitchen range and went to fill the kettle. Her mother and brothers would be in soon and Shirley would have their tea on the table waiting for them. Mum had made some lovely plum jam in the autumn and there was a fresh loaf, also some almond tarts and rock cakes and a batch of mince pies.

Lifting her head, Shirley put the letter out of her mind. If Richard had something to tell her he could tell her himself.

11

Janet looked at the smear of lipstick on the handkerchief she'd taken from her husband's jacket pocket and her throat caught with tears. She hadn't been looking for proof of her suspicions, but the jacket needed cleaning and Ryan had asked her to take it into the shop for him. Had he left the handkerchief there deliberately, wanting her to see it?

Janet felt the tears turn to anger as she grabbed a pair of scissors from the dressing table and cut the offending article to shreds. For a moment, she was tempted to cut the jacket up too, but something stopped her. It was her favourite jacket and she'd bought it for Ryan herself – but now she flung it to the ground in disgust. How could he do this to her?

Shaking her head, she picked the jacket up again and gathered her coat, gloves, bag and scarf. She was meeting a friend in town for coffee and a snack lunch and she would be better doing that than sitting at home brooding. At least she knew now for certain that Ryan had something going on, but she wasn't sure it was a full-blown affair yet.

Was she hiding from the truth? Janet blinked hard to clear her vision as she started the little Austin car her husband had bought for her. It gave Janet the independence she needed living in the country and she loved it and was grateful for his gift. However, that didn't stop her suspecting her husband was cheating on her. If she'd known about the lipstick before, she would have told him the holiday in Scotland wasn't on and taken Maggie to her mother's for Christmas, but it was too late now. Everything was booked and Maggie was looking forward to it; she'd told all her friends and they envied her.

'I wish Bob would take us to Scotland for Christmas,' Susie Briggs had moaned. 'I'll be stuck in the kitchen all day feeding his family while he sits in front of the fire scoffing and listening to the King's speech on the wireless.'

'You should ask for help,' Janet had retorted. 'When we go to Mum's, we all help with the cooking and the washing up, Ryan and Maggie included.'

'As any civilised family would,' Susie had said. 'Bob's lot expect me to wait on them like a slave – and daft me does it every year. Some folk don't know how lucky they are...'

Janet reflected that Susie didn't know how lucky she was. Her husband Bob might be lazy around the house and expect to be waited on, but he worked hard, providing Susie with nice clothes, a lovely home and a little car of her own and he was faithful to her – that meant more than all the rest. She really couldn't complain and Janet had had no cause for complaint either – until they lost the baby and then that awful miscarriage followed, leaving her tired and miserable.

'You need a break,' Ryan had announced back in October. 'We'll go to Scotland for ten days at Christmas and then perhaps you'll be more like yourself...'

Instead of the moaning Minnie she'd been of late, Janet had recognised what he hadn't said as truth. She didn't actually complain much, but she didn't smile either and even Maggie had told her she wasn't much fun these days.

'My friends do things with their mums,' she'd told Janet once or twice. 'They come to the school fete and help with the concert and things – and they take their daughters to dance lessons and the pictures on Saturday afternoons. Fay and Freddie go roller-skating. I never go anywhere fun...'

'I took you to see *Snow White* at the pictures...' Janet had protested, but Maggie had pulled a face.

'That was months ago. I wanted to see *Bambi*, but you said you hadn't got time – and you didn't come to my school fete day either...'

Janet knew she'd spent too much time crying in her bedroom after the miscarriage and she'd avoided the school functions, because the other mums looked at her with sympathy because they all knew she'd lost another baby. She saw them eyeing her, thinking how useless she was – 'Can't even give her husband a child...' was what she imagined they whispered to each other.

Janet pulled across the road, startled when a car coming towards her hooted loudly. She hadn't signalled her intentions! Guilt and a shock of fear went through her. She couldn't dwell on the things that upset her when she was driving or she might end up in an accident, causing harm to herself and others.

Her car parked, Janet took Ryan's jacket into the cleaners, glad to be rid of it. She made a beeline for the café where she was due to meet Susie. At least for the next couple of hours she would have no chance to dwell on her wrongs and it would give her time to decide what to do. Should she confront Ryan and risk an all-out row? It would be better than letting things drag on, but what happened then? Could Janet justify turning their lives upside down because of a smear of lipstick? Maggie wasn't Ryan's daughter, but she thought of him as her father and would be upset if they parted – and where would Janet go? Could she demand that he moved out? Could she afford to keep herself?

The questions buzzed at her. Janet had a part-time job, but she was used to buying whatever she wanted and that would have to stop if Ryan paid her only a small allowance. After all, she couldn't claim maintenance because Maggie was Mike's daughter not his. And that was only the financial side. What about missing him? What about the pain and heartbreak of a split and possibly a divorce? Maggie would never forgive her.

Janet realised she was caught between a rock and a hard place. Whichever way she chose, it would be painful now that she suspected that Ryan was cheating on her, because she would never be able to trust what he said...

'Oh, Mum,' she whispered to herself. 'I wish you lived nearer.'

Janet knew she was guilty of pushing her mother away. She'd done it before when Mike was missing and when he'd died; she'd done it again when her mother brought the Christmas presents down, shutting her out and keeping a distance – and now all she wanted was to weep in her mother's arms. Perhaps she would ring her later and tell her what she'd found, but would Peggy understand? Would she tell her to pull herself together and make the best of things?

Janet needed a shoulder to cry on, but the habit of keeping it all inside was strong and she knew that the moment her mother asked questions, she would clam up and be unable to speak about her pain. It was something inside her that made her unable to reach out when her mother was sympathetic, especially over the phone. She tended to bottle things up inside, withdraw into herself rather than talk about her worries. Perhaps if her mother were here, a touch of the hand might make it all come tumbling out, but the telephone was so impersonal.

Sighing again, Janet walked swiftly towards the café. She couldn't tell Susie the truth, because her friend probably wouldn't believe her about Ryan, because she liked him, so she would just have to put on a brave face and make out everything was fine.

* * *

Peggy picked up the receiver and then replaced it. She'd had a strange feeling all day that Janet was in trouble and yet when she'd taken their presents down the previous weekend, her daughter had shut her out, pretending everything was fine. Her manner and the look in her eyes had told Peggy that Janet's life was far from fine and she'd tried to talk to her, but Ryan had come into the room and Janet had shut down. She'd smiled and laughed as if nothing was wrong, giving Peggy beautifully wrapped gifts for all of them and talking non-stop about her holiday in Scotland.

Just before she'd left to drive home, Ryan had got Peggy alone for a moment.

'I'm worried about Janet,' he'd told her. 'Something is wrong, Peggy, but she won't let me in – she has shut us all out, even Maggie.'

'It happened once before, after Mike died so suddenly,' Peggy had told him with a frown. 'I tried to help her, but she went away from us all. She wouldn't talk to me until she'd found her own peace, Ryan.' Peggy had looked him in the eyes. 'Is everything all right from your side? Has she reason to be hurt?'

'None,' Ryan had replied firmly. 'I know we've lost the babies and I've told her enough is enough. Yes, I would've liked a son and I grieved as much as she did when we lost our son and then the miscarriage made things worse, but I don't want to lose her, Peggy. It's silly to risk her health for nothing...'

'You've told her this?'

'Yes, but I don't think she's listening.' Ryan had frowned. 'She blames herself for losing the babies, but it isn't her fault – I don't blame her, Peggy. I can't bear to see her like this...'

'Then make her understand that,' Peggy had advised him. 'She has to come out of this and realise that losing a child is terrible, but it isn't the end of everything. She still has so much. I just want to see her on form again, get her sparkle back.'

'Yes, I know.' Ryan had looked at her wretchedly. 'I'd give anything for her to have another child for her sake, but I just want her, Peggy – I'm beginning to fear for her sanity...'

'Rubbish!' Peggy had said sharply but there was no time to say more because Janet and Able had come into the hall and were hugging. Able seemed to reach her daughter when Peggy couldn't and she'd seen tears in Janet's eyes.

'What's on your mind, hon?' Able asked as he entered the hall and saw her hovering by the phone.

'I was wondering whether to phone Jan...'

'I should if I were you,' he said with a loving smile. 'She was a bit down when we were there. I told her we both loved her and she was welcome to come to us if she ever needed a break – or a home...'

'Is that why she was hugging you?' Peggy asked. He was such a lovely, kind man, no wonder she loved him! 'What did she say?'

'She just hugged me,' Able said. 'I wish she would open up to you – to both of us.' He smiled at her. 'Your daughter keeps things inside too much. I think she imagines Ryan is upset with her because she can't give him a son, but he adores her. You can see it in the way his eyes follow her all the time...'

'I worry about her, Able...'

'We could go down again if you wish...'

'No, we have too much to do this week,' Peggy said. 'All those bookings for special lunches and the cakes I've promised to regular customers. Besides, she's travelling to Scotland at the beginning of next week and then we're off to London. I'll telephone her at the weekend and then I'll go down in the New Year if the weather permits.'

12

Rose saw the stall selling walnuts and other Christmas treats as she walked to the market that weekend. Surely it was the one she'd shopped at before but he'd moved his pitch, perhaps because he didn't have a proper license. Some of the stalls that set up for Christmas had not been given an official pitch or permission to trade. She measured her steps and then stopped as Nobby's cheeky smile flashed out at her. He looked a bit bedraggled, his hair sticking up stiffly, as if it needed a good wash, and she thought he was too thin, because his trousers hung on him. They were probably his father's cutdowns, she thought. The mother in her wanted to take him home, give him a bath, some better clothes and a good meal, but she knew she mustn't interfere. The boy was proud and would resent it if she offered charity.

'After some more of them walnuts, missus?'

'Yes, please,' Rose agreed. 'I'll have a box of your sticky dates too – and what are those Brazil nuts like?'

Rose had planned to buy those from her usual stall in the covered market and was conscious that Nobby and his father were robbing the legitimate traders of their rightful trade and felt a bit guilty. Yet, she'd come across his stall despite taking another route and the half-starved look in Nobby's face made her get her purse out and buy more than she'd intended. Tom would love the nuts and the lad needed to earn a few shillings or he would likely go without his supper.

'Good,' Nobby promised. 'Me and Dad ate a pound between us last night and there wasn't a bad 'un in them!'

'I'll have two pounds then please,' Rose said. 'Tom likes those as much as the walnuts. So that's a pound of walnuts, two of Brazils and a box of dates...'

'Five bob to you then, missus – me dad said to let you have them at a good price if you came...'

'Where is your dad then?' Rose asked, because there was no sign of him.

'He went ter meet a mate and left me ter mind the stall fer half an hour. Yer've just missed him...'

Rose nodded and paid over her five shillings. She smiled and walked on, relieved that Jim Broad had not been there to disturb her with his knowing looks and the smile that made her vaguely uneasy. The nuts would be good, the best she could find in the market, but she'd avoided an embarrassing encounter and that was a good thing. She'd made up her mind to walk past if Jim had been there, but since he was elsewhere no harm had been done, because Nobby deserved a helping hand even if his father was too familiar for Rose's liking.

Her Christmas shopping was all but done now apart from last-minute food and Rose was planning to look for a new dress for Christmas Day. Tom had given her a five-pound note for herself, which was a small fortune.

'I've already got a surprise for you,' he'd said, smiling and clearly pleased with himself, 'but you need a pretty dress for the day. We've been invited for tea with Sheila and Peggy, so you'll want somethin' new – and you'll choose better than I shall...'

Rose had scolded him for spoiling her again, but she was pleased because it would be lovely to have a new dress to wear for Christmas tea after all the cooking and clearing up was done. She'd seen something in a local shop she liked and walked determinedly in the right direction. Her best black patent shoes were still good, so she would spend all the money on the velvet dress she'd liked in Matthews' dress shop. It was situated close to the covered market and Rose popped in every now and then to see what was new.

The midnight blue dress was available in her size and when she tried it on, Rose knew it suited her down to the ground. She happily paid for it and left the shop carrying the distinctive bag. It was a beautiful dress, full in the skirt with little puffed sleeves and a squared neckline, hugely expensive, but just under the five pounds Tom had given her. She would save the few shillings change and buy something for the children another day.

'Been treating yourself?' a voice asked just behind her and Rose spun round to be confronted by a pair of mocking eyes. Her heart sank as she saw the look Jim Broad gave her, but she controlled her mounting unease, frowning at him.

'As a matter of fact, my husband treated me,' she said in a cool voice, reminding him she was married to a good, generous man.

'So would I, if you were mine,' he said in a suggestive voice that made her go hot under the collar. 'You'd pay for treating you would, Rose.'

'I don't recall giving you permission to call me Rose,' she told him frostily. She hadn't wanted to offend him in front of Nobby when he'd done it the first time, but his son wasn't here now and it was time to nip his flirting in the bud before it got out of hand! 'I'm Mrs Barton to you, Mr Broad, and don't you forget it...'

'You like the way I look at yer though, I know yer sort...'

'You are quite wrong,' Rose said, angry now. 'I bought from your stall, because I liked your son – and it's obvious you neglect the lad. When did he last have a good meal? However, if you persist in annoying me, I'll – I'll report you to the council for illegal trading...'

Rose wasn't sure why she'd threatened something she wouldn't dream of doing, but something in his familiarity and his assumption that she liked him looking at her had made her angry and reckless.

His grin disappeared and he looked at her as if he would like to hit her but didn't say a word.

A flicker of fear went through her and she wished her hasty

words unsaid but couldn't bring herself to take them back. After all, he was trading illegally, she'd guessed it because his pitch wasn't a regular one and the council frowned on traders taking pitches that weren't licensed. Sometimes they turned a blind eye over Christmas but would soon move him on once it was over.

Rose walked on by, forbidding herself to turn around and see if he was watching her. She knew he was and it made her uncomfortable. What was it about her that had made him think he could be so familiar?

It wasn't the first time it had happened to Rose. Before she married Tom, she'd got it all the time in the pub. Men seemed to think she was fair game and flirted with her outrageously. Since her marriage, the locals had treated her with proper civility, perhaps out of respect for Tom – but Jim Broad was different. Rose recognised the look in his eyes. He was dangerous and she would do her best to keep out of his way in future.

* * *

Tom approved the dress when Rose tried it on for him. It made her look sensual and beautiful, enhancing the flame of her hair that seemed even redder under the electric lights. He felt a sharp surge of desire and a warm glow of possession, because she was his and her lips would be soft and warm, inviting whenever he kissed her. Tom had been lucky to get her. He understood that she'd taken him on the rebound after Jimmy's death and sometimes felt a little guilty that he hadn't given her time to get over it properly. Was she happy – did she truly love him?

From the moment Rose had first walked into the corner shop where he was then working and teased him, Tom had adored her. He was younger than Rose and at the time he'd never expected she would ever look at him. She'd been engaged to a brave soldier and Tom had been merely a cadet. His brief service in the Army had made a man of him and the work he did had built muscles as hard as iron. Not many men in the lanes were bigger or stronger than Tom these days; he was well respected, known as a good tradesman and there were always men willing to stand him a drink in the Pig & Whistle. Tom took his turn and bought as many pints as he was offered, but he never drank more than one himself, because he preferred to keep his wits about him, and he would never go home to his Rose the worse for drink.

'I'm glad you like it,' Rose was saying. 'I'll take it off now, Tom. I don't want to spoil it before Christmas.'

'You always look lovely,' Tom said and caught her hand as she turned away. 'You are satisfied? You don't regret marrying me?'

'Of course not,' Rose answered swiftly. Tom saw something in her eyes for a moment, but then it was gone. 'You're the best of husbands, Tom, and a wonderful father – and I love my kids and my life. I'm so lucky...'

'That's all right then.' Tom let her go to take off her special dress, scolding himself for his flash of doubt earlier. He shouldn't let himself remember that Rose had loved Jimmy first and taken him on the rebound. She was a wonderful wife and the loving mother of their children. It was stupid to let his own insecurity cloud his mind! 'Is supper nearly ready?' he asked when she came back to him, wearing her everyday clothes. 'I could eat a horse...'

'I made a shepherd's pie this morning; its heating in the oven and I've got beans in tomato sauce with it and fruit, jelly and ice cream for afters.'

'That's a feast,' Tom said. 'What have I done to deserve it?'

'I made the jelly for the children,' Rose said and her smile teased him. 'We're having what they didn't manage to eat for their tea...'

'Ah, I might have known,' he said, but he was laughing. Rose spoiled the children. Most kids in the lanes would have a bit of bread and jam for tea if they were lucky. Some of them didn't even get jam on their bread, poor little devils. Rose was always making jellies, blancmange and custards for her family.

Suddenly, the small clouds disappeared and Tom knew he'd been worrying for nothing.

There was only just over a week to Christmas now and Tom was looking forward to his annual break. He normally took ten days off at Christmas to be with his family, because it was a special time and he was usually so busy. He really looked forward to that time, though he knew his neighbours might have little jobs they would beg him to do – most of them took him ten minutes at most and he made no charge. Fixing a loose screw for a woman living alone, changing a light bulb for Alice or fetching the coal in for old Mr Coulson opposite the pub were things Tom had always done to help his friends and neighbours, but that wasn't work to him. It made a break to walk over the road, fix the leak under Mrs Butler's sink and then go home for a cup of tea and a bun with his Rose. It was when he got into knocking down walls, building walls and fixing new kitchen sinks that he was back to work.

Tom smiled contentedly as his wife set their plates on the table and he smelled the delicious pie. He was a lucky man.

13

'Can I take my skates with me?' Fay asked as Peggy was packing their cases. 'Will I be able to go skating when we're staying with Aunty Sheila?'

'If you wanted, you could probably try ice-skating,' Peggy told her and saw her daughter's eyes light up. 'You can take your roller skates, but you'll be able to borrow ice skates and boots at the rink...'

'Mum!' Fay rushed at her and hugged her. 'I've wanted to try for such a long time but we never could... can I really?'

'It was too far to take you during school term and you only broke up yesterday,' Peggy said. 'I thought this holiday would be a good chance for you to try. I'm not sure if there will be time before Christmas because we'll arrive late tonight and I'll have a lot to do tomorrow, unpacking and settling in – but you should get to skate several times while we're there, if you enjoy it, because we shall stay until the New Year, if Sheila can put up with us that long...'

'You're the best mum ever...' Fay popped a kiss on her shoulder, which was as high as she could reach.

'There will be a rink we can easily get to on the bus or the underground,' Peggy told her, feeling happy as she saw her youngest daughter's delight at the prospect. She glanced at Freddie. 'Do you want to try as well, love?'

'I don't mind having a go, Mum,' Freddie said. 'I'll come and watch Fay and go on with her if she likes. I'm happy either way – but do you think there will be a football match on up there?'

'I'm sure there will,' Peggy reassured him, looking at her son fondly. 'Your brother Pip will know and your father will take you – Chris might like to go too...'

'Chris likes reading and making models more than sport, Mum. I'm not sure he and Pip go to football matches.' Freddie nodded wisely.

'Well, there's sure to be a match on for Boxing Day,' Peggy told him. 'There are fixtures all over the country and London probably has several scheduled over the holiday, because there are different clubs. West Ham will be playing, I expect, and Arsenal...'

Freddie nodded and smiled. Arsenal was one of the most famous clubs and he'd love to get to one of their matches if he could. 'And you will enjoy meeting all your friends, Mum. Are you looking forward to it?'

'Yes, I am, love. I'm planning on taking you both to a pantomime at Olympia, too. They have some wonderful productions on there. I took Pip to see *Aladdin* when he was your age and Janet loved *Cinderella*. I'm not sure what is on this year, but there will be lots of exciting things going on in London, Father Christmas in the stores and...' She smiled because Freddie was too big for Father Christmas visits now. 'We might see a good cowboy film at a matinee one afternoon.' His grin told her that she'd hit on a treat he would like.

'Why don't we live in London now?' Fay asked. 'I could go ice-skating every day after school then...'

'Don't you like being so near to the sea?' Peggy asked. 'In the summer, you go to the beach every Sunday. You couldn't do that in London.'

'I don't like swimming in the sea,' Fay said. 'I prefer the indoor swimming pool when I go with my school. I know there is an indoor pool in London, because Dad took us when we were little.'

'Yes, he did,' Peggy agreed. 'We thought it would be a better life for you in the country though.'

'I like it here,' Freddie said. 'We have lots of sports – football in the winter, running, jumping and cricket and tennis in the summer.'

Peggy smiled at his enthusiasm. Able shared his love of sport and despite his war injury, when he'd lost most of his left arm, he made little of it and could manage to play football in the garden and bat with one hand, though his aim wasn't good and they normally played on the beach rather than in the garden where his erratic swing might have sent the ball through next door's window!

'You could play all those games in town,' Fay said, scornful of her brother's pastimes. 'I can't ice-skate here. It's too far to get into Truro every time...'

'Yes, it isn't easy, but if you really want to do it after you've tried it, Fay, I could perhaps find time to take you in once a week...'

'I need to practise every day if I'm going to skate in the Winter Olympics.' Fay pouted and Peggy's heart sank. Taking Fay for practice every day just wouldn't be possible with her busy routine at the café.

'Well, you don't know if you will like it,' Peggy said to placate her, but she felt distressed. Fay could be so difficult at times and, like a terrier with a bone, she just wouldn't give up.

'Can I take my football boots, Mum?' Freddie asked. 'I've cleaned them and put them in my bag, so they won't make a mess in the case.'

'Yes, of course you can,' Peggy agreed, though she wasn't sure he would get a chance to use them. A visit to a match could be arranged, but where would he play? Boys played football in the lanes, but they didn't wear special boots; you needed a muddy field for the studs.

'Nearly ready, hon?' Able asked, entering the bedroom. He eyed the three big cases already packed. 'We're only going for twelve days or so not forever.' His eyes danced with amusement.

'Worse luck,' Fay said. 'I wish we lived in London...'

'And why is that?' Able asked, watching his daughter's face.

'So, I can go ice-skating every day after school,' Fay supplied promptly.

'Ah, I see,' Able said, suppressing his laughter. 'I suppose that's because the World Ice Skating Championships will take place in London next March?' He laughed as Fay made a face at him. 'What about Sundays on the beach?'

'I don't like the beach,' Fay said. 'Can we live in London, Dad?'

'I don't know,' Able replied. He looked at his son. 'I think that needs a lot of thought and discussion. How does Freddie feel about moving to London?'

'I don't mind – as long as I can play football,' Freddie said obligingly. 'But you and Mum have worked hard to make the café a success, Dad. It shouldn't be us who decide...'

Able looked at Peggy, his brows raised. 'I think it all depends how your mum feels about things. We have a lovely home here and a good business, but I can make coffee and pancakes anywhere...'

'It's just Fay being fanciful,' Peggy said, because her daughter often had whims. Peggy sometimes felt a bit nostalgic about her good times in Mulberry Lane, but she'd settled well here. 'She doesn't even know if she will like ice-skating yet – or if she will be any good at it...' She turned away to finish her packing. 'Can we get all this stuff in the boot, Able?'

'Plenty of room,' he assured her and picked up the heaviest case. He was very strong despite his disability and Peggy knew he exercised to keep himself that way. 'Freddie, you carry that little one and I'll come back for the rest.'

'I can bring one,' Peggy said, but Able had already gone.

She moved the other heavy case to the top of the stairs and then picked up a lighter one and carried it down. If she tried to take the heavy case down, it would make her husband cross. He'd told her once he might be missing an arm but wasn't an invalid and she hadn't repeated her mistake by offering unwanted help.

Able soon had the car packed and then applied his energy to getting the children into the back seat. Coats, books and games to play on the way went in after them and then Peggy slid into the front beside her husband.

'Have we all got everything?' she asked, looking round at the twins, who nodded. 'The lights are switched off and everything is locked up – I think we can go, Able?'

'Sure...' He glanced in the mirror. 'Anyone want the bathroom before we leave?'

'No, thanks,' Freddie said and Fay just shook her head, impatient to be off.

'Here we go then...' He smiled at Peggy. 'Have a rest while you can, love.'

'I'm fine, Able. If you want me to drive for a while, just pull over and we'll change.' He drove his specially adapted automatic car easily these days and had passed his English driving licence test, even though he already possessed an American licence.

'We'll stop for a drink and a sandwich somewhere,' he said, 'but I want to get there by supper time if we can.'

'We should be all right, unless we get stuck in traffic nearer London.' Peggy nodded. She was looking forward to seeing her son and his wife and child again.

'It will be easier being a Sunday,' Able said. 'Besides, we couldn't leave before or the kids would've missed their school nativity play and party, and we had bookings at the café yesterday for your special turkey dinner.' His eyes twinkled at her, because Peggy had put on a lovely Christmas dinner for the regular and elderly customers at a special low price and the café had been packed out all day.

'They did enjoy it so much,' Peggy said. 'We broke even on it, Able – and I wanted to say thank you to our regulars for their custom all this time.'

'Did I tell you how much I love you, Peggy Ronoscki?' Able said with a smile that made her heart flip. 'There were a lot of happy folk and I think you enjoyed it too...'

'I did,' she admitted and sighed. 'It's good to know we've got three whole weeks off though, isn't it?'

'Some of our customers were a little put out we were closing for the next three weeks, but I told them we needed a rest and most understood, except for the young ones. They won't have anywhere to come for their pancakes and coffee.'

'Did you deliver all your presents to your school friends?' Peggy glanced back at the twins and received a nod from Fay and a smiling affirmative from Freddie.

'We took them in on Friday, Mum.'

Fay had been chosen to play Mary in her school nativity play this year – something she'd taken seriously. It had been performed the previous Saturday and all the parents had been invited. It had been quite a success and Fay had been full of it for a few days, but now she was back to talking non-stop about her ambitions to be an ice-skating champion. She was drawing something on her pad now and held it up to show Peggy a picture of a girl on the ice. It was quite good, but Fay was good at a lot of artistic things, a bit like her elder brother, Pip.

Janet and her family had gone up to London on Thursday, taking her daughter out of school a few days early, because they were breaking their journey to Scotland overnight and calling in to see Sheila. Maggie hadn't minded, because her school party had been on that afternoon, and she'd come home laden with stuff she'd made in class. Peggy had had a brief phone call on Saturday evening to say that they were all well and about to catch their train up to Scotland and that Pip had sent his love and was eager to see them all. They were going up on a sleeper train and would arrive nice and fresh in the morning.

Peggy nodded and smiled. Long journeys in the car were easier now the twins were older, because they amused themselves with books and games. She had biscuits, bottles of squash made up and some fruit sweets that helped if anyone was feeling sick. Hopefully, there would not be too many stops and they would arrive before it got too late in the evening.

* * *

It was dark by the time Able drew up outside the Pig & Whistle and Peggy could see the lights on upstairs. The pub was closed, of course, because it was Sunday, and Peggy was pleased there was no one around to see them arrive tired and bedraggled.

She got out and went to the door, using the old-fashioned knocker to let Sheila know they had arrived. The big thick door flew open before she had managed to get the twins out of the car and start to unload. Sheila came out, beaming and opening her arms wide. She embraced Peggy and then the twins flew at her, being hugged and kissed with Sheila's customary warmth.

'Hello, you two,' she said. 'I'm glad you're here. I was beginning to worry.'

'Happy Christmas, Aunty Sheila!' the twins chorused. 'We've brought lots of presents.'

'That's lovely,' Sheila said. 'Chris still believes in Father Christmas don't forget – at least, I think he does...'

'No, he doesn't,' Pip said coming out to greet them. 'He's like me and I never did...'

Sheila made a little face at her husband and Peggy moved towards her, taking her arm to squeeze it. She whispered in Sheila's ear, 'He did until he was six and saw his father filling his stocking...'

Sheila smiled at her. 'I thought you would be here an hour ago...'

'We stopped a couple of times and ran into a bit of a traffic jam in central London,' Peggy said. 'The journey was fine up until then, but we had a nice lunch and then we all needed to visit the toilets and these things take time.'

'As long as you're safe here now,' Sheila said, ushering them in. Pip smiled at her. 'It's lovely to have you all here – Happy Christmas. Everyone was looking for you all night, wondering when you would arrive.'

'I knew they would be late. It's a long journey and you need lots of stops with children in the car.' Pip came forward and hugged her. 'All right, Mum? I hope it wasn't too bad?'

'No, the twins were very good and it's wonderful to be here,' she said and smiled at him. 'Happy Christmas, darling, and to you, Sheila. You both look well. I'm so glad to see you – is Chris still up?'

'In bed but still awake. He's making a model of a racing car,' Pip said. 'I left him to fix a tricky piece by himself and he'll come to say hello once we get upstairs...' He took the heaviest case from Able. 'Let me take that, Able. I'll come back and help with the other stuff.'

'I can get it all in the hall and then lock the car,' Able said. 'Should I run it under the arch?'

'I think it might be safer,' Pip said. 'Those who know it belongs to you and Peggy won't touch it, but some of the lads from further away will have the wheels off if you don't watch them.'

Able laughed. 'I'll take it round the back yard then,' he said. 'I shan't be in your way?'

'Plenty of room for all the cars,' Pip replied. 'Sheila doesn't bother to drive. She takes a bus or I drive her where she wants to go – I tell her she should learn, but she can't be bothered...'

'Living in town you don't have to bother with a car so much,' Able agreed. 'Peggy learned, because in the country you do need it. You can wait hours for a bus to come and sometimes they just don't turn up.'

'It wouldn't suit me,' Pip said. 'I've thought about it, but I can get to meetings here or at de Havilland's factory by car or train and Sheila likes living here.'

Able nodded, his eyes reflecting laughter. 'Fay wants to live here so she can ice-skate every day after school. She's going to be an Olympic skater – so she says...' Both Fay and Freddie had gone rushing up the stairs to the private floor, where a warm fire awaited them in the sitting room.

'That sounds like my baby sister,' Pip said and roared with laughter. 'You spoil her, Able. I pity her husband if she ever marries. She will lead him a right dance.'

'You're probably right,' Able agreed. 'I think it was because I didn't know about them for a long time. I felt lucky to be alive after what happened and it was such a bonus to discover I had twins and to be able to marry Peggy...' He shook his head. 'I'll get the car round and be right in.'

Pip went in and closed the front door. As Able returned to the car, he saw a woman peering at him from a bedroom across the road.

She waved furiously at him and he realised it must be Alice, an old friend of Peggy's. He waved to her and then blew her a kiss. She immediately sent one back, so he knew he'd done the right thing.

He drove through the pub arch and into the large back yard. Pip's car was standing there under a carport and Ryan's car had been parked behind it while they were in Scotland. Pip must have had the carport put up since they were there a couple of summers previously and Able could see that it would help protect the vehicle from ice and snow, though the rain might still get under. Apart from that, everything looked much as it had the last time they'd been here. Most of the rebuilding, like Bob's shoe repairs next door, then the boarding house that did bed and breakfast, and the tea shop Sheila ran, which was next door but one to the pub, and on the site of the old bakery that had been bombed and pulled down, had been rebuilt in the first years after the war. Since then, nothing much had happened to Mulberry Lane, not like some parts of London which were being pulled down to build what the old Londoners thought of as towering monstrosities in the form of new apartment blocks.

Able parked out of the way and then lifted the bonnet and put an old blanket underneath the hood. It helped to stop the engine freezing and his car wouldn't much like being left out in the cold; Able had a large double garage at home, which had room for both their cars. He hadn't truly realised how much of a luxury it was. Living where they did might have its shortfall when it came to ice rinks and theatres, but there were definitely benefits too.

Able knew that he and Peggy had a good living from their café. He'd used part of his savings to set them up, but they never spent all they earned and he had a nice balance in the bank again now. He could afford to buy a decent property in London if Peggy wanted to return to the city.

Able wasn't sure how she felt. He knew she loved the cottage and they had made it very comfortable, but there would be no need to sell. They didn't own the café outright, but the lease was coming up for renewal quite soon. It would be simple to renew and then sell the goodwill, because it was a thriving business.

Still, he was jumping the gun, because so far it was only Fay who wanted to live in London, and that was for a silly reason. She had some idea of being a famous ice skater. Lots of young girls wanted to be ballerinas, but very few made it into the ballet company, though hundreds took lessons. Fay's passion for skating might be just a passing phase, perhaps because she'd read about the World Championships coming to London next year. Besides, Peggy would have the last word. Able was easy either way. His wife and the twins were his life, and, as he'd said earlier, he could do his job anywhere.

He arched his shoulders, feeling the ache of a long drive, even though Peggy had insisted on taking over for a couple of hours to give him a break. He smiled as he thought of his wife. Marrying Peggy was the best thing he'd ever done and he walked towards the lights of the kitchen feeling content with his lot.

The back door of the pub was open now as he walked towards it. Able caught the smell of Christmas baking and cinnamon as he moved closer. Entering, he saw the table was piled with freshly cooked mince pies, apple pies, cinnamon biscuits, scones and a loaf of delicious bread, as well as an egg and bacon quiche and sticks of celery in a glass vase. Sheila had kept supper for them despite the late hour and Able was hungry even though they'd eaten snacks and stopped for a drink and a light lunch on the way.

Sheila's food looked good and the quiche, mince pies and scones were still warm. She had dishes of pickles on the big table and the children had come back downstairs and were washing their hands at the sink, drawn to their aunt's table by the sight of buttered scones with cream and home-made jam.

'I thought I'd have a light supper this evening,' Sheila said, smiling. 'I didn't want to cook a proper meal in case it spoiled.'

'This looks proper to me,' Able said. 'That celery smells wonderful, Sheila, and I love your pickles. Peggy makes them too and they are so much better than the shop-bought ones...'

'Peggy gave me the recipe,' Sheila replied. 'I hope they will taste as good as hers.'

'I'm sure they will,' Able said. 'I'd like some of those sausage rolls and a slice of quiche, Sheila. I'm starving and I can't wait to taste that celery and those pickled onions...'

The twins had been joined by their cousin Chris, who was showing them a model car he was building. They were into the scones and jam with dollops of thick cream on top, but Able helped himself liberally to the pickles and celery to accompany his savouries.

'These are lovely,' he told Sheila. 'The pickled onions are really crisp and delicious and that celery is good.'

'It's Fen celery,' Sheila told him. 'I buy it from the market and they only ever have it at Christmas. Mick Butler always has it and he saved me half a dozen sticks because it sells out so fast, I'd never get any otherwise.'

'Delicious,' Able said and sipped the glass of pale ale Pip had poured for him. 'This is so nice, Sheila. We do get a bit fed up with preparing everything ourselves after we get home from a day in the café, so it's nice to just walk in and find everything on the table.'

'I made apple pie for afters,' Sheila said and glanced at Pip. 'It won't be as good as Peggy's, but I hope you will enjoy it.'

'It looks just as good to me,' Peggy smiled. 'This quiche is delicious, Sheila. You must give me the recipe for it – there is something a little different and nice about it.'

'I've used Red Leicester cheese,' Sheila said, 'and a little mustard. It just gives it a bit more flavour – and it sells well in the pub.'

'I really like it,' Peggy told her. 'You're a very good cook these days, Sheila. I expect it is all the practice you get with the pub and the shop to bake for...'

'It is a lot sometimes,' Sheila agreed. 'I couldn't manage if it were not for Maureen...'

'She is a big help to you, but she enjoys it,' Peggy remarked. 'She tells me how much fun you have together. It's nice to have someone you can rely on. I don't always have that at the café. Some of my staff are good, but others leave a lot to be desired. I know I should be tougher, but it's hard when you know someone really needs the job.'

'Yes, I suppose so,' Sheila replied, smothering a sigh. 'I don't think I'd want to carry on if I hadn't got friends to help me. Maureen and Rose are both a big help.'

'Yes, old friends are the best,' Peggy agreed. 'I have made a couple of good friends where we live, but not as many as I had here...'

'You were here so many years,' Sheila said. 'Do you miss it at all?'

'I miss people,' Peggy told her. 'You and Pip and my grandson – and Maureen, Rose, Alice and Tom – lots of others too.'

'You don't regret moving away?'

'No, we've done well for ourselves,' Peggy said. 'Living in the country, it's easy to source good food and the air is fresher, and we're not far from the beach,' she smiled. 'We've brought a big hamper of country food, Sheila, to help out over the holiday.'

'Lovely,' Sheila said. 'We always get through mountains of stuff at Christmas.'

'We do too,' Peggy said. 'Though not as much as we did here – I had the big party every year then.'

'But don't you miss the hustle and bustle?' Sheila probed. 'I'm sure I would. The country and the sea are lovely for a holiday or long weekends...'

'Yes, I agree,' Pip chimed in. 'You're a Londoner, Mum. I didn't think you would stick it this long.'

'I don't suppose I should if it weren't for the café,' Peggy admitted. 'We're always so busy, I don't notice where I am much and it's nice to relax at weekends.'

'You could do that if you lived in London,' Pip said, looking at her pointedly.

'Yes, I suppose so...'

'I want to live in London,' Fay spoke with her mouth full of jam and scone. 'I could go ice-skating every day after school...'

'Don't talk with food in your mouth, Fay,' her father said.

She pouted at him and swallowed quickly. 'I think London is better than the country. In the winter, there's nothing to do – and I like a swimming pool better than the beach...'

'Fay, eat your supper and don't talk nonsense,' Peggy said a little more sharply than she intended.

Fay pulled a face and subsided, but she had a stubborn look in her eyes and Able knew that she wouldn't let it go. His daughter never gave in; it was something she got from him, though he was more subtle when he wanted something. His dogged nature had got him through his pain during the war when he'd been injured and half out of his mind, so he couldn't blame Fay for her nature when he knew she got it from him.

'We'll see,' he said to placate her. 'Your mum decides what we do, Fay. If she decided it would suit her better in London, we would look for a place to live.'

'I can solve that one right now,' Pip said and there was a gleam in his eyes. 'The bed and breakfast place is to let again. The couple who took it on have split up. Maria went off with a Canadian engineer and Roger has been trying to run it with help from a few casual workers. He told me he'd had enough and was handing in his notice to the landlord after Christmas. He had bookings for the holidays, but January is slack, so he says he'll try to get out of it and, if not, he'll sell his lease – he has another five years, so he may be lucky enough to find a buyer for it...'

Able saw that Pip was looking directly across the table and knew the information was aimed at him. He glanced at Peggy, but if she'd heard, she wasn't responding. She was talking to Sheila in a low voice. It looked like they had secrets to share, but when he raised his eyebrows, Peggy just smiled and took a bite of her pickled onion.

'These are shallots,' she said. 'I love them done like this, Sheila, much better than the onions that were all we could get during the war. I haven't seen many about this year. Where did you get yours?'

'In the market. We get lots of interesting food these days,' Sheila told her. 'It was difficult for a while after the war ended, but things are getting much better now. I bought some sticky dates this week. Last year they were still scarce, but this year I found a stall selling them and some wonderful almost wet walnuts and Brazils too.'

'Yes, I got wet walnuts and we had locally grown cobnuts earlier in the year, but I didn't find any sticky dates,' Peggy said. 'I suppose you get the pick of everything that comes in from abroad these days.'

'Yes, living in town has its compensations,' Sheila agreed with a smile. 'How have you found the tinned salmon situation?'

'We get it every now and then,' Peggy said. 'Canadian red salmon is lovely, but it sells out as soon as it is on the shelves. I've had pink, but it's not as nice, is it? I think we're still failing to supply all we need as a nation...'

'The Government says we have to pay our way and that restricts what we can import,' Sheila said with a little smile. 'Maureen's wholesaler saved us half a dozen tins of red salmon for Christmas – wasn't that good of her to think of us? I've bought some fresh salmon and pickled it. I think it will be nearly as good, but we'll see what you think, Peggy.'

'There are some good fishmongers where we are,' Peggy told her. 'I buy fresh fish every week – and I got some lovely king scallops last week, which were delicious, but they haven't had any fresh salmon for ages.'

'Yes, I like scallops poached or fried, but neither Pip nor Chris will eat them,' Sheila said. 'I can't often find them in my fishmonger's – they sell as soon as they come in.'

'I suppose we do well with fish, crab and lobster – anything from the sea or the local farmers,' Peggy agreed. 'It's strange how things are better in some ways there and here in others.'

'Swings and roundabouts,' Sheila said with a nod. 'All in all, I think there is more variety in town.'

'You might be right.'

'Can we get down, Mum?' Freddie asked. 'Chris is going to let me help build his model car.'

'You can have half an hour,' Peggy said, glancing at her watch, 'and then I want the pair of you in bed. It's nearly eleven.'

'Chris should be there now,' his mother put in. 'You can have another half an hour as it's Christmas, Chris, but after that it's bed for all of you.'

'Yes, Aunty Sheila...' Fay and Freddie said in chorus. They scrambled down from the table and disappeared into the hall and up the stairs to Chris's room on the second floor, the sound of their excited giggles floating back to the kitchen, where everyone else had started on the apple pie and cream.

'This is very good,' Able said warmly.

'Thank you...' Sheila glanced at her husband across the table as if seeking his approval.

'She's improving,' Pip said and smiled at her. 'It used to get a bit burned round the edges, didn't it, love? She's worked hard for that little shop of hers though – I'm proud of her.'

Able noticed that Sheila's eyes filled with tears, though she blinked hard to flick them away. He frowned. Pip was a bit thoughtless sometimes, because that remark seemed to belittle his wife's cooking to him – or was there a little discord between the two? He wasn't certain, but he had noticed something once or twice. He rather thought Sheila might be hiding something, though he wouldn't mention it to Peggy until he was sure.

14

Maureen came rushing into the kitchen the next morning. She had Matty in his pushchair and Gordy by the hand, a pile of brightly wrapped Christmas gifts in the tray under the pushchair.

'Peggy,' she cried as her friend rose to greet her. 'Happy Christmas! I couldn't wait to come around to see you! Shirley wanted to visit. but she is meeting her friend Carol this morning. She'll pop in later and say hello...'

'Happy Christmas, Maureen love,' Peggy said. 'I was just thinking of coming to yours, so you beat me to it. I've got lots of bits and pieces for you – have you come to work or just to see me?'

'Rose is helping Sheila this morning,' Maureen said. 'I've got the morning off and then I'm in the shop this afternoon.' She smiled at Sheila. 'I'll get my pair out of your way in a minute. I just had to come and see Peggy.'

'Why don't you go upstairs?' Sheila suggested. 'The twins and Chris have eaten and gone up there already. I think Able and Pip went out a few minutes ago...' She smiled oddly. 'Christmas secrets, I think – I caught them whispering and looking secretive.'

'Yes, we'll give you space so you can work,' Peggy agreed. 'I can make us some coffee upstairs and I'll give you a hand with finishing those cakes later, Sheila.'

'Thanks, Peggy. Maureen and I are a little behind on the last-minute orders.'

Peggy held out her arms for Matty. She looked at Maureen in surprise as she felt his weight. 'Gosh, he has grown since I saw him in the summer!'

'Yes, he has put on several pounds,' Maureen said. 'The nurse at the clinic said he's doing really well.'

'I can see that,' Peggy agreed with a smile. 'He's beautiful, aren't you, my little love?'

Gordy was pulling at Peggy's skirt. He'd remembered who she was and wanted her attention. 'Aunty Peggy,' he said. 'I've grown too – I'm nearly six now...'

'Yes, I know you are,' Peggy said and smiled at him. 'You're doing well at school your mummy says.'

'Gordy was top in his class for sums,' Maureen said. 'Gordon says he takes after him. He was always top in mathematics.'

'You're not bad yourself,' Peggy said, reminding her. 'You could add up a shop bill without a pencil and paper, as I recall.'

'Yes, but that was it – I'm no good at logarithms or algebra. Gordy and his father do problems for fun at night.'

'Well, that is clever,' Peggy said. 'Pip and Laurie used to do the *Sunday Times* crosswords together. I could never manage them...'

'Nor me,' Maureen said, making a face. 'What does Able do with Freddie?'

'They play football in the garden and cricket on the beach when it's fine, also table tennis in the new conservatory when it's cold outside – any kind of sport or active games. Able is pretty good at most of it, though his batting goes a bit awry sometimes.' She smiled lovingly. 'Fay used to like roller-skating but now she wants to try skating on ice, and she likes colouring books. Freddie likes jigsaw puzzles with lots of pieces.'

'It's strange how different people can be,' Maureen said. 'Shirley studies nearly all the time. I'm hoping she will take some time off for fun now that Richard is home for a few days – but he doesn't have long. He returns to medical school on Monday morning.'

'That's Boxing Day,' Peggy said, looking surprised. 'Is he working at a hospital then?'

'Yes, it is a part of the training to work on the wards,' Maureen said. 'He does the theory a couple of days a week and the practical the rest of the time. I suppose he is what you call a student doctor now.'

'Time flies,' Peggy shook her head in wonder. 'Is Shirley training yet?'

'She has another few months at school and then she will go to college when she's eighteen. Her father hopes she'll get a place in London, though Richard went down south for his training. She might want to follow him; however, he may be looking for a placement up here by next autumn, which is when she'll be starting her training.'

'She is still keen on becoming a doctor then?'

'Oh yes, she never has her nose out of her books,' Maureen said. 'Sometimes I worry about her, Peggy. She has seemed a bit quiet lately and I've wondered if it is all too much for her...'

'Have you asked what is wrong?'

'I don't like to pry.'

'You should ask her,' Peggy suggested. 'If she isn't like herself, then something might be upsetting her. She won't tell you unless you ask.'

'No, you're right,' Maureen replied, a relieved expression in her eyes. 'You see how much better things are when we talk! I've been holding back for fear of pushing my nose in – and perhaps Shirley needs help...'

'I've found her a sensible girl and she adores you. Talk to her, Maureen, and see what is wrong.'

'I shall.' Maureen hesitated, then, 'Has Sheila told you her news yet?'

'What news?' Peggy frowned. 'I noticed something last night – she hasn't had a row with Pip, has she?'

'Not to my knowledge, but it might be coming.' Maureen shook her head as Peggy quizzed with her eyes. 'No, it isn't my secret, but I think Sheila should talk to you herself.'

'Now you've got me worried, Maureen. She isn't ill, is she? I thought she looked a bit paler than usual last night...'

'No, she's not ill.' Maureen bit her lip. 'I shouldn't have said anything, but I thought she would have told you.'

'Told me what exactly?' Peggy gave her a straight look. 'You can't leave it there; I'm thinking all kinds of things – they're not breaking up?'

'No, of course not – but you will probably need to speak to Pip, because he may be upset when she finally tells him. I've told her she should...' Maureen looked uneasy. 'Really, it's good news, but I've said too much now.'

Peggy stared at her and then her eyes widened. She glanced at the children playing by the fire, but they were all busy with various games and jigsaw puzzles. The answer suddenly dawned on her. Of course! She'd seen that look in a woman's face before.

'Is she having another child?'

Maureen's face gave her the answer, though she didn't speak.

Peggy worked it out for herself. 'And Pip has no idea – what is she thinking of?'

'I don't know and I'm not sure she does,' Maureen said. 'She just went ahead and removed the cap without consulting Pip. You knew, of course, that she was advised to have one fitted years ago?'

Peggy nodded, because Sheila had asked her advice before going to the clinic.

Maureen looked a bit guilty for having revealed Sheila's secret. 'You won't tell anyone I let it out, will you?'

'No, of course not, you didn't mean to,' Peggy reassured her. 'I do understand how she feels, of course I do. Sheila wanted a big family. It was unfortunate that the first one made her so ill, but she needs to be careful.'

'I'd like a little girl too,' Maureen admitted, 'but Gordon put his foot down and said enough was enough – and, in a way, I'm glad he did. I'm sorry I didn't have a little girl, but I've got Shirley so I've made up my mind to be satisfied.'

'Sensible woman,' Peggy said. 'Sheila is not thinking straight at the moment – but if she's pregnant there's no more to be said and Pip is a fool if he makes a fuss over it. She will need him to help her.'

'I've told her I'll do more hours and I'm sure we can find another cook to help out until she's over the birth...'

'I think she'll need help for quite a while,' Peggy said and looked thoughtful. 'One son is enough to look after and run a business; two children of differing ages can be difficult. I was lucky that the twins were beginning to grow up when I moved away. When I lived here, I had so much help.'

'Yes, during the war years, you had Janet and Anne as well as me, and then Rose too,' Maureen agreed, 'but even then, it was not always enough.'

'Not always,' Peggy affirmed. 'I daresay Sheila will find helpers if she advertises.'

'Perhaps, but they need to be exceptional cooks,' Maureen said. 'You can't have hit and miss when you sell your cakes professionally. I mean, everyone knows they are home-made and we don't pretend otherwise, but they have to be perfect.'

'Your cakes are better than they produce in the professional bakeries,' Peggy said. 'That's why you sell out every day. They are fresh, moist and delicious.' Peggy frowned. 'It will be a lot for you to do, Maureen, if Sheila is off work a long time.'

'We'll have to see what happens,' Maureen sighed as Matty let out a squawk of indignation and demanded to be put down. 'I ought to go. I have a lot to do this morning.'

'You will be in the shop this afternoon?' Peggy asked and smiled as Maureen nodded. 'I'll pop in and give you a hand. It will be a chance to meet local people and Able is taking the twins to the ice-skating rink this afternoon. I thought I'd let him do it and see how they get on.'

'I'll look forward to it.' Maureen kissed her cheek. 'It's lovely having you here for a few days – though it's never long enough – but we can have a good chat later.' She paused at the door and looked back at Peggy. 'Gordon is taking Shirley and me to see Alec Guinness in *Oliver Twist* this evening and she's really looking forward to it. Alice is coming to ours, to sit with the little ones. I'd like to take Gordy, but I'm not sure he would sit through the film.'

'Probably best not yet. They don't really take it in at that age – unless it's *Bambi* or a Walt Disney.'

'That's what I thought,' Maureen said and smiled. 'I'll see you later – I'm so glad you're here, Peggy.'

* * *

'Fay was brilliant,' Able told Peggy when they were alone in their room that evening. I wished you'd come with us to see her, hon. She took to that ice like a swan to water, gliding across it as if she'd done it all her life. By the time her session finished, she was twirling and twisting with the best of them – she loves it and I think she deserves to have regular lessons.'

'Oh, Able,' Peggy said with a sigh. 'Is she that good? I must admit I'd hoped she might not like it and would give up the idea. You know what it means, I'll be taking her into Truro or Exeter every weekend and it still won't be enough.' She frowned. 'I don't know where she got the idea from – though we did take her to see that pantomime on ice last year in Truro. I suppose that's what made her think she would like to skate.'

'She's good,' Able said, 'really good. I think we owe it to her to give her a chance, Peggy. Even if it means you having time off work to take her in on Saturdays and perhaps Sunday too.'

Peggy looked at him thoughtfully. She would need to see for herself, but if Fay really did have a talent, they would have to help her develop it somehow. 'I doubt that would be enough for her if she really loves it. What about Freddie?'

Able smiled fondly. 'He just about kept his balance, fell over once but recovered and got better. I think he quite enjoyed it. Freddie likes any sport, but he wasn't bothered.'

'If I was ferrying Fay to and fro to the rink, he would have to come too. It would be hard to fit in his football practice and the youth club.'

Able nodded his agreement. 'The youth club might have to go,' he said thoughtfully. 'Freddie mustn't miss his football – and it will be hard for you... unless...' His gaze met hers steadily. 'Fay could catch a bus to the rink by herself if we lived in London. She is quite capable, especially if Freddie goes with her sometimes, and we could take it in turns to fetch them home later.'

'What are you suggesting?' Peggy said, looking at him in surprise. 'You wouldn't give up all you've worked so hard for just because Fay might be good at ice-skating?'

'She is good, Peggy, believe me.'

'We couldn't move to London just for her, though – could we?' she was asking herself as much as Able, because although she'd thought of it before, it had seemed foolish to uproot again when they had such a good life in the country.

'It wouldn't be just for Fay, though she is a big part of it – you all are. Freddie will settle anywhere; he's like me. I'll find a football club for him and a place he can go to play. I think our son might have it in him to be a sportsman professionally if he gets the right chances, Peggy, and he'll have more of those up here than in the country...'

'You're really serious, aren't you?' Peggy was astounded. 'After just one session? I thought we were all right at the café?' She'd been too busy to consider it before, but imagined Able was content as he always seemed to be.

'We are fine,' Able said and smiled at her in the way that made her heart catch. 'But perhaps we could do things better, hon?' He moved to take her hands in his. 'If you'd seen her, you would understand. She'll need to be taught, of course, but she's a natural – and it made her so happy. Besides, I've thought for a while that we're both working too hard. That café is a gold mine, Peggy, but if we stay there, it will suck the life out of us and then what good is the money? I'd rather have more family time – and if it works better for our kids here...' He raised his brows at her.

'We do work long hours at the café,' Peggy agreed. 'But our lovely home at the cottage...'

'Will still be there for holidays and long weekends and maybe we'll retire there. We don't really spend much time doing the things we talked about, Peggy. The café has taken over our lives and it has to be that way if we're to make money, but there might be another way...'

'I'm not sure I understand,' she said, frowning. 'We looked for a place in London before we moved and they were all too expensive or awful...'

'That was then,' Able said. 'Pip and I went to look at the boarding house they run as a bed and breakfast here in the lane this morning. There are two doubles, a single, and a family room for a couple and one child. It's been completely refurbished and it makes a reasonable living, booked most nights all year long, apart from January and February, so the present landlord says. We could do better, I know. I could help you cook breakfasts and we can get someone in to clean and make beds. If you left a casserole, I could put it in the oven and even serve the evening meal if some customers want it...' He paused and Peggy knew he was reading her thoughts. 'You would be here to take Fay until she gets used to going alone on the bus and help Sheila if you wanted – an occasional stint in the bar perhaps... as much or as little as you wanted.'

'Could we afford it?' Peggy asked, her mind working furiously. Sheila was going to need far more help than either Pip or Able realized. 'What about the café?'

'I can sell the lease.' Able smiled. 'I've been approached a couple of times. People know we're busy and I'll get a few thousand for it – and the owner is offering the boarding house on a ten-year lease, which means that the twins will be grown up by the time we have to renew.'

Peggy frowned. 'You haven't signed anything?'

'Of course not. I would never do that without talking to you, hon, but we'll have to move fast if we want it.' Able paused and reached out to lightly caress her cheek. 'I'm easy either way, hon. I've got you and the twins – and I can work anywhere. As I told you, I can make coffee behind any counter and serve plates of breakfast, sandwiches or egg and chips wherever – even in the Pig & Whistle.'

'You and my son have been busy...' Peggy said, unsure whether to laugh or feel annoyed that they'd been planning behind her back. 'I'm not sure I want to move back to the lanes, Able.'

'Then we'll have to arrange ice-skating lessons for Fay in Truro somehow...' He shrugged. 'It's your decision, Peggy. I'll go along with whatever you want...'

Peggy smothered a sigh. The trouble was, she wasn't certain what she did want. Being here with her friends around her, she knew a feeling of contentment and belonging. The idea of the bed and breakfast house was appealing, because it would cut down the hours she was forced to work, giving her more time for her family and to help out where she was needed – and if Sheila had another baby, she would like to be around more. Peggy had missed seeing Chris grow up and she'd regretted that, but by moving to London she would be further away from Janet and Maggie. It was a dilemma and she felt as if she were being torn in two.

'Don't worry about it, hon,' Able said and moved closer, bringing her into him and kissing her softly. His hand caressed the back of her neck. 'It was just a suggestion and you don't have to do anything you don't want.'

'I'm not sure what I want,' Peggy told him. 'I've been happy where we are, Able – but, like you, I would be happy anywhere with you and the twins, and sometimes the work is a bit too much. I do have more friends here and I miss them, particularly Maureen and Sheila. It's something I need to think about. I'd need to talk to Janet too...'

'Janet can come up to town whenever she likes,' Able told her. 'She could stay with us for as long as she likes. We would still have plenty to do.'

Peggy nodded, lifting her face to his as he nuzzled her, feeling the comfort of his loving embrace. Whatever they decided, it would work out fine as long as she had Able and her family.

15

Janet looked around the cosy log cabin set in the beautiful scenery of Scotland and felt a sense of peace. They were right up in the north, the nearest big town, Inverness, and they'd been here four days and with each day she seemed to feel easier every time they returned to the peace of their cabin. The fire was so welcoming and giving after the icy cold outside, and the smell of the pine logs made her feel better than she had in a long time. There was even a Christmas tree, thoughtfully provided by the hotel owners. Janet had piled their gifts underneath it as soon as she'd unpacked on their first evening.

The one thing the cabin lacked was a telephone, so to ring her mother she had to go up to the hotel, but, as Ryan said, the point of coming to a place like this was to get away from it all and at home his office was forever ringing him at any time of day or night. He'd continued to work for the Government after the war and still travelled far too much for Janet's liking. Having him here at the cabin was nice, because she knew he wouldn't retire to his study for hours at a time.

The fully equipped kitchen meant that she could make tea and cook breakfast for them each day of their stay, but they went up to the hotel, which was just a short walk through the wonderful grounds, to have lunch and afternoon tea. Janet had done some shopping in the village store before they moved in, and she had plenty of snacks as well as sweets and biscuits to keep Maggie happy. However, Ryan said it was a holiday for her as well as them and she was not to cook lunch or bother about an evening meal.

The first meal they'd had soon after their arrival had been delicious. Roast Scottish beef, lovely crispy potatoes, parsnips and cabbage chopped with butter, salt and pepper and a Yorkshire pudding with gravy that was to die for, all of it accompanied by a hot horseradish that was the best Janet had tasted. Afters had been fruit compote with light sponge and cream for all of them, and the raspberries had been delicious.

The hotel keeper had told her that Christmas wasn't an official holiday in Scotland, but they kept it for the English and foreign visitors who liked to stay with them. They held their own celebrations at the New Year for Hogmanay.

'We'd been asked so many times if we opened over Christmas, we decided to make it special,' Mr Mackenzie had told her with a smile when she'd asked questions. 'My grandfather would have told me I'm a disgrace to my name for not keeping the Lord's birthday quiet and respectful, but he didn't have to recover from two lots of death duties – my father and grandfather died within two years of each other and I'm still paying off the taxes.'

'This place must take a lot to upkeep...' Janet had sympathised with him, because the huge but beautiful old house would have been impossible to keep going if they hadn't turned it into a hotel.

Her husband's presence behind her made her turn towards him, smiling a little uncertainly. She'd felt lighter since coming here, but the shadow of finding two lipstick-stained handkerchiefs in his jacket pockets still hovered at the back of her mind.

'Are you ready, love?' Ryan asked, with Maggie at his heels. Both were dressed warmly in coats, boots, scarves and wool hats, gloves on their hands.

'I was just looking at the fire,' she said, glancing back at it to hide her uncertainty. 'Do you think it will last while we walk and then have our lunch?'

'I'm sure it will,' Ryan said. He bent down to add another fragrant log, replacing the big fireguard. 'I'll soon have it going again even if it burns low, Jan.'

'All right,' Janet said and smiled at him. 'Where are we going this morning?'

'Maggie wants to walk down to the lake and see if she can spot Nessie,' Ryan said with a naughty smile. 'She says Angus McPhee told her that Nessie often makes an appearance on misty mornings and it's pretty misty this morning.'

'Yes, it is,' Janet said and pulled on her thick coat and fur hat. She took Maggie's hand and they left the log cabin with all its comforts and started walking.

Pine Tree Lodge Hotel had once been the laird's castle and was set in huge private grounds; there were half a dozen cabins hidden amongst the fragrant trees so you seldom caught sight of the other holidaymakers, unless you went up to the hotel itself. Most people had lunch and afternoon tea there and some couples had an evening meal. Janet knew her family would prefer the home-cooked treats she'd brought with her for supper – sausage rolls, Christmas cake, mince pies and almond biscuits she'd baked and transported in tins. They didn't eat a big meal at home at night unless Ryan had been away and then it was just the two of them after Maggie was in bed, so they would be satisfied with lunch and a good tea at the hotel and then a snack in the evenings.

The mist was quite thick as they walked the three miles or so down to the lakeside. Janet wondered at the knowledge that her daughter was happy to walk such long distances here, when at home she grumbled about walking to the shops, but she was entranced by the woods and the creatures they saw. It had been a thrill for them all to see red squirrels leaping from branch to branch and they'd even caught sight of a stag in the distance on a clear day – but the prize as far as Maggie was concerned was the monster that legend said dwelled in the murky depths of the loch.

'You know it's just a story, don't you?' Janet said as her daughter skipped ahead, pouncing on fir cones she stuffed into pockets to take home with her. Maggie had several pebbles, fir cones and bits of strange-shaped wood she'd taken back to her bedroom in the cabin and planned to take home with her. 'The monster is unlikely to exist...'

'Angus says it does,' Maggie said innocently. 'He told me he has seen it twice on misty mornings.'

Janet glanced at Ryan and saw the laughter in his eyes. 'Are you sure it wasn't at night on his way home from the pub?' he asked in a teasing tone.

'Oh Dad!' Maggie said and gave him a little punch on the arm. 'Angus told me that's what people always say when he tells them he's seen Nessie – but he says I'm likely to see it, because it is only the pure of heart who can.'

'Pure of heart?' her father mocked. 'He doesn't know you then, miss.'

Maggie's laughter rang out, because she loved his teasing. She caught his hand and he looked down at her, the love in his face evident to Janet. Her heart contracted with pain. Ryan loved Maggie. He truly thought of her as his daughter and Maggie adored him – more than she did her mother, Janet sometimes thought. How could he risk all that for a silly affair? Yet she knew he wouldn't for a casual fling and that was what hurt so much, because he must really love whoever he was seeing or he wouldn't throw away all they'd had. It was the only reason Janet could think of that he would leave those handkerchiefs there for her to find, because he wanted to quarrel – as an excuse to part because of her nagging. So far, she'd managed to keep her recriminations inside, but the thought was there, burning at the back of her mind the whole time.

They were approaching the lake now. It looked vast despite the mist that wafted across the deep waters and Ryan halted Maggie a safe distance from the edges of those treacherous depths. Monster or no monster, a tumble into the icy lake could only result in tragedy for a small girl, so he held on tight to her hand.

'Come on, Nessie,' Maggie said in a low voice that Janet could only just catch. 'I'm wishing just like Angus told me.'

Janet was about to say something to ease what could only be disappointment for her daughter when she saw something move out in the lake. There was too much mist to be certain, but it was a dark shape rising from the water, though, of course, it might just be a cloud of mist rising.

'Look, Daddy,' Maggie cried excitedly and pointed towards the dark shape out in the middle of the lake. 'She's there – Nessie has come for me just like Angus promised, can you see her?'

Ryan looked in the direction his daughter pointed and just for a moment he hesitated as though there was something he couldn't see clearly and then shook his head.

'There was something there,' he said in disbelief. 'I'm not sure it was Nessie – it might have been a bird or a cloud or something...'

'I saw it too,' Janet said and shook her head. Like Ryan, she didn't believe in the monster. Common sense told her it was a myth, a legend put about by locals to encourage tourists, but she had seen something and, if she were honest, it did look vaguely like one of the long-lost dinosaurs that had died out hundreds of years ago.

'I saw her, truly I did,' Maggie insisted.

'I saw something,' Janet agreed with her daughter, 'but it must have been a boat or a big bird or something. The monster is just a fairy story, Maggie.'

'Angus told me you would say that,' Maggie replied happily. 'He said if I came down in the mist, I would see Nessie and I did. I knew where to look because he told me where she appears and I saw her clearly. She's real, I know she is, and she came just for me because I wished her to appear.'

'Well, you're a lucky girl then,' Janet said and shook her head at Ryan, who looked as if he was about to explain about myths and legends. Later, she would tell him that she thought Angus must have somehow set up a pretend monster in the lake for Maggie's sake. No doubt the locals thought it was amusing to trick visitors and keep the legend of the monster alive. However, it was Christmas and if Maggie wanted to believe, then let her. She'd only recently stopped believing in Father Christmas and Janet didn't want to take all the magic from her life – but she would have a private word with Mr McPhee.

* * *

'Ach, lassie, there's no need to fash yourself,' Angus said when she taxed him about it at the hotel. 'Your little lassie has an open mind and she saw Nessie right enough. 'Tis only true believers who really see her. Others will see a dark shape and their minds block the truth, but if you want to see her, you will.'

'And you weren't out there in a boat waving something about to deceive us?' Janet looked at him chidingly.

'Nay, I would'na do that to your lassie,' Angus said and looked so earnest that Janet was puzzled. 'I told her the legend and 'tis my belief her own mind supplied the rest.'

'My husband saw a dark shape. I saw what looked like a long, arched neck…'

'Aye, that would be Nessie,' Angus nodded. 'So, you've not closed your mind to the magic of this world yet then, lassie.'

Janet was still unconvinced and suspected him or some other local of somehow arranging the sighting – but there was enough doubt in her mind to leave it there. She didn't feel like complaining to the management, even though it wasn't entirely fair to play such a trick on her daughter. Maggie was enjoying the magic of their stay, which had begun to work for Janet the moment they'd stepped into their cabin.

'Do many people get to see Nessie then?' she asked.

'Nay,' he said and his eyes twinkled. 'There are hundreds look for her every year. They come with their cameras and their special equipment and they go out on the lake on clear days and never see a whisper of her. So, they go back where they came from and say we're tricksters and it's all nonsense – but they don't look at the right time. Nessie will only come if she wants – how do you think she's avoided capture or death all this time? Too smart for the lot of them, she is!'

'I think that is very convenient, Mr McPhee.'

'Aye, well you would, but young lassie understands.'

'I see – thank you...'

Janet knew that he had defeated her. She didn't believe that she'd seen a prehistoric monster out there in the lake, but she couldn't disprove it either.

'I doubt you got much out of him,' Ryan said when she joined him as they waited to be shown to their table in the dining parlour. 'He appears a simple soul, but he can be devious if he chooses, I dare say.'

'Yes, perhaps,' Janet said. 'I asked him a lot of questions and he seemed genuine but...'

'You know it is a myth, don't you? Please don't tell me he's got you fooled too, Jan,' Ryan said.

Maggie was talking earnestly to one of the other children staying at the hotel over Christmas. She came back to them, glowing with excitement.

'Did you know there's a fancy dress party on Christmas after-noon? We can borrow costumes from the hotel and if we look good, we might win a prize – another holiday here in the summer.'

'Would you like to come back here in the summer?' Ryan asked her.

'Yes, please,' Maggie said, her face lighting up. 'They have special games near here then and we could go deer stalking – not to hurt or frighten them but just to watch. There are golden eagles that nest in a secret location – we have to go blindfolded to see them – and all sorts of fetes and things going on...'

'We'll have to see what we can do then,' Ryan promised. 'It depends on what your mother would like to do...'

'We'll see how things are in the summer,' Janet said. 'It's certainly lovely here, Maggie, but the sea is nice near where we live and you like swimming, don't you?'

'Yes, Mum, but I love it here – it's special, don't you feel that?' Maggie asked innocently. 'Can we pick our fancy dress costumes this afternoon please? And then there's a competition for us all to play in the meeting room before tea. It's for children and their parents, so we can all play together... It's darts and a game called pin the tail on the donkey and others...'

'Sounds fun,' Ryan said. 'I'm a dab hand with the darts.'

'Yes, all right,' Janet said, giving into the pleading look in her daughter's eyes. 'I'm up for it – if your father is...'

'I'm here to please my two favourite girls,' Ryan said and smiled at them. 'Whatever you want to do, I'll play my part.'

His smile seemed to caress them both and Janet's heart caught with pain. He seemed so loving and she wondered if she'd been mistaken. The lipstick on his handkerchief might have got there innocently. Perhaps she'd been punishing herself for nothing, or perhaps the affair was over?

Janet forced a smile. This was a magical time for her family and she would be a fool to ruin it. She would wait to ask Ryan about that lipstick until they were home. In the meantime, she would join in all the fun – and she would find a moment later to telephone her mother from the kiosk at the hotel and ask her how she was getting on at Sheila's.

16

'I was going to try and ring this evening, but I wasn't sure if they could reach you. It's a bit of a nuisance you haven't got a phone in the cabin, though I suppose it would be too much to expect. They would have to have them in all the cabins and that would be expensive,' Peggy said when Janet telephoned after tea. It might not be possible either, because many people who wanted the telephone these days had to accept a 'party phone', which meant other people were also using the same line and when you picked up the receiver, you might listen in to the other party's conversation. It was expected that you hang up and wait to make your call, but some folk were blatant about listening in. 'Are you enjoying yourselves?'

'Yes, it's wonderful,' Janet replied enthusiastically. 'There is so much to do here, Mum, and the scenery is lovely, majestic. We're only a few miles from Loch Ness and we walk there most mornings after breakfast.'

'Have you seen Nessie?' Peggy teased and Janet hesitated.

'Maggie thinks she has. Ryan saw a dark shape and I saw something – it seemed to have a long neck...'

'One of the locals is playing tricks on you,' Peggy said and laughed.

'I shouldn't be surprised. Though, when I asked him, he seemed genuine – but I know it has to be that...'

'Unless you'd been drinking too much malt whisky...'

'It is certainly delicious. Ryan has bought half a dozen bottles to take home, but I'm not a big fan. I prefer wine.'

'I don't mind a good whisky,' Peggy said. 'Ask Ryan to get a couple of bottles for me please. Able likes a glass sometimes and so does Pip.'

'That was a habit he picked up in the war – Pip I mean,' Janet said. 'How is everyone up there, Mum? Have you had all your friends to visit you? Is Pip all right and Sheila and Chris?'

'I've seen Maureen and Alice, they both came straight round, and a few of the others in the lane. Pip is the same as always and Sheila is making a fuss of us. Her food is lovely and there is so much of it, we shall all get fat! The rest of the news is good and not so good,' Peggy said. 'I can't talk about it yet, Jan, but I'll tell you when we get home. I'm so glad you're enjoying yourselves. Give Ryan and Maggie my love. I hope she likes what we bought her for Christmas.'

'She's being spoiled silly this year,' Janet said. 'This holiday is orientated towards the children a lot and she's having fun – we won her a fur muff in a competition this afternoon. It's made of rabbit fur but so warm for her hands and she loves it. There's a fancy dress on Christmas Eve and we could win another holiday here if we got first prize.'

'It sounds fabulous,' Peggy said. 'The twins might like it another year – but at the moment all Fay wants is to learn to ice-skate like a professional.'

'That girl is thoroughly spoiled,' Janet said. 'Next month it will be something different.'

'No, I don't think so. She is serious about it. Able took her and he said she was good, so I'm going to take her tomorrow. If she is as good as he says, then I have to make sure she gets those lessons.'

'Won't that be difficult for you – it's a trip into Truro every time. How often would she need to skate? It's surely too far after school.'

'That is the problem. If she is serious about it, she needs to train at least once a day if she wants to get anywhere in competition, so I'm told, and perhaps more,' Peggy said. 'If she is good enough to skate for Britain, as she hopes—'

'Mum! That's nonsense,' Janet said. 'You know what Fay is like – she'll get fed up in a few months, probably as soon as the World Championships are over, and plague you for something else.'

'She might,' Peggy admitted. 'I think Fay takes after her father... she has big ambitions.'

'Yes, she does,' Janet agreed. 'You'll find it hard to keep up with her demands, Mum – unless you stop working so much and that might not be a bad thing...'

'Unless we made changes...' Peggy said. 'Able suggested selling the lease of the café and moving back up here so that Fay could just get on a bus herself – we could run the boarding house next to the pub...'

'You wouldn't!' Janet cried, sounding shocked. 'Just for a little girl's whim.'

'There are other reasons,' Peggy said, prevaricating because she couldn't tell her about Sheila just yet. 'We should keep the cottage for holidays of course...'

'What about Maggie and me?' Janet demanded. 'I should hardly see you...'

'You don't come very often anyway,' Peggy said truthfully. 'You could get on a train and come to London, stay with us in the school holidays, whatever you wanted. There would always be a place for you in my home wherever I was, Jan.'

'That's not the point,' Janet said, a resentful note in her voice. 'If I needed you, you weren't too far away.'

'I'm always there, on the end of a phone, wherever I am – and, besides, when I came down recently, you were clearly upset but you wouldn't tell me anything...'

Janet was silent for a moment. 'I couldn't, Mum. I was hurting too much to tell you, but I wanted to. I'll come and see you when you get back.'

Peggy heard the note of distress and softened immediately.

'Good. I've been worried about you, love. I'm sure you can sort it out whatever it is...'

'I wish I could think the same,' Janet said sadly. 'Have a good Christmas, Mum. Please don't make any decisions too quickly. Make sure it is right for you as well as Fay.'

'If I do it, Fay won't be my only reason – and not even the most important,' Peggy told her and hesitated, then, 'I'm glad you're having a lovely time. Happy Christmas, to all of you, my darling. Give my love to Maggie and Ryan.'

Peggy put down the phone on that note. Janet's distress at the idea of her moving had upset her, but her daughter could be selfish. She complained that Fay thought only of herself, but Janet was much the same, so where did they get it from? They had different fathers and Able didn't have a selfish bone in his body, so it must be from her. Peggy frowned. She hoped she wasn't selfish and she did have to think very carefully, because if she was thinking of changing her life again, it must be to help those she loved, including Janet and Maggie – and that meant she was going to be torn apart by her emotions whatever she decided.

* * *

Peggy was shocked by how good her youngest daughter was on the ice. Fay had only put ice skates on twice in her life, but she was twirling and gliding like a beautiful swan over the ice. She'd had years of practising her roller-skating so whether that had helped, Peggy couldn't tell. Freddie, on the other hand, looked like the amateur he was. He'd roller-skated for a while and he could stand up and just about skate on the ice, but Fay's tricks were way out of his league.

'She's so good...' Peggy breathed and Able nodded his agreement. 'Even when you told me she could skate, I didn't imagine she could do it like that.' Even as she spoke, Fay almost took a tumble but recovered and went on skating as if nothing had happened.

'She is great,' Able said just as a woman dressed in purple

trousers and a warm cable-knitted jumper skated up to where they were sitting.

'You're Fay's parents, aren't you?'

'Yes – Peggy and Able,' he said as the woman offered her hand.

'I'm Sara Anderson. I train the youngsters to skate and we look out for kids with potential – but Fay is exceptional. How long has she been skating?'

'This is the second time on the ice, but she's been roller-skating for three years...'

'Twice? That's unbelievable!' Sara Anderson looked shocked and a little disbelieving. 'The roller skates would help with balance, but it is a different skill – your daughter is a natural. I thought she was good, but now I realise she is fantastic. With a little help from my colleagues, she could do really well in the sport...' She frowned. 'Are either of you skaters?'

'I did ice-skating during the winter as a lad back in the States,' Able said. 'I won a speed championship when I was fifteen...'

'That must be where she gets if from,' Sara replied and looked pleased. 'It is up to you, of course, but I feel she has a future in the sport – if she has the proper training.'

'It's what Fay wants,' Peggy told her. 'The only trouble is we're just visiting for the holidays.'

'That's a pity,' Sara Anderson looked disappointed. 'It's a shame to waste a talent like that... if there's any way she could stay up here – with relatives or something...'

'How often does she need to train to have a chance?' Able asked.

'We'd like up to two hours a day,' Sara said. 'We usually take the children of her age for a couple of hours after school and then we'll do a three-hour session on Saturdays – Sundays too if a big competition is coming up,' she smiled at them. 'We take the children through regionals and then up to the national competition level – and after that it's international...'

'If it could be arranged,' Peggy asked thoughtfully, 'how much would all that cost?'

'You pay her bus fares, you buy her skates and her costumes. My colleague, Mark, and I, train her for free...'

'The tuition is free? Why is that?' Able asked, frowning.

'The London council pays for our time,' Sara said. 'We need youngsters to enter the big world competitions in the future. Britain hasn't won many ice dancing gold medals and we're hoping to train the ice dancers of the future. Other countries have far more facilities than we do in this country and that's why we've started this scheme. We spot those we think might have a chance and we guide them through small competitions through to the world stage. It's up to you and Fay of course, because it takes dedication; she would need to give up all her other hobbies to become really good. Otherwise it is just for fun.'

'What do we do if we decide it could be arranged?' Peggy asked, still thoughtful.

Sara fished in her pocket. 'Here's my phone number. Give me a call and we'll talk more when you've decided.' She smiled. 'I'm going to have to go – one of my most promising pupils has just arrived.' She waved her hand. 'Robert...' A young lad waved back to her, sitting down on a bench to pull on his boots. 'Give me a call...' Sara said and skated off in the direction of the boy.

Able looked at Peggy as Freddie skated up to them. He grinned and sat down, bending to take off his skating boots. 'Fay is so good, isn't she, Mum? I bet she could skate for Britain one day if she tried...'

'Yes, perhaps,' Peggy said. 'How would you feel about coming with her, Freddie? You wouldn't have to skate all the time, but you could sit and wait and bring her home safely...'

Freddie nodded. He was the same age as his sister in years but older and wiser in his thinking. 'I could come with her, Mum, and watch and talk to other kids. I might play ice hockey too – they've got a team here...'

'What about your football?' Able said.

'If I had practice, Mum would have to bring her...' Freddie was thoughtful. 'I'd miss it if I really had to, Mum, but I like my football...'

'Yes, I know,' Peggy agreed. 'I think we could work something out. I can come with Fay sometimes and sometimes your dad might pick her up – and other times just the two of you could catch the bus...'

'That means we'd be living in London,' Freddie said and frowned. 'Is it what you and dad want?'

'I'll do whatever you all want,' Able assured him. 'How do you feel about it, Freddie? You like your school and you're in the football team – it means starting again if we move. We want to be fair to both of you...'

Freddie looked at him in silence, then, 'I like living where we are, Dad,' he said. 'I would never have asked to move – but Fay is my twin and I want her to have her way. This means so much to her and I can make new friends, work hard to get into my new school's football team. I don't mind, honestly.'

'You would be willing to do that for Fay?' Peggy asked and he grinned easily, so like his father, it caught her heart.

'It's no big deal, Mum,' he said in a very modern and grown-up way. Sometimes Peggy thought he was more like fifteen than nine years old... 'Fay will be miserable if she can't skate now. She's talked about nothing else for weeks and that was before she tried it and found out how good she was...'

'She'll give us no peace unless we take her in to Truro or bring her here,' Able said, looking at Peggy with a twinkle in his eyes.

'Don't tell Fay we asked you,' Peggy told her son. 'We haven't decided yet. It is a big thing to move away from a thriving business and leave the friends we've made in the country.'

'Is it such a big wrench?' Able asked as Freddie accepted some coins from him and went off to buy a hot drink of cocoa for all of them. 'You've got far more friends here than down there, Peggy – and a ready-made business to walk into – to say nothing of helping Sheila and Maureen...'

'What about Janet and Maggie?' Peggy said, looking up at him as he rose to his feet. 'You don't need to answer, I know what you'll say –

and you're right. Janet is capable of coming to us in London and she doesn't need us. All she needs is to sort out her own life.'

Able nodded to show that he agreed and went off to take the loaded tray from his son.

Fay skated up to the side of the rink and looked at her mother.

'Did Miss Anderson speak to you, Mum?'

'Yes, she told me she thinks you're quite good,' Peggy said, refusing to get her hopes up too soon. It was too early yet to know if Fay was as good as they thought, because neither she nor Able were impartial enough. Fay could skate and looked lovely on the ice, but doing it well enough to win competitions was another thing. 'With lots of training, you might be good enough to enter competitions one day – and that means a couple of hours training every day for years, even if you don't feel like it. You can't shirk it for a couple of days just because you want to do something else...'

'I want to skate more than anything in the world,' Fay said, her expression earnest and pleading. 'I would train so hard...'

'If we could find a way, it couldn't mean the end of your schoolwork,' Peggy said. 'You would still have homework to do and you'd still need to pass exams at school.'

'I know and I'll work hard, honestly I will – but I can't live without this,' Fay cried passionately, throwing out her arms to indicate her love for the ice around her.

'Well, your father and I will think about it and find out more, but that is only thinking about it, Fay, nothing more.'

'You're the best mum ever.' Fay looked excited and Peggy felt the tug on her heartstrings. How could she refuse her beloved child something she wanted so badly?

'I'm not promising anything, but we might be able to work something out...'

Fay's face lit up as if a light bulb had been switched on inside her. 'Thank you, Mum! I promise I'll be good and do everything you tell me...'

'Here's our lovely hot cocoa,' Peggy said and took her mug, her eyes moving round her family as she sipped the hot sweet drink. She was pretty contented right now and knew that she would enjoy accompanying her daughter to the rink some days and to mix up her working hours accordingly. The facilities and opportunities for Fay were far greater here than at home and she knew in that moment she would give in to her youngest daughter's pleading.

She knew Janet was going through a bad patch in her marriage and that made it harder to decide, but Peggy's mind was almost sure of what she ought to do, it was so simple really. Her oldest and dearest friends were here and it was her younger daughter's life she was considering. Able and Miss Anderson believed Fay had the ability to do great things and Peggy could not deny her daughter the chance. Freddie and Able were so easy-going that it didn't matter where they lived, both would and could adjust, and if Peggy looked deep inside, she knew that her own life would be better back in the lanes.

She'd done nothing much but work since they'd opened the café. The long hours had meant that she only had a short time on Saturdays and Sundays to take the children out and make the most of the beaches and the beautiful countryside. Whereas if they went down for holidays in the spring and summer, they would have cover for the boarding house and enjoy far more time to themselves. Here in London Peggy would not be as tied, because she would have friends who would help out and the hours were not so long. Breakfasts, an evening meal and the rest of the day to please herself. And that would be such a relief.

Peggy looked at her husband and saw that he could read her thoughts. How did he know her so well? Yet he'd understood that despite her love for the cottage and the wonderful business they'd made, Peggy's heart still remained in London. She'd always belonged here and although she would never have moved back for her own sake, this opportunity for her daughter was giving her the excuse she needed.

She laughed and shook her head at her family as they looked at her inquiringly. It didn't matter if Fay's passion wore out or she wasn't good enough to skate for Britain, she would go on to do other things – and the move would still benefit them all. Freddie would have plenty of chances to follow a top football team here like Arsenal, and if he wanted to play football for a good club when he left school, he would have more chance of being spotted in London than in the country.

Peggy started to count the reasons for the move. It would mean an easier life and, quite honestly, she was ready for it. Four and a half years of slogging in the café was enough, and if Able could sell the lease as easily as he thought, they would be able to afford to take on the boarding house easily. She would talk to her husband about it when they got home.

'Another half an hour on the rink and then we have to go home,' she told her daughter, who had finished her hot drink. 'Freddie, would you like your father to take you home now?'

'I'm all right, Mum,' Freddie said. 'Do you see that man in the black polo-necked jumper? He's Mark and he runs the ice hockey team. If Dad will come with me, I'll ask him what I have to do to join...' Able nodded to his son and the pair of them walked off in pursuit of the trainer.

On the ice, a group of skaters was singing Christmas carols and some of the lads were chasing after the girls with sprigs of mistletoe. Peggy could smell the mouth-watering scent of chestnuts roasting somewhere. It was nearly Christmas and she decided to let her problem go. Plenty of time to think about it in the next few days – she would speak to Sheila and ask how she felt about having them live next door but one.

Peggy smiled. Freddie was talking to the man he'd called Mark, laughing and nodding eagerly, already adjusting his life to make things better for his twin. She should follow his lead. She would talk to Janet about things when they got home after the holidays, nothing was decided yet, but it could all fall into place so easily. If Able sold the lease, they could take on the bed and breakfast place and make it busy and profitable, just as they had the café. It would be a good life and already she knew her decision was made, but she'd keep it to herself until after Christmas.

17

On Christmas Day, Rose yawned and woke to the sounds of her children's excited voices. It was still dark and she groaned, because it was too early, but the children were already awake and calling to each other in anticipation. She could hear Jenny talking to Jackie, urging him to look at the presents that Father Christmas had brought him. Now wide awake, Rose nudged Tom in the side and he woke with a little snort of disgust.

'What's wrong?' he muttered, still caught in the clutches of sleep.

'The children are awake and opening their stockings. They will want their big presents next...'

As if on cue, Jenny opened their bedroom door and peered round. She was clutching the little wooden hand mirror that Rose had put in her stocking, together with sweets, an orange in silver paper and some hair slides, a broach with red glass stones and a bracelet of painted beads.

'Father Christmas has been, Mummy,' she told them and pulled on Jackie's hand. He toddled behind her, clutching the little wooden elephant that had been in his stocking, together with other small trinkets. 'Can we have the presents from under the tree now please?'

Rose had told her children that the presents under the tree were from Mummy and Daddy and other people they knew, while the stockings at the end of the bed came from Father Christmas. It was the only way to explain the gifts from friends and family, Rose believed, without exploding the myth of a friendly old gentleman who came down the chimney at night.

'Do you realise it is only six in the morning?' Tom groaned. 'It's the one day a year I don't have to get up...'

'Says who?' Rose said and tugged on the covers until she remembered that he wasn't wearing anything underneath. Tom had claimed his present the previous evening and his pyjamas were lying in a heap by the bed. She gave a little giggle and left him modestly covered. 'You two go downstairs and we'll be there in a moment, and make sure Jackie doesn't fall, Jenny.'

As they took her at their word and ran from the room, Rose got out of bed and pulled on her warm cotton robe, covering herself. She laughed at Tom, who was still groaning.

'I'll make a cup of tea, but you'd best get up – you can go back to bed after the presents.'

'Slave driver,' Tom muttered into the pillows.

'Don't blame me, blame two excited kids,' Rose said good-humouredly. 'They've seen all those presents and it has been agony for them to wait – put yourself in their shoes.'

She left Tom burying his head under the sheets but knew that by the time she had the kettle boiled he would be downstairs and waiting for the presents to be opened despite his moans.

She could hear Jenny in the sitting room. Near the fireplace was the plate with crumbs where Tom had eaten the mince pie left out by Jenny for Father Christmas the previous evening, because she thought he would be hungry. She'd insisted on leaving a carrot for the reindeer, but Rose had taken it back to the kitchen because Tom had refused to eat it.

Jenny was now busy reading the labels on all the parcels, or trying to, and itching to sort them out and start tearing the paper off, but her reading was not quite good enough yet for her to be absolutely sure of the words, so even though she might think a parcel was for her or Jackie, she hadn't started to dole them out when her mother carried the tea tray through and put it down on the little glass-topped coffee table by the fireplace.

It was cooler in the sitting room than the big kitchen, which was warmed by the range, so Rose turned the one-bar portable electric fire on for a while. Tom had bought it because they didn't often have a fire going in the front room and if someone called they could warm up the sitting room quickly rather than take them into their comfortable well-used kitchen. The front room normally only got used properly on Sundays and at holiday times. Tom would get a good fire going in here later and for the whole of Christmas, but the electric would warm it up while the kids opened their presents.

Tom entered wearing his trousers and a warm shirt. They were his working clothes but clean on that morning. He'd obviously taken them from his wardrobe. She smiled because he hadn't shaved and he looked rugged and handsome in his red-checked shirt.

'Tea is ready,' she said. 'Milk for you two.'

Jenny took hers and gulped it down, putting the empty glass on the tray before Rose had finished pouring their tea. She was fingering a big parcel that she clearly thought was for her.

Rose smiled and nodded at her. 'Yes, that one is from Daddy and me – and you can open it. Give the red parcel to Jackie...'

Jenny did as she was bid and Jackie sat staring at his parcel. He laughed and patted it, but Jenny was tearing off her silver paper in a flurry of excitement that only increased as she saw the wonderful doll's house that Tom had made so painstakingly for her. He'd painted it black and white to look like a Tudor manor house and the whole of the front opened. Inside were pieces of furniture that Rose had bought from a specialist shop and some tiny little dolls to live in the house.

'It's wonderful...' Jenny breathed as she peered into the little rooms. 'All these things... it's just like a real house...'

'You've got a mummy and daddy doll and two little children,' Rose said, watching the pleasure in her daughter's face.

Jackie was still patting his present, unsure of how to get the paper off. Even as Rose thought about helping him, Tom was on the floor, squatting by his son, helping him to expose the large pedal toy inside. It was made of wood, shaped like a horse with a mane of hair, red leather reins and a trolley that could be pulled along or sat on and pedalled.

Tom sat his son on the horse's back and pushed him forwards, bringing a chuckle of delight from Jackie as he felt the movement under him. He didn't seem interested in the other parcels, even though Tom tried to tempt him to open the train set he was itching to set up for his son.

Rose sat on the floor beside Jenny and watched as she took the tiny pieces out of the house one by one, examining them carefully before putting them back in their place.

'You can rearrange the rooms as you like,' Peggy said, 'and there are lots of bits you can collect to go in your house, darling...'

'It's lovely, Mummy,' Jenny said. 'I love the little tea set and the parasol...'

'Yes, they are sweet,' Rose said. 'There are so many pretty things you can buy for your house, Jenny. Every so often you can buy something with your pocket money...'

'I love it,' Jenny said, 'but the children are wrong – it should be a big girl and a little boy...'

'They didn't have a boy the right size,' Rose said. 'We'll have to see if we can find one another day.'

Jenny nodded happily, still taking other pieces from the house to examine them. The furniture was gilded for the sitting room and painted for the bedrooms and brown wood for the kitchen,

Tom had brought yet another parcel for Jackie to open and inside was a large fluffy dog that immediately had the little boy reaching for it. He held it to his face, his smile lighting the room.

'Who is that from?' Rose asked her husband.

'Peggy brought it last night – it's from her family,' Tom replied.

He picked up a parcel in green and gold and handed it to Jenny. 'This is from Aunty Peggy and Uncle Able, and the twins...'

Jenny tore the soft wrappings of coloured tissue paper off and discovered a pretty pink cardigan with pearl beads sewn over the front and a faux pearl bracelet on elastic that just slid on her wrist.

'Oh, that is pretty – aren't you a lucky girl?' Rose said as Jenny held the cardigan to her face. 'You must thank Aunty Peggy and Uncle Able nicely when we go to tea this afternoon.'

'I can wear my new cardie...' Jenny chortled, 'and my bracelet.' She slipped it over her wrist.

Rose got up to distribute the other parcels. Alice had bought the children small gifts and Maureen had bought them interesting parcels too. Tom was helping his son to discover what was inside his gifts and looked up with a surprised smile as Rose put some parcels at his side.

'Are all these for me?' he asked. 'People shouldn't – for the kids, yes, but I don't need anything...'

'You have friends,' Rose said. 'The green and gold one is from me – the others are from Sheila and Pip, Maureen and Gordon, Alice, and Peggy and Able – oh, and those two little ones are from customers you've helped.'

'Good gracious,' Tom said as he opened Peggy's present, which was wrapped in brown paper but tied with a red ribbon and looked a bit shocked. 'An electric sharpener for my tools – that must have been expensive...'

'And very thoughtful,' Rose said. 'Peggy knows you so well.'

Tom's other presents included whisky, cigars and cigarettes from his customers and a beautiful silk scarf from Maureen. Rose had bought him the cine camera and a soft wool jumper in dark blue. He smiled at her, a thrill of excitement in his eyes.

'A home movie camera! Just what I wanted, love...' He laughed and kissed her enthusiastically, clearly touched by her thoughtful present. 'You shouldn't have spent all that money on me, Rose. I know it must have taken a lot of saving – but I love it. It's the best present ever, except for you and my kids.' He bent his head over the instructions and nodded. 'I'll have films of these two growing up – and so many memories. I can hardly believe it, Rose – that you should save up all your money to buy me this...' He was thunderstruck.

'Now you can take pictures of the kids all the time...' Rose said, laughing. She'd known he would be pleased, but he was so thrilled it made her feel good inside.

'Aren't you going to open yours?'

'Yes, now Jenny has finished opening all hers.' Jenny was surrounded by books, puzzles, a doll and some extra dolly's clothes.

Rose opened the large parcel first containing the new coat Tom had bought her first. It was a russet colour with a big black fur colour and suited her beautifully when she slipped it on. There was also a silver bracelet from Jenny and Jackie, which Tom must have helped them buy for her and could have charms hung from it, some gorgeous perfume from Sheila and Pip, a lovely tan leather handbag from Maureen, a pair of black leather gloves from Peggy and a pair of sheer black nylons from Alice.

'Anyone would think you'd all got together to choose these because they will all match,' she told Tom in delight.

He grinned at her. 'Peggy rang and asked what you needed. I told her the colour of your new coat. Maureen didn't ask, but she always knows what everyone likes anyway.'

'Yes, she does,' Rose agreed. 'We have done well. I hope our presents pleased as much as we liked ours.'

She reflected how lucky they were. It wasn't many years since Tom started in business with hardly a penny to his name and these days his industry and business sense had made him not rich but perfectly able to give his wife and children a good living and presents like these at Christmas. Not all the folk living in the lane were as well off, like Alice. But Rose had bought her a large box of staples from Maureen's shop, including sugar, tea, biscuits, tinned fruit and tinned salmon and a nice box of Milk Tray chocolates – all the things that Alice considered treats. She'd also made her a large cherry cake and some mince pies, and Tom had given her ten pounds for a present. That money meant Alice could pay her coal bill in the cold weather and she'd cried when she saw what he'd given her.

'That husband of yours is too good to me, Rose,' she'd said. 'They threw away the mould after they made Tom Barton.'

Rose had been affected by the old lady's tears, but she'd reassured her that Tom was grateful for all she did for them, looking after the little ones when she was needed.

Times were still hard for some in the lanes, especially the older folk who had no way of earning a living. Some younger men were in full-time employment these days, builders particularly, because London needed rebuilding after the devastation of the war. Tom had got in at the right time, and his business was founded on goodwill and the way his neighbours felt about him. Everyone went to Tom when they needed a job done and knew he never cheated them. With a reputation like that, he'd brought in work from all over London and now employed another man and two young lads to help him. He was now comfortably off and could probably have taken on more labour, but refused to run before he could walk and was still working just as hard himself as the men he employed. Tom wanted more than just comfort. He wanted to give Rose and his children all the things his father could never have aspired to give him.

Looking around her comfortable living room, Rose smiled with satisfaction. A fresh green Christmas tree had made its appearance for Jenny's first Christmas and Tom got her one every year now; she added new glass balls to it every season, and it had a fairy on top with a star on her wand.

Jenny was still playing with her doll's house. It was obvious that it was her best gift by far, though she'd liked all the others – but this was the thing she would play with all Christmas.

'That was a good idea,' Rose told her husband. 'The miniature bits and pieces are expensive, but we can get more as we go along.'

'It took me ages to make the house and make it look right – but the small things are even more fiddly,' Tom said.

'That's why I found a specialist who makes them,' Rose said, smiling at him. 'They are so intricate, Tom. I've even got a little newspaper on the table in the sitting room. The writing is so tiny, you need a microscope to read it, but it tells you the latest news for miniatures and gives the name of the shop I bought it from.'

'Good advertising for them,' Tom said. 'How much did that cost?'

'I paid five pounds for all the bits I put inside.'

'That is a fortune,' Tom said, looking at her as if she were mad. 'It didn't cost me that much to make the house.'

'Not in materials perhaps, but how many hours did you put in? I'll bet you could have earned more than ten pounds doing something else...'

Tom laughed. 'Got me!' He stood up. 'How about we all go and have breakfast – who wants bacon and scrambled egg?'

'Me!' Jenny cried, jumping up. She clutched her new cardigan, which seemed to be the most popular of her other gifts. 'Can we have some tomatoes out of a tin with it please?'

'Can we, Mum?' Tom asked Rose as she scooped up her son, who clung to his new fluffy dog as if his life depended on it, horse, train and cars abandoned.

'Yes, as it's Christmas, you can have fried bread too...' Rose said, laughing as Jackie chortled in her ear. 'You too, Jackie. We'll all have a lovely breakfast and then our dinner – and then tea with Peggy and Sheila and God help our waistlines...' She smiled at her husband. 'I'm going to pop over the road a bit later and make sure Alice knows I'm expecting her for Christmas lunch. When I asked her, she said she didn't want to intrude, but I shall make her come, whatever she says.'

'You get on with whatever you like,' Tom said after they'd eaten. 'I'll fetch Alice over myself – and I'll pop into a couple of others and make sure they're all right too.' Tom smiled at his wife. 'We're lucky, Rose, and we can spare a bit for those that aren't. I'll take a packet of fags and a bottle of brown ale to old Mr Giddings. His daughter will fetch him to dinner later, but I'll have a word before he goes.'

'That's why I love you,' Rose said, laughing. 'Get off with you then, but don't bring the whole street in for lunch...'

Tom grinned, because he knew his Rose wouldn't mind if he did, but it was only Alice who was in danger of being alone this Christmas. Her friend Maud had died two years previously. Until then they'd often shared Christmas lunch or tea, but Tom had looked after her since and she would sit down with them for lunch even if he had to carry her.

* * *

Across the road in the Ashley household, the excitement was just as intense and the adults were woken every bit as early. Sheila went down first and stoked up the range so that it would be warm in the main kitchen, where the big goose she'd bought would be cooked later that day. Upstairs, children's voices were exclaiming over gifts found at the end of their beds. The main presents were in the sitting room upstairs and Sheila returned carrying a large tray of food to munch, because she knew her family. They would all want biscuits and mince pies with the tea and coffee Peggy was making in the small family kitchen.

When the whole family was assembled, the present giving began. The twins and Chris took the parcels round to the adults and then dived into their own. Soon there were piles of torn wrappings, tissue paper, coloured paper, gold stars that had been painstakingly cut out and stuck on, discarded ribbons and piles of gifts everywhere: puzzles, games, records, book tokens, sweets, clothes and individual gifts the children had wanted, including Chris's guitar. Everyone thanked everyone else, enjoying the atmosphere of so many animated faces and excited chatter. Fay was twirling a new dress against her and looking at her new ice skates with adoration. Freddie had a football, some kit and a small box camera from his parents, as well as books, puzzles and a smart penknife that did all sorts of things, like take a stone out of a horse's hoof. It was called a Swiss Army knife and Freddie was pleased to bits with it.

Tea, coffee and orange squash was drunk, mince pieces and chocolate biscuits eaten, chocolates and fudge shared. When all the excitement died down, Sheila declared breakfast would be in an hour so that she could prepare the big cockerel and goose she'd ordered for Christmas. The goose had been partially cooked the previous evening so that everything would come together and they could eat at about two o'clock.

'I thought we would have goose, this year,' she'd told Peggy earlier. 'Maureen is having turkey on Boxing Day, so it makes a change – and Pip likes goose better than turkey anyway.'

'Able likes turkey, but we ate the one I brought up with us the other day, so he won't mind – he never minds anyway whatever I choose...'

Peggy helped Sheila clear up when the children had departed to their bedrooms to take their loot back. Fay had a book about ice-skating from her parents, as well as numerous other gifts from her aunts and uncles and friends. She declared that she was going to read and the two boys decided to make a model car in Chris's room. He had a large table to lay the pieces out on and Freddie was going to help him with his new project. Pip had given Freddie a model ship to build, but he wanted to watch Chris at work before he opened his own model.

'I might save it and make it after Christmas,' he told his brother. 'He'd already thanked his parents for the football kit and the camera, as well as various puzzles and books. From other family and friends, he'd had more books, puzzles, a jumper from Maureen in red and a model of a tiger in glass from Janet and Maggie. Uncle Ryan had given him two pounds to spend as he liked, but he'd decided to save it until he saw something he really wanted.

'Maureen makes lovely jumpers,' Sheila said as she looked at the one Maureen had knitted for Fay when they cleared up before going down to the main kitchen. 'That green lacy pattern looks professional. I don't know how she finds the time. She's always busy – how does she do that?'

'I suppose she likes to knit and listen to the wireless in the evenings, or when she's sitting down at home before fetching Gordy after school,' Peggy said. 'She always did knit well.'

'Yes,' Sheila agreed as they walked downstairs together. 'But then,

Maureen is always thoughtful with her gifts. She bought you that pretty nightdress and my petticoat is so pretty.'

'Yes,' Peggy agreed. 'I bought a lot of leather gloves this year – for adults. It was easier than trying to buy clothes or knitwear when you're not sure if someone has lost weight or put it on. Hands don't change in size.'

'That's true,' Sheila said and looked at her mother-in-law. They were alone now and she saw the question in her eyes. 'No, Peggy, I haven't told him yet. I wanted to get today over. It would be awful to quarrel on Christmas Day.'

'The longer you leave it, the more annoyed he will be,' Peggy said and touched her hand in sympathy. 'Remember that Pip loves you, Sheila, but he expects you to trust him and tell him things.'

'Yes, I know, but it is so difficult...'

'What is difficult?' Pip asked, entering the kitchen at that moment. 'Can't you get that goose in the oven? I told you it was too big...'

Sheila looked at Peggy for help, but Peggy's expression was bland. Sheila ought to be the one to tell him her secret, but she was clearly too nervous and looking to Peggy for help. It wasn't Peggy's place to tell Pip that his wife was pregnant, but Sheila was lost. Never one for beating about the bush, Peggy cleared her throat.

'Sheila has something to tell you, Pip. She has saved it for today to tell you as a surprise, an extra present if you like...' Her words invited Sheila to tell him the truth, easing the way for her by pretending she'd meant it as a surprise gift.

'What do you mean?' Pip stared across the kitchen at Sheila. 'You bought me a new wristwatch – what more could I want?'

'What about a new addition to the family?' Peggy prompted.

There was hesitation and fear in Sheila's eyes, but also a faint appreciation of the way Peggy had made it sound like she was keeping her secret as a special gift for him.

'New addition – you haven't bought a dog? I know I said I'd like one but—'

'I'm having a baby,' Sheila blurted it out in a rush. 'Peggy guessed as soon as she got here, but I asked her to keep it a secret until today...'

The colour had leached from Pip's face, leaving him ashen. Fear for his wife leapt into his eyes. 'You're joking... That bloody cap! I knew I should have used something...'

'No, Pip,' Sheila said. 'I took it out a while ago. I wanted another baby...'

'No! You didn't – why? What on earth did you think you were doing? Risking ...' He looked furious. His gaze stabbed at his mother, angry that she'd known before he did and feeling it was a women's conspiracy. They'd clearly discussed something he felt was just between him and his wife. 'How dare you do this to me? After what you went through when Chris was born – after what I went through thinking you might die...'

'Pip!' Peggy said sharply. 'Be careful what you say. Sheila wanted another baby...'

'She should have asked me how I felt first,' Pip said and rounded on his mother in temper. 'You interfere too much, Mum. Keep out of this! This is between Sheila and me – and Chris. What is he going to do if his mother dies?'

'That's foolish talk...' Peggy told him, because Sheila was trembling and looking as if she wanted to cry. 'You should welcome the chance of another baby and don't take it out on Sheila, she needs your love and understanding. It's a time to be close and love one another.'

'I'm not taking it out on her. Sheila knows I didn't care about a big family as long as I had her and Chris,' Pip said. He looked accusingly at his wife, still too upset to think of her. 'What do I do if you're ill? I can't run the pub or bake cakes...'

'No, but I can,' Peggy said, causing both Pip and Sheila to pause and look at her. 'I wasn't going to say until after I'd spoken to Janet – but Able and I are going to buy the lease of the boarding house and move back to the lanes. We're doing it so Fay can skate every day, but also I'll be here to help look after things for you and Sheila...'

'Oh, Mum, are you doing it for me?' Sheila was crying now, the

tears dripping down her cheeks. 'Your lovely cottage and the café...
you can't give all that up just because of me...'

'You're a part of it, Sheila, but not all. Able and I have talked and
we're both of the same mind. We shall keep the cottage for holidays
and that café is damned hard work,' Peggy said, smiling at her. 'It will
be easier for us back here. Able can pull pints and make coffee. He
can do breakfasts and I can bake cakes and apple pies for the shop –
and help out in other ways. You needn't worry about that side of
things, Pip, so don't be angry...'

'I'm not angry, not really. I was shocked and upset. The business
isn't my main worry...' Pip scowled at her, as if half accusing her of
encouraging Sheila, but he'd calmed down now and his expression
became concern rather than anger. 'You both know what I'm upset
about...'

'I'll be all right,' Sheila said. 'I asked my doctor before I did it, Pip
– he doesn't agree with the hospital. He said that just because I was
so ill last time it doesn't mean that I shall be this time. I may have to
take it easier as the time goes on, but if Mum is here...'

'I'll make sure she rests,' Peggy said. 'I'm going to leave you two
together to talk now. I'm sorry if I caused the row, Sheila, but you had
to tell him.' Sheila inclined her head to acknowledge it and Peggy
looked at her son. 'Pip, remember it is Christmas...'

Peggy went out and Sheila heard her talking to Able in the hall.
They went upstairs together.

Her eyes met Pip's. 'I'm sorry I didn't tell you,' she said. 'I know I
should have said something, but it was in my head and it wouldn't
stop... so I just did it. I wasn't sure it would happen and since I found
out I've been hesitant to tell you, because I knew you would be
upset...'

'Oh, Sheila...' Pip's voice broke and he moved towards her,
putting his arms around her, holding her as if he thought she would
snap in two. 'It's just that I love you so much and I nearly lost you the
last time. Yes, of course I should be pleased if we had another child –
but I couldn't bear to lose you, my love.'

'I know...' Sheila choked back a sob. 'I know I should have talked about it, but I was afraid you would talk me out of it and I long for another baby... I'd like a little girl.'

'You might get another boy,' Pip said and smiled oddly. 'You can't choose things like that, love.'

'I know...' She smiled at him tremulously. 'Are you very cross with me?'

'I am – and I'm not. You're my wife and I do understand and I love you, but you have to promise me – this is the last. You will never do it again...'

'I promise,' Sheila said. 'This one but no more.'

Pip smiled down at her. 'Then there's nothing more to say – but if there are complications and it's you or the child, I shall choose you, do you understand?'

'Yes, but I pray there won't be,' Sheila said tearfully.

'Well, it's done now and we'll hear what the doctors have to say – in the meantime, is there anything I can do to help with Christmas dinner?'

'I'm fine, Pip,' she said and smiled. 'Don't start wrapping me in cotton wool just yet – besides, Peggy will be down to help with the cooking soon. She only went to give us some privacy.'

'I'll peel the spuds,' Pip said, taking the knife from her. 'Do we want all these?' Sheila nodded and he smiled. 'Why didn't you tell me rather than Mum?'

'I didn't tell her, she guessed. Women notice these things more, Pip.'

He grimaced, clearly still annoyed with Peggy. 'My mother is going to explain herself to me. If she knew, she should've told me...'

'She guessed, Pip, but I wanted to get Christmas over.'

'Don't worry, I shan't spoil it,' he promised. 'I feel a bit upset you couldn't trust me, Sheila – how long have you known?'

'The doctor confirmed it a couple of days before Peggy arrived.'

'Well, you should have told me,' he said. 'I'll ask Mum to come down and give you a hand with the rest...' He put the peeled potatoes in water and dried his hands.

Sheila sighed as her husband left the kitchen. Peggy had forced the issue and that had helped her to break the news, but she knew Pip hadn't completely forgiven her, even though he wasn't going to have a big row while they had company. He was brooding about it, though, and she sensed that one of these days they would have it out properly. Pip was hurt and she could hardly blame him, because she was in the wrong. He was right when he said she should have talked it over with him; Sheila knew she'd stepped over the mark when she went ahead and removed her cap without telling him. It was almost as if she'd used him to get what she wanted and he might well resent that – and she knew he would worry about her. Pip kept things inside and one of these days it would come out in harsh words, because that was the way he was.

18

Maggie was delighted with all the gifts she'd received. So many that she didn't know what to play with first. Her parents had bought her pretty clothes, shoes and a silver bracelet she could collect charms for, as well as books and some scented talcum powder, and a pretty glass pot for her dressing table at home. Her relatives in London and her granny had all sent gifts: a lovely book with pictures of a ballerina and a pretty nightdress from Grandma Peggy, and Grandad Able had also given her two pounds to spend as she liked. Grandma's friends in London had sent books, puzzles and sweets, and Aunty Sheila had sent her a pair of fur slippers and a hairband with silk flowers on it.

In the fancy dress competition, the previous afternoon, they'd won third prize for going as a witch, wizard and their cat. Maggie had been the cat and had a wonderful time prancing about in her costume and purring at people. The prize for coming third was five pounds, which her parents thought excellent, but Maggie thought poor. She'd wanted the first prize of the return visit to the hotel, because all the other prizes were money. Ten pounds for second, five for third, two for fourth and so on down to five shillings for the eighth entrant, who had been a little boy dressed as Nessie.

He'd had a silly costume in Maggie's opinion, because he didn't look a bit like the beautiful creature she'd seen out in the lake, all shimmering and white in the mist. It had seemed to Maggie that Nessie had a curious light about her, but neither of her parents had seen it, which made her wonder why not. She'd seen the vision so plainly, just as Angus had described it to her.

When she'd seen Angus on Christmas Eve and given him the small box of cigars, she'd chosen for him herself, Maggie told him what she'd seen and he'd nodded and smiled at her.

'You're one of the lucky ones, lassie. Not many see her as clear as that – I have, as I told ye, but most don't believe me. I saw her twice. The first time I wasn't even looking for her, but she just popped up in the lake and waved her long neck at me...' His kind eyes had smiled at her. 'Now don't ye be telling anyone that, young Maggie. They'll think we're both mad because those that don't believe can't ever see her. They've lost the magic, do ye see?'

'I believe you, Angus,' Maggie had told him earnestly. 'And I know what I saw – she was so beautiful. People say she is a monster, but she's not... she's lovely'

'From the mouth of a child,' Angus had said and nodded. 'There's many a man I could wish had your sense, lassie. Now away back to your parents, because they will worry...'

'Yes, I know,' Maggie had said and looked at him with an anxious frown. 'I don't know why, but they aren't very happy. It's been better here – better than at home – but it's still not the same as it used to be...'

'Grown-up folk get themselves in terrible tangles,' Angus had said. 'You'll just have to love them both and show them the way.'

'Yes, I do, I shall,' Maggie had said and smiled at him. 'If I went to the loch by myself, do you think that Nessie would come closer?'

'No!' Angus had said and looked startled. He'd touched her arm urgently. 'You must not go alone, Maggie lass. It is too dangerous. Promise me you won't – please.'

'All right, if you say I shouldn't, I won't,' Maggie had promised him and smiled. 'I'm glad you told me about Nessie, Angus. It was so lovely to see her.'

'Now you be sure to have a lovely Christmas Day and don't go to the loch alone...' Angus had warned. 'And remember what I said – don't go back. Nessie only comes very rarely...'

Maggie had nodded and run back to her parents. Her mother had smiled at her and asked her if Angus liked the gift she'd given him.

'Oh yes,' she had said happily. 'He was very pleased and wished us a Happy Christmas.'

'Good.' Maggie's mother had smiled at her and given her a kiss. 'It has been a lovely time up here, hasn't it?'

'Yes, Mummy. I love it here. I wish we could come again.'

'Perhaps we shall,' her mother had promised but in that vague way adults had when they didn't want to commit themselves.

Maggie had gone to bed in a haze of excitement and woken up to the sun shining in her window. She'd stretched and got up to open her gifts with her parents and they'd all had a lovely breakfast of bacon, eggs and fried bread with tomatoes, with a bit of black pudding, because that was special to Scotland, but Maggie didn't eat it – but then something had happened and now they were quarrelling in their bedroom. They were trying to keep their voices down so that she shouldn't hear, but she knew they were both upset and her mother had shouted that her father was a cheat and that she hated him.

Trying to shut out the harsh words she could hear coming from the bedroom, Maggie felt the tears squeeze out from under her lashes and blinked hard because she couldn't bear for her mother and father to quarrel like this – it was so hurtful and frightening too.

Her mother was saying that she couldn't trust him and he'd called her neurotic. Maggie had no idea what that meant, but it sounded awful. How could they say things like that to each other on Christmas Day? Maggie could not believe it was happening. She loved them both so much – why couldn't they love each other and be nice to each other as they once were? What had happened to make her mother so miserable that her voice was sharp all the time? Maggie longed for them to be as they used to be.

As easy together as they'd all been on the morning they saw Nessie at the lake – or loch, as Angus called it. Maggie remembered how they'd laughed and her father had teased her. Why were they quarrelling now?

Hearing her mother weeping frantically, Maggie jumped to her feet, grabbed her coat and hat and gloves and went out of the cottage quickly. She couldn't bear to stay there and hear them arguing like that – it was breaking her heart. She would go for a walk on her own, perhaps as far as the lake, to see if Nessie was about, although it wasn't misty and Angus said she only came in the mist. In her distress she'd forgotten her friend Angus's advice about not going alone...

* * *

Janet swiped at her eyes, looking at Ryan reproachfully as the heat began to drain out of her. 'Are you in love with this girl?' she demanded. 'Do you want to marry her?'

'Her name is Serena, and, no, I don't want to marry her, nor do I want a divorce,' Ryan said. 'I told you it was nothing – just a bit of fun at the Christmas party...'

'I don't believe you,' Janet accused miserably. 'It happened more than once – please don't lie, because I found a handkerchief in your pocket twice and the same lipstick was on it both times. I just can't trust you...'

Ryan stared at her in silence and then sighed. 'All right, if you want the truth – it has happened a couple of times. The first time was at the party and I'd had a few drinks, but the second... well, she came on to me, and I was mad at you for being so buttoned-up all the time, and so I kissed her, but that is all, Janet. I give you my word; it hasn't gone beyond kissing. It might have done, but I came to my senses in time, told her I was sorry but I didn't want an affair, and that's all there is to it.'

'Do you expect me to believe that?' Janet gave him a bitter smile. 'You don't want to make love to me these days.'

'What makes you think that?' Ryan asked, looking angry. 'I thought that's what we did last night? I can't believe you've done this, Janet – and on Christmas Day too...'

Janet didn't understand why the quarrel had started either. She'd got up feeling rested and relaxed, opening presents with Maggie and Ryan, but then something had just made her snap at him. She wasn't sure why – perhaps because she'd gone to a lot of trouble to buy him a lovely cashmere sweater in a blue-grey that went with his best slacks and a book he'd been wanting, and his present to her had been a very expensive bottle of French perfume – but one she disliked and had told him months ago that she hated. If he ever listened to her, he would never have bought it, but it felt to Janet that Ryan hardly knew she was around these days. If he couldn't even be bothered to check what kind of perfume she liked, it meant he just wasn't interested...

It was a stupid reason to quarrel, of course, but it had all been building inside for so long and she couldn't believe he'd spent all that money on perfume she wouldn't wear, but in truth that had merely been the last straw. Really, it was months of uncertainty and feeling a failure, and that damned lipstick on the handkerchiefs in his pocket.

Now she was defensive and miserable and wished she'd kept it all inside as she usually did. She replied resentfully, 'You'd been drinking and were in a Christmas mood last night – before that we hadn't made love for ages. When I put my arms around you at home a couple of weeks ago, you said you were too tired.'

'I was – and a bit guilty because of that kiss,' Ryan said and his eyes met hers, because he was angry too. 'Would I be entirely to blame if I had strayed? You've been on edge for months, moody, tearful. Nothing I did was right; even Maggie couldn't get you to smile when she told you about her part in the Christmas play at school. I thought you'd forgotten how to until we came here. Suddenly, you were the way you used to be, laughing with Maggie – and that's why I made love to you last night, because you seemed more like your old self.'

'Ryan!' Janet blinked hard. 'I know I haven't been a good wife—'

'And what is that supposed to mean?' Ryan demanded. 'I don't give you marks for how you perform, in bed or anywhere else. Damn it, don't you know how much I adore you – how much I love you and Maggie? You're my life. I couldn't live without you.' He ran his fingers through his hair. 'Serena meant nothing to me – yes, she is attractive, and I thought about sleeping with her, but I didn't. The reason I didn't is because I had too much to lose – you and my daughter. I love you both and I didn't want to lose either of you...'

He was so clearly telling the truth that Janet found she was crying, her tears spilling over and running down her cheeks and into her mouth. She dashed them away. 'I'm sorry; I didn't mean to say anything. Now I've spoiled it all—'

'Nothing is spoiled, love,' Ryan said and moved to take her in his arms. 'I didn't know those handkerchiefs were in my pockets. Serena must have wiped away the lipstick and put them there – I knew she wanted an affair, perhaps more, and maybe she thought if you found them it would force me into a divorce, but I'd never have gone with her. I'll ask to have her moved to another department or I'll change my job...'

Janet sniffed and blew her nose on his handkerchief, which was plain white with his initial in the corner, not striped round the edges like the ones she'd found. If she'd thought about it clearly, she should have known there was something wrong about them at the time, because he never used that kind, but she'd jumped to conclusions. 'Would you do that for me?'

'I've been thinking of it for a while,' Ryan said. 'As a matter of fact, I've been offered work up this way, an hour or so's drive out of Edinburgh – it's one of the reasons I brought you and Maggie up for a holiday. We would keep the house back home, maybe let it to people for a holiday – just those we can trust – but rent up here somewhere for a few years until the end of the contract – which is for five years – and this place would be close enough to visit at weekends.'

'Move to Scotland? Maggie would love that,' Janet said and

looked at him inquiringly. 'It would mean you were home more, wouldn't it?'

'Yes. I thought it might be better for all of us.' Ryan looked at her. 'Do you think Maggie would be prepared to change schools? I've made inquiries and there's a school she could go to where they teach in English, but Gaelic lessons are also available if she wants them...' He frowned as the thought suddenly came to him. 'She's a bit quiet, isn't she? Do you think she heard us arguing?'

'She must have...' Janet looked at him anxiously, but he was already on his way, wrenching the door to the big sitting room open. She could see past him, see that Maggie's presents were all on the floor where she'd opened them first thing, all of them together. 'Maggie! Where are you...'

Ryan was already searching – her daughter's bedroom, the tiny kitchen and the bathroom. Janet saw the answer in his face as he returned to her. 'Where can she have gone?' he asked and the fear was in his voice and his eyes. 'Where would our little girl go, Janet? To the hotel to find friends? To the lake?' His voice rose higher in fear, 'To see that damned monster she thinks is there?'

'No...' Janet was terrified. 'She wouldn't, Ryan. She knows it is dangerous.'

'If that stupid fool has encouraged her...'

'He wouldn't...' Janet told him and ran to the window to look out in panic. 'I heard him tell her not to go to the loch alone.' There was no sign of Maggie anywhere and she rushed over to the door but Ryan was in front of her, scowling, and grasping the handle.

'He filled her head with this nonsense,' Ryan accused as he opened it and peered out into the mist. 'If anything happens to her, I'll hold him responsible.' He cupped his hands and called Maggie's name but there was just an eerie silence.

'No,' Janet said fearfully. 'If anything happens, it is my fault for quarrelling with you at Christmas. I spoiled it for her – it's my fault, Ryan...' Her voice rose as the hysteria caught hold and he slapped her once across the cheek, not hard enough to hurt but enough to stop her. The tears came then and he grabbed her, holding her tight against him, stroking her hair. Janet moved in protest. 'Ryan, we have to look for her...'

'Yes,' he said and stood back. 'It's not your fault, Jan. Please, don't blame yourself – it isn't your fault we can't have another baby and it isn't your fault Maggie went off. We'll find her. I promise you; we'll find her—'

'If anything happens to her I'll never forgive myself,' Janet said and she knew that Ryan would never forgive her either. Maggie was too important to them both. In her desire to give birth to a son, she'd let that fact escape her – and then she'd been foolishly jealous over a Christmas kiss that meant nothing! She'd let her feelings of resentment boil over at Christmas and that was unforgivable.

'Oh, Maggie...' Janet felt the silent tears trickling down her cheeks. 'Forgive me...'

Ryan moved away to grab his heavy overcoat and scarf. He looked at her with frightened eyes. 'I'm going to search for her,' he said and sounded scared. 'Stay here in case she comes back, Jan.'

'Do you think we should raise the alarm?' she asked.' Call the police?'

She felt the panic rising inside her as he shook his head and opened the door, letting in the icy cold and the swirling mist. Earlier, the sun had been shining. When had the mist come up? Why hadn't she noticed? Why had she neglected her daughter because of foolish jealousy? What would she do if Maggie had fallen into the loch as the locals called it...?

As the door slammed behind Ryan, Janet sank to her knees, her head bent in prayer. Oh God, let her little girl be all right. Please let Ryan find her before she became ill or was taken from them. Please let her be all right. Please let Maggie be safe...

Why wasn't there a telephone nearer than the hotel? She wished they'd brought the car up instead of leaving it in London, but they hadn't needed it here. There was a courtesy car at the hotel so they could shop in the village and a bus stop just a short walk from the hotel if they needed to go further; buses only ran twice a day and that meant she now felt isolated, something that hadn't bothered her until this happened. She wanted desperately to talk to her mother, to tell her Maggie was missing, but she had to stop here in case Maggie found her way back.

Janet swiped at her eyes. It was time she stopped feeling sorry for herself, stopped dwelling on her own pain and looked after her daughter. If Maggie was returned to her safely, she would do whatever she wanted – she would never ever neglect her again. Please God, let her have the chance to make it up to Maggie and to Ryan too, though he had some making up to do of his own. Please let Maggie be safe…

19

Sheila looked at her husband as the family were eating their Christmas lunch. Everyone else was laughing, tucking into the mounds of lovely food and thoroughly enjoying themselves. Pip just kept staring at her as if she were a stranger he'd never seen before. When his mother spoke to him, he answered politely, but it was easy for Sheila to see he was still upset with her. He was keeping himself on a tight rein, because it was Christmas, but he couldn't completely forgive her yet despite the way he'd held her and kissed her earlier.

Sheila felt the sting of tears but choked them back. She couldn't let her grief spoil Christmas for everyone else – but she loved Pip so much. She didn't want to lose his love and she knew this was her fault, because she ought to have told him what she wanted and discussed it before she just went ahead and removed the contraceptive cap. He had a right to be consulted in the matter of a second child, of course he did. Supposing he couldn't forgive her?

The delicious food seemed to stick in her throat, but she swallowed it down.

'This goose is delicious,' Able told her and she saw sympathy in his eyes, as if he'd picked up on Pip's anger. 'Did you buy it in London?'

'No, it came up from a farm in the country – Tom Barton has a customer he's done work for and he orders his own poultry from this farmer's son and I asked if he would get me one. Last year, I had to make do with big cockerels because I couldn't buy one, I liked the look of.'

'We get our turkeys from a local farm. Peggy cooks two or three and we do sandwiches in the café for a couple of weeks before Christmas – or with either jacket potatoes or chips and salads.'

'I'd like to do that for the pub,' Sheila said, 'if I could be sure of getting a decent supply. I've seen more about this year, but I bought chickens and cockerels for the pub snacks and everyone seemed to like them.' She pushed her own problems to the back of her mind. 'Everyone still talks about Peggy's Christmas parties. I've never started the tradition. At first, it was just too difficult to get decent food and then it seemed pointless...'

'I did it to thank my customers for their trade,' Peggy said, picking up on their conversation. 'Folk went without a lot in the war and I knew a bit of extra food was always welcome then. It was a lot of work and I'm not saying you should do it – but if we still lived here, I'd bring it back in some form.'

'Why?' Pip asked almost rudely. 'We buy a few drinks for regulars – that should be enough...'

'It was a feeling of wanting to help during the war and they were all friends. They still are. I've met so many old friends since we've been here this time and I offer them all a free drink...'

'Taking advantage that's what they do,' Pip replied harshly. 'You're too soft, Mum, that's why I never encouraged Sheila to start it.'

Peggy looked at him and frowned but didn't say anything. She glanced at her wristwatch. 'I thought we might have heard from Jan before now. They should be at the hotel eating their lunch.'

'Perhaps they will ring later,' Sheila said. 'They might have got up late or be having too much fun.'

'Yes, I suppose so,' Peggy said but still looked puzzled, as if slightly concerned. Sheila wondered why she should be – was Janet having marriage problems too? No one had told her anything, but Pip would know. He and Janet were still close.

She looked at her husband and smiled. He didn't respond and her heart sank. There would be a quarrel at some point, perhaps when they retired for the night – or maybe he'd just sulk and hold it inside him until the visitors had gone.

'If you're anxious, you could telephone the hotel,' Able said to Peggy. 'They're probably having the time of their lives.'

Peggy sent him a loving smile and reached for his hand. Seeing the perfect love and trust between them, Sheila felt her throat close with emotion as regret flooded through her. Would Pip ever look at her that way again? Or had she ruined it all?

She fought her misery and smiled at her son as he tucked into his lunch. He was thrilled with all his gifts, but the thing he'd shown the most interest in was the guitar and Sheila knew that she would always wish that she'd bought it for him herself and ignored Pip's instructions to give him a bike. Her son would never know that his mother had been instrumental in getting him his heart's desire.

For a moment, Sheila's guilt gave way to anger. Why should she always do what Pip decided? She'd wanted to give her son a guitar and she'd wanted another baby – so did she really deserve Pip's black looks?

Fighting down the wave of misery, she looked at Peggy and forced a smile. 'You can ring the hotel later, Peggy, but I'm sure Janet is fine – as Able said, she's enjoying herself too much to think of ringing just yet.' She looked around the table at her guests. 'Does anyone know what time the King's speech is on the wireless?'

'I think it may be on now,' Peggy said, frowning. 'It will be repeated this evening anyway. We can listen to it then...'

It was easy to see she was worried and Sheila felt a bit cross with her sister-in-law. Janet was a bit careless where her mother was concerned. She shut her out and she didn't seem to appreciate how lucky she was to have a mother like Peggy, because what possible reason could she have to neglect ringing her mother on Christmas Day?

20

Janet paced the floor ceaselessly after Ryan had gone. Every few minutes, she looked through the window, peering into the gloom of the mist, tempted to go out and start searching for her beloved child and yet someone had to stay here in case Maggie returned. She would be cold and frightened if she found the cabin empty.

Where was she? Had she gone to the loch alone and fallen in? Was she lying somewhere in the woods, unconscious? Had someone abducted her?

Guilt swept through Janet, making her pain unbearable, and she grabbed her coat, knowing that she couldn't wait here alone a moment longer. Just as she reached the door, it opened and Ryan stood there, his face pinched, nose red with the cold. The bleak look in his eyes told her he hadn't found her daughter.

'She hasn't come back?' he asked, though it was obvious as he entered. 'Where the hell is she? I looked for her at the lake – funnily enough, it is clearer down there – but there's no sign of her.' He passed a shaking hand over his face. 'I thought I'd check in first – now I have to go to the hotel, Jan. We need a search party – and the police...'

'The police?' she said in a hollow voice and her heart clenched with fright. It was so ominous. A child lost in the woods while her parents argued – if anything happened to Maggie, everyone would point fingers. They would say they were careless parents...

'I know – I don't want to do it,' Ryan said, 'but I've looked thoroughly from here to the water and there's no sign of her. It's freezing cold out now and she's too young to be wandering alone in the dusk, Jan. I have to do something...'

'Let me go, I can't bear the waiting...'

'It's best you're here to look after her if she returns. I'll go, Jan.'

Janet looked at him, close to giving way again, hysteria rising. Where was her baby? No matter what Ryan said, if anything had happened to Maggie, she would blame herself – but even as she struggled to put her fear behind her, the door of the cottage opened and Maggie entered, followed by Angus. She was laughing, unaware of their ordeal, and he was carrying an armful of scented pine logs and smiling at her.

'Maggie!' Janet screamed in relief. 'Where have you been? We've been so worried. Daddy has been out searching for you...' She rushed to the little girl and flung her arms around her, holding her close as the tears ran down her face and she stared over the girl's head at Ryan.

He looked as if he might collapse into the nearest chair, but he was looking at Angus, waiting for an explanation, more in control than Janet and able to ask, 'Where did you find her? I walked for miles, to the loch and back and all around...'

''Tis a pity there's no phones in the cabin,' Angus replied with a sympathetic shake of his head. 'No one realised at first that she was on her own...'

'She was in the hotel?' Ryan was close to exploding, but Jan looked hard at him and he calmed down.

Angus shook his head. 'Playing in the gardens with a wee laddie she'd met during the Christmas party. I was bringing these logs down for ye when I met the pair of them playing hide-and-seek,' he told them cheerfully. 'Yon lassie told me she was on her way to the hotel to play with her friends and have something to eat, but I said she should wait for her mother and father – so we came back together.'

Maggie had been released by her mother and was looking at her father doubtfully. He held his arms out to her and she ran to him, looking up at him anxiously.

'Are you cross with me, Daddy?'

'No, I'm cross with myself for not looking after you better – your mum and I were worried that you'd gone to the loch.' Ryan shuddered, his eyes meeting Jan's in shared distress. 'We love you, darling, and it would break our hearts if anything bad happened to you.'

'I wouldn't go to the loch alone.' Maggie looked at him with innocent eyes. 'Angus told me I mustn't go there on my own, so I thought I'd find friends to play with at the hotel, because you were quarrelling,' Maggie said and looked at Janet. 'You've been crying, Mum – why?'

'Because I'm silly,' Janet said. 'I thought things were too good to be true up here –but Daddy says we can come and live in Scotland for a while, would you like that?'

'Yes, please,' Maggie said and smiled, running to hug her mother. She looked across at Ryan. 'Shall we be near the loch'

'A few hours' drive away. We'll be nearer Edinburgh,' Ryan said. 'However, there are other lochs to visit and mountains and woods, all the things you like – and we can come here to stay for weekends often if you want...'

'That's good news, lassie.' Angus had made up the fire for them. 'I'll be on my way then. I've others to deliver logs.' He nodded approvingly at Janet, smiled at Maggie and then winked. 'I told ye there was magic up here, did'na, lassie?'

Maggie gurgled with joyous laughter. She went to hug her father after Angus had gone. 'I didn't believe him at first, Daddy,' she said and laughed as he bent to lift her in his arms and kiss her, before setting her down again. 'I thought it was just a story – but I did see Nessie and now my wish has come true.'

'Did you wish to come and live here?' Ryan looked at her oddly.

'No,' Maggie said with a shake of her head. 'I wished for Mummy

and you to be happy again.' She looked from one to the other. 'You
are – aren't you?'

'Yes,' Ryan said softly. 'I think we shall be, darling – that's truly
Christmas magic for you.' He smiled down at her. Janet moved closer
to him and he put an arm about her, hugging him to her for a
moment. 'Shall we walk down to the water and see if we can see
Nessie again before we go up to the hotel and have something to eat?
We've missed dinner, but I dare say they will find us a nice sandwich
and soup or something.'

'Yes please,' Maggie said and laughed in delight. 'Wear that pretty
red cardigan Auntie Maureen made you, Mummy. Red suits you and
it is such a happy colour.'

'Yes, it is,' Ryan agreed, 'and it does suit you, Jan darling. Let's all
decide to be happy together – the three of us. It is all we need to be
happy, the three of us together, isn't it?'

'Yes, it is,' Janet agreed. 'I'll put the cardie on now. Thank you for
reminding me that red is my colour, Maggie.' She smiled at her
daughter. 'I'd forgotten how much I like it.'

'I told Auntie Maureen when she asked me in the summer. You
were always smiling when you wore red, Mummy.'

'We're all going to be happy again now,' Ryan said. 'Let's make the
most of this holiday – and then we'll come up again in the spring
when we've found our new home.'

21

'I'm still a bit worried about Jan,' Peggy said when Maureen and her children joined them for tea, having eaten their dinner with a cousin of Gordon's. 'I suppose she's just been too busy...'

'That girl wants a good shaking,' Maureen said and looked cross for a moment. 'Don't let her spoil your day, Peggy. Sheila has put on a magnificent spread for us all – though I expect you helped.'

'As much as she would let me,' Peggy said and smiled fondly at her friend. 'It's lovely to be with you today. What did Gordon buy you? Anything nice?'

'Yes, he bought me a lovely dress and shoes from him and Shirley – and he got me a television for the kitchen and a new iron.' Maureen pulled a face. 'Gordon likes gadgets; he would get me all the latest bits and pieces that come out if I'd let him, but I mostly like my old things – I do well with my flatirons I put on the range, but this is electric. I hadn't seen one before, not close up. I suppose it might be easier. I haven't tried it yet...'

'Able got one for me last year,' Peggy reassured her. 'I'd clung to my old-fashioned ones, but I find it is easier – especially if it's a warm day and you don't want to heat the range up too much, but I don't have a television in my kitchen. Oh my, you are posh,' she chuckled as her friend pulled a face. 'No, really, I think it is lovely, Maureen.

It's more than anyone I know has. Gordon is always ahead of the times with things like that. You should be grateful you have such a thoughtful and generous husband. We both, have come to that...'

'Yes,' Maureen nodded at the wisdom of her words. 'Well, have you all had a good day at the Pig & Whistle?'

'Lovely – except that Pip is sulking...'

'He knows then?' Maureen said and glanced at Sheila, guessing what had caused Pip's mood. Peggy nodded but didn't add to that, because Rose and her family had arrived. Sheila was taking coats, fussing over the children and trying to get them all organised so that she could serve tea. Looking at how her daughter-in-law responded to Rose's little boy and her daughter, her face lighting up with love and happiness, Peggy suddenly understood how much it meant to Sheila to have another child. She would have to have a word with Pip, make him see things from Sheila's point of view instead of his own.

Sighing, she acknowledged to herself that Pip was very much Laurie's son. Her first husband had sulked when things didn't go his way and it looked as if Pip did much the same. That made her sympathise with her daughter-in-law more, because she'd suffered from Laurie's moods much of her married life. While they'd been young and in love, they'd always made up their quarrels in bed, but later in life it had become more serious and the quarrel over Janet's marriage had been the last straw on the camel's back. After that they'd started to drift apart and when the war had separated them, it had been inevitable that their marriage would end one way or another. She'd been sad that Laurie's illness had left him to die amongst strangers, but by then there had been nothing left for either of them.

For a moment a cloud passed over Peggy, but then she looked at Able and smiled. He was giving Rose a hand with her smart new coat and talking easily to Tom. Just as he met her eyes, the phone shrilled.

'You get it, Peggy,' Sheila said and smiled at her. 'I'm sure it will be Janet.'

Peggy nodded and went out into the hall. It was a bit chillier here and she shivered as she reached for the phone. Since the morning, her senses had been telling her something was wrong and now it was stronger than ever. She put the receiver to her ear and spoke into the mouthpiece.

'The Pig & Whistle...'

'Mum...'

'Jan, love – are you all right? Is Maggie all right?' she asked as soon as her daughter spoke.

'We're all right now – how did you know?' Janet asked and sounded unlike herself. 'It was terrible, Mum. I had to wait in the cabin in case she returned and couldn't get to a phone...'

'What happened?' Peggy asked. 'I sensed something...'

And then it all poured out: the quarrel with Ryan, Maggie's disappearance, her pain and distress. Tears were in her voice as she talked, telling Peggy of all the fear and suspicion, as well as the terror of thinking Maggie might be lost for good.

'I was so worried, Mum!'

'Of course, you were. It must have been terrible in that cabin on your own – unable to ring me or anyone. I wish I'd been able to comfort you, love. I'm so sorry.'

'It's all right now,' Janet said. 'They got us jacket potatoes and warmed some turkey up, so it was nearly as good as a proper dinner – not like yours, of course, but good when you're hungry and we were all starved by the time we got there. Maggie and Ryan have gone back to the cottage. I told them I would ring you and they wanted me to say thank you for all the lovely presents. Maggie loved all hers – and I love that silver bracelet you bought me, Mum. Just what I wanted.' She paused for a moment, then, 'We all love it up here, Maggie particularly. It shook me when she disappeared like that, but until then we'd had a really good time.'

'Maggie is all right so don't let it spoil things, Jan love. I'm glad you rang, and that you all liked your presents – but get back to your family now. I'll talk to you when we get home. I've got some news, but it will wait until I see you.'

'Yes, I'll come up.' Janet sounded a bit strange. 'I've got a lot to tell you, too.'

Peggy stared at the receiver as it went down. Janet hadn't told her everything, but at least she knew why she'd had that strange feeling since mid-morning. Thank goodness Janet had rung, because otherwise she would have been awake all night!

Returning to the big room where everyone was gathered about to sit down to their tea, everyone looked at her expectantly.

'Maggie disappeared for a short while,' she said into the sudden silence. 'Ryan searched for her and couldn't find her and Janet was desperate, but one of the locals brought her back – she'd been playing near the hotel with another child...'

'Is she all right?' Able and Sheila asked in the same breath.

'Yes, Janet says she's fine. Just wandered off while she and Ryan were getting ready for lunch – and they missed the proper lunch, but the hotel got them something later. She's only just been able to ring, because they don't have phones in the cabins.'

'That's a bit awkward, isn't it?' Tom said. 'These days you'd think they would have a phone for the guests.'

Peggy shook her head. 'I expect it would be too expensive to install and, besides, the hotel isn't that far away and they can ring from there – if Ryan had gone there first, Maggie would have been back with them in no time, but he thought she might have gone to the lake alone.'

'Janet must have been frantic,' Rose said, looking concerned. 'How awful for them.'

'Yes – they've been having a wonderful time and that must have spoiled it a bit, but Janet says they love it up there and they're staying on until the end of their holiday.'

'Did Jan say why Maggie wandered off?' Pip asked, but Peggy shook her head. Janet had told her about the quarrel, but she wasn't going to pass that bit of news on, because it was Janet and Ryan's private business.

'I'm glad they're all OK,' Maureen said and smiled lovingly at

Shirley, who was sitting Matty in the high chair they'd brought with them. 'I couldn't bear to lose any of my children.'

'I wouldn't wander off,' Shirley said, returning her smile. 'And I'd make sure Gordy and Matty were safe too.'

'I know you would, love,' Maureen said with a fond look. 'I've been lucky to have you, Shirley.' Her daughter's smile lit up the room. 'You're a big help to me – Janet doesn't have anyone like you.'

Peggy saw the girl frown and knew that, like others, she would be wondering how Janet had allowed her daughter to stray in a place where she might get lost and could fall into a deep lake. A shudder went through her as she thought what might have happened and the horror that would have brought. No wonder Janet had sounded so odd!

'As long as it all turned out all right,' Sheila said. 'Come on, everyone, let's have our tea.'

Her words broke the atmosphere and everyone talked and laughed again, thanking each other for presents and commenting on the lovely spread on the table. Dishes of red salmon mashed up with pepper and vinegar, thick slices of cold goose, ham and cold roast pork, together with fen celery, sliced tomatoes and cucumber in vinegar with a little sugar, pickles, generous slices of bread, baked the previous day and kept in the fridge to make certain it was fresh and not dry, buttered thickly. As well as the various pickles, there was mustard, redcurrant jelly to accompany the cold goose and a bowl of crisps for the children. Able kept pinching them from Fay's plate, making her giggle, while Freddie slid his share over to her so she didn't lose out.

It was a lovely atmosphere and Peggy relaxed. She noticed that even Pip seemed less tense and angry than he had at lunch and wondered what had made the difference. She wished that Janet and her family were here to share in the joy but knew that things were better for her daughter than they had been for a while – perhaps the fear of losing Maggie had made both of them realise how much they already had. Now, they'd been given a second chance, and if they had any sense, would make the most of it.

* * *

Sheila looked at Pip uncertainly as she closed their bedroom door for the night and walked towards the bed. He didn't say anything, so she sighed inwardly and began to take off the skirt and jumper she'd worn for tea. The jumper was new and one of his presents to her, along with the gold locket and chain he'd given her, which she was also wearing.

'Chris loves that guitar Mum gave him,' he said suddenly, bringing her out of her thoughts with a start.

'Yes, I thought he would,' she agreed. 'His teacher told me how musical he is...'

'I was wrong about that,' Pip admitted and looked directly at her. 'I know I'm not always right, Sheila. I also know that I have a habit of forcing you to accept what I say. I can be a bit bossy at times, without really knowing or meaning it – is that why you didn't tell me what you intended to do?'

Sheila hesitated, then, 'In a way,' she admitted. 'I knew you would say I mustn't risk it – and I wanted another child so badly...' Tears stung her eyes as she looked at him sadly. 'I asked my doctor what he thought and he says I should be fine – and he will keep an eye on me. I know I should have discussed it with you. I did try once, but you weren't listening...' she blinked hard. 'Please forgive me, Pip...'

'It's me that should be asking you to forgive,' he said quietly and came around the bed to her. He looked contrite now and a bit ashamed. 'I was a pig earlier on, Sheila. It is just because I'm so frightened...' He caught his breath and she saw his hand tremble with the force of his emotion. 'I just can't bear the thought that I might lose you – but I have no right to deny you the chance to have another child and I shouldn't dominate you so much.'

'You don't – well just a little sometimes.' Sheila smiled at him. 'I don't mind – you always were bossy, but I loved you then and I love you now.' She hesitated, then, 'Can you accept what I've done?'

'You're a wonderful wife, Sheila. If you couldn't discuss something that important with me, I'm at fault...'

'No, I should have done, Pip. I'm sorry – but I'm not sorry I'm pregnant. I really want another baby.'

'I'd like a little girl – or another boy,' he admitted, smiling at her. 'I do love kids and seeing all those faces at our table.' He moved towards her, taking her hands and looking into her eyes. 'I love you so much, darling. Promise me you will tell me if you feel anything unusual – it doesn't matter how small it is. You need taking care of for a while.'

'I think your mum will come and help out, Pip,' Sheila said. 'She seems to have made up her mind, but I shan't take it for granted.'

'Able says it will be better for her. Living down there hasn't worked out quite as they thought – the hours are too long and they can't get enough of the right help. Besides, Janet doesn't visit often – she acts as though she doesn't need anyone, but I know that is an act.'

'You know your sister as well as anyone – how could Maggie have slipped off like that?'

'Perhaps her and Ryan were arguing.' Pip frowned. 'She as much as told me she thought he was having an affair.'

'She couldn't have thought that!' Sheila exclaimed. 'Ryan adores her.'

'I told her not to be an idiot and she slammed the phone down on me.' Pip looked rueful. 'That can't have helped her. We're pretty close and when we quarrel it puts us both out of sorts.'

'Yes, I've noticed,' Sheila said. 'I knew something was wrong lately. I thought I'd upset you.'

'No, why should you?' He shook his head. 'You're a wonderful wife and mother, Sheila. I may not tell you enough, but I'm proud of the way you keep the pub running and that shop of yours.' He grinned. 'I'll let you into a secret, but you mustn't tell Mum...'

Sheila nodded, looking at him in wonder as she waited.

'Your almond macaroons are twice as good as Mum's. She tried them a few times years ago and they were either too chewy or too sweet. You get them perfect every time.'

Sheila laughed; she couldn't help it. Pip looked surprised. 'I didn't think my cooking was up to Peggy's standard in your eyes.'

He made a face at her. 'Maybe at the start you had something to learn, but I think you could give her a run for her money on most things now. Your Christmas cake was delicious and so were those sausage rolls.' He opened his arms to her. 'Kiss me and tell me I'm forgiven?' he invited and she went into his arms without hesitation, giving herself up to the sweetest kiss she'd known in a while.

Sheila wasn't a fool and she knew it wouldn't all be sunshine and roses from now on. Pip was stubborn and sulked if he didn't like something and it would happen again – but when it mattered, he loved her and he was big enough to apologise when he knew he was wrong.

'Happy Christmas, darling,' she whispered against his chest. His face nuzzled into her hair as he held her close. 'I love you.'

'I love you, too. I don't always deserve you – but I'll never stop loving you and I don't want to lose you.'

'You won't,' she promised, but of course she couldn't guarantee that. Every woman risked her own life to carry a child. Most did so safely, but some were unlucky. Sheila knew she was more at risk than some – but pray God, she would come through, because her family needed her.

22

'So, what do you think of the private rooms?' Able asked Peggy as they walked round the top floor of the boarding house two days later.

Boxing Day had passed without incident, all the men of the family off to watch Arsenal's match after lunch at Maureen's and back to tea at Rose's house. The pub had been open for a couple of hours in the morning and again in the evening but had closed at nine instead of the usual ten, with normal service having been resumed that morning. Peggy had been up early and helped prepare fresh cheese and onion flans, salads, a shepherd's pie and more sausage rolls, because Christmas closing was over and for the landlady of the Pig & Whistle life had returned to normal. However, Pip was off work for a few more days and he'd actually volunteered to serve in the bar Boxing Night and he was in the bar again that morning. Peggy had smiled approvingly and he'd hugged her and apologised for being rude to her on Christmas Day. He'd been just the same as a little boy and Peggy had forgiven him, smiling to herself. She loved and understood her son and always would.

Peggy looked at her husband now as he asked the question for the second time. 'Will they do or shall we look for something else?'

'Sorry, love, my mind was wandering.' She smiled lovingly at him. 'I think they're all right. Adequate at the moment, but we'll make them home, Able. A bit of paint and our own things will transform them.'

'What will you bring from the cottage?'

'Clothes and the children's things mostly,' Peggy said. 'We'll leave our furniture at home – the cottage is still home, Able, and always will be. It's there whenever we want or need it. I'll buy what we need here, new beds and the rest of it. I may bring some of my cooking things and crockery.'

'You've got far more than you need at home.'

'Yes, I know. I shall buy more here as we go along, but I'll need certain things here to start me off.' Peggy nodded and made a note on her lined writing pad. 'We've got plenty of linen and stuff to bring back, but tables, chairs, we can get all those from the second-hand shops in the East End.'

'Wouldn't you rather buy new?' Able asked. 'We have money...'

'Beds only,' Peggy said and smiled. 'We may need some new bits for the guest rooms, but most already have decent furniture we can buy cheaply. For our own use I prefer traditional; Georgian or Edwardian are the periods I like, if I can find things at the right price.'

'Similar to what we have at the cottage,' Able agreed and smiled. 'I like your taste, Peggy, so I'll be content with whatever you choose.'

'It will be fun,' she said and smiled up at him. 'We're so lucky to be able to afford two homes, Able. Most folk can't afford one...' She frowned, thinking about her neighbours and the poverty some East Enders still endured every day.

Peggy had always helped out those she could, and she knew Tom made sure Alice was all right and old Mr Giddings, too, from what Rose had said. Peggy would find time when she got settled back here to do what she could for others too. Rose had talked about a young lad she'd seen on a market stall before Christmas. She'd wished she could help him, but the stall had disappeared and she didn't know where the family lived. Peggy thought she might join a committee to help out a bit and decided she would ask Tom.

He had his finger on the pulse and would know if there were folk in need in the lanes.

'Sometimes I feel a bit guilty,' she said to her husband. 'We've got so much when you look around you...'

'We've worked hard for what we've got,' he told her with a smile of satisfaction. 'For us personally it is just a case of changing our workplace – and we'll give it a few years and see how we feel then, but I think perhaps we moved to the country too soon. The cottage will be great in a few years when the children have left home...' He saw that she still looked concerned and smiled at her. 'You'll find folk you want to help, Peggy, and I'll never stop you – I remember you were always taking pies and food to those in need...'

'Yes, I did and no doubt I'll do it again,' Peggy said and sighed. 'I did love the cottage, Able, but I must admit I thought we'd have more free time down there, but it didn't work out that way. To be honest, I'm still reeling from the shock because until I saw how good Fay was on the ice, I hadn't thought of moving back. I enjoyed the café and the friends we had down there.'

'Yes, but we were both working too many hours and that wasn't what we planned.'

'No, it wasn't,' Peggy agreed. 'I have to admit I found it tiring sometimes – but I shall be sorry to tell April I'm leaving. I'm sure whoever takes on the café will want to retain her, but it won't be the same.' April was the best of her staff at the café; they got on well and she'd always been reliable.

'She might want to move to London,' Able said. 'She could help us out here if she wanted – serving breakfasts, evening meals, helping with the tea shop or the pub. It would be a varied job and flexible hours...'

'I could ask, I suppose.' Peggy didn't think April would want to uproot her life; she still couldn't believe she'd agreed to it so easily herself. Yet she knew that what she was doing was for them all – it meant help for Sheila, Maureen and Pip, extra fun for the children, and the chance for Peggy to do more of the things she liked. Yet most people would think she'd gone mad agreeing to such an idea.

'You do that, hon,' Able said. 'Have you seen all you want here?'

'Yes, for the moment,' Peggy agreed. 'How long exactly do we have to sort out things here and at home?'

'March the thirtieth,' Able said. 'Time to settle our affairs, let folk know and hopefully sell that lease...'

'It isn't long,' Peggy said, frowning. 'I'll need curtains here as well as furniture, but I shan't have time to make them.'

'Get a firm in to measure and make them,' Able suggested. 'Sheila will let them in for you and make sure everything gets done to your liking.'

'Tom will decorate and do small jobs for us,' Peggy said confidently. 'I don't need any structural work carried out just yet, but he will find someone to give it all a good clean for us. I want professional standards, Able. I've seen cleaner...' She ran her fingers along a door ledge. 'I know the last proprietor was trying to do it all alone, but no one can do everything.' She nodded. 'We'll stop on a couple of days or so to get things sorted – give me a chance to look for furniture and make lists of what I need Tom to do here.'

Able nodded his agreement. 'We'll have things spick and span before we move in and advertise it as under new management – that should bring the customers in. Especially, when word spreads that Peggy is back in the lanes.'

She laughed as she saw the look in his eyes. 'I am excited, Able. Everyone I meet wants to know if it's true.'

'So why do I see that little worried look at the back of your eyes?'

'Janet...' Peggy said. 'I feel so guilty, Able. Am I letting her down – her and Maggie? Ryan too. He told me how worried he was for her when we visited. If she was ill and I wasn't able to get to her...'

'How many times have you tried to help her and been shut out?' Able said mildly. 'You have to let go, Peggy. Janet is old enough to live her own life and you're not helping by trying to fix everything for her.' He smiled to take the sting from his words. 'She knows there is always a home for her here, hon. It is up to her what she makes of her life.'

'Yes, I know – and we have to think of ourselves,' Peggy said but it wasn't easy to just let go. Jan would always be her little girl and she tended to want to protect her even though she was a grown woman. 'Let's go back to the pub. Sheila will want to hear what is happening and so will the twins.'

'You are certain this is what you want?' Able looked into her eyes. 'Don't do it if it makes you unhappy...'

'I'm like you,' she replied, smiling at him. 'As long as I have you and my family, I'm fine.'

'Then, we should tell everyone and I'll get on with the contract for the lease – have you told the twins for definite?'

'They know we're coming back to London,' Peggy said but nodded. 'They will need to choose their own room and see where they will be living.'

'Fay isn't much interested in anything but ice skating just yet,' Able said. 'Freddie might get to choose his room this time rather than letting Fay have all her own way.'

Peggy laughed. 'She can be selfish – does she get it from me, do you think?'

'Doubt it – perhaps from my father.' He gave her an odd smile. 'He could be a bit of a bastard, but my mother was worse, more than a match for him.'

'Who knows where these things start? She has always been the demanding one. Poor Freddie has to put up with such a lot, but he's so good with her.' Peggy shrugged her shoulders.

'Freddie doesn't need a lot,' his father said affectionately, 'but we should look out for him, Peggy – can't have him sacrificing everything he loves for his sister. I've spoken to a couple of people about schools. Freddie is bright and I don't want him losing out on his education – and there's the football to consider. I've been told about a private day school. He will get a good grounding in maths and English, languages too – but they're dedicated to sport and I believe that's our son's future.'

'Can we afford private tuition?' Peggy frowned.

'Why not?' Able said mildly. 'The house I did up in Mulberry Lane will fetch a good price now and its lease is coming up for renewal soon – once the tenant moves out, I could sell and invest the money for Freddie's future.'

'You're such a good father,' Peggy told him. 'I hadn't even thought of anything other than a state school.'

'I've been thinking of it for a while,' Able told her. 'My son deserves the best, hon. If we'd stayed where we were, we might have had to send him to board somewhere, but here he can come home each night – and he's quite keen to try ice hockey too.'

'So, it will benefit Freddie as well,' Peggy mused and gave him a loving smile. She knew she was storing up all the ammunition she would need to deflect Janet's recriminations. Her eldest daughter would feel she was being abandoned for other people's sakes and Peggy would have to find good reasons to explain her choice. However, she didn't feel like an argument over the phone and decided to leave it until Janet visited and she could talk face to face.

* * *

'Is everything all right? Did you speak to the landlord about the lease?' Sheila asked eagerly when Peggy and Able came into the kitchen. She'd been baking cakes as the shop was now open again. The smell of them was irresistible and Able helped himself to an almond macaroon. 'Are they OK?' Sheila asked as he munched happily.

'Lovely,' he assured her. 'I love these.'

'I love them too and they sell well,' Sheila said. Her confidence in her cooking had grown since Able arrived. 'Chris loves them – and I know Pip does as well.'

'Pip loves anything with almonds,' Peggy agreed. 'I prefer coconut and so do the twins. I'm afraid I don't make these often enough...' She smiled at Sheila. 'Next time you make them, I'll watch what you do – you make them better than I do. Macaroons are not my biggest success...'

'I make them most days, because they sell out,' Sheila said and Able looked pleased.

'I'll be one of your best customers,' he promised.

'You don't have to pay,' Sheila assured him.

Pip came in then and immediately went up to her with a worried expression on his face. 'You're not overdoing it, Sheila?'

'No, I'm fine,' she reassured him. 'Honestly, Pip, I feel wonderful – why don't you sit down and have coffee and a macaroon.'

'They're good,' Able assured him. 'Will you think I'm greedy if I have another?'

Sheila laughed and assured him there were plenty. 'I made three dozen,' she said. 'Maureen took two dozen into the shop and I kept these for us. I've made a coconut cake, Mum – and some madeleines and three Victoria sponges. I fancy a madeleine myself…'

The children crowded round the table and started helping themselves to the sweet treats and soon the plates were empty. Sheila smiled; glad she'd filled her tins as well as the table. Three children and extra adults could eat an awful lot of cake…

'Save space for your lunch,' she warned. 'Peggy made us a ham and chicken casserole and that will be ready for two-thirty.'

The pub would close at two-fifteen until six-thirty that evening. Even though it was still the holidays for many folk, the regulars wanted a drink or two and they had to alternate staff to keep it going. The door had been open since ten-thirty that morning and Pamela Makepeace was working extra shifts until she went back to her technical college after the holidays. She was still training to be a secretary but said she wanted to keep working in the bar some evenings to earn extra money. Pamela loved nice clothes and the money she'd earned over Christmas was being saved to buy an outfit in the style of the latest Christian Dior fashion.

'I'll go through to the bar if that is all right with you,' Peggy said. 'I think I might have seen Alice on her way over and I'd like to find out for myself how she's doing. Tom told me he thinks she has a bit of a struggle these days.'

Sheila looked thoughtful as Peggy left them. 'Why is it everyone tells Peggy? I've asked if Alice was managing and she always says she's fine...'

'Mum used to send her an apple pie or something even when she was working in the pub – I doubt Alice can afford to feed herself properly now she no longer has lodgers,' Pip said.

Sheila felt upset. Why hadn't he told her before? She wouldn't have let one of Peggy's friends go short if she knew, but she supposed she was still a newcomer despite her years in the lane and Alice's pride wouldn't allow her to say she couldn't manage on her meagre income.

'I'll send her something tomorrow,' Sheila said to no one in particular. 'What does she like?'

Pip didn't answer, but Able smiled at her. 'A nice big meat casserole would last her a few days, because she can warm it through and add vegetables to it,' he suggested.

'Yes, that's a good idea,' Sheila said, looking relieved. 'I know Peggy makes a lot of them – I'll ask her advice.' She wasn't one for many casseroles except on bitterly cold days, but, for Alice's convenience, she could see the reasoning behind Able's words and she thought how kind and understanding he was. 'We do a lot of things differently,' Sheila said, 'but I can't tell you how grateful I am that you and Peggy have made such a big change to help me...'

'We're pleased to help,' Able assured her gravely. 'Don't feel you have to be grateful, Sheila. I think this change was coming – Peggy has been working far too hard and this is as much for her as anyone. I would never have dreamed of telling her she was doing too much, but in her heart, I think she knew it – she was just too stubborn and brave to admit it.'

'Mum is always like that,' Pip said. 'She never complains and it's silly, because she would just have gone on until she was ill. I never wanted her to leave and I'm glad she's coming back. If Janet had any sense, she would get Ryan to bring her to London more – after all, he's got that little flat. He stays there when he's working up here and she is stuck at home. She should put her foot down...'

'Perhaps she will when she knows her mother is here,' Able said. 'I think Janet needs to make a few changes for the sake of her family as well – but she isn't the easiest one to persuade.'

'I'll persuade her if I get the chance,' Pip promised. 'I'll ring her when she's back home and see what she has to say for herself.'

Christmas was almost over, though the decorations weren't down yet and they were still clearing up the bits and pieces Rose had made. Tom was already back at work and he'd been discussing the changes Peggy needed at the boarding house, because she wanted it done as quickly as possible and he had a couple of other jobs to finish as well.

The nuts she'd bought for Christmas were long gone. Rose had done well with those and wished she'd bought a few more. Tom had asked if she thought the market would have any left or any fresh stock and she knew he wanted her to try to buy more – but Rose was reluctant, because of where the nuts had come from. She would buy if the lad was there on his own, but if Jim Broad was there, she might walk away and buy elsewhere, even though they might not be as good, because although she'd taken to Nobby, she didn't much like his father.

As Rose approached the spot where the stall selling nuts had been, she saw there was a big notice from the council saying it was illegal to park a barrow there or to trade without a licence. Someone must have reported Nobby's father to the council and they'd been moved on. Rose felt a pang of pity for the young lad, because he'd been hoping for a stall of his own, but she doubted the council would give him a licence at his age. What would happen to the family if the father had lost his pitch and couldn't get another?

Rose couldn't do anything to help them. If Nobby had been on his own, she might have tried, but Jim Broad made her a bit nervous and she would do better to avoid him and put the family's plight out of her mind. Shivering in the bitter air – it felt cold enough for snow – she hurried on.

She entered the covered market, inhaling the special scent that it always held: spices, citrus fruits, fish, meat and the scent of a stall-holder's hair oil as she lingered by his display of Christmas goodies now at knock-down prices. Rose saw a box of crackers with pictures of Father Christmas at a shilling and considered buying them for the next year, then decided that the fun of Christmas was buying in the last few days. She walked on, looking for bargains on various stalls, bought some small oranges that she was assured were sweet and a pound of walnuts. They weren't the same as they'd had at Christmas but looked as if they might be nice.

'Deserted me have yer?' the voice behind her startled Rose and she swung round just as the man caught her about the waist. Pressed against him, she looked up at Jim Broad in shock, her eyes widening, lips parting as he bent his head and kissed her. Just like that! In the market, in front of everyone, without a care for her reputation.

'How dare you!' Rose struck out furiously, catching him a hard blow to his nose in her distress, to the accompaniment of jeers from watching stallholders and laughter.

He put his hand to his nose and she saw a smear of blood, though she hadn't hit him that hard; her ring must have caught the skin.

'That's taught yer, Broad,' one of the men said. 'Go on, ducks, give the bugger another. Bloody cheek, that's what I say.'

'If Tom Barton hears about this, he'll kill yer,' another of the jeering onlookers entered the fray. 'Shouldn't want ter be in yer shoes when his missus tells 'im!'

'It were just a joke,' Jim said, looking uncomfortable as the other men sent hard stares towards him. He held up a limp piece of mistletoe. 'I've been carryin' this around hopin' fer a Christmas kiss.' As Rose glared at him frostily, his unease increased. 'I thought yer would like it,' he muttered. 'Yer've been givin' me the eye...'

'In your opinion,' Rose said angrily. She didn't care that she had quite an audience. 'I bought some nuts from your son, because I admired his enterprise, even though you were trading illegally. I had no desire for your advances whatsoever. Please go away and stop embarrassing me. I shan't bother telling my husband, because he would come after you and that might lead to trouble for him – and, quite frankly, Mr Broad, you're not worth it. My Tom is worth a thousand of you!'

'So, it was you told the council on us – bitch!' Jim Broad snarled furiously. 'I knew someone did... I'll get even wiv yer...'

'Don't try or my husband will teach you a lesson...' Rose said, too angry to realise what he was saying or to see the reaction her words had caused.

'You're right there, missus!'

'Clear orf you clown,' one of the traders yelled. 'Yer not wanted 'ere – go back where yer come from. If she reported yer ter the council, yer deserved it...'

'But I didn't...' Rose said; her words were lost in the storm of abuse from all sides as the market men gathered and shook their fists at him. The traders formed a protective circle. Rose realised that they were enjoying the spectacle and that some of them knew Tom well and meant to protect her if need be, but she'd had no need. She was more than a match for this fool.

'That's told yer...' a large man with a red beard loomed up to Jim Broad menacingly. 'The lady don't want yer botherin' 'er – and yer ain't worth the drippings of me nose. Yer ain't wanted 'ere neither. I've made up me mind and after the way you treated this lady, I shan't sell me stall ter yer – and if any of us see yer hanging around here again, yer'll wish yer were back in Bermondsey where yer came from. Sling yer hook, mate, and watch yer back if yer come near our patch again, pinchin' our Christmas trade.'

'Yeah, bugger orf,' several voices were raised against him. They were angry he'd dared to assault and embarrass Rose, but even more furious that he'd set up his unlicensed barrow and stolen trade from the legitimate market at Christmas.

He turned without another word and slunk away, but not before sending a look of such bitter anger at Rose that, had she been alone, she might have feared physical retribution for his humiliation.

She looked at the red-bearded man, feeling a little shaken now it was over. 'Thank you,' she said. 'He looked at me oddly when I shopped with him – but I didn't think he would dare to do that...' She frowned, feeling vaguely guilty. 'I felt sorry for his lad...'

'Yeah, the lad is all right,' the trader agreed. 'I thought about lettin' the boy take over me spare stall – but not after Broad behaved the way he did to you, Mrs Barton.'

'Oh, I think he knows his advances are not welcome now...' Rose smiled.

'Yeah, you told him, Mrs Barton,' he said and smiled. 'I'm Red George. Tom has helped me out more than once and for two pins I'd have knocked the bugger down, sneaking up on yer like that...'

'He isn't worth the bother it might cause you,' Rose said, 'but thank you for your help.' Her gaze swept round the men as they dispersed and returned to their stalls. 'It might not have been so easy without all of you, thank you!'

She saw smiles and nods and, collecting her senses, she went to the nearest stall and bought brazil nuts, pears and Cox's apples. After that, she continued her search for the freshest foods and bargains, buying some pretty pink knitting wool to make Jenny a new bobble hat and some mittens, because it was colder again and it might snow soon.

Rose was thoughtful on the way home. She'd told Jim Broad that she wouldn't bother telling Tom what he'd done, because he wasn't worth it, but now she wondered if she ought. Red George wouldn't tell him, but others might gossip and the women in the market had stared without speaking. The tale would get back to Tom eventually and it might get stretched in the telling.

* * *

Tom heard the story of the way Rose had been grabbed and kissed by a rogue market trader before the day was out. One of his customers told him – and he heard the full story, of how Rose had hit him and stood up to the man who had insulted her.

'She gave him what for good and proper,' Benny Hall said with a grin that held no malice. 'You've got a right one there, Tom – your Rose hit him on the nose and I reckon she might have broken it, 'cos it were bleedin' as he went orf wiv his tail between his legs. Told him she weren't interested in his advances and you were worth a thousand of 'im. She's right an' all, smarmy bugger. Opening his stall just afore Christmas and selling them nuts, pinchin' our trade, and the bugger hadn't got no licence for our patch neither.'

'He came here and wanted me to fix the wheel on his barrow,' Tom said, 'asking questions – personal things. I should've hit the so-and-so then... Grabbin' my Rose like that...' His eyes glittered with anger and his hands clenched as he thought what he'd like to do to the man who had dared to upset his Rose. 'He wants a good thrashing...'

'Red told 'im to sling 'is 'ook,' Benny chortled at the memory. 'I doubt he'll come sniffin' round 'ere again in a hurry.'

'If he comes near us again, I'll make him sorry...' Tom growled. 'Where does he live?'

'Yer don't want ter go lookin' fer trouble,' Benny said uneasily. 'I told yer 'cos yer might 'ave 'eard it wrong and I didn't want yer thinkin' your Rose did anythin to encourage the bugger. She told him straight.'

Tom nodded, but the anger was simmering inside and he knew that if he ever saw Jim Broad again, he would knock him down. No man embarrassed his wife like that and got away with it... though it sounded as if Rose had put him in his place right enough.

'Looked at 'im as if 'e were something the cat 'ad dragged in from the gutter,' Benny chuckled. 'She's a right madam your Rose when somethin' upsets her...'

'Rose hates anythin' like that,' Tom agreed. 'She used to get it sometimes if she worked in the pub – but I sorted one or two of them out. Rose never knew, of course, but I gave one bloke a damned good hiding and he spread the word.'

Benny nodded, smiling at him in shared pleasure. 'I 'eard about that, mate. It's what a few of 'em need – especially the cocky ones. Locals know to leave your missus alone, but he comes from Bermondsey.'

Tom nodded his expression thoughtful. 'It might prove worthwhile to pay him a little visit...'

'Nah, leave it alone, Tom,' his friend said. 'Red put the wind up the bugger – I doubt we'll see 'im 'ere again in a hurry...'

'Maybe yer right...'

The glare faded from Tom's eyes as his anger cooled. Benny was talking sense. Tom didn't need to get involved in a brawl if the culprit had been scared off. He had his good name and a business to look after and he didn't want bother with the law. Rose had handled the incident well and Tom's friends had seen Broad off – but if he bothered Tom's wife again, he would have to be taught a lesson.

* * *

Jim walked quickly until he was out of sight of the marketplace and the rotten devils that worked there. Self-satisfied buggers! Just because they all had licences and could work legitimately, they looked down on him for setting up an illegal stall. He'd lost his licence two months before Christmas because of persistent late payment of rent. It wasn't his fault. He was still paying off the debts he'd run up from when he first got back from the war. His mind shied away from that terrible time. He'd learned that his wife had been cheating with that bloody Canadian flier while he was fighting the war and he'd taken to the bottle. On top of all he'd suffered out there, it was just too much – and then she'd said he was a bully and run off with her lover.

Jim scowled bitterly. Women were the devil! He'd flirted with that red-haired beauty at Christmas and she'd loved it – he'd swear she had, but then when he'd given her a little kiss, she'd created hell.

Jim's scowl deepened. He'd wondered who had reported him to the council and now he thought he knew – it was the red-haired vixen! What a bitch she was and he'd like to show he a thing or two.

The resentment and worry churned round and round in his head. He'd straightened himself out after Ginny left him for that bloody Canadian. His mother had made sure of that, threatening she'd report him to the welfare and get the kids taken away if he didn't stop drinking, and so he had – but no matter what he did, he couldn't get right – they were all against him. Every bugger was out to get him. The bloody council had warned him he wouldn't get a licence unless he had a proper pitch and could pay his rent in advance; they'd told him he'd be reported to the police if he set up on the side of the road again without a licence – and now that bugger had refused to sell him a pitch in the covered market. How the hell was he supposed to make a living?

Jim clenched his fist as the bitterness and anger stirred inside. It had all started when his wife ran off. Women were the root of it – and that red-haired bitch had landed him right in it. She deserved a fist in her mouth, but there were other things Jim would like to do to her. The more he thought about the way she'd hit him and cheeked him, and them buggers in the market had jeered and laughed, the angrier he got. It churned inside him, making him want to strike back, making him sick to his guts.

He needed a drink or three, Jim's head came up as he saw the pub before him. It was one of the few that hadn't banned him. He would have a few beers before he went home to think what he'd like to do to that bitch... let her just wait...

24

Rose was waiting for Tom when he got in for his meal that evening. She looked upset and he thought she'd had a little cry earlier. Her eyes met his, but even as she opened her mouth to begin, he smiled at her.

'I know, love,' he said. 'I've heard what happened three times – but a mate told me the true version and I'm glad he did, because it got a bit twisted. It seems you handled the situation well...'

'I'm sorry, Tom,' Rose said and her expression was troubled. 'I bought our Christmas nuts from his stall and they were so good I went back and got more – even though he kept giving me the eye. Perhaps I shouldn't have done, but I didn't encourage him – at least, I didn't mean to. Sometimes, men seem to think I'm flirting when I'm not...'

'It's not you, love,' Tom told her firmly. 'It's the way you look – something about you that men like and fancy. Even if you toss your head and walk off in annoyance, you look sexy. It isn't anything you do deliberately. I saw it the first time we met and I fell under your spell. You only had eyes for Jimmy back then and I would never have got a look-in if he hadn't been sent on that mission...'

'No, Tom,' Rose said and moved towards him, placing a finger to his lips. 'You were young then and Jimmy was a man and I did love him – but he chose to volunteer for those dangerous missions by taking that course and that means he was prepared to risk what we had for...' She shook her head, tears in her eyes. 'I don't know why – for King and country or because he wanted excitement – it hardly matters. He didn't think of me... he took what he wanted and then left me.' Her eyes sparkled with tears. 'You would never have done that, Tom. You've loved me and the children, treated us as if we're precious... you're worth a hundred of any of them...'

Tom grinned down at her. 'Only a hundred? You told Broad it was a thousand...'

Rose's eyes flew to his and saw the teasing light there. She started to giggle. 'Oh, Tom, I do love you – it's different to the way I loved Jimmy, but it's stronger and better. He would never have looked after me and loved me as much as you do.'

Tom gave a little groan and reached for her, drawing her close and kissing the top of her head. He inhaled the wonderful scent of her and felt a familiar shaft of desire. No wonder other men fancied his Rose – but she was his. Somehow, all the doubts he'd held since their marriage melted away. He didn't know quite why, but he was quietly confident now. Tom didn't need to chase after Jim Broad and smash his face in – Rose had given him his comeuppance herself.

* * *

'Wot's wrong then, Dad?' Nobby looked at his father's brooding expression and shivered inside. He hadn't seen that for a while – it had been there a lot after Nobby's Ma left but not for the past year or so, but now it was back with a vengeance.

'Nuthin' ter do wiv yer,' his father muttered. 'Mind yer business, Nobby, or I'll give yer a clip of the ear.'

'Yer look like yer found sixpence and lost half a crown,' Nobby joked and dodged as his father's fist went for his ear. 'Yer were all right this mornin'.'

'Soddin' buggers!' Jim's sudden outburst made Nobby retreat. This was bad. His father hadn't been in a mood like this for an age.

He saw the bottle of whisky on the table and knew he'd been drinking hard. 'Make a fool of me would they – I'll show that bloody tart and the rest of 'em. Bloody women... they're all the same!'

Nobby retreated to the curtain that divided the one shabby room they slept, ate, cooked and lived in. There was an outside lavatory and neither of them washed much, using public baths when the nits made themselves a nuisance, or a quick wash all over in a bowl behind the curtain if they wanted to smell sweeter for the customers. His father hadn't bothered much after Nobby's mother left and his drinking had resulted in them being thrown out of one lodging house after another. Nobby had thought things were turning the corner once they got the barrow. His father had pulled back from the brink and his grandmother had taken charge, forcing him to stop drinking and get out to work. She'd threatened to take his kids away and after that he'd straightened himself out.

Life had gradually got back to being pretty good. Nobby's father had been talking of getting them better rooms – a little cottage or at least two rooms with running water and an inside toilet. Now, he was suddenly sullen and drunk again and Nobby shuddered inside. Sober, his father could be fun and good to his sons, but drunk he was violent and a bully.

Nobby looked at his younger brother, who was sleeping peacefully. Gran had told him that he should go to her if his father ever went back on the bottle. They'd all hoped it wouldn't happen. Gran said it was the war and Nobby's mother deserting them like that, but Nobby remembered his mother's voice crying out in pain before she went.

'You're a devil, Jim Broad – a vindictive devil and you can be so cruel. I'd have stayed if you'd treated me decent, but now, I'm off...'

'Clear orf wiv yer fancy man,' Nobby's father had answered and he'd heard the sound of blows and a scream followed by tears. 'Get out yer bitch!'

Nobby's mother had tried to take Robbie with her, but his father had thrown her out with nothing save the clothes she was wearing. Nobby's brother had wept, but Gran had come and told their father to stop shouting and, gradually, things had got back to what they should be.

Nobby wondered what had turned his father sour all of a sudden. He frowned as he tried to think of anything but couldn't – unless it was that pretty woman who'd bought nuts from them. She'd been a little like Ma but younger and prettier and his dad had tried to flirt with her, even though she was having none of it. She'd gone off with a flounce and Nobby had seen his father watching the sway of her hips – he'd fancied her something rotten. Yet there wasn't anything in that to upset him surely?

Shaking his head, Nobby lay down on the mattress beside his younger brother. He stirred and muttered in his sleep and Nobby hushed him. 'It's all right, Robbie, it's only Dad. If he gets violent, we'll go ter Gran's...'

25

Peggy smiled as the chorus of voices greeted her arrival behind the bar. The news of her taking over the bed and breakfast had got out and everyone cheered and clamoured to talk to her. For a moment she was besieged by customers wanting to shake her hand or kiss her cheek, to tell her how pleased they were she was returning to the lanes. She laughed with excitement; there were at least twenty of her older friends and customers in that night and she ordered a round of free drinks for them all.

'It's where yer belong, Peggy...' said Millie Seymour from the house almost opposite. 'Bloomin' good news, that is an' all!'

'It's the best news I've heard for years,' Alice told her and toasted her with her milk stout. 'We're all pleased as Punch over it. When Tom told me, I couldn't believe me ears – you comin' back to the lane.' She shook her head in wonder. 'And you with that lovely café at the sea and that cottage...'

Alice hadn't visited them at the sea, despite invitations, but she'd seen photographs and Maureen had told her all about Peggy's home and business.

'Family is more important...' Peggy told her with a smile. 'Friends too – old friends are the best. New friends are good but not quite the same. We go back a long time, Alice.'

'We do that,' Alice agreed. 'I remember when you came here as a young bride, Peggy love. You were as pretty as a picture and all the lads wanted you – but you only had eyes for your Laurie then...'

'Yes, we were happy then. Your Alfie was alive then, Alice.'

'Aye, just about,' Alice agreed, sadness in her eyes. 'He couldn't hardly get his breath, but he hung on for me as long as he could, poor soul.' She shook her head. 'It was the first war that done for him, gassing it was...' Alice gazed into her glass as if she could see into the past. 'You should 'ave seen my lad in those days, afore he went orf to the trenches. Big and strong, he were, Peggy. Alfie could pick me up wiv one hand in them days.'

Peggy nodded. She'd heard the story many times, but Alice was lost in her thoughts.

'Two wars we've been through, Peggy – terrible wars, though you'd hardly recall the first...'

'I wasn't very old when it ended,' Peggy said, 'but I can just remember some things – we didn't know quite as much about it as this last time, but I remember my dad coming home... He never got over it, though, and died too young.' She smiled at her old friend as she saw the memories in her eyes. Alice would be all right now Peggy was back, she would see to that – might suggest to her that she give up her house, which was far too big for her, and move in as a full-time boarder. She would have to choose the right time and put it diplomatically, but she reckoned she could take Alice as a boarder for what she paid in rent and make life comfortable for her in her last few years. She just had to be careful not to hurt Alice's pride.

'Aye, you're right there,' Alice agreed. 'We went without stuff and the Zeppelins were frightenin', but it was the men in the trenches bore the brunt of the first war. We took it on the chin this time, lass. I don't know how I'd 'ave managed it if hadn't been for you.' She grinned at Peggy suddenly. 'I didn't care about them bombs when I was sittin' in the cellar wiv you and drinkin' stout and singin' me songs.'

'You kept us all goin',' Peggy told her with a smile. 'It was good – wasn't it, Alice? I don't just mean in my cellar, but the way we all stood together and helped each other out. You'll have to come and help me when I get back.' The smile in the old lady's eyes made her feel good.

'It got us through,' Alice said and finished her drink. Peggy picked up the glass and refilled it, but to her surprise Alice shook her head. 'It's time I bought you one, Peggy love – what will yer 'ave?'

'I'll have a half of lemonade shandy then,' Peggy agreed. 'I'm thirsty but not for spirits. I've been cookin' all afternoon – why don't you have a slice of apple pie, Alice?'

'Don't mind if I do,' Alice said, 'and a drop of your custard – no one makes it like you do. Young Sheila is a decent cook, but she can't make custard – serves cream or ice cream. I like me custard warm, I do.'

Alice accepted a generous slice of warm apple pie covered in creamy custard. She smiled her satisfaction and ate it with relish. Peggy put a little glass of port and lemon out for her to sip afterwards. She'd taken Alice's money for the shandy because she'd wanted to buy her a drink, but this was a special night and it was her treat for the customers who had come flocking in at the news.

'This is the busiest the pub has been for ages,' Sheila whispered as she passed Rose behind the bar. 'It's you that has brought them in, Peggy.'

Peggy smiled and nodded. She'd known that they would be busy once the news got around that she was handing out free food and drinks. It was a party night, though not quite like her Christmas Eve party, when everything had been free. Peggy had bought everyone a drink, but now the customers were buying their own, but the food was free. Every table was full and the bar was two deep all the way along.

She'd asked Rose to come in and give a hand. Sheila had enough to do, though she was there to share in the fun and excitement, but Pip and Able were sorting out a few things round at the boarding house, overseeing the departure of the present host and making sure that the furniture they'd agreed to buy was left in situ. Their stay had extended beyond the original twelve days planned, but they'd shut the café for three weeks and so had no reason to rush back, and Sheila was glad of the help.

'It's like the old days,' Rose said as she pulled a pint of bitter. 'I'm really glad you're coming back, Peggy. If you get stuck for anything – cooking or cleaning, you know I'll help if I can...'

'Thanks, Rose,' Peggy said and smiled. She'd been inundated with offers of help from everyone and it made her feel wonderful. Everyone was pleased and excited because she was returning and it made her wonder why they'd ever gone away. She did love the cottage; it was beautiful, and the area was lovely, fresh air and nice scenery, but something about London had tugged at her heart. She would never have suggested a return if her family hadn't wanted it, but she couldn't help being pleased by all the fuss everyone was making over her.

Peggy had begun to make lots of plans for the future. Her bed and breakfast, and evening meal if required, would not conflict with her daughter-in-law's trade at the pub. They had different customers. Some of them might choose to eat in the bar at lunch or the evening if they chose, but the breakfasts were part of the service and the evening meal would be optional. Besides, Sheila would be so glad of her help that she wouldn't be counting a few lost sandwiches at the bar – if that was the result. Peggy's customers would, she thought, mainly be travelling salesmen, though she was open to having a permanent lodger if it was someone like Alice.

It was similar to what she'd done before at the pub but would give her more free time than she'd had prior to the war. When you thought about it, Peggy had hardly stopped working since she arrived at the Pig & Whistle as a bride and it would be a pleasant change to cut down a little. Even if she gave Sheila and Maureen a hand with their cakes sometimes, it would be more like fun than work – and a couple of nights behind the bar each week would feel like a treat.

'You look thoughtful,' Alice said, smiling at her. 'Penny for them?'

'I was just thinking how lucky I am.'

'Nay, lass. Yer make yer own luck – and anything you get yer give back in spades.'

'She's right,' Sheila said and smiled lovingly at her. 'I'm the lucky one to have you for my mother-in-law.'

Peggy laughed and shook her head as Maureen came up to them. 'I can't stop long,' she said. 'Shirley was meeting her friend Carol this evening; she felt a bit down because Richard had gone back to medical school, and so Gordon told me to come by myself. I didn't want to leave him, but he said I should – so do you need a hand for half an hour?'

'Yes, why not?' Peggy said. 'Rose has been here an hour and that's all I asked for; she needs to get back to Tom now.'

'I'm all right for a bit longer,' Rose said and smiled at them. 'Tom said to come and enjoy myself – he's content reading his magazines and looking out for the kids.'

'Maureen is here now,' Peggy said. 'You go home, Rose love. I know you're busy. Sheila will square up with you another day.'

'This one is for free,' Rose laughed. 'I wouldn't have missed this for the world, Peggy – but I'll get off home if you're sure?'

'Maureen is here for a while and the crush is nearly over,' Peggy said. 'It's icy tonight, Rose, make sure you don't slip over out there.'

'I shan't – goodnight then. Sheila, I'll be here on Friday night as usual. Night, Maureen, Peggy...' Rose went through the hall to the kitchen to fetch her coat.

Peggy smiled at Maureen. 'It's almost like during the war – only better, because there are no bombs...'

* * *

Rose slipped out of the back door of the Pig & Whistle just as Peggy came through to the kitchen. She waved and called goodnight again before going into the freezing cold. After the warmth of the bar, it felt bitter out and she pulled her fur collar up around her neck to keep out the cold. She would hurry home to Tom and get warm. A nice mug of cocoa each and they would get to bed. Tom had a big job on and would be up early in the morning.

It was as she walked out under the arch that someone launched themselves at her, grabbing her, first by the arm and then by the throat, as he forced her back into the shadows and against the wall. The stink of his breath told Rose he'd been drinking, but there was another smell that alerted her to the identity of her attacker.

'Let me go,' she gasped as he pushed his knee between her legs and used one hand to fumble at her skirts. 'Don't be a fool – I told you I didn't want anything to do with you...'

'Sod what yer want,' Jim Broad muttered viciously as the hand around her throat pressed harder against her windpipe, cutting off the scream so that it was merely a whimper. 'Yer ain't so big now wivout all yer friends around yer.'

Rose did the only thing she could and stabbed him in the leg with her high heel shoe. It didn't hurt him much, but he jerked back and his hold on her throat eased. Rose screamed three times before his arm came across her throat, blocking her air again. As he held her, she scrabbled and fought him with all the strength she had, her gloved hands unable to do much damage as she clawed at his face and eyes. However, she managed to poke her thumb in his eye hard. Once more the pressure on her throat eased and Rose screamed again. Her voice wasn't much more than a croak and as he hit her hard across the face, Rose knew she was losing the battle. She was going to be raped and there was nothing she could do to stop this brute from having his way.

Even as the despair swept through her, she pushed with the last of her strength and cried out for help. Dimly, as though through a mist, she heard the sound of pounding feet and men's voices and then they were on him, dragging him off her. She was nearly unconscious, but she knew the voices – Able and Pip had her attacker. They were struggling with him, fighting, and he was yelling his head off and swearing.

Rose sank to her knees and then Able had his arm about her, helping her to her feet, supporting her as she swayed unsteadily.

'It's all right now, Rose,' he said. 'We heard your scream, but we were upstairs in the bed and breakfast and it took us a few moments to get down here.'

Rose tried to whisper her thanks, but she had no voice left. She was hardly aware of what was happening, though she heard Pip swear.

'Damn it! The bugger got away.'

'Let him go, Pip. We'll have the law on him. We both saw what he was trying to do – they will lock him up and throw away the key, if I have my way...' Able growled while supporting Rose as she swayed between consciousness and the faintness that was coming over her in waves.

'I'm out of practice,' Pip said ruefully. 'He threw a lucky punch and I let him get away – the bastard.'

'You're bleeding,' Able said to Rose and then looked at Pip. 'Give me a hand with Rose. We'd better get her home. She doesn't want everyone to see her like this.'

Rose vaguely remembered being carried between the two men. She glimpsed Tom's face when they told him what had happened, the fury and the concern as he swept her up in his arms and carried her up the stairs.

'Will you call the doctor?' he asked Able. 'Thank God you were both there. It has to be that so-and-so Jim Broad. No one else around here would do anything like that to my Rose. I thought the bastard had cleared off after he was warned. I should have gone after him, but I didn't dream he would try anything like this.'

He looked at Rose as if hoping she would confirm his suspicions, but although she did try to say something, no sound came from her bruised throat. She lay in her bed as Tom bent over her and tenderly stroked her cheek. Tears were on his face and she reached up to touch him, trying to tell him it was all right, but she couldn't. She was crying now because she could see his pain.

'Just rest, my love,' Tom said gently and gave her his loving smile. 'The doctor will come and I'll look after you – I'll kill that devil. If he thinks he can do this to you and get away with it...'

'No, Tom...' it came out as a hoarse whisper, hardly discernible, but he understood. 'Be careful...' She didn't want anyone to harm Tom. 'Love you...'

'And I love you, Rose – but that man has to be punished. For what he's done, I'd swing for him...' She clutched at him, but he bent and kissed her forehead. 'Try and sleep, dearest. I'll thank Pip and then the doctor will be here.'

Rose felt the tears on her cheeks, but closed her eyes because she felt so weak. She heard the murmur of voices outside the room as Pip tried to talk sense to Tom, but she knew how stubborn he could be and felt chilled. Tom would do something terrible, if not tonight then in the future...

* * *

Rose might have slept or swooned. When she woke, Maureen was with her and so was the doctor. He smiled down at her cheerfully.

'Come back to us then? Well, you have a few bruises and your throat is going to be sore for a while, but no real harm done.'

'I'll see Doctor Gorton out,' Maureen told her. 'I'll be back in a moment, Rose.'

Rose tried to get up once she was alone but fell back because she felt so weak. Had the doctor given her something? She thought he must have because she couldn't think straight or move properly.

Maureen came back after a few minutes and sat on the bed. 'I'm sorry, Rose. None of us had any idea or we would have walked home with you – the rotten bastard. Everyone is up in arms and the police have been informed. Tom says they're worse than useless, but everyone is talking to him, calming him down. He wanted to search for that evil devil tonight, but they've made him see sense – for now anyway.

'He mustn't...' Rose croaked and then took the glass of water Maureen held and swallowed a little. 'Trouble...'

'He's been told to let the law handle it,' Maureen said. 'Able was very good – said with him as witness the culprit will go to prison.'

'Not Tom...' Rose said and swiped a tear from her cheek. 'So angry...'

'Not with you, love,' Maureen said and smiled at her. 'Tom adores you, always has, and his children. Don't worry, we'll all look out for you – and I doubt Broad will dare try it again.'

Rose was worried about Tom rather than herself, but she couldn't keep her eyes open. The world was slipping away, taking her into a deep sleep as the bedroom door opened and her husband entered.

'How is she?' he whispered.

'Worried about you – that you'll go after that beast and thrash him.'

'If the cops don't get him, I shall,' Tom said harshly. 'I've listened to Able and the others and I'll wait – besides, I don't want to leave Rose and the kids while I don't know how she is. I'm not daft, Maureen. I'd never do murder, even though I felt like it when I first saw what he'd done to my Rose.'

'She wasn't raped,' Maureen said. 'Pip and Able got there in time. The bastard hurt her, but he was stopped before he could do more. Pip is furious with himself that he got away, but at least he stopped him...'

'Yes, I know and I'm grateful – and I'm trying to be sensible, Maureen – but you ask Gordon how he would feel if it was you.'

'I don't need to, I know. Something similar once happened to me and if Rory hadn't managed to kill himself in a drunken fit, I think Gordon would have done it without blinking. But what would have happened to me then? Think of Rose and your children, Tom. That man isn't worth going to prison for – you could even hang.'

'I know,' Tom said. 'But the police had better catch him and soon or I shall... and if I don't quite murder him, I'll make him wish he was dead!'

26

Shirley looked at her mother's anxious face and knew she was worried about Rose. It was awful her being attacked like that only yards from her own home – and it was no wonder that Tom was angry and threatening to kill the man that had hurt her. Shirley had heard her parents talking about it the previous evening.

'Tom sounds calm and sensible,' Shirley's mother told her father as they all sat drinking their bedtime cocoa. 'But I know him too well – he is simmering underneath and if the police don't find that devil soon, Tom will go after him. He has quite a few friends who would help him too...'

'A vigilante group?' he asked with a lift of his brows. 'I know something similar has happened in the past, but surely Tom wouldn't be such a fool?'

'I don't know, he thinks the world of Rose. I've never been sure she gave as much back, but she was really shaken by the incident, so I know it wasn't her fault.'

'She would be a fool to risk all she has with Tom,' her father agreed and her mother nodded. 'Rose made a mistake once, but I know she loves her children and she cares for Tom in her own way.'

Their conversation had passed on to other things then, but Shirley could tell her mother was worried about Tom and what he might do, which meant she couldn't burden her with her own troubles. Shirley was churning inside, her unhappiness making her wish she could cast herself into her mother's arms and tell her what was worrying her, but with her Mum worried over Rose and Tom she had to keep it all in.

Shirley had been so excited at the thought of Richard coming home for Christmas, but in the event, he'd only spent three days with her and two with his family before returning to his other life. He'd spoken of how wonderful it was when he'd given Shirley her gift, which was a pretty silk scarf in pink and a small bottle of Evening in Paris cologne. Shirley had given him a fountain pen and propelling pencil set which he'd said he'd loved.

'Hopefully, I'll manage to keep this from going astray,' he'd told her. 'Katie says she's never known anyone for losing pens the way I do – and she gave me a silver propelling pencil too.'

Shirley's present was as much as she could afford, but it wasn't silver or expensive and she'd felt disappointment that his friend from college had given him a better one. She hadn't said anything, nor had she mentioned the poison-pen letter she'd received. Shirley didn't know who it had come from, though she'd wondered if this Katie person had sent it to make trouble – but why would she do that? She didn't know Shirley's address, did she – or had she seen a letter he was sending to Shirley? If he'd asked her to post it for him or she'd looked in his pockets... Was she kind of girl who would do that? Perhaps she didn't want him to have another close friend – which might mean she was serious about spending her future with him.

The idea had made tears sting Shirley's eyes, but she still hadn't asked – hadn't told him about the letter or her suspicions, because it would sound as if she were jealous. Shirley knew there was an element of jealousy in her hurt feelings. Not that Richard had implied there was more than friendship between them. He'd been happy to be home, interested in her exam results and all that was going on in the lanes and enjoying his holiday.

'We work so hard,' he'd told her. 'You'll realise when you get to college, Shirley; it's a real slog once you're classed as a junior doctor even though you're still studying, so many hours when you just have to be on call for routine stuff. And the patients expect you to know everything and tell them why they're still in pain even though the op went well.' He grimaced. 'You need to be dedicated, because otherwise you'd give up. I'm so damned tired all the time.'

As if to prove his point he'd fallen asleep on her shoulder twice, once in the pictures and again when they had a little time to themselves at his house. He'd apologised when he woke up; she'd shaken her head, but she'd hoped he might kiss her, tell her how much he missed her – even that he loved her, but he hadn't said a word. Even their kiss under the mistletoe was brief and passionless, as if he were kissing a casual friend or his sister – and that hurt.

'I'm sorry we haven't had longer together,' Richard had apologised when she'd gone with him to the station to see him off. 'I know I haven't said anything, but I had an idea for the summer – I'll get several weeks off then and I thought we might go away together, as friends, of course – to Cornwall, a sort of working holiday – or even abroad – if we could raise enough money. I thought we might do seasonal work at the sea – Katie says there's plenty going and a lot of the other students do it to earn money and have fun. You could share a room with another girl. You might like Tosy, she's a bit like you, Shirley.'

'Tosy?' Shirley had questioned. 'That's an odd name isn't it?'

'Yes, her name is Tori, but she doesn't like it and claims she's a bit of any idiot, so someone nicknamed her Tosy and it stuck.'

Shirley had laughed. 'It sounds as if you all have fun?'

'We do – it's a good crowd and we go out as a group and sometimes as pairs. I think you would like Tosy.' He'd smiled. 'You could ask your father and see what he says – your mum might be on your side, if you want to come, of course?'

'I'll think about it,' Shirley had said and felt a pang of regret as she heard the announcer call the arrival of his train. 'You'd better go, Richard. I'll write to you – tell you what I think and what Dad says.'

'I should've asked him, but I thought he might refuse and I didn't want to spoil Christmas,' Richard had said and then hesitated. 'I enjoy your letters, Shirley – they were all that got me through when I was first in college. You do know you're my special friend?' He'd looked hesitant, uneasy, as if not sure of his ground.

Shirley hadn't answered, because she'd always believed it until recently and now she just wasn't sure. Besides, it wasn't enough for her any more; she wanted to be more than a friend.

'You're still so young – and so serious and I know you have to work hard,' Richard had murmured in a soft voice she could hardly catch above the noise of the busy station. 'I should've said more, but I don't want to ruin what we have...' He'd leaned closer and kissed her cheek. 'I must dash. Don't forget to write.'

He'd hastened away to catch his train leaving Shirley bewildered and uncertain. Why had he left it until the last moment to tell her about his summer plans and why kiss her cheek if he meant more?

Shirley had brooded on it for a while and then decided that he hadn't meant more than friendship and it was just in her mind, because she was growing up and had wanted to experience her first real kiss that Christmas. She knew she couldn't have anything more yet; she was too young for marriage and it would be years before she finished her training. To become romantically involved was a complication she didn't need... and yet – and yet, her heart was breaking because Richard was older and there were other young women who might be ready to exchange kisses and caresses... to make love...

The very idea made Shirley hot all over. She wasn't ready for that yet, but a kiss on the lips would be nice. Perhaps men didn't want to stop at that – perhaps once they kissed, they wanted more and that was why Richard hadn't kissed her, because she was too young for that kind of thing.

Katie was the same age as Richard. Perhaps she didn't mind if the kissing went further... Jealousy seared Shirley as she pictured her Richard in a passionate clinch with this unknown girl.

She shook her head, knowing she was being foolish. She couldn't begin to understand what that side of life was like yet and she needed to concentrate on her studies – so given Shirley wasn't ready, she couldn't complain if Richard found someone who was – someone who wanted to explore the passion of love. The letter had said that he was having an affair and that had rankled at the back of her thoughts. She ought to have kept the letter and shown it to him rather than burning it, but she'd just wanted to get rid of it – and now it was too late. She probably wouldn't see Richard again for months and it wasn't the kind of thing you could write about.

Shirley sighed. Mum was always so busy lately and didn't want to bother her. Shirley wanted someone to listen to her and yet knew she wouldn't impose her troubles on her mother. Her silly thoughts were just that and after what had happened to Rose, Mum had far more to think about.

* * *

Shirley seemed quiet again that evening. Gordon had gone down to the pub to fetch a couple of bottles of the pale ale he enjoyed and they were alone. Maureen was beginning to worry about her, but she didn't want to ask questions that her stepdaughter might resent. Shirley was as much loved as if she'd given birth to her and she relied on the girl for so many things these days. Shirley didn't often go out with friends because of her studies – in fact, the only friend she bothered with much was Richard.

Maureen wondered if that was altogether healthy. She didn't mind the two being close, but perhaps she ought to go out with other friends more. Richard was nearly four years older and away at medical college and Shirley needed to go out and have a bit of fun more often. She'd spent some time with Richard while he was home, but she didn't seem as happy as she usually did after one of his visits.

'Is something wrong, love?' she asked now. Maureen didn't want to interfere, but if something was wrong, she couldn't just ignore it. 'You seem a bit quiet – is it all right with Richard?'

Shirley hesitated, then, 'He asked if I wanted to go on a working holiday to Cornwall in the long summer holidays...'

'Oh... that has come out of the blue, hasn't it?' Maureen asked. 'Why didn't he speak to me or you father?'

'He didn't want Dad to get cross and spoil Christmas – it's just as friends, Mum. Other girls and boys will be going and I can share a room with a girl called Tosy.'

'Do you know this girl or anything about her?' Maureen asked, frowning. 'I'm only asking because your dad worries and you've never been away from us before.'

'But I shall be when I start medical school,' Shirley reminded her. 'I'll be seventeen next year, Mum. I'm not silly – besides, Richard is someone I've known all my life. Don't you trust him to look after me?'

Maureen's frown disappeared. 'Yes, I do, darling. I suppose I hope you two might get married one day – you've been such good friends and you're both dedicated to helping the sick. It seems an ideal match...'

Shirley hesitated, then, 'I think Richard may have met someone else he likes better in that way, Mum. She's nearer his age and I think...' Shirley shook her head but looked upset again.

'What do you think, love?' Maureen asked gently.

'I'm not sure...' Shirley took a deep breath. 'If I tell you something, will you promise not to tell Dad?'

Maureen hesitated. Was her daughter going to tell her Richard had seduced her? Gordon would half kill him if that was the truth. 'Unless you're in trouble, I promise – if it's that I'll have to tell him.'

To her surprise, Shirley laughed. 'He hasn't even kissed me, Mum. I hoped he might this Christmas, but even under the mistletoe it was just a peck on the cheek.' Her cheeks went pink. 'I had a horrid letter from someone – it wasn't signed, but I think it was this girl Richard is friends with... it said he was sleeping with her.'

'Oh, Shirley love!' Maureen said, immediately concerned. 'That was awful for you – did you keep it?'

'No, I burned it,' Shirley said. 'It was vile and filthy, Mum. Dad would have been furious. I've been a bit miserable thinking about it, but then, just before he caught his train, Richard told me about his plans for next summer and he sort of hinted that I was special to him, but he couldn't say anything or kiss me properly because I'm too young...' Her wide eyes filled with tears, making Maureen's heart ache with love for her.

'Shirley, my sweet innocent daughter...' Maureen smiled. 'You've just confirmed my belief in Richard as an upright, trustworthy young man. I always thought he was more than fond of you, but he's right you are still very young. Richard is taking care of you, darling. He probably wants more than is right or proper just yet and doesn't want to risk losing his head and taking it too far. It must be a dilemma for him, Shirley. He has to finish his exams and then he will still have to establish himself as a GP or in a hospital – and you need to study hard if you're to do the same. You can't afford to get pregnant.'

Shirley swiped at her eyes. 'So, you think I'm worrying for nothing?'

'I think that Richard loves you and one day you may marry...' Maureen hesitated, then, 'Men are a little bit different to us, Shirley. Sometimes they want or need to have sex – and they have the ability to remain detached. In other words, Richard might have a brief fling with another woman in college if she is free with her favours without caring about her reputation...'

She saw Shirley's eyes widen and she looked thoughtful, and then she nodded. 'I sort of understand, Mum. Something like that happened to you before you married Dad, didn't it?'

'Come and sit here and let me explain,' Maureen said gently. Shirley joined her on the battered old kitchen sofa. 'I knew Rory long before I met your dad. Your mum was still alive back then. I thought I was in love, but things didn't work out. Rory came back into my life when I was nursing and it was during the war. Bombs were falling on the hospital and we both knew we could die. I went to bed with him even though I felt it was wrong to make love without marriage, and then I fell for Robin. Rory was going to marry me, but I discovered he'd been having an affair with another nurse at the same time as he'd been with me and I broke it off...'

'He wasn't very nice, Mum.' Shirley touched her hand. 'I remember having tea with you before you went off to nurse and then you came back a year or so later and married Dad – and you had our darling Robin. He wasn't Dad's, was he?'

Maureen shook her head and leaned in to kiss her cheek.

'Your dad had been kind to me and I liked him,' Maureen said, still in that same gentle tone. 'When he offered to marry me, I wasn't in love with him, but it was a way out because I would have been in a lot of trouble – my father would have refused to speak to me and everyone would have thought me shameless to have a child out of wedlock...'

Shirley looked at her thoughtfully. 'A girl at school said something like that to me once. I hit her...'

'Yes, I remember,' Maureen said and smiled. 'I'd always liked your dad a lot and after we married, I fell in love with him. He was so lovely to me, Shirley, and he always has been. He loved Robin as if he was his father – you know that...'

'I loved him too,' Shirley said and her face reflected her sadness at the memory of Robin's death. She smiled suddenly. 'I'm glad I told you, Mum. So, it doesn't mean Richard loves this Katie person even if he goes to bed with her?'

'He probably won't be the first and he'll know that,' Maureen said. 'Besides, I think he really cares for you, Shirley. You tell him to write to me and ask if you can go on this working holiday next summer and I'll do my best to persuade your dad.'

'You're the best mum in the world!' Shirley said and threw her arms around Maureen and hugged her. 'I love you so much!'

'I love you, darling. You know you're my special girl, don't you? I don't know what I'd have done without you all these years.'

Shirley smiled and looked happier than she had for a while. 'I know,' she said. 'I feel much better now. I should have told you before – you always make things better.'

'That's what mums are for,' Maureen said. 'Go and write a nice chatty letter to Richard, darling. Tell him how much you enjoyed being with him and you're looking forward to spending the summer with him if your dad will let you – and that I'm going to persuade him, but I need a responsible letter from him, telling me about the arrangements, so I know you'll be safe.'

'Thanks, Mum,' Shirley said and ran off to fetch her writing things.

Maureen smiled as her stepdaughter sat down and started to write, a smile on her face. If only she could solve Tom's problem as easily, but when a man's pride was injured it was no small thing and Tom was smarting, itching to get his hands on the man who had hurt his Rose.

27

'How is Rose now?' Peggy asked as she stood in Tom's office that morning, her coat on and all ready for the journey home, which they would break for one night to make it easier, because of the icy roads. It was the first day of January and they had a lot of work to do when they got back. They'd already stayed over their original time, seeing the New Year in with Sheila and Pip and all their customers and friends in the pub, and were only leaving now because they had to sort out the lease at the café. Able wanted to keep it going until he could hand over to someone else and that meant getting back to work in a few days.

'She's a lot better, but it upset her and she's not her usual self.' Tom looked angry. 'I'd like to thrash the life out of that devil...'

'Promise me you won't do anything stupid,' Peggy said. 'I do know how you feel, Tom, and we'd all like to thrash the bugger for you – but you have a family and a business to think of. I'm relying on you to smarten up the bed and breakfast for me, love.'

'I know, Peggy, and I know you're the best friend I could ever have,' Tom replied with a warm smile. 'I'm more than happy you're coming back to the lanes. I'm probably the last one to have said it, but I really mean it.'

'I'm glad too,' she told him. 'I shall be popping up every so often on the train and we'll be taking over in March – all being well. Able says if he needs to, he'll stay on at the cottage to finalise things so I can get started up here, but hopefully we'll all be able to come together.'

'Anything you need fetching from the shops for the bed and breakfast, you only need to give me a ring.'

'I know I've got good friends here and you're one of the best, Tom. I care about you – you were like another son to me and I won't have you go to prison – or, worse, hang – for that bastard. Do you hear me?' She gave him a stern look and Tom burst out laughing.

'You look like my Army Sergeant Major, Peggy,' he jested and saluted her. 'All right, I give you my word. I shall not go looking for Jim Broad – but if he comes near Rose again, I'll thrash the life out of him.'

'If he attempted it for a second time, I think you would be within your rights to do that,' Peggy agreed. 'Hopefully, the police will get him first – and be assured that every person in this lane will be on the lookout for him. If comes anywhere near the pub or your home, the police will be alerted and your wife will be protected.'

Tom nodded. 'I've been told by several of the men that they'll scare him off if he even shows his face at the market. I've got a lot of friends and I could have taken at least a dozen men to corner him and give him a hiding if I'd chosen. I'd like to batter his face to a pulp, Peggy, but Rose is recovering and she begged me not to make things worse and so I'm leaving it to the police for now.'

'Good,' Peggy smiled at his words. 'I can go home with an easy mind now, Tom. I know you for a man of your word and I know you won't let me or Rose down.'

'I value what I've got too much,' Tom said. 'Rose didn't encourage the rogue; she told him to leave her alone in front of witnesses, so if it comes to court and he makes out she encouraged him there's a dozen as will stand up and call him a liar.' He smiled his satisfaction. 'Rose is my wife and she loves me – I shan't risk throwing all that away.'

'That's what I wanted to hear,' Peggy said.

She left him feeling easier in her mind. Maureen had told her she was sure Tom would go after Jim Broad and half kill him. Jack Barton had done that with the man who'd raped Ellie – one of Maureen's friends who no longer lived in the lane – and Janet's first husband had witnessed it and done what little he could to stop that evil creature getting away. Poor Mike had been desperately ill and Janet had always believed the chase had brought on the relapse that killed him. Jack had done the thrashing and Ellie's first husband had finished the rapist off, through a hired killer. In the end, Ellie's husband had murdered one of the most-loved residents in the lane – Mrs Tandy, because she refused to tell him where his wife had gone – and Ellie had fled from London. Maureen had had one letter but since then no one had heard anything from Ellie.

That had been during the war and things like that had happened back then, but time had moved on and the police wouldn't stand for it now; even if they could cover it up, it would haunt Tom. So, Peggy had done what she could to dissuade him and she thought he'd seen the sense of it for himself. He might want to smash Jim Broad's face, but he would leave it to the police to arrest and punish him – unless he was foolish enough to make another attempt on Rose...

Surely, he would have more sense? Peggy thought that the rogue market trader would know that he'd made enemies in this part of London and that he could go to prison for what he'd done. He would stay in his own part of town and keep clear of Tom and his legion of friends.

* * *

'Where is Dad?' Robbie Broad asked his older brother and shivered with cold. There was no fuel in the house and it was freezing. They'd eaten the last bit of stale bread that morning with a slice of streaky bacon each and now there was nothing left of the Christmas food, which had kept them going thus far. 'I'm 'ungry, Nobby.'

'Yeah, me too,' Nobby said and picked up one of his father's old jackets, draping it around his younger brother's shoulders. It was five days since they'd seen their father. He'd been drinking all over the festive period, sullen and bad-tempered, leaving Nobby to cook their food and look after his sibling.

'I don't know where he's...' he broke off as he heard heavy boots on the stone stairs leading down to the basement room which was all they could afford in this old house. 'It might be 'im now...'

His hopes were dashed as someone knocked on the door. The brothers looked at each other. Gran didn't call often, but when she did, she just opened the door and called out their names. No one else ever came here. Their father had no friends and if he met any other men – or women – he did so away from his home.

'Are you in there, Mr Broad?' a loud voice demanded. 'This is the police. We just need to ask you some questions...'

Nobby shook his head at his brother and put a finger to his lips. He went to the door and opened it a crack, peering round it at the large policeman in a constable's uniform.

'Me dad ain't 'ere,' he told him. 'What yer want him fer?'

'It's a little matter of assault,' the police officer said. 'How old are you, lad?'

'Sixteen,' Nobby lied instinctively because he knew the coppers would have the council round if he thought young children were living alone. 'We ain't seen Dad fer a few days. He went out to buy some whisky and he didn't come back.'

'May I come in please?' the police officer asked. 'It's cold out here.'

'It's cold in 'ere an all,' Nobby said but reluctantly allowed him in.

He sensed the officer's critical gaze travelling around the shabby room, taking in the lack of a fire and the basic furniture, barely enough for their needs.

'Have you got any food?' he asked gruffly and Nobby saw pity in his eyes.

'We ate the last this mornin',' he replied with a shrug. 'Yer needn't feel sorry fer us. We'll go to Gran's and she'll give us a meal later – and I'll find a job. I've left school. Dad was goin' ter get me my own barrow, but he started drinkin' and forgot...'

'Drinks a lot, does he?'

'He used to, but then he stopped – he started again just around Christmas. Somethin' upset 'im...' Nobby shrugged. 'When Gran knows, she'll sort 'im like she did last time.'

The officer put his hand in his pocket and gave Nobby half a crown. 'Buy some wood for your fire, lad,' he said. 'If I were you, I'd ask your Gran to take you in – and I'd look for that job. You're too young to get a trader's licence for yourself yet and yer dad isn't likely to be able to get a barrow for yer to trade on his licence, if he has one...'

'What has he done?'

The police officer looked at him for a long moment and then nodded. 'You're a sensible lad, so I'll tell yer – even though you don't look older than twelve. Your dad is in big trouble. He attacked a woman in Mulberry Lane. When we find him, we'll arrest him and he'll go to prison for a few years I should think.'

Nobby dropped his head. He knew the woman concerned. His father hadn't been able to take his eyes off her, flirting with her at the stall and watching her walk away. Nobby had thought it was just a bit of fun until his dad came home from the market swearing that she'd humiliated him and ruined his chances of getting an indoor stall for them. He'd been after buying it for Nobby and they'd planned on moving to better rooms once the stall started paying. Something had gone wrong that morning and Nobby's father had started drinking – and now he'd ruined everything...

'I'm sorry, lad, but there's no point in lying to you. After I've gone, you should take your brother and go to your gran's. If you stay here, you'll likely catch your death of cold – and you need an adult to look after you both or the social will be taking you into care.' He smiled and Nobby decided he wasn't bad, giving him a half crown and what he knew to be good advice. 'It's just a friendly word, lad... What happened to your mother?'

'She went orf after Dad beat her up too many times,' Nobby said truthfully. 'She would've taken us, but he wouldn't let 'er...'

'If you know where she is you could write to her – if you can write?'

'I can,' Robbie piped up. 'Nobby can too. Mum taught us – and I'm going to grammar school when I'm old enough, leastways, that's what Mum said.'

'Good for you, lad,' the officer said. 'I'm Constable Rogers – and if you need help, you just ask for me down the Nick – do you hear? I'll do what I can to find your mum…'

'I know where she is,' Nobby blurted it out. 'She wrote to me - told me we could go to her if we wanted.'

'Then that's just what I'd do if I were you.' Constable Rogers nodded to them. 'I'll leave you lads to it, then – but I have to report what I found. I should take what you want and go to your Gran's soon as you can or you'll have the council lot after you.'

Nobby gave him a considering look. 'You're all right,' he said. 'I'll write to the address me Mum give us and we'll go to Gran's for now. I can find a job where she is as well as 'ere.' He raised his head. 'I'm sorry me dad done what he did, sir. It were the war what changed 'im. He always had a bit of a temper on 'im, but when he come back, he were different – violent, and he found out Mum had a bit of a fling wiv a Canadian pilot and went mad… he gets mad at women now… says they're all cheatin' bitches…'

'Yes, the war has a lot to answer for,' the constable agreed sadly. 'I'm off then, lads. Don't forget – go to your gran's before they come and take you into care.'

'Yeah, we shall – and thanks.' Nobby shut the door behind him and looked at his brother. 'You'd better 'elp me pack our things,' he said. 'We ain't comin' back ter this dump.'

'What about Dad?' Robbie said uncertainly. 'He'll fetch us back and give us a 'iding…'

'Nah, he won't,' Nobby said. 'He's lying low somewhere, Rob, keepin' out of the way of the cops – either that or he's chucked 'imself in the river.'

'Do you think he's dead?' Robbie's eyes opened wide.

'I don't know,' Nobby replied. 'He's got money stashed away. I daren't touch it before, but I know where it is and I'm takin' it for us – if he comes after it, I'll give it back, but until then it's our secret.'

Robbie looked at him fearfully. 'He'll half kill yer, Nobby.'

'If he does, I'll tell him the cops was goin' ter search the place so I hid it,' Nobby said. 'They'll either get 'im, Rob, or he'll end up in the river or on a ship...' He screwed up his eyes. 'I never told the copper, but he talked about going on a merchant ship once...'

'They won't take him if he's drunk,' Robbie said. 'He served in the war, but they demobbed him afterwards – remember he was bitter because he couldn't get work on the liners? It's why he started the market stall.'

'I don't think he 'ad a proper licence,' Nobby said. 'Not for Spital-fields anyhow. I reckon he lost it over somethin' he did wrong back in the summer and that's why we tried a new patch at Christmas. We used to go different places every day so the council wouldn't cotton on and come poking their noses in.'

'He quarrels with everyone,' Robbie agreed. 'Can we carry everything?'

'We'll take our clothes and bits,' Nobby said. 'We ain't got much, Robbie – and we'll leave Dad's stuff. If he comes back for 'em that's OK, but if not, I'll sell what I can or leave them to the landlord. I bet Dad ain't paid the rent this month.'

'Dad ain't got much either, only a few clothes,' Robbie said.

'There's Grandad's silver watch and a silver cigarette case he brought home from the war – I think he took it orf a dead sailor. It's engraved wiv someone's name and it ain't 'is.'

'You mean 'e pinched it?'

'Probably,' Nobby said. 'If the bloke was dead, I suppose he just took it.' He shrugged. 'I'll take them and the money. If Dad comes looking fer 'em, he can have 'em, but if he don't, they're ours.'

Robbie nodded. 'I'm glad you're 'ere, Nobs, I shouldn't know what to do if yer weren't...'

'We'll 'ave ter leave London if we go to Mum,' Nobby told him. 'We could stay wiv Gran if yer like.'

'I want ter be wiv Mum,' Robbie said. 'She's in Canada, ain't she?'

'Nah, she's down in Brighton, 'ere in England,' Nobby said with a grin. 'She wanted 'im ter think that, but they've got a lorry business down at the coast and she told me I could work for Frank – that's her bloke...'

'Yeah, I know.' Robbie nodded, a smile coming to his eyes now. 'Mum's smart, ain't she? If Dad knew where she was, he'd have gone after her. I can go to grammar school down there, can't I?'

''Course yer can,' Nobby said. 'As soon as Mum comes to fetch us, we can slip off and tell no one – especially not Gran, 'cos she would tell Dad...'

'Yeah, I know – she hates Mum,' Robbie said. 'She's all right with us, but she wouldn't let us go to Mum.'

'So, we'll keep this to ourselves, right?'

Robbie agreed, watching as his brother moved a small chest of drawers and removed a floorboard, taking out a small leather pouch. He slipped it inside his jacket breast pocket and picked up his bundle.

'I ain't sorry ter see the last of this place – come on, Robbie, let's go.'

'Are yer goin' ter lock up?'

'Nah – I don't care who gets in now,' Nobby said. 'Dad would break the door in if he 'ad to, but this way he can get in and out quick if he wants – and he won't know fer sure if it was me that took his money.'

28

Peggy shivered as she entered the cottage. The kitchen range must have burned low and that meant Sandra next door hadn't been in today to make it up. Fortunately, it wasn't freezing so they hadn't come home to burst pipes, but it wasn't like Sandra to let Peggy down – so perhaps something had happened to throw her out of her routine.

'Don't worry, love, I'll soon have it going again,' Able said. 'I've been wondering if we should have some other sort of central heating installed – gas or oil-fired. I know we like the range, but we'll have to sort it out before next winter.'

'Sandra would come in and keep the range going once the weather turned,' Peggy said. 'I'm sure she would have come as soon as she could, Able – she's very reliable.'

'As a rule,' he agreed, 'but we can't always rely on friends doing favours, Peggy. I'll look into it because I don't want to let the cottage. I could pay for a caretaker to come in now and then...'

Peggy nodded, because Able was just talking aloud. He would sort it out himself; he was very good at managing their affairs and she didn't have to worry. In the winter, it was nicer to have someone keep the heat on rather than draining it all down, as he'd done that the first winter when they hadn't been living in the cottage.

Peggy looked around her kitchen. She really did love this place and she would miss it. For her it had been a home and a whole new life. The café was always busy so she hadn't spent as much time in her garden and exploring the countryside as she'd expected, but that would happen in the future. Peggy wanted to come back here when it was just the two of them. The children and grandchildren could come for holidays – and perhaps great-grandchildren one day.

A smile drew her mouth up at the corners as she thought of her family. The twins were in their bedrooms, arguing and laughing as they usually did. Both were excited about the move. Freddie had already joined the ice hockey team, even though he couldn't yet play and was in the reserves, and he'd been to three football matches over Christmas. Chris had told him that his school had a football team and Freddie was hoping to get into it. Sheila had promised to put Peggy in touch with the headmaster and Peggy would do all she could to get Freddie into the same school as Chris.

Peggy unpacked various baskets and bags. They'd stopped to shop on their way home and she was cooking them pork chops, mashed potatoes, carrots and sprouts, followed by an apple pie she'd made yesterday and brought home with some warm custard she would make – as soon as the range was warm enough.

Just as she was unpacking her last basket, the back door opened and Sandra popped her head round the door. 'You are home then,' she said. 'I'm sorry I didn't get in to make the fire up this morning, Peggy. I've kept it going until now, but last night I had an urgent phone call and I've been up all night at the hospital.'

'Oh no, I'm so sorry – is it your father?'

'No, unfortunately, it was my mother this time,' Sandra said. 'That's why I couldn't leave until now. My father was crying and as helpless as a kitten without her and she was taken into hospital with a heart attack. Her next-door neighbour went around because Dad was making a noise and she rang the ambulance and then me. I went straight to the hospital and I've been there all the time with him. He can't understand what is happening and I've had to arrange a paid helper to go in with him at home.' Sandra sighed deeply. 'If anything happens to Mum... I suppose I shall have to take him in with me. He can't be alone and I don't want to push him off in a home, or some kind of mental hospital. The infirmary would take him, but it's awful there – more like the old workhouse, I imagine. I visited once to see one of Mum's friends and it smelled of disinfectant and urine. I'd hate Dad to go there. I did make some inquiries about help at home and I may be able to get a woman in to just be around, help with dressing and stuff like that, so that I can get out sometimes...'

'Oh, Sandra, I'm so sorry,' Peggy said, because she'd seen the illness in her own family with her father's mother, though Gran had been a tough old lady and struggled alone almost until the end when she'd become bedridden and Peggy's mother had looked after her. 'While I'm here, I'll be glad to fetch the children from school – but we're moving back to London, as I rang and told you.'

'Yes, I shall miss you a lot,' Sandra said and looked upset. 'Even more now...' Tears welled up and spilled over, running down her cheeks. 'Mum has been so brave and good, looking after him all this time – never finding fault, protecting him and letting him think everything was normal. It isn't, and without her, he'll discover that very quickly. I can take care of him, but not the way she did – and I'll need help. Fortunately, the kids love him and while they're around he can play with them; he's actually still good at playing games they enjoy.'

'It is so sad for all of you...'

'We had a really nice Christmas. Dad seemed better with all the family around him and Mum was happy when we visited her in hospital. She kept saying how lucky she was to be alive. I cooked Christmas dinner as normal and the kids and my brother and Ken kept Dad amused.' Sandra sighed. 'It's a pity Mum didn't let us know she was feeling ill sooner. We might have avoided her being rushed into hospital – and Dad getting into a state the way he did.'

'He was frightened,' Peggy said. 'Out of his home and confused as to what was happening.'

'He still keeps asking where Mum is,' Sandra continued, clearly distressed by the trauma of it all. 'I tell him, but the next minute he asks again and I get a bit impatient. I don't know how Mum coped all this time – no wonder it took its toll on her.'

'Saying I'm sorry doesn't help you,' Peggy said. 'If I can do anything while we're still here...'

'I know,' Sandra said and then gave a little sob of despair. 'Would you give me a hug?'

'Of course.' Peggy put her arms around her and hugged her tight. Sometimes, when things were at their worst, words were useless but a hug certainly helped. Sandra's troubles made Peggy feel guilty again, because she wanted to do more to help her friend, but the decision was made and she had to go ahead with the move for her family's sake.

'My brother Rodney says he will take him when he's home, on leave, sometimes,' Sandra said, her mind still running on her father's incapacity. Her brother Rodney was in the Army and unmarried, so he couldn't offer to take his father in or even split the problem with her, except when he came home for a leave. 'I know he means well – but it is going to be a big problem for us...'

'Perhaps your mother will get better and be able to look after him again,' Peggy suggested. 'She has obviously been neglecting herself, but now the doctors will treat her and she may get back to almost her old self.'

'They can't manage that big house any more,' Sandra said. 'Ken thinks they need to sell and either find a smaller place or move into residential care together. The money they get would help with care too, because I'm not sure we can manage otherwise. I obviously can't do the office work and that means employing a secretary.'

Peggy nodded her understanding, because an illness such as Sandra's father unfortunately had turned a family upside down. The affected person needed so much attention that it took a lot of time and care to keep them clean and happy.

'I suppose your parents might find a residential care home that caters for couples,' Peggy agreed. 'It isn't like the old days when the workhouse split up families and husband and wife. However, I'm sure if they had some savings, you could find someone to help out, on a daily basis, Sandra.'

'Yes, perhaps, if Mum gets well enough to come home...' Sandra's expression was lighter. 'I always feel better after I talk to you, Peggy. Ken told me not to dwell on the worst, but Mum looks so ill...' she gave a little sob. 'Why did it have to happen? Dad was always the clever one...'

'I know. It's strange, isn't it?' Peggy said and looked at her sympathetically. 'I don't know much about the illness at all, but I know it's unfortunate and very upsetting for everyone.' She pressed Sandra's hand in sympathy. 'The range is hot enough for a kettle now – sit down and I'll make tea. My lot can wait for their supper.'

* * *

After Sandra had gone and Peggy's family had eaten, she told Able about her friend's distress. He nodded in sympathy and then smiled.

'You can't solve the problems of the world, hon. I know Sandra is a good friend, but she has to face up to whatever happens next. She has a good husband, her brother and children – and if her mother isn't capable of taking care of herself and her husband, she'll have to find a way. Perhaps someone to go in and cook their meals and help with washing and bedtime. I dare say there are good-hearted women who would help for a few pounds a week.'

'Yes, I think there must be,' Peggy agreed. 'Folk here aren't as poor as they were in London in the years between the wars, but it isn't that easy for most. I'm sure she'll find a way.'

Able put his arms around her, looking into her face. 'And you're quite sure you want to move back to London?'

'You know I am,' Peggy said. 'I just felt sorry for Sandra and wished I could promise to help her.'

'Yes, of course you do – but you can't do everything, love,' Able said. 'Sandra is upset, but she'll get used to the idea and find a way to manage.'

Peggy nodded. 'What have you decided about the cottage? We

can't ask Sandra and Ken to look after it now; they have enough to worry about.'

'I'll be putting in proper central heating,' Able said. 'The cottage should be a pleasure not a liability, so I'll spend whatever I need to make sure I don't have to ask my neighbours to see to the range. Sandra certainly wouldn't want the responsibility and no one else is close enough.'

Peggy agreed. 'Will it stretch you financially?' she asked doubtfully. 'On top of the move and everything?'

'I've had an offer for the property in Mulberry Lane,' Able said. 'I was going to try to hang on to it, because the rent is useful, but now, I think I'll sell. I've nearly doubled my investment there and it will free up some funds for what I need to do here and keep us going in London until the business picks up.'

'We were doing so well at the café...' Peggy looked at him, trying to read his expression. This move was a lot to expect of her husband. He had a good business and plans to make it even better and now he was being asked to move back to a lane in London, away from all he enjoyed. 'Did anyone ask you how you felt about all this, Able?'

'You did – and so did Freddie,' he said and grinned at her. 'I told you I was easy and I haven't changed, hon.'

Peggy moved towards him, slipping her arms about his waist. 'You would tell me if you weren't happy about something?'

'I love you, Peggy Ronoscki, and nothing else matters,' he said and kissed her. 'Stop worrying about me. You have enough to do, packing and keeping everyone else happy.'

Peggy nodded. 'Yes, I know Janet is going to have something to say about all this...'

Able smiled at her. 'Janet is a lovely girl, but she does tend to be a bit thoughtless, Peggy. I'm afraid that this time, you have to put others first.'

* * *

Peggy felt like a whirlwind had hit her after the calm and peace of

Christmas with her family in London. They were immediately busy at the café and at home she was busy sorting out what they would need in London and what could be left here. The children's clothes would be needed, because they grew so fast that by the time they came down in the summer, anything left here would probably no longer fit. They both wanted to take all their possessions, though Peggy persuaded them that the older toys they never played with could safely remain in their bedrooms.

'Your dad is going to have someone come in regularly to clean and check things over, so it will all be safe,' Peggy told her children as they pounced on stuff they couldn't possibly leave behind yet would probably never touch once they had it in their rooms. A rocking horse and a large metal pedal car were reluctantly left in Freddie's bedroom. Fay's doll's house was left in situ after a long debate. The cot with her collection of dolls was also left, because she decided she didn't have time to play with them now that she was going to be a famous ice skater. Fay had been told that she would have to train hard to be accepted into the British team when she was older and that she might never make the grade, but she was completely convinced she would win championships and no matter what her parents or anyone said she held to her beliefs.

'I don't want to give my dolls away, Mum,' she told Peggy seriously. 'I want to keep them here in the cottage and one day I might give them to my daughter – when I'm as old as you.' She eyed her mother, considering. 'Of course, I shan't be an old lady for years and years... and I shan't marry until I've won lots of medals and retired from the rink...'

'No, you won't be an old lady for many years,' Peggy said, hiding her smile. 'But don't get your hopes up too high, love. Just because you're going to have lessons and learn ice-skating, it doesn't mean you'll win anything.'

Fay gave her a confident smile. 'You wait and see, Mum – I'm going to be really good on the ice, Miss Anderson said so. You're so old-fashioned, you don't understand...'

Peggy turned away, half-laughing and half-rueful. Fay wasn't intending to be rude to her mother, just saying things the way she saw them. She understood that she must seem ancient to the twins sometimes, because she'd had them late in life, but Able said she was still young and beautiful to him, and Freddie just said she was his mum and he loved her. Fay loved her too, but she wasn't as thoughtful or loving as her brother, at least not outwardly. A lot of people thought she was a selfish little madam, but Peggy loved her and knew that the slight deafness in one ear didn't help her. It had been caused by a childhood illness and the wooden bead she'd put in her ear when very small. It had festered and caused some damage before anyone realised what was wrong with her. Sometimes Fay missed what was said if the speaker was turning away and she hated it, becoming sullen and angry rather than asking people to speak clearly for her.

Dismissing her daughter's opinion of her age, Peggy thought about starting her packing. She had brought tea chests full of her possessions when she'd moved out of the Pig & Whistle and now she began to fill those same chests with things she would be taking to the private rooms above the boarding house in Mulberry Lane. Most of it was cooking utensils, the children's bits and pieces and other items they all felt they couldn't leave behind.

It was amazing how much extra stuff they'd collected in the few years they'd been living at the cottage. Especially the gardening tools Able had acquired, which resided in the garage, except on the rare days he had time to cut back a few bushes and mow the lawn. Whoever came to check on the house would need to keep the garden tidy too or it would get out of hand.

'At least we don't need to take any of that stuff,' Peggy said, eyeing the packed shelving. 'If you get someone to look after the garden, they may use them...'

'I'll need my toolbox,' Able said and collected some spanners that had strayed from the smart box Peggy had bought him as an anniversary present. 'I know Tom Barton will do any difficult jobs, but I like to tinker sometimes.'

'You must take what you need,' Peggy agreed and sighed as she looked round. 'We've been happy here, haven't we? It seems sad to be leaving just as we were getting it all the way we'd hoped it would be...'

'Yes, it is a pity in some ways,' Able said, 'but it will still be ours, Peggy. We're not leaving for good and we'll have summer holidays and one day we'll retire here and grow ancient together.'

His smile reassured her. Able was slightly younger than Peggy, but she never felt too old for him, because he loved her and expressed his love in every way possible.

'I'd best get on,' she said. 'Janet and Maggie are coming up this afternoon and they will stay for a couple of days...'

'The twins are back to school tomorrow,' Able said, frowning. 'I would've thought Maggie ought to be back too.'

'Janet says she's explained to her school that she needs to take Maggie out for a couple of days – I don't know why.' A frown wrinkled Peggy's smooth forehead. 'She's hinting at something important and changes for them all – I hope she isn't going to tell me she's leaving Ryan...'

'Didn't she say they had a lovely Christmas – apart from the scare over Maggie getting lost?'

'Yes, but somethin' is goin' on and she won't tell me until she comes, which is worrying me.'

'You worry about that girl too much!' Able retorted. 'I've told you, Peggy, you have to think of yourself and others for once. Janet is old enough to make up her own mind now.'

'Yes – but I do want her to be happy. She went through a lot with Mike...'

'I know and I'm not unsympathetic towards her, Peggy – but she brings a lot of it on herself.'

Privately, Peggy agreed but didn't answer. She had never quarrelled with Able, but a couple of times they'd drawn back from the edge of angry words and both times it had been over Janet. Peggy's daughter was difficult and moody and she did shut her mother out, but that didn't stop Peggy loving her and being anxious about her. Much as she adored her other children and Able, she still loved Janet and wanted her to have a good life. She'd been lucky to find Able and she wanted the same kind of happiness for her daughter.

Sandra was waving to her from her back door as Peggy returned to the kitchen. She saw her friend was smiling and went to greet her and draw her in to the warmth of the kitchen. A kettle was about to boil on the range and Peggy made a pot of tea, bringing out a large Madeira cake and some almond macaroons as well as some jam tarts with coconut on for the children.

'How is your mum this morning?'

'Sister says a lot better,' Sandra replied, beaming at her. 'I told you yesterday she'd come out of it well and now she's sitting up eating tea and toast. I'm going to visit her this afternoon – and my father is coming with me...'

'Has he settled in your spare bedroom?'

'He wanders a bit in the night, looking for his things,' Sandra said, 'but Ken takes him back to bed and he's all right. Sometimes, he's as right as rain and you wouldn't think there was a thing wrong with him – and then he gets confused. It's working better than I feared anyway...' She saw the morning paper lying on the kitchen table and frowned. 'I don't like the sound of that – we've asked America for a stock of atomic bombs.' She shivered. 'It would've been better had that thing never been invented in my opinion.'

'I feel the same,' Peggy agreed, 'but Able says the bombs they exploded in Japan shortened the war and he's right – I just don't like them...' She folded the newspaper and put it to one side. 'I'm more interested in your dad than that gloom-and-doom rag. Have you decided what to do – what does your husband think?'

Sandra sipped her tea. 'Ken is back to work on Monday and I know it will be harder to cope then – but I've found a lady who says she has some experience with the illness and she's promised to come in and help when I need to shop or fetch the children.' She smiled wryly at Peggy. 'I panicked that first night, but it's better now...'

'Good. I know it is hard for you,' Peggy said. 'When I'm around, I'll always help, you know that...'

'Yes,' Sandra agreed and munched an almond macaroon. 'I love these, Peggy. Are they a new recipe?'

'Yes, my daughter-in-law's. She and Maureen run a little tea shop...'

'I remember you told me. I should be a regular customer if I lived near enough if all her cakes are this good... still you always make good cakes, whatever sort they are.'

'I love cooking, always have.' Peggy smiled. 'However, the café was a bit too much like hard work. I'll have more time in future to cook what I like and experiment, though it will still be a busy and fulfilling life.'

'What will Janet say to you returning to London?'

'I expect her to tell me I'm a fool, but I know I'm doing the right thing.'

'That's all you can do.' Sandra thanked her for the tea and stood up. 'I'm cooking an early lunch tomorrow so that I can get off to the hospital for two o'clock visiting.'

Peggy waved her off and washed up, then prepared the roast. In contrast to Sandra, they would eater lunch later that Sunday – at about three – so that Janet and Maggie could eat with them.

* * *

'That roast beef was delicious, Mum,' Janet said when she came up that Sunday afternoon, 'and Able's horseradish is the hottest I've tasted. Lovely, thanks.'

'Can I get down now, Mum?' Maggie asked after finishing her portion of ice cream and strawberry jelly.

'Yes, if you've finished – Mum, is it all right if Maggie shows the twins some of the things she got for Christmas?' Janet asked her.

'Of course,' Peggy agreed and smiled. 'Yes, you two can get down now.'

The three children disappeared into one of the other rooms, leaving Janet and Peggy to clear the table together.

'Do you need any help?' Able asked.

'No, you get on with whatever you need to do,' Peggy told him. 'We can do these.'

'Shall I wash or wipe?' Janet asked and Peggy handed her a clean tea towel.

'I'll wash, Jan – you tell me about your holiday.'

'It was really beautiful, Mum,' Janet said as she wiped the first glass. 'The cabin was quaint and very warm and the fire smelled lovely – we loved the walks and the hotel was fabulous.'

'Sounds as if you enjoyed yourselves – apart from Maggie's disappearance. That must have terrified you...'

'It did – especially as it was my fault. I started the quarrel that Maggie overheard and that was the reason she went out on her own...'

'Not a very pleasant way to end the holiday,' Peggy said and turned to look at her. 'So, what do you want to tell me? I know there's something on your mind...'

Janet took a deep breath. 'Ryan is taking a job in Scotland and we're moving up there for a few years – he thinks the contract is for five years but may be renewed...'

'Moving to Scotland?' Peggy stared at her blankly for a moment because it didn't sink in. Here she was, worrying over how Janet would take the fact that she was moving to London and her daughter was going all the way up to Scotland and she hadn't even hinted at it or asked how she would feel. That was typical Janet! For a moment Peggy felt angry and then she suddenly saw the funny side of it and started laughing. 'Oh, Jan, you do take the biscuit! There I was worrying about returning to London and leaving you in the lurch and you're off to Scotland just like that without a thought...'

'I know, I'm sorry I didn't warn you...' Janet looked apologetic. 'I made all that fuss when you said you might move back to London – and now I'm going even further away. It means we shan't see each other much – perhaps twice a year in the holidays.'

Peggy counted to twelve because ten wouldn't have been long enough. 'What does my granddaughter think of the move?'

'She loves the idea – and Ryan asked her. She thinks anything he says is wonderful, so it wouldn't have mattered what I thought.'

'So, what do you think?'

'I'll see more of Ryan,' Janet said. 'He won't have to come down to London more than twice a year and he says he'll try to make it coincide with school holidays so we can all come.'

'I might see as much of you as I do now,' Peggy remarked sharply and Janet flushed.

'That's not fair, Mum. We've seen each other several times this year…'

'Because I came down to you,' Peggy reminded her. 'This is only the second time you've been here in over a year. If I bring the twins to Scotland for a holiday in the summer, I'll probably see more of Maggie than I have here.'

'I'm sorry, Mum.' Janet had the grace to look ashamed. 'I know I've been a pain these past few months…'

'Yes, if I'm honest, you have,' Peggy agreed. She smiled at Janet ruefully. 'It isn't the first time, Jan, but it doesn't stop me caring about you. If you think the move will make you content, I'm all for it – and we're moving back to London as soon as Able can sell the café lease. I'm packing our stuff now and I'll be popping up every so often to make sure things are progressing, though I know I can trust Tom to get on with it.'

'So, you've made up your mind then?' Janet nodded. 'I hope it's what you want, Mum, and not just for Fay's sake.'

'It was for Fay in the beginning, her and Sheila – as you know, she's having another baby and Pip isn't sure how he feels about it.'

'I know; he told me she was risking her life and he's pretty cut up over it.'

Peggy frowned at her. 'Sheila is thrilled and Pip has to accept it for her sake. Once the baby is here, he will be over the moon, but I know he's worried he will lose her. She went through so much last time…'

'He feels a bit hurt that she just went ahead without talking to him about it,' Janet said. 'I told him to forget it and remember he loves her and just take care of her. He got annoyed and said he thought I'd be on his side – I told him I am. There's more than one way to lose the one you love and I should know...' Janet blinked hard. 'I almost drove Ryan away, Mum – I shut him out the way I did you. I don't mean to do it but I can't help it... it's as if I can't bear to let anyone in because it hurts too much to lose them...'

'I know.' Peggy wiped her hands on a towel and went to embrace her daughter. For a second, Janet stiffened and then she relaxed and hugged her mother, giving a little sniff as the tears ran. 'We all love you, Jan darling. Please don't shut us out.'

Janet nodded and swiped her cheek with the back of her hand. 'I'm an idiot, Mum – but it hurt so much...'

Peggy knew that she was talking of losing first her home and then her husband in the war. Janet had curled up like a hedgehog then, all prickles and defensive, because she couldn't face her pain and she'd done it again when she lost her baby.

'It's all right now, though, isn't it? Ryan does love you. I know he does, darling.'

'He could have had an affair, but he didn't,' Janet said and smiled mistily.

'Of course, he didn't – he loves you, always has. You couldn't have thought he would?' Peggy gave her a look of disbelief.

'I found lipstick on some handkerchiefs in his pocket. That's what caused the row. He said nothing happened, because he had too much to lose... she kissed him when he was a bit squiffy at the office party.'

'It happens, but if love exists it goes no further,' Peggy said, nodding her understanding. 'I doubt if Laurie would have gone astray if the war hadn't happened.'

'You wouldn't have had Able or the twins,' Janet said and smiled at her. 'I know Able makes you happy, Mum. He was the best thing that ever happened to you. Even before the war, you and Dad – you weren't truly happy. He took you for granted and you let him, because you were busy and you had your friends.'

'Yes, I know,' Peggy agreed. 'I think a lot of marriages are like that,

Janet. I would never have thought of anyone else if Laurie hadn't been so nasty to you – and to me – but I'm fulfilled now. I want you to be as content as I am, love.'

'I think I shall be now,' Janet said a little tentatively. 'If we're together more. I've stopped worrying about having another baby. We've got Maggie and each other – why do we need more?'

'You don't,' Peggy said and kissed her cheek. 'I'm so pleased you've realised it for yourself, darling. Happiness is what you make and pass on to others and only you can do it.'

'You make everyone feel better. In the war, everyone came to you with their problems,' Janet said and smiled lovingly. 'Next time I start sulking, give me a kick up the pants, Mum.'

'All right, that's a promise,' Peggy laughed. 'So, when are you thinking of moving to Scotland? And whereabouts will you be living?'

'I think we'll be moving in March, a similar time to your move to London, Mum – and Ryan says he needs to live within an hour or so of Edinburgh.'

'So not near Loch Ness then?'

'No, that's further up north. He's going up before me to meet his new boss and look for a place to live. I'll be at home packing, because we're taking our stuff with us and letting the house on a five-year lease.'

Peggy nodded and smiled to see Janet looking enthusiastic. She could only hope that this new mood would last, but Able was right. Peggy couldn't solve her daughter's problems, Janet had to do that for herself and it looked as if she'd made a good start.

29

'I'm not sure I think that is a good idea,' Gordon said to Maureen when she showed him the very polite letter that Richard had sent her expressing his hopes that they would allow Shirley to go on his working holiday with him and promising to take good care of her. 'She's only sixteen – and very young with it...'

'I think you underestimate your daughter,' Maureen said with a little smile. 'Shirley is very responsible – and wise beyond her years. This might be good for her, Gordon. She has worked so hard for her exams and hardly ever goes anywhere with friends. Don't you think she deserves a treat? After all, she'll be going to college in the autumn, so why not let her have a little fun in the summer?'

Gordon frowned and sighed. 'She's still a little girl to me, Maureen. I couldn't bear it if anything happened to her...'

'Do you think I don't feel the same? I love her and she's been an angel to me. I shall miss her so much when she goes to college. She's such a help to me with the children that I'll probably have to cut down some of my working time once she leaves home.'

'And why not?' Gordon said with a frown. 'Sometimes I think you do too much, love. You don't need to work so many hours.'

'I know we don't need the money these days, because you've

made the grocery shop so successful,' Maureen said. 'I do it for the friendship and companionship.'

'Yes, I know.' He smiled at her. 'I've been tempted to ask you to stop, but I know Sheila is a friend – but perhaps when Peggy is back you could cut down a little? Peggy can help and you'll want time to be with her, too...'

'You know me too well,' Maureen agreed. 'If Peggy helps, we'd be finished hours sooner – or we could alternate mornings. I know it will be easier for us all with her in the lane again. I've discussed it with Sheila and we're going to offer her a third of the business for the cakes. She's such a good cook that she'll fit right in and none of us need the money. We all do it for love and friends, and the locals love it.'

'I know. I'm always being told what a marvellous baker you are.' Gordon smiled. 'That's it then, love. I'll manage a morning off once in the week this spring and summer – get someone in to help in the shop for a few hours – we can take Matty out somewhere together. Make the most of it before he goes to school. He's hardly been to the zoo more than once and I want to take the children for a nice long holiday in the summer, somewhere for just them and us.' He smiled at her. 'They premiered *The Third Man* this week, so it should be on at a cinema near us soon – I'd like to see that. We might go out for dinner and then catch the second house if you like.'

'We've never done that – we've never done any of those things,' Maureen ran to put her arms around him and hug him. 'I love you, Gordon, and I think that is a wonderful idea. We can ride into the country or have a picnic in Epping Forest or lunch out at a nice pub.'

'Now, you're talking,' Gordon said approvingly. 'I've wanted to tell you not to work all the time for ages, but I knew you wouldn't let Sheila down and now you won't have to.'

'No – and it's all because Peggy is coming back to the lanes.'

Gordon laughed. 'You women! I've never known anything like it. Anyone would think you and Peggy were joined at the hip...'

Maureen beamed at him, because he wasn't cross. She'd been a bit worried that he resented her working, but he just wanted to spend a little more time with her and in future they would arrange it so that he could – now that her father's old shop was making a decent little profit and all Gordon's hard work had paid off. They had money for all they wanted and enough to help out a few neighbours now and then, too.

'So, what about Shirley's holiday?' she pressed home while he was pleased with life. 'I know she'll behave, Gordon, and Richard is a good lad – he'll be sensible too. He cares about her – you can tell that from his letter – they just want to have some fun together...'

'Yes,' Gordon grinned at her. 'So, did I, when I was a lad. Her mother was only eighteen when I married her – and we were content enough until she became ill. I trust your judgement, Maureen, and I know you're right. Shirley won't get into trouble, because she has to study for years. She's a bright girl, my daughter.'

'Yes, she is – so may I write back and tell Richard to arrange it?'

'Yes, I don't see why not – but tell him if anything untoward happens to Shirley I'll blame him...'

'Yes, I think he knows that,' Maureen said, hiding her smile.

* * *

Shirley was delighted when Maureen told her that her father had given his permission.

'I'm writing to Richard and I shall put him on his honour to look after you,' Maureen said. 'I know you're a bright girl, Shirley, but when you're young and you fall in love things can get out of hand quickly. However, we're trusting you both – and I know you will both respect that.'

'Yes, Mum, we will,' Shirley said though her cheeks were pink. 'Thank you for persuading Dad – I bet he didn't agree at once.'

Maureen laughed. 'He wasn't too much trouble, love. Your dad loves you and he just wants to protect you and make sure you have a good life...'

'I want that too,' Shirley said. 'Some of the girls I went to school with are working in factories and courting – one of them got married at Christmas, as soon as she was sixteen. Her husband is in the Army and she's six months pregnant.' Shirley looked a little upset. 'Myra's father hit her and threw her out, but her mother signed for her to get married and helped her find somewhere to live when her husband comes home – it's just a couple of rooms, but she's happy.'

'I think that is sad,' Maureen said. 'It breaks up a home and if he doesn't see his grandchild, he will always regret it...'

'Myra is going away as soon as they can get into married quarters,' Shirley said. 'She says they may be posted somewhere abroad, and she can't wait to get away.'

Maureen nodded. 'If that is what makes her happy – but it's still sad. Janet's father never forgave her because something similar happened to her. Mike married her despite her father's objections, but it started the rift between Laurie and Peggy. Janet and Mike were happy together until the war wrecked their lives.'

'That was so sad,' Shirley agreed and went to put her arms about Maureen. 'I know you would always forgive me – but it would make you and Dad unhappy if I did something silly, so I promise I shan't. Do you believe me?'

'Yes, I do,' Maureen said and kissed her. 'I should love you whatever you did and I'd forgive you – but your dad's pride would take a tumble and that is something you wouldn't enjoy, love.'

* * *

Shirley took her time over her letter to Richard. She spoke of all the things that she enjoyed at school, Peggy coming back to the lane and her father's unease over her going on holiday with him and his friends.

Mum persuaded him for us. She is always on my side and she trusts me to be sensible. We shall of course, because we both have a long way to go to become doctors – me years longer than you.

I do care about you lots, Richard. I hope you know that there is no one as special to me as you – and I don't think there ever will be. I know you're older and if you liked someone else and wanted to be with them, I would understand. You're my best friend and I want it always to be that way – and more one day. I think the world of you, but I think you know that.

Take care of yourself and think of me sometimes – but enjoy your life, Richard. I can't ask you to wait if you want more than just friendship.

If you get home one weekend for a few days that would be smashing.

Sending you my love and friendship,

Shirley

She read her letter through several times but couldn't think of a way to improve what she wanted to tell him. Surely, he would understand and know she was in love with him? Shirley couldn't expect him to remain faithful to her for years and she wanted him to know that if he had feelings for someone else it need not ruin their friendship. Only if he committed his love to her would she feel betrayed if he broke that promise – as yet it hadn't happened. It hurt to know that perhaps there was someone he wanted to kiss and touch, but she had a lot of growing up and learning to do and how could she blame Richard for wanting what she couldn't give yet?

At the railway station, Richard had hinted at his feelings being more, but he was afraid to commit. Was it because he knew that if he made love to her it wouldn't stop at kissing? Shirley sighed, because she hadn't got around to thinking beyond that yet, though she'd understood her mother's warnings to behave. It was something for the future, but she wasn't ready to think about it yet.

30

Rose looked uneasily over her shoulder. She couldn't help feeling that someone was watching her and it sent shivers down her spine. Tom had asked her if she wanted him to accompany her on this, her first trip to the market since she was attacked, but she'd insisted that she go alone. If she let Jim Broad make her afraid, she would never go anywhere alone again and Rose was not prepared to live her life in the shadows. Yet, she couldn't help glancing over her shoulder now and then. No one was there, of course. It was sheer imagination. Her attacker wouldn't dare show his face around here again, too many folk were on the lookout for him.

'Good morning, Mrs Barton,' one of the stallholders said as she approached his display of fruit and vegetables. 'It's nice to see you here again.'

'Thank you, Mr Soames,' Rose said. 'Are those potatoes good for making chips and mash?'

'These are best for mashing – and these are the best for chips,' he replied. 'I do like a nice King Edward for chips. They crisp up lovely in the pan.'

'Tom likes a few chips when we have sausages,' Rose said. 'I'll have some of each please – two pounds of both, and some of those

Brussels and also some carrots and a stick of celery, a pound of little oranges and four bananas.'

'That's a lot to carry,' Mr Soames said, smiling at her. 'Would you like my lad to deliver them for you this afternoon?'

'Would he?' Rose beamed at him. 'That is so kind of you – I've got more shopping to do and the veg is very heavy.'

'Much too heavy to carry,' he agreed. 'I'm always happy to send round your order. Tom would do the same for me – he fixed my shed up a treat and for half the price anyone else would charge.'

Rose smiled, paid him and moved on. Tom was so popular in the lanes and surrounding district and she was lucky to be his wife. She'd realised just how lucky these past few days as her husband fussed over her long after she'd recovered from her bruises. He'd treated her as if she were a princess, never once questioning her. Tom assumed she'd given that man no encouragement and she felt close to tears when she thought of his perfect trust in her. She knew now that no man could ever replace Tom in her heart and the lingering regret she'd felt over Jimmy had gone. It was sad that he'd died, but it had been his choice to volunteer and Rose was happier now than she'd ever thought she could be – apart from the slight shadow of the brutal attack on her outside the Pig & Whistle.

She wanted to tell Tom how much she loved him but couldn't find the words. Her heart was filled with gratitude for all she'd found as Tom Barton's wife and she felt privileged to be Mrs Barton. One day she would find the words to tell him all the thoughts that teemed inside her head.

Rose finished her shopping in the market and was about to start out for her home in Mulberry Lane when she caught sight of someone lurking behind one of the stalls. Her heart caught with fright, because she knew it was Jim Broad – and he was watching her. She could sense the menace in him – an anger that had driven him back to the covered market where she habitually shopped even though he must know the police were on the lookout for him.

For a moment the panic ripped through her and she wanted to

run, but then she took a deep breath and thought carefully. Tom had friends here and she only had to ask for help.

Looking round, she saw that Nick Soames was looking at her. She took a deep breath and walked towards him, willing herself not to run. She mustn't panic – must not allow herself to fear attack or she would never be able to shop alone again.

She reached the stall she was heading for and looked at the market trader who had been so kind to her earlier. 'You will think I'm foolish – but I think I'm being followed.'

'You're not foolish and he's been spotted,' he replied with a grim look beyond her. 'We've been watchin' 'im, Mrs Barton, and the police are waitin' ter grab him if he approaches yer – but they'll get the bugger after you leave the market. We didn't want to frighten you...'

'I'm leaving now,' she said and summoned a smile. 'Thank you all so much for taking care of me.'

'It's a pleasure, Mrs Barton – Tom is a good mate to us and we'd do the same for any of our women.'

'Yes, thank you,' Rose said and smiled. She walked away, resisting the temptation to look back, knowing that she was being protected. Suddenly, she heard a cry and then shouts and scuffling and glanced back hurriedly. She was in time to see several men, including two police officers, grappling with a man she believed was Jim Broad – although he looked nothing like the bright-eyed man who had sold her walnuts before Christmas. Unkempt, unshaven and wild, he fought those who attempted to restrain him, breaking from them and charging after Rose like a wild bull.

From somewhere, Rose found the courage to stand her ground and not run. Fear rippled through her as she smelled the foul unwashed stench of him and saw a touch of madness in his eyes.

'Bloody bitch...' he said and sprang at her. 'I'll teach yer...'

Rose never knew where her courage came from but instead of screaming or trying to get out of the way, she swung her arm and hit him full square in the face with her heavy shopping bag and, unbelievably, he went down, stumbling and then sagging to his knees before her.

'You're a fool,' Rose said coldly as he looked at her in a daze. 'You've ruined your life for nothing...'

Jim just stared at her, too dazed and stunned by her blow to move. She thought he must be drunk or weak from lack of food and before he could struggle to his feet the police had cuffs on him.

Rose drew a deep breath and then heard the sound of clapping. 'Well done, Rose! That showed the bugger.'

'Freddie Mills couldn't have done better – and that's afore that American so-and-so give 'im a battering!'

There was a chorus of laughter at the joke about the British boxer who had recently had a hammering from his American opponent; applause and cheers followed for Rose's moment of courage. However, her knees were feeling weak and for a moment she thought she might faint, but then she recovered and grinned at the group of admiring men and women who had witnessed her stunning blow.

'I'd give the same to all bullies. You stand up fer yerself, love. Give the buggers 'ell!' one of the market women said.

Suddenly, Rose was laughing. All her fear had gone. She'd shown Jim Broad she wasn't afraid of him and she'd do the same to anyone else who thought she was vulnerable.

'I intend to,' she said to the woman, who was grinning at her. 'Not my Tom, though – he's the best...'

A few more cheers sounded in her ears as she walked out of the market. Rose smiled to herself as she quickened her step. She would pop into the office to see her husband before she collected her children from Alice. She felt as if she were walking on air and couldn't help smiling. How on earth had she managed to swing that heavy shopping bag with such force? It had a tin of pineapple in for Tom's favourite cake and that was probably what had floored her attacker.

It was funny the way he'd looked at her with that stunned expression. Rose was glad the police had him in custody; she couldn't feel it in her heart to pity him yet, despite his terrible condition, though she felt sorry for his lads. Those kids were innocent and she couldn't imagine what sort of lives they must have been leading with their father drunk most of the time. She would ask Tom to make inquiries, see how they were managing without their father, though, by the look of him, he hadn't been back home in weeks – and that meant the children might be in difficulty.

* * *

Granny Broad sighed. She was getting on a bit to have the care of two growing lads. It had been all right when Jim wasn't drinking; he'd given her money to help and they took more notice of their dad than they did her.

She rubbed at her chest. That pain was bothering her again. She ignored it as much as she could, because she'd never trusted doctors. They'd told her it was free to go to the hospital now, but she wasn't sure that was true. Folk said stuff but then you got a bill you couldn't pay and that caused trouble. Besides, she remembered her father rubbing at his chest. He'd just had a bit of a pain, but then he'd gone in the infirmary, caught pneumonia and never come out. She would manage as best she could for as long as she could and not breathe a word to the lads. If their father sobered up and came home soon, he might be in time to take over before she went...

'Mrs Broad?'

Granny looked round with a scowl on her face as she saw who had entered her kitchen by the back door. She hated coppers as much as most folk round here – interfering busybodies always trying to catch folk out!

'I understand the lads are staying with you for the moment – so I thought I'd best come and tell you—'

She glared at the young officer. 'Got 'im, 'ave yer? Can't yer leave the man in peace fer a bit?'

'You know he attacked a young woman, Mrs Broad?'

'Serves the bitch right for encouragin' 'im, leading him on,' she snarled. 'My boy's been let down by women, that wife of his were no better than she should be, carryin' on behind 'is back.'

'The young woman he attacked is happily married and did not encourage him,' the officer said. 'I came to tell you that Jim is in custody – but he is very ill, ma'am. He is under guard but in the infirmary and if you wish to see him, I suggest you go soon. The doctors think his lungs are severely damaged and he may not have long to live...'

'My poor boy,' Granny Broad screwed up her face, anger and tears mixed as she stared at him. 'And who is to look after them boys now then?' she demanded. 'I'm too old. You never think of folk like us – hauntin' my poor lad until he's nearly done ter death.'

'Your son brought his illness on himself,' the officer replied mildly. 'If he'd given himself up, he would have had care and attention long since...'

'Get out of me 'ouse!' Granny picked up her long-handled broom and shook it in the policeman's direction, though she was too weak to do any damage had he been attacking her.

He looked at her with pity. 'The lads would be best with their mother.'

'That bitch ain't 'avin 'em!' she yelled. 'Now, leave afore I hit yer wiv me broom...'

The young officer went but not without one last sally. 'Tell the boys to visit if they want to see their father alive.'

Granny made a rude gesture at him and he left. She breathed hard and then went to sit down as she fought for air. Her boys were out, the youngest at school, Nobby looking for work. Tears filled her eyes, but she dashed them away as a sign of weakness. Tears never did anyone any good!

Her Jim was dying in the infirmary and she hadn't got long. What was going to happen to them lads?

She knew the police officer was right and that she'd done wrong hiding the letter that had come for Nobby a few days back. It had come from the bitch that had ruined Jim's life, cheating on him while he was fighting the enemy – but perhaps it was the only chance her son's lads had...

Hauling herself to her feet, Granny felt the pain strike at her chest. It was sharper now than ever before. She pulled herself slowly across the kitchen, staying upright with difficulty until she reached the dresser where she'd hidden the letter. She wrenched open the drawer and took out the letter and then gave a terrible cry as the agony seared through her.

Sagging to her knees, she sank to the floor and fell forward, twitching for a few moments before lying still.

She was still lying there face down when Nobby got back later that afternoon and found his young brother trying to wake her.

'Has she fainted?' he asked Robbie, but his brother looked up, distress in his eyes.

'I think she's dead,' he replied. 'She's got a letter for you in her 'and, Nobby. Do yer reckon it's from Ma?'

'It might be,' Nobby said and knelt down by his grandmother. She felt icy to the touch and he recoiled, shocked by his first encounter with death. 'She's gone. I'll fetch the cops. They'll know what to do...'

'Shouldn't we get a doctor?' Robbie asked doubtfully. They looked at each other, shocked and apprehensive.

'It's too late fer that.' Nobby said.

As they looked at each fearfully, uncertain what to do, a knock came at the door and then it opened and someone came in.

Nobby rose to his feet, staring at a man he knew by sight, because he'd been to his builders' yard with his dad, but had never spoken to before. It was Tom Barton of Mulberry Lane, because his father had complained about that bloody Tom Barton after they'd left.

'Me Gran's dead,' Nobby said baldly as Tom Barton looked at him. 'I was just goin' fer the police...'

'Let me see...' Tom knelt down and touched the old lady's face. She'd died in some pain by the look of it. 'Yes, I'm afraid she's gone – so you two can't stay here. I'll take you back with me and we'll call in to the police and let them deal with this.'

'Do yer think someone hurt her?' Robbie asked fearfully.

'Your father has been arrested if that's what you're thinkin',' Tom said, guessing why the boy looked scared. 'Perhaps the news brought on a heart attack – it looks like that to me, but the police may want an autopsy...'

'We'll be all right 'ere.' Nobby said with an attempt at bravado.

'Rose would never forgive me if I left you two alone,' Tom said and smiled at him. 'She's cooking sausages and chips when I get back and I reckon she'll have plenty for you two...'

'Ain't you married to the lady what me dad hurt?' Nobby frowned uncertainly.

'Yes, but she wasn't badly hurt – and she doesn't blame either of you.' Tom waited as the boy digested this. 'I know she'd like you to stay for a while – just until the police sort things out for your gran...'

'He's right, Nobs,' Robbie said. 'We ought ter go – we can't stop 'ere and the cops need ter know.'

'Thank yer, Mr Barton.' Nobby hesitated, and then inclined his head. 'Me Ma's written ter me, so I reckon we'll be going to live wiv 'er soon, but we'll come to yourn tonight and see what she says when she comes ter fetch us. If yer missus doesn't mind...'

'Rose will only mind if I don't bring you,' Tom assured him. 'Is there anything you want to bring with you?' The boys shook their heads. 'We'll get off then. I don't know about you lads, but I'm starvin'.'

31

'No one but you would have taken them in like that,' Tom said, looking at his wife with adoration. 'After the way their father behaved towards you, Rose...What's more, if you hadn't sent me round there to check they were all right, I don't know what would have happened to them with their granny lying there dead on the floor.'

'It was hardly their fault,' Rose said. 'I liked the eldest lad when he served me on the market; he was cheeky but as bright as a button – and his brother is a nice polite boy, nothing like their father.'

'Chalk and cheese,' Tom agreed. 'I'll speak to the local nick later and ask if there was foul play or if their gran died of natural causes – though we know Jim is in custody and I've heard he might be very ill.'

'Half out of his mind with fever so the constable said,' Rose agreed. One of the local officers had called at the house to tell her and she'd told Tom when he got in, making sure Jim's sons didn't hear. Time enough to tell them when they'd settled down a bit. 'I wonder how much of his illness is down to the war, Tom. He blamed his wife for leaving him to go after another man – but Nobby told me he beat her something awful.'

Rose had got over her shock and distress at Jim's sudden assault and could think more clearly. Something had made the man the way he was, though she'd played no part it in and his attitude towards her was irrational. The constable said drink did that to a man and Rose thought he was probably right. For some reason Jim had transferred his resentment to her. It made no sense, but then when your brain was soaked by strong whisky, what did?

'Some of the men came back from the war that way,' Tom agreed. 'Men who never showed any sign of aggression before the war changed completely. I suppose they must be haunted by what happened and the black moods are a result of it – and if his wife cheated him, it may have made him hate all women.'

'It didn't happen to you,' Rose pointed out. 'You fought, Tom, and you were wounded twice – but it didn't change you.'

'No, thank goodness,' Tom said. 'I'd rather top myself than lift a finger to you or the kids – but I think the reason I stayed sane was you, Rose.'

'Me?' she stared in surprise. 'I wasn't even your girlfriend, Tom.'

'That didn't stop me thinking about you or loving you,' he said. 'Even if you hadn't married me, I'd still love you and want you...' He grinned in the way that made her heart race and Rose knew how lucky she was and always had been to know a man like Tom.

'Would you have taken no for an answer?'

'Probably not,' he said and put his arms about her. His eyes dwelled on her with love, more love than she could ever deserve, even though she would strive to in future. 'How could I when I couldn't get you out of my mind?'

'I'm glad I did say yes,' Rose told him. 'Perhaps at the start I wasn't as much in love as you, Tom – but I am now.'

'That's good,' he said and bent his head to kiss her. 'Because I don't know how I'd get through a day without you.'

'Daft!' Rose said, blushing and giving him a little push. 'Go on with you, Tom Barton. I've got work to do before I go to bed.'

'Yes, bringing those kids back for you to feed put you behind,' he said. 'You didn't mind, Rose?'

'I'd have minded if you'd left them to fend for themselves.' Rose gave his arm a squeeze. 'Jenny was a bit suspicious, but Jackie didn't mind – he liked Nobby, because he played with him and his train set...'

'I couldn't have left them alone in that place with their grand-mother dead,' Tom admitted. 'They reminded me of myself and my brother...' Tom's younger brother had been reckless and got in with bad company, which led him to being killed on a bomb site while searching for plunder from a bombed-out jeweller.

'I thought perhaps they did,' Rose said and smiled. She put her arms about his waist and hugged him. 'The work can wait – what if we have an early night?'

The look in her eyes made Tom chuckle. He swept her up in his arms and carried her upstairs. 'I hope those two rascals are asleep,' he murmured, 'because the spare room is too close for comfort and we're not quiet when we make love...'

'After the amount of sausages, chips and fried onions they ate, they will sleep for a week.'

Tom laughed and nodded, carrying her in his strong arms up the stairs and into their bedroom. His Rose was a lovely girl and so sweet and giving that it was no wonder she had him twisted round her little finger.

* * *

Rose lay awake for a while after Tom slept. She reflected that she'd never enjoyed lovemaking as much as that night. Tom was a far more caring, giving lover than Jimmy had ever been, and perhaps that was the first time she'd ever given herself to him completely with no reserve. She wondered if he'd known the difference and what he would think if he had and smiled a little. She'd always considered herself a lucky person and now she understood that she really didn't lack for anything. Tom had filled the empty space in her heart without her truly knowing it was happening.

She snuggled up to his side and breathed in the slightly musky smell of him. Tom always smelled good and he made her feel safe –

safe and happy. Even so, she was pleased that she'd stood up to the bully who had attacked her. It really was the only way. Had she run and let the market men deal with Jim, she would always have been afraid. Seeing him crumble before her and the look of astonishment in his eyes was empowering – and that had helped her to understand herself in a way she never had before. It was the reason she could leave the shadows behind and go forward into the future.

Rose stroked the bare arm of the man she loved and smiled. It was good to know you had a man who loved you and would protect you, but it was even better to know you could look after yourself.

* * *

'Do yer reckon they're asleep now, Nobs?' Robbie asked after the faint noises had stopped in the room next door.

'Yeah, I should fink so,' Nobby said. 'They were at it fer a while – but he didn't 'urt 'er – not the way Dad used ter 'urt Ma.'

'What does Ma's letter say?' Robbie asked, though his brother had told him three times already.

'She's comin' up on the train tomorrow and she wants us to meet her in the market. She said ter bring what we could, but it didn't matter if we couldn't get our stuff 'cos she'll buy us new clothes as soon as we get home.'

'Has she got money now then?' Robbie wrinkled his brow, because he remembered his mother as always being short of a few shillings when it came to buying food and clothes.

'She's got a good job and a place to live,' Nobby said. 'She never went orf to Canada like she told Dad. She just wanted a chance ter get on and make a home and now she has.'

'Will her bloke be there?' Robbie asked warily.

'No, she said he were fer a bit, but then he got fed up wiv the business he was running and wanted 'er ter go back to Canada, but she wouldn't because she wanted ter be near us, so she stayed and now she's managing a shop wiv livin' accommodation over the top and it's near a good school fer you, Rob.'

'I want ter learn proper,' Robbie said with satisfaction. 'I'm glad she didn't go to Canada – but I'd go wiv 'er if she asked...'

'Yeah, I reckon,' Nobby said. 'We'd better get some sleep now – and after breakfast we'll say we're going home, but we'll grab our stuff and go to meet Ma in the market like she said...'

* * *

'Cor, that was smashin',' Robbie told Rose when he'd cleared his plate of the last scrap of toast. 'Yer a good cook, missus – I'd like breakfast like that every day.' His grin brought a smile from Rose, but she didn't answer or offer any more food.

'Do you want me to bring a barrow so you can manage more of your stuff?' Tom asked when the boys told him what they were doing after eating their fill of toast, streaky bacon and scrambled eggs.

'Nah, we don't want much,' Nobby said. 'I reckon they'll clear Gran's stuff out to pay fer the funeral. I don't think she paid in fer it – she thought me dad would pay when she went.'

'Would you like me to organise that for you?' Tom asked. 'The police told me someone needs to be responsible. Have you got any preference, boys?'

'Nah,' Nobby said. 'Just as long as she's buried proper – and if her stuff pays fer it, that's good. If not – I'll earn what's owing when I can.'

'You don't need to worry,' Tom told him. 'I'll make certain it is all done right and if there's anything left over, it will belong to you and Robbie.'

Nobby nodded. 'I dunno know why you're helpin' us, Mr Barton, but yer all right.'

Tom grinned. 'Remember, this is your home until your mother comes for you – and I'm ready to help all I can.'

Nobby shuffled his feet then. A part of him felt bad about sneaking off without telling Tom Barton where he was going, but he knew that folk always interfered and he didn't want anyone to stop them leaving with their mother that afternoon.

* * *

Ginny Barton saw her sons coming towards her and gave a glad cry as she ran to them and threw her arms around the two of them, hugging them as the tears streamed down her face.

'I thought you might have trouble getting away?'

'Nah, Tom Barton didn't suspect nuthin'...'

Nobby nudged his younger brother, but it was too late.

'What is it to do with Mr Barton?' she asked, puzzled. 'I've heard of him, he's the builder from Mulberry Lane and I went to his yard once to ask about a leak in the roof, but yer dad wouldn't let me have it done. No, I didn't mean him; I meant your dad and your gran might try ter stop you.'

'Gran's dead of a stroke and Dad's been arrested – Mr Barton told us he ain't well, might not have got long ter live.' Robbie paused for breath. 'Mr Barton come ter see if we was all right and saw Gran on the floor after she 'ad her attack. I weren't sure what ter do. He took us to the cops ter tell 'em about Gran and then 'ome wiv 'im fer the night and they fed us proper...'

Ginny gasped. 'That's awful! I left your dad because I couldn't take any more of his brutality, but I never wished him harm – and your gran was all right, even though she didn't like me...'

'Dad attacked a woman,' Nobby said. 'It was Mrs Barton – and the police arrested him for it, but he was took bad. I ain't been to see 'im yet 'cos I was afeared the cops would stop us comin' ter you. I should like ter see 'im though – and Rob would too.'

'They won't try to stop you now that I'm on my feet with a home and a good job,' she said and frowned. 'I think I'll visit your dad in the infirmary and you can come too if you want – but before we do that, I'm going to thank Mr and Mrs Barton for looking after you when your gran died.' She put an arm about her younger son's shoulder. 'You can show me where he lives, can't you?'

* * *

Rose looked at the woman with the young boys and then smiled. 'You're their mother – I can see a likeness, to Robbie in particular. Come in and have a cup of tea, please.'

'That is very kind of you, Mrs Barton, but we shan't intrude. I just came to thank you and your husband for your kindness to my boys – all the more so after what Jim did.' She shook her head. 'He can be violent when he's been drinking – he wasn't as bad before the war, but afterwards he'd changed so much that in the end I couldn't live with him. I wanted to take the boys then and leave, but he wouldn't let me. Now I have a good home and a job and I can look after them.'

'I'm glad about that,' Rose said and looked down at Jackie, who was pulling at her skirt. She picked him up, kissing his cheek. 'Tom is arranging your mother-in-law's funeral through the police – and they've agreed her furniture can be sold to pay for it. If that's all right with you, we'll send on any surplus if you leave an address.'

'Thank you, that's real good of you,' Ginny said, smiled and jotted something down on a notepad Rose provided. 'I'd heard Mr Barton was a decent man – one of the real old Londoners. I'd be grateful if you'd go ahead with Mrs Broad's funeral. We never got on and she wouldn't want me clearing her stuff. However, if Jim should die, I'll arrange the burial through the infirmary or the police. I'm still his wife, even though we've lived apart for a few years, and I have some savings.'

Rose nodded her approval. 'I'm glad you've told us, Mrs Broad, otherwise we should've worried about those two.' She smiled. 'You've got two bright lads and I'm sure they will do well now.'

'Yes, we'll be all right now,' Ginny said. 'I'm sorry for what Jim did, Mrs Barton – but he's not fully responsible for his actions. The war did that to him and I suppose I did the rest when I left him...'

'You shouldn't blame yourself too much,' Rose said. 'I would say the war played the biggest part.'

'You may be right – anyway, thanks for what you did.'

'You're welcome.'

Ginny nodded and walked away, leaving Rose gazing after her.

Nobby turned around and grinned. 'We're okay, Missus Barton. We've got Ma now...'

Rose nodded and smiled. Nobby looked happier than she'd ever seen him and Robbie was sticking close to his mother's side. The boys would do all right now and she was pleased they'd been able to help, even if only for a little while.

* * *

'So, she's happy for Mrs Broad's stuff to be sold and the funeral to go ahead,' Rose said when Tom came back from arranging the funeral. 'And she said she'll be arranging the funeral for her husband if he dies, so we can pay anything left over to her and the kids.'

'I wish I'd caught her,' Tom said. 'I'd have saved her a trip to the infirmary. Jim Broad died in the night, peacefully I'm told, so the poor devil is at peace at last.'

'May God take pity on him,' Rose said with a little shudder. 'His wife told me how the war changed him. It was a terrible waste of men's lives, Tom. Not just those who died.' Rose could pity him now that he was no longer a danger to her or the children.

Tom nodded and put his arm about her. 'They're going to clear Mrs Broad's things today and they've paid me seventy-five pounds. She had a nice old oak dresser and a few bits of silver.' He frowned. 'It will pay for the funeral and she doesn't have many debts – a week's rent owing. I've got the book and I'll see it gets paid. There will be at least forty pounds left for the boys and their mother.'

Rose nodded. 'She gave me her address. You can send it to her Tom, with an account of what you've spent out.'

'Will do, as soon as it's all settled,' he said. 'I've decided not to work today, Rose. How about we take Jackie and visit the zoo? We'll pick up Jenny from school later and take them both for ice creams and fish and chips.'

'Tom?' Rose was surprised. He seldom took time off during the week, preferring to work hard for his family. 'That sounds wonderful, but why?'

'Because I love you and the kids – because life is too short and it might have been you dying in the infirmary or me...' He grinned at her. 'Come on, love, let's make the most of it! I've got a job to finish for Peggy, so once I get started, I shan't be able to take a holiday.'

'All right, give me five minutes to find our coats,' Rose said and giggled with excitement. 'Come on, Jackie darling, Daddy is taking us to the zoo.'

32

'You're back then, love.' Peggy had been reading a story in the news-paper about the death of the famous author George Orwell. He'd been too ill to enjoy the success of his wonderful book *Animal Farm* and she felt sorry that such a man hadn't had time to know how much his work was appreciated. However, when the door to the kitchen opened, she looked at her husband expectantly as he entered. He'd been to speak to one of the men who had asked him if he would sell the lease to the café and he'd been confident of getting a straightforward sale. However, she could see from his expression that things hadn't gone just as he'd hoped. 'You didn't sell the lease then?'

'He tried to knock me down by a thousand pounds,' Able said. 'I refused his offer and he said he's not interested at my price.'

'Oh, Able, he told you he really wanted it when he approached you...' Peggy felt disappointed. She'd spent the weekend packing stuff she wanted for London, but what would happen if he couldn't sell the lease to the café?

'That was when I didn't want to sell,' Able told her grimly. 'Now, he thinks he has me over a barrel so he wants to grind me down – but I'm not for grinding. I'll hang on to it for a bit if I have to.'

'But how will you run it if I'm in London?' Peggy's heart sank.

The last thing she wanted was for Able to remain here while she worked in London – all their bright plans to spend more time together would be lost. 'We really needed that sale...'

'Should I have taken his offer?'

Peggy looked at him for a moment and then shook her head. 'No, he was trying to cheat you.' She was silent, then, 'Supposing I asked April if she would consider managing it for us and let her take on her own staff?'

'She could do it,' Able said and looked relieved. 'I suppose one of us would have to come down now and then to see how things were going...'

'It isn't ideal, but it's better than you having to stay here – and it's better than you having to go back and offer that horrid man your business for nothing.'

'Speak to her at work tomorrow,' Able said and sighed. 'Any chance of a cup of coffee and a slice of apple pie, hon?'

'Yes, of course, and it's just fresh from the oven,' she said with a smile. 'Don't worry, Able. We'll work it out somehow – why should you give away what we worked so hard to build?'

Peggy served him coffee and apple pie and sat down with him to enjoy hers. The children were quiet upstairs and she knew they'd rediscovered some of their older toys while packing what they wanted to take with them and were playing board games that made them laugh every now and then. It was time they were in bed, but she was disinclined to harry them. Childhood should be fun and they would find their beds when they were tired.

As the telephone rang, Peggy got up to answer it, expecting it to be Janet. Her daughter rang two or three times a week in the evenings. She was in the middle of packing herself, ready for the move up to Scotland, and excited enough to want to tell her mother all about it.

'Peggy, is that you?' Hearing the voice of April, Peggy frowned. 'I wanted to ask a favour...'

'Of course,' Peggy said instantly. 'If you need a few hours off...'

'No, it's the opposite,' April came back with a laugh. 'I've had a bit of luck – my great aunt left me a few thousand pounds and I wondered... Would you and Able sell me the lease to the café?'

'You know he is asking four thousand pounds?' Peggy said, feeling shocked, because this was the last thing she'd expected. April had been a bit quiet when they'd told her they were selling, but Peggy had thought she was worried about her job. She'd tried to reassure her by saying they would ask whoever took over to keep on the present staff.

'Yes, I know. He told me the price on Friday and that's what gave me the idea – Aunt Mabel left me eight thousand pounds. I can afford the lease and I'll have enough to see me through for a few months until I start to show a profit.'

'Have you thought it through – who you will employ to cook?' Peggy asked, pleased but not wanting to jump in too quickly. She owed it to April to make sure she understood what she was taking on.

'I'll do what Able does,' April said. 'I've watched him often enough and I think he'll give me the recipe for his pancakes?'

'Of course, he would... but there's all the other stuff...'

'My sister is a good plain cook, Peggy, and she wants a little job – and Mum is a terrific cook like you. She would come in for a few hours. I can find women to wash up and to serve – it will be mainly a family thing.' Her voice rose high with excitement. 'Please tell me I'm not too late...'

'Oh no, love, you're not too late,' Peggy said. 'I'm delighted you want to take it over and as far as I'm concerned, it is yours – but I'm going to fetch Able. You need to talk to him, April.'

'Able – come and have a word,' Peggy said, summoning him from the kitchen table. 'It's April and she has a little proposition for you...'

Able came back ten minutes later with a gleam in his eyes.

Peggy was washing up the cups and plates and smiled at him. 'Did you say yes?'

'Of course, I did – and I promised to show her everything. I'll teach her all I've learned, Peggy, and I'll throw in the jukebox that I've ordered. I was going to sell it elsewhere, but since it is April who wants the café, I'm having the jukebox installed for her at no extra charge.'

Peggy knew it had cost him two hundred pounds, so it was a generous gesture and would ensure that the café attracted all the young people that April got on so well with on Saturdays. She might lose one or two older couples on a Saturday, but they would learn to come in on another day. The coffee and pancake trade would probably increase by two or three times its current volume.

'Are you glad you didn't sell it this afternoon now?' Peggy said teasingly and he caught her by the waist and danced her around the kitchen.

She laughed and then caught sight of her young son in his pyjamas. Freddie was watching them and grinning, a picture-perfect version of his dad in a younger form.

'Can anyone join in?' he asked and came to put his arms around them both, giggling as his father whirled them all about the kitchen. 'What's happened, Mum?'

'Your dad sold the lease to April – you like her, don't you?'

Freddie nodded his head and smiled. 'Yeah. She made me a smashing pancake when Dad wasn't looking last Saturday. Filled with blueberries and cream.'

'I wondered where the last of those berries went,' Able said and picked his son up in one arm, laughing. 'I shan't be able to do this soon – especially if you keep stealing my blueberry pancakes.'

'You're all mad.' Fay's voice from the doorway made them all look at her. 'I'm starving, Mum – can I have a slice of apple pie please?'

'Yes, you both can – and then it's off to bed with you,' Peggy said. 'It is school in the morning and just because we'll be moving soon it doesn't mean you can miss it.' She spoke firmly but with a smile on her lips. 'And you'll be starting a new school soon after we move...'

'Come on, Fay,' her twin commanded. 'I'll get the plates and you can bring the pie from the pantry. Mum isn't a servant. We can get our own supper.'

Peggy moved as if she would fetch what they wanted, but Able held her arm. He mouthed the words at her, 'Let them do it.'

Peggy smiled and stood back, watching her son organise their supper. How grown-up he seemed. When had he become the dominant twin? Peggy hadn't noticed it happening. When they were little, Fay always got her own way in everything and Freddie let her – he still did in some things, but, when he spoke with authority in that calm way, his sister took notice.

Fay looked up suddenly. 'Aunty Sheila said I could go up sooner than you if I wanted and stay with her so that I can start my lessons on the ice.' She pulled a face, because Peggy had only found time to take her into Truro once a week since they got home and it wasn't enough for Fay, which was why she was impatient to move.

Peggy nodded. 'Yes, I know – but would you want to do that? It won't be long before we all move – wouldn't you rather wait?'

'I've only been ice-skating three times since we got back,' Fay said, pouting. 'I want to skate every day.'

'If that's what you want,' Able said decisively. 'We'll take you up on Sunday and leave you there.'

'What about the café the next day?' Peggy asked with a frown.

'April wants to have the decorators in and discuss a new colour scheme.' He shrugged his shoulders. 'We'll be back by Tuesday, but she's ready to go on the lease and it will be done and sealed in two weeks at most.'

'So, we're more or less handing over to her?'

'Yes.' Able smiled. 'I'll spend the rest of this week teaching her the ropes and then take next Monday off...'

Peggy nodded. It made sense and she felt relief. As far as she was concerned, the sooner the move came now, the better – even if it would mean rushing Tom. She wouldn't disturb him on a Sunday evening and tell him of their change of plans, but first thing on Monday.

'That's the phone...' Able said and touched her arm. 'Now this time I'm betting it is Janet...'

33

Peggy rang Tom first thing on Monday morning and told him they would be ready to move three weeks earlier than she'd expected. 'Our buyer is very keen,' she said, 'and she has the money in the bank, so there is no bank loan. I know I can't push you to have it all finished – but if you could get the living accommodation done...'

'I've done most of your rooms already,' Tom said, 'but I'll get my men on to it and we'll finish them this week – the bed and breakfast rooms will take a bit longer.'

'That's wonderful, Tom,' Peggy said. 'I shan't mind waiting for them to be finished, because I'll have time to set up, buy bits and pieces – and also to help Sheila and Maureen.' They already had the keys to the bed and breakfast and Able had insured it, even though they hadn't intended to move until the first week or so of March. Now they would be there sometime in February.

'That's great,' Tom said warmly. 'It will be good to have you back, Peggy. We have a lot of catching up to do, but I'll tell you when I see you – I'd better get straight on organising your decorating.'

Peggy smiled as she replaced the receiver. Able came into the hall, carrying her tins filled with the results of her baking. She'd made three apple pies, three Bakewell tarts and three treacle tarts, which should be enough for a Tuesday and the casual visitors who popped in for a coffee and a cake.

'Tom says he'll have our rooms ready on time. The rest will be on schedule – and that gives me time to go visiting and buy whatever I need for the guest rooms.'

'You'll be able to put Janet, Ryan and Maggie up when they stop over in London,' Able said, nodding his approval. 'They won't care if their rooms aren't redecorated. Janet didn't want to go to their flat, because it isn't central...'

Janet had telephoned the previous evening to ask if Peggy thought Sheila was up to having visitors. She and Maggie wanted to take a break in London, before journeying the rest of the way to Scotland on the train. Now, as things had worked out, Peggy was sure she would be able to have her daughter and granddaughter to stay at the bed and breakfast house and that would be a pleasure. It all seemed to be working out well and she felt a flutter of nerves. When things went too well, it sometimes seemed that was exactly when it could all go wrong.

She breathed a silent prayer. 'Please let everyone be well and let nothing go wrong with the plans...'

* * *

Fay went down with a cold that week and was in bed over the weekend, which meant that they couldn't go up to deliver her to her Sheila's care. However, she was feeling too sorry for herself to mind and didn't even plague her mother to take her to the ice rink. Fortunately, the rest of the family stayed clear of the sickness and Fay went back to school for her last few days at the end of the following week. She and Freddie came into the café that Friday afternoon and burst into tears, Fay was so upset that even the comfort of one of her father's special pancakes couldn't cheer her up.

'What's wrong?' Peggy asked her. 'Was someone unkind to you at school?'

Fay shook her head miserably. 'They all hugged me and kissed me and cried and said they didn't want me to leave...'

'Oh, is that all?' Peggy hid her smile of relief. 'Saying goodbye to friends is always hard, Fay. It was the same for me when we left Mulberry Lane – and I missed them, but I wrote to them, talked to them on the phone and saw them at holiday times. And I made new friends – besides, think of what the future holds for you, and you will still have us and Freddie.'

'Yes, I know.' Fay sniffed and then looked at her father speculatively. 'Can I have another pancake with cream, honey and nuts this time please?'

'I don't see why not,' Able said and looked at April. 'Why don't you make pancakes for us all?'

'Love to,' she said and grinned. 'If I can please your kids and Peggy, I've got no worries.'

They laughed and went to sit down, waiting for April to make her mix and whip the cream before placing their favourite flavourings in front of them.

Fay and Freddie scoffed theirs. Peggy and Able ate slowly, tasting and considering before passing a verdict.

'I think you're about ready to go,' Able said. He smiled at her in his easy way that made him so popular with the customers. 'We shall be at the cottage until Wednesday, April. Closing up and packing the last of the stuff we need to take with us – so if you need us...'

'I'll shout,' she said but looked confident. 'On Monday the decorators start. I'll be open again on Tuesday, but I'll have a new menu – though I'll be keeping the pancakes.'

Peggy nodded. 'I would do the same, April. We all have our favourites.' She got up to hug her. 'That was a delicious treat – almost as good as Able's and that's high praise. I wish you all the luck in the world.'

'Peggy is prejudiced in my favour,' he said, smiling at them both. 'The pancake you made me was spot on, April. I couldn't do better myself.'

'Then I'm happy,' she said, looking at their faces. 'I am going to miss you all – but I'm excited.'

'That's as it should be,' Peggy assured her and then turned to Fay. 'It's how you should be feeling, darling – a little sad to leave friends but excited for the future.'

Fay nodded and then giggled. 'I am, Mum – but I shall miss Carrie and Silvia.' They were her special friends at school and she'd suddenly woken up to the fact that she wouldn't be seeing them in future.

'Then you can write to them and visit when we come down for holidays,' Peggy said and looked at her son.

Freddie hadn't said a word, but she saw a sadness in his eyes that wouldn't be erased by another pancake. It had cost her son dear to give up his football clubs and his friends, but he hadn't complained and he wouldn't. Freddie had accepted the move for his twin's sake and he would make new friends... slowly. It was a good thing he had Chris in London, because even though Pip's son was younger, they got on well – both of them serious and thoughtful boys.

'All right, love?' she asked softly and he smiled.

'I'm fine, Mum. Don't worry about me. Pip has promised to help me get a season ticket for Arsenal – it's only a part of the year, of course, but it should be fun. Dad wants to go to the matches as much as I do.'

'Yes, your dad will take you.' She smiled and squeezed his shoulder. Freddie was her special one, perhaps because she'd come close to losing him when he was born. Or perhaps it was because of his lovely nature – he was just so much like his father that when he smiled it made her heart catch.

34

Maureen shook her head over the final death toll for the crew of HMS Truculent, the submarine that had been accidentally rammed and sunk in the Thames Estuary in January 1950. Sixty-four men had lost their lives, despite the efforts of the Navy's top divers to attempt a rescue, which was a terrible waste of life and an awful way to die. On top of India becoming a republic and severing ties with Britain and that dreadful murder, where the body of a man called Stanley Setty had been dumped from a light aircraft over the Essex marshes, it had been a turbulent month.

She put the newspaper aside with a little shiver as the kitchen door opened and her daughter entered the kitchen that afternoon.

'Did Richard get off all right?' Maureen asked her. 'Was he pleased that we said you could go on that working holiday in the summer?' Richard had come down for a flying visit over the week-end, surprising Shirley and his family and Maureen had seen the happiness in her daughter's face when she'd opened the door to him.

'Yes, to both questions,' Shirley said and beamed at her mother. 'I know I have you to thank for getting Dad's permission to go – and please don't worry, Mum. I shan't let you down.'

'You could never let me down, Shirley love,' Maureen said, smiling at her fondly. 'Whatever happens in your life, I shall always be here for you. I want you to know that and be sure of it. Your dad has his pride and men are a bit touchy where their precious daughters are concerned – but he loves you more than you could ever imagine.'

Shirley rushed at her and hugged her tightly. 'You really are the best mum in the world – do you know that?'

Maureen laughed and hugged her back. 'You're the best daughter, I know that – and now you can set the table for tea if you will, love. I've got a bit of baking to finish off and then your dad will be coming home for his meal.' She smiled at her daughter. 'I was a bit late with my work because I put the wireless on and sat with Matty to listen to that new children's programme on the BBC – *Listen with Mother...*'

'Was it good?' Shirley asked.

'I think Matty enjoyed it,' Maureen said. 'It was a nice story, but he likes the illustrations in his books best, so he enjoys the stories I read while he looks at the pictures.'

'Perhaps they will put something like it on the television one day,' Shirley suggested. 'He could watch it then while you got on with your baking.'

Maureen nodded. 'I suppose so. It was a lovely present, Shirley, and must have cost your dad a pretty penny – but I'm not sure I know how to work it properly.'

Shirley smiled fondly. 'It's easy, Mum. I'll show you. When I told my friends at school about it, they were all envious – but I'm a bit like you, there isn't much on I really want to see.'

'I suppose we're lucky to have broadcasts in London,' Maureen admitted. 'Peggy is looking forward to having a TV – they couldn't get it down there at all.'

'They've only just started transmitting to the Midlands, but we're lucky in London, we get most things first – and if they start putting on more good films, as they've promised, you'll be glad Dad bought it for you.'

'I'd like to see that new film at the cinema. It's called *The Blue Lamp* and it's about a police officer called PC George Dixon I read in the paper where the critics say it will have us all queuing up to see it...'

'You should treat yourselves when it comes here,' Shirley said. 'I'll look after Gordy and Matty.'

'You're a lovely girl,' Maureen said fondly. 'I'm glad you're my daughter, Shirley.'

* * *

Maureen watched her daughter as she finished her homework and then went up to bed with a book. There was a change in Shirley. She'd seen it coming at Christmas and this last visit from Richard had completed the change. Shirley was grown-up, a young woman not a child. Maureen didn't think the two youngsters had become lovers yet, but she expected it would happen soon. They were in love and passions ran high when you were young.

For herself she'd never had the time or the inclination at Shirley's age. Maureen's mother had been an invalid during her teenage years and she'd spent much of her time looking after her or serving in her father's grocery shop. When she had fallen in love, she'd been denied her chance of marriage until later when her father had married again.

Gordon was her second lover and he'd become her everything. She hadn't thought she would love Gordon so passionately when she agreed to wed him, but his kindness, tenderness and love had deserved a response and she'd found it was easy to love him. Yet Maureen understood that a young girl might want to make love before marriage, even though it wasn't wise or sensible. She'd done her best to warn Shirley of the pitfalls and, to be truthful, she wasn't too worried because she knew Richard would marry Shirley if anything happened. He was obviously in love with her.

Maureen offered a silent prayer that the young couple would be sensible during the long summer holidays. She wanted Shirley to achieve her ambition to become a doctor and she wanted Gordon to be proud of his daughter. However, she'd made sure

Shirley understood that she would always support her whatever happened.

Was she wrong to be so liberal in her views? Having a child before marriage was still frowned on in the lanes and the gossips loved to point the finger of shame, but Maureen couldn't condemn what she knew was natural and had happened to so many young girls in the last war. She wouldn't encourage it and Shirley knew that, but she would still be there to love and support her if the worst happened – and when young folk were in love, well, accidents happened, didn't they?

'You're thoughtful this evening?' Gordon put his arm about Maureen's waist. 'Have I done something to upset you – or are you just thinking about your Peggy coming back to the lane?'

Maureen laughed at the teasing note in his voice and put her concerns for Shirley out of her mind. 'She will be here by the end of the week,' she said, smiling at him and moving in for a kiss. 'I am happy she's coming, Gordon, but I was just as happy, watching little Gordy's reaction to the animals at the zoo when we took him. He loved the monkeys and the elephants. I want to buy him a toy elephant, Gordon. He was so fascinated by them. I should think Hamleys will have them if I go up to the West End.'

'Yes, I expect so – and Gordy did love them,' Gordon said. 'I think it was because the keeper put him up on her back. He called her Nellie and she tucked away a fair few bananas while we watched.'

'Yes, she did,' Maureen said. 'I know he'd like a puppy or a kitten of his own, but I worry about pets in town – there's nowhere they can run free safely.'

'No, that's why I've said we shouldn't buy a dog,' Gordon agreed. 'They need a good place to run and you can only do that in the country.' He looked at her thoughtfully. 'What do you think to a pet rabbit? We could have a hutch in the back yard and Gordy could pet a rabbit safely – if you don't mind him bringing it in to the kitchen sometimes?'

'Rabbits don't make a lot of mess,' Maureen said. 'Yes, why not? He can have a cardboard box with some straw in his bedroom – and the rabbit can go in the hutch some of the time and come in at others.'

'You're a lovely woman,' Gordon said and kissed her, his eyes meeting hers teasingly. 'I suppose there's no chance of an early night?' It was his way of letting her know he wanted to make love to her.

Maureen smiled and moved closer, a little smile on her lips. 'You're a lovely man, Gordon Hart, and I'm glad I married you. Come on, let's go up – I don't think we'll bother with cocoa tonight.'

35

'Right, you two,' Peggy said, looking round at the children as they scrambled into the back seat that Friday evening. They were going to drive through the night while the roads were quieter and stop for drinks, food and perhaps have a sleep if they found somewhere safe to park up for a while. Able suggested they might stop somewhere and take a room if they all felt too tired, but he wanted to keep going if they could manage it. 'Have you got all you wanted – nothing forgotten? We shan't be down for at least a month or two, so if you haven't got everything, it will wait until we come for a visit.'

'I packed all my things into the tea chest you sent up by carrier,' Freddie said. 'I don't need anything I've left in my room.'

'Good – what about you, Fay? Did you pack the dolls and games you want?'

'I don't play with dolls much now,' Fay said grandly. 'I'll be too busy with my ice-skating lessons.'

Peggy nodded as Able got into the car beside her. 'Everything off, locked and done?'

'Yes – but Ken will be checking once a week for us,' Able said. 'He offered when I told him I was still looking for a caretaker. He will ask around, and, if he finds someone, I'll pop down and fix it up. Sandra is busy looking after her father – and her mother will be coming home soon.'

'Yes, I know,' Peggy said. 'She told me that Ken had suggested they have an extension built so they can have her parents with them and look after them. The old family house can be sold and the money invested in case they need more care in future – but Sandra thinks she will manage once her mother is home.'

'They were lucky she pulled through – that heart attack might have killed her.'

'She'd just been doing too much, carrying the burden alone, but now she has Sandra and Ken to help her and together they can keep Sandra's father happy. He just needs a lot of attention.'

Able smiled at her. 'She told me you'd helped her just by talking things through calmly. She panicked at first, as anyone might.'

Peggy nodded and looked at the twins. 'We're off then. I hope Tom got our room finished. He said it was nearly done when I rang and I didn't push him, because he's so good.'

'I'm sure he will have finished if he promised he would,' Able said. He looked round at his children. 'We'll stop for something to eat at that nice little café we used at Christmas for breakfast – all right?'

'Yes, please, Dad,' Freddie said. 'I want egg and chips please. They don't cook them like Mum does, but they're all right with lots of tomato sauce.'

'I want a milkshake and an iced bun,' Fay chimed in and her father frowned.

'You can have the milkshake, but you need to eat a proper meal, Fay – and don't pull a face at me. If you don't eat the right things – and that includes greens and fruit – you won't be strong enough to skate professionally.'

Fay looked at him in a considering way for a moment and then smiled. 'All right, Daddy. I'll have egg and chips like Freddie with a tomato – and then an iced bun.'

Able shot Peggy an amused glance and saw the slight shake of her head. Wisely, he didn't argue. He would order egg and chips all round and make sure it was eaten and then see if the children wanted the sweet things after. They had been spoiled a little because the sweet treats were always on offer at the café, but they were growing up now and it was time to make sure they ate properly rather than just choosing the pancakes he made so delicious that one was never enough, for his customers and his children alike…

* * *

It was nearly dusk on Saturday before they reached Mulberry Lane after stopping several times for meals, drinks of tea and fizzy lemonade for the children and one long rest where they all went to sleep in the car. The journey had been quiet and relatively easy, Peggy and Able sharing the driving between them and not needing to seek out a room. Because they'd driven through the night, there wasn't as much traffic on the roads and they'd made good time, the long journey tiring but not as exhausting as it might have been had they not stopped for comfort breaks.

Peggy stood outside the door of the bed and breakfast looking at it. It had enough rooms to be called a boarding house or a small hotel, but she didn't want to run it as a hotel, because that involved too much work. Keeping it to bed and breakfast, with some visitors choosing the evening meal option, would give them more time to themselves. Now that she was here, she felt her stomach spasm with nerves. It had been a huge decision and she'd plunged into it without giving it much thought – had she made a big mistake? For a moment she wanted to turn around and drive straight back to the cottage.

'Looks good, doesn't it, hon?' Able's arm about her waist steadied her. 'You can smell the paint. Tom has been busy.'

Peggy realised that all the windows and doors had been painted outside. She hadn't expected that much to be finished. She hoped he'd finished inside first.

Able unlocked the door with his key and they all went in, switching on the lights as they went. Everywhere smelled of fresh paint and glue. New wallpaper had been hung in the downstairs hall and it looked really bright and welcoming. Able was bringing in the various cases and baskets, dumping them in the hall.

'I'll carry some upstairs to our rooms, Dad,' Freddie offered and picked up two heavy baskets. He struggled manfully upstairs with them and dumped them on the landing, before running down the hall to his own room. 'My packing case is here...' The larger items had been sent on by carrier a couple of days ahead of them and his voice floated back down the stairs to Peggy, who had stopped staring and picked up a suitcase to take up herself.

She walked to Freddie's room and looked in. Tom had painted it in the blue and white colours her son had chosen, fitting the shelves he'd wanted for his sports trophies and his model cars.

'If you leave the chest for the morning, your dad will open it for you,' Peggy said. 'This is your case. You can unpack that tonight.'

'Thanks, Mum. I'll go back and see what else I can carry up for Dad.'

'Good boy.'

Peggy wandered back down the landing to her kitchen. She opened the door and went in, smelling the freshness of paint and cleaning fluid. Someone had put milk in her refrigerator and fresh bread was in the enamel bin on the new pine dresser she'd ordered. Tom must have seen all her things in, just as he'd promised.

She'd bought a new kettle and that stood ready to use. Filling it with water, Peggy looked about her with satisfaction. At the moment it looked bare and not a bit like home, but she would soon have her things unpacked and that would make it feel right.

The hollowness she'd experienced outside was receding. As Able had told her the previous night, they still had the cottage and would visit when they had time – but this was a new adventure. Peggy was back in Mulberry Lane, but not in her pub. She was the landlady of a bed and breakfast house. It would involve some cooking but she would have time for helping Sheila and Maureen – and for taking her children where they wanted to go. She would also be surrounded by friends and suddenly it felt like coming home.

Able came into the kitchen carrying a box filled with stuff she'd

brought from the cottage – foodstuffs, spices and cooking ingredients. He grinned at her. 'It will be better when we can smell apple pie
rather than paint – but it's nice, Peggy. Tom has done a lovely job for
us.' He placed a sheaf of envelopes on the table. 'I found these in the
letter rack downstairs – they're mostly for you...'

Peggy looked at what were obviously cards and smiled. She
wouldn't mind guessing that they were welcome home cards from
Maureen, Alice, Sheila and a whole lot of others in the lanes.

'We're home, Able,' she said and the relief surged through her. 'I
wasn't sure – right up to the moment I came in here, but now I know.
We've done the right thing.'

'Of course, we have,' he said and grinned, aiming a kiss at her
cheek and finding her lips. 'It's going to be an adventure, hon – fun
for the kids and for us. We'll be busy and yet we'll have more time
than we did running the café – and I'm looking forward to it.'

Peggy laughed, looking up at him with love. How could she have
doubted even for a moment? It didn't matter where they were, as
long as they were all together. If she had Able and her children, she
was home. She could even hear the voices of people calling to each
other as they entered the Pig & Whistle. Peggy wouldn't go in this
evening; she wanted to get some of their things straight and the
morning would do to check up on her friends and Sheila's family.

* * *

'I couldn't wait to come and have a look,' Maureen said as she arrived
the next morning, a pretty vase of cut flowers in her arms. 'Happy
homecoming, Peggy. I'm so glad you're back... Besides, I'm nosey. I've
been wanting to look around, but Tom wouldn't let us. He said you
had to be the first, so he kept all the doors locked. I tried to peek
when some stuff was delivered, but he wouldn't let me...'

Peggy laughed and took the vase, sniffing the flowers. She hugged
her friend and thanked her. 'Tom has made a wonderful job – and
he's done everything, even downstairs. He kept telling me it wouldn't
be quite finished, but it is.'

'Tom likes to tease,' Maureen said. 'He's been a different man since all that trouble after Christmas. Once the police arrested that awful man, he and Rose took the kids in for a night – did he tell you what happened?'

'No – not a word, tell me.' Peggy gasped as the story unfolded. 'Well, I'm glad their mother turned up to take them home with her.' She smiled at Maureen comfortably, because it was just like old times. 'Let's have a cup of tea and then I'll show you all over the place.'

'Yes, I told Gordon I'll be an hour or so and then I'll get dinner ready.'

Peggy nodded. 'I'll need a couple of days to get sorted and then I'll be helping you with the cooking for the cakes. Is Sheila all right?'

'She seems fine to me,' Maureen said and smiled. 'Pip watches her like a hawk but I think she is blooming.'

'Good – let's hope it continues that way,' Peggy said. 'It was about the seventh month when she got ill last time, so Pip is right to watch – but we'll all be here to keep an eye on her and see she comes to no harm if we can help it.'

Maureen nodded. 'Gordon has been teasing me for days. He says I'm like a kid at Christmas because you're coming back.'

'I'm glad to be back,' Peggy said and knew she meant it. 'I think we're all going to have a lot of fun.'

Maureen nodded and sat down at the table as Peggy made the tea. It was as if the years between had never been and nothing had changed. 'When is Janet coming to stay?'

'At the end of next week,' Peggy told her. 'They are sending all their personal stuff up to a house Ryan has hired in Scotland and they're going to rent their house out for a few years.'

'Rent their lovely house?' Maureen looked shocked. 'No, really? I don't think I could do that if I had a home like Janet's.'

'She was a bit dubious, but Ryan thought it was sensible. What they don't need in Scotland will be stored and their home will be let unfurnished – so no one will use their things.'

'Even so...' Maureen shook her head. 'You didn't think of doing it with the cottage?'

'No, not once,' Peggy said. 'Able asked a friend to look after it until we can find someone permanently – and he'll either pay him something or buy him a gift every now and then. We'll go down for a weekend sometimes, once we're organised and have things up and running.'

'That's a good idea,' Maureen said. 'Will you find someone to run the bed and breakfast while you're away?'

'Yes, I shall try to get someone who can do the breakfasts and Tom has already offered to be on hand to make sure he can put things right if any problems crop up. Rose says she doesn't mind giving me a hand in reception now and then and I'll get an assistant on a regular basis once we're up and running properly.'

'I was going to tell you – Dot's daughter is looking for a job. She says that Pearl is a good worker and only got the sack from her office because she had to take a few days off to look after her daughter – Pearl is a single mum. Her husband was killed in the war and she has one daughter, Jane, who is a teenager and prone to colds and bouts of tonsillitis.'

'Poor Jane,' Peggy said sympathetically. 'You tell Dot to send Pearl to see me. If she doesn't mind mixing office work with reception and a bit of waiting at table for breakfast, she sounds ideal for me. I'll be able to trust her to look after things while we're away, and Jane can help out too sometimes, if she wants.'

Maureen nodded thoughtfully. 'I told Dot you'd say that and she says Pearl would jump at the chance to work here. She needs an understanding boss who won't sack her if she can't come in once in a while.'

'Good grief, no,' Peggy said. 'We all have to make allowances for children being unwell. There were days when I couldn't get to the café and then Able and one of my staff managed alone. I pre-baked apple pies and cakes and it was just the salads and things like ham and chips they had to cope with. Of course, Able usually managed to persuade the customers to try the pancakes...'

'He wouldn't need to persuade me,' Maureen said. 'The cherry and almond cream he put in mine last time I was visiting with you was so delicious. I had withdrawal symptoms when I got home.'

'Yes, I love that one too,' Peggy smiled. 'Until Able showed me what he made I'd never thought of adding more than lemon and sugar to pancakes.'

'It's traditional,' Maureen agreed, 'but we didn't know what we were missing.'

'He's talking about offering a variation at breakfast for our customers,' Peggy said and laughed softly. 'It will be interesting to see how many would go for pancakes with maple syrup, cream and nuts rather than bacon, egg and fried bread.'

Maureen sighed. 'My mouth is watering. I could just eat one of those right now – but I'm not sure which I'd choose first thing in the morning.'

Peggy nodded and sipped her tea. 'I know which the kids would go for given the choice – but I'm not sure about my travelling salesmen.'

'Is that who you think will stay here?'

'I imagine so. When we did bed and breakfast at the Pig & Whistle, it was always men who travelled for their work.'

'I think you'll find things have changed a bit since then,' Maureen said. 'In the summer last year, they had families staying here – tourists from abroad and people who came to London to see a show and couldn't afford the posh hotel prices.'

'That sounds even more interesting,' Peggy said. 'It looks as if Able might win the little bet we had after all...'

Maureen looked puzzled, so Peggy explained.

'He thinks we'll get a more varied clientele than I expected.'

'Able is right,' Maureen said. 'Your husband has a business head on him, Peggy.'

'Yes, he has,' Peggy agreed. 'I thought we might need to sell the house he bought after the war and so we had it valued – it has more than doubled what he paid.'

'Are you selling it?'

'No – we sold the lease for what Able wanted so we don't need to,' Peggy said. 'He bought the lease here and we've spent a bit on freshening it up – but otherwise we're all right. We're not rich, but we don't want for anything...' She nodded and then changed the subject, bringing up the election; she'd been listening to the results on the wireless the last few days. 'I didn't like them putting Churchill out in the election after the war after all he did for us, but we've done all right under Labour – What do you think of the results this time?'

'Gordon says he thought it would be a tight squeeze.' Maureen shrugged. 'I don't suppose it makes much difference to us, though Gordon grumbled when they devalued the pound last year. It made everything dearer for people. Our customers kept coming, but some of them had to cut down on their orders.'

Peggy nodded thoughtfully. 'I think most folk in work are better off than we were before the war. I know we are, but I'm not sure how much of that is down to Able's ability to run a business or the change in society since Labour got in.' She frowned. 'Alice is feeling the pinch – I'm going to do what I can for her and old Mr Giddings, too.'

'We're about the same as you, better off than we were,' Maureen said. 'Gordon makes a decent living from the shop – far more than my father ever did – and I earn a few pounds to spend on the kids, but I know of a family around the corner that could do with some help. I took them a few bits from the shop at Christmas, made out they'd won a special prize by being the seventieth customer that week. Ruby pretended she believed me. Her husband would refuse charity, that's why I had to make up the story of the raffle.' She looked thoughtful, then, 'Did Sheila tell you what we'd decided?'

Peggy shook her head. 'I haven't seen her this morning. I thought she might pop in, but she hasn't yet.'

'We thought you might take a third share partnership in the tea shop – split the work and the profits between us.'

'You don't need to do that,' Peggy said. 'I'll be glad to help for nothing.'

'I'm sure we'll—' Maureen began but got no further as they heard feet pounding up the stairs and a woman rushed into Peggy's kitchen. 'What is wrong, Dot?' Maureen was on her feet at once. 'Sheila...'

'Took bad she is...' Dot said, gasping for breath. 'I didn't want ter leave her, but she told me to come and fetch Peggy.'

'I'm coming now,' Peggy said and reached for her thick cardigan, pulling it on over her dress and apron. 'Tell me, Dot, what was wrong with her?'

'She looked proper queer and then she fainted,' Dot said. 'Knocked her mixing bowl on the floor and smashed it.'

Peggy nodded, her heart racing as she ran down the stairs and out of the back door, through the side passage and into the lane, Maureen pounding behind her. She hurried under the arch to the pub yard and in through the stable door, which was opened at the top to let in the air. Sheila was sitting in a wooden armchair by the fire looking pale but otherwise fine.

She looked at Peggy apologetically. 'I'm sorry, Mum. I fainted and because Pip is so worried about me, I panicked and sent Dot for you...'

'No apology necessary,' Peggy said and smiled at her. 'I'm glad it was just a faint – but we're going to let Maureen take over the baking this morning and I'm taking you to the A & E at the hospital.'

'I'm fine now,' Sheila protested.

'Good – but we're still going to the hospital, just to let them check you over, love.' Peggy put a firm hand on her arm. 'I'll get the car out and take you myself – where is Pip?'

'He took Chris to an exhibition of old cars somewhere.

'Right, I'm not taking no for an answer.'

'All right,' Sheila agreed and smiled at her. 'It did make me feel pretty groggy for a while, I must admit.'

'Better to be safe than sorry,' Peggy said. 'I know how much this baby means to you, Sheila – and how much you mean to Pip and Chris.'

Sheila nodded and made no further protest as Peggy fetched her coat and borrowed one of her jackets for herself.

'What about lunch?' she asked. 'I may not be back in time to get it...'

'Able will put the casserole I made in the oven – there's enough for your family as well as mine. Stop worrying and look after yourself, Sheila...'

'Thanks, Mum, but I'll tell Pip I felt a bit faint and that's why you invited us over. I don't want to lie to him.'

Peggy nodded and took her daughter-in-law's arm. Had she not been next door, Sheila wouldn't have let anyone take her to the hospital, because she would have carried on and cooked dinner. She was too stubborn to give in, but this way she had no excuses left.

36

'You needn't have come down just to take us up to London,' Janet said to Ryan the following Friday night. 'You've spent hours on the train all the way from Scotland and I could have managed.'

'I didn't want to leave the move entirely to you, it wouldn't be fair,' Ryan said and put his arms about her, kissing her softly on the lips. 'I almost lost you, Jan. I thought our marriage might be over – travelling down to see you safely to your mother's is nothing.'

She lifted her face for his kiss and felt the sting of tears. 'I thought so too before Christmas – that was a magical holiday, Ryan. I hope Maggie won't be disappointed when she sees her new home,'

'Oh, I don't think so,' Ryan said with a secret little smile. 'I think you're both going to love our new house, Jan.'

'Well, I suppose a modern place will be nice,' she agreed, though privately she'd been a bit disappointed with Ryan's choice. It looked like a soulless modern-built house on the edge of a village – practical, as he'd told her when she asked why he'd chosen it, but not pretty or romantic.

'Yes, I think you'll be pleasantly surprised,' he said and the twinkle in his eye increased her suspicions.

'What are you up to, Ryan?'

'You'll see next weekend,' he said and shook his head. 'You'll get no more out of me, Jan – you have to wait and see.'

She looked at him, but he was so pleased with himself that she couldn't get cross, although why he imagined that she would like a red-bricked semi on the edge of a village, she had no idea. They'd been so much happier since Christmas. She'd thought he would know she would hate a house like that but didn't want to argue again. Perhaps it was all he could find to rent, and she cared more about being with him in Scotland than the actual house. They could always get out for long walks and visit the hotel they'd all loved. 'As long as we're together more that is all that matters,' she said and smiled. 'Maggie is so excited – about visiting London with her gran for a week and then Scotland...'

'I'm excited too,' he said. 'Shall we get an early night so we can get up early and be ready for the removals van?'

'Yes, that's what I'd planned,' she said and put her arms around him. 'I'm glad you came – I just think it was a long way on the train for you.'

'I'm here now and the service from London is quicker and easier. That's why I'm glad you're breaking your journey with Maggie. I'll come to London with you, leave you and catch a train back, and then I'll be waiting for you when you arrive in Scotland.'

* * *

'How lovely to see you all. I didn't expect Ryan too,' Peggy said as she welcomed them to her new home. 'It's fine, though. I've got a spare room for Maggie – and you've got my best guest room, Jan. You can tell me what you think of it in the morning.'

'Something smells good,' Ryan said as they followed Peggy upstairs. 'What have you been cooking?'

'Able is cooking pancakes,' she said and laughed over her shoulder. 'He's working on a new recipe and the kids are testing it out for him. Chris is here as well, even though it's long past his bedtime. Sheila is having a rest this week...'

'She isn't ill, is she?' Janet asked, frowning.

'No, just a little tired. The doctor said she needs to rest for a week and then halve her working hours. He hasn't asked her to stop – just to rest in the afternoons. So, I'll be helping with the baking and my new assistant will take a turn in the tea shop for a few afternoons a week. We've got it all worked out.'

'New assistant?' Janet stared. 'You move fast, Mum. I thought you would hardly be settled in yet.'

'Pearl needed the right sort of job and I needed the right sort of young woman,' Peggy told her. 'She is Dot's daughter – Dot works with Maureen and Sheila, washing up and helping generally, but her daughter is a trained typist and bookkeeper. However, she doesn't mind what she does as long as it fits in with looking after her daughter.'

'Another of your lame ducks, Mum?' Janet asked with a shake of her head.

'Far from it,' Peggy said. 'I think Pearl will turn out to be a treasure. I like her a lot and she can do a lot of things I really need help with.'

'So, you're happy with the move then?'

'Very much – what about you?' Peggy asked when they were alone in the bedroom she'd prepared for them. Ryan had paused on the landing to talk to the children and she'd sensed something wasn't quite right.

'I had a bit of a pang when all our stuff was moved out and I handed the keys over to the estate agent. He's arranging a clean and the tenants move in next week. I hope they will love our house.'

'No one could live in that house and not love it.'

'No.' Janet looked at her mother and then the words came rushing out of her, 'I want to move to Scotland to be near Ryan, Mum – but I don't like the house he's chosen. It is modern and it looks soulless...' She sighed. 'I didn't want to complain. It's probably all there was close to his work...and we're only renting so I suppose we can move if we find something better...'

'Have you told Ryan how you feel?'

'No – I didn't want to spoil things. We've been happier recently. If I start questioning and moaning...'

Peggy nodded. 'Wait and see, love. It may be better than you think.'

'Let's hope so.' Janet agreed. 'At least we've got a week with you before we get there and I've been looking forward to it, Mum. We haven't spent enough time together these past years.'

* * *

'I've just seen an advert for tickets for the World Ice Skating Championships next month and I'm going to try and buy some,' Able said as he brought the newspaper in that morning. He liked to walk to the corner and fetch it, chatting with everyone he met and Gordon at the shop, before bringing it back. Glancing at Janet standing in the hall with Maggie, Peggy and her suitcase, he smiled. 'You're ready to leave then – it doesn't seem five minutes since you got here.'

'We enjoyed it,' Janet said and smiled at him. 'But Ryan will be waiting for us. I've told Mum I'll try and get down later in the year – stay for a couple of weeks.'

'You know you'll always be welcome to stay here,' Able nodded at Janet as they heard the taxi she'd booked to take her to the station draw up and hoot outside in the street. 'This is your second home – and we love having you and Maggie.' He smiled at the little girl and then slipped her a ten-shilling note. 'Pocket money for the journey.'

'Thank you.' she said and went to hug him.

'Thank you, Able,' Janet said and she too hugged his arm. 'I've not always been sure of the things Mum has chosen to do these past years – but marrying you was the best decision she ever made.'

'Thank you, Janet,' he said and smiled at her in his easy way. 'I love Peggy more than I can ever say – and in my opinion Ryan feels the same about you. Be happy, Janet – and believe in your husband. If you do, you'll have a great life together.'

'Yes.' Janet looked at him. 'I think so too – and I've got something to tell you and Mum, but I need to tell Ryan first.'

Able nodded. 'We're on the telephone – and only a train ride away.'

Janet nodded and turned as her mother came downstairs to say goodbye. She was carrying a small basket packed with food for them to eat on the train.

'Have a good journey, love, and don't be too disappointed in the house,' Peggy said. 'I'm sure it can't be too bad or Ryan wouldn't have taken it.'

'No, of course not,' Janet said and hugged her. She held out her hand to Maggie, who was whispering to Fay. 'Come along, darling. We need to catch our train.'

* * *

'Where are we going?' Janet glanced at Ryan as he drove them away from the station. At first, she thought she recognised some of the scenery from their holiday at Christmas, but then she realised she hadn't been this way before and it was all different. Ryan turned off and followed a long winding road that travelled for ages through a deep valley and out the other side. She could see mountains topped by clouds in the distance and there were thick woods covering some of the slopes. 'It is very beautiful here – but it seems a bit remote...'

'We're about an hour and a half or so from Edinburgh,' Ryan told her. 'There's a decent-size village with shops, Jan, and a train station. So, if you want to shop in town, you don't have to drive; you just hop on the train.'

'But where...?' she asked as she saw a village that boasted a high street, two public houses, a hotel and a shop or two.

Ryan drove straight through and down another narrow road for some minutes, and then turned into an impressive gateway.

'Are we going to a hotel?'

She was puzzled as she looked about her. Ryan was grinning like the Cheshire cat and Maggie pointed through the window excitedly.

'Is that a castle, Daddy?'

Glancing through the trees, Janet could see the imposing turrets of a castle before Ryan turned left and stopped – outside a wonderful old thatched cottage.

'This is your new home,' he said. 'It's the lodge keeper's cottage and belongs to the Laird McPhee; it has been a holiday let – but he was looking for a long-term lease to help his finances and was happy to rent it to me for five years...'

'Ryan!' Janet stared in amazement at the beautiful old house. It was like something off a picture postcard and she couldn't believe it would be her home for the next five years or so. 'How did you find such a wonderful place – and why did you show me that awful modern house?'

Ryan laughed in delight. 'I wanted to surprise you, Jan – and it was Maggie's friend Angus who told me about this place. He is the Laird's cousin and knew it was standing empty.'

Janet helped Maggie out of the car and picked up a basket of supplies from the back seat, but she couldn't wait to get inside, her heart beating wildly with excitement as Ryan unlocked the door. Someone had lit a fire in the cosy parlour, where their furniture fitted perfectly. A vase of fresh spring flowers stood on a table by the fire and there was a plate of delicious-looking scones with a bottle of malt whisky waiting on the sideboard.

'Who baked these?' Janet said, lifting the plate to sniff the gorgeous aroma of fresh baking.

'That was the Laird's wife, Mairie,' Ryan told her. 'She does tours of the castle in the spring, summer and autumn, and she has a little café in the village too – which she runs with the help of friends. They need the money because the castle is always wanting repairs. I happened to mention what a good cook you are and she wondered if you might like to give her a hand,' Ryan grinned. 'The Laird is writing a war novel based on his father's experiences in WWI and Mairie needs to help him with typing and his notes – so she could really do with more help...'

'I can type a bit,' Janet said and smiled as he nodded. It looked as if Ryan had chosen this place with care, thinking of her happiness as well as his work.

'Maggie will attend the village school, where the Laird's children go, so you can take her in and fetch her and fit in whatever else you want to do during the day. You'll have plenty of chance to make friends here, Jan.'

'Yes,' she smiled at him. 'It's the sort of thing I can do... even when...' She hesitated and then took a deep breath. 'Don't get anxious, Ryan. My doctor says everything looks normal – but he thinks it is probably a Christmas baby...'

'Baby? I can't believe it...' Delight followed by doubt flickered in his face. 'That's wonderful news - as long as you're all right?'

'I couldn't say before, because the first couple of months are when it was likely I would miscarry, but the doctor says he thinks I'll be fine this time.'

Ryan nodded, coming to put his arms about her and hold her carefully. 'I'll find out about hospitals and doctors up here, love – but if Peggy wants to come and look after you nearer the time, don't push her away like you did before.'

'No, I shan't,' Janet said, smiling at him. 'I will invite her to stay here with us – not until much nearer the time, though. Besides, I should imagine Mairie will know things like that, Ryan, about doctors and midwives...'

'Yes, she has three children, but you mustn't shut your mother out, love...' He looked thoughtful. 'Have you told Peggy and Able yet?'

'No. I wanted to tell you first and I wanted to be sure I wasn't going to lose it before I said anything.' Janet smiled. 'I went to a specialist in London and he said I could visit if I needed him – and if I let him know in plenty of time, he would visit us here. Apparently, he has some relatives in Scotland and could combine the business trip with pleasure.'

'We must telephone Peggy tonight and tell her,' Ryan said. 'Your mother is such a sensible lady and I'd like her to come and stay a bit nearer the time.' He counted back on his fingers. 'At Christmas – so that means September...'

'Yes, middle to end of September, I imagine,' Janet said and smiled because Ryan had taken it so easily.

'Mummy...' Maggie came running back into the cosy parlour, banishing Janet's thoughts. Her daughter had been exploring all over the cottage. 'I've found my room with my things in – and the window overlooks a field. There is a pony in it...'

'Yes, Maggie,' Ryan said, smiling at her. 'The pony belongs to your friend Angus and he says that if you'd like to learn to ride it, he will come and teach you on Saturday mornings, and Sunday too if you want.'

'He's beautiful – sort of red and white,' Maggie said excitedly. 'Can I ride him, Mum?'

'Yes, of course, if you want to,' Janet agreed. 'I'm quite sure Angus will look after you – and it will be nice for you to ride out in a place like this.' She looked at Ryan. 'Are we allowed to go where we like on the Laird's estate?'

'Yes, that goes with the cottage,' he said.

Janet looked at him and smiled. 'It seems that life is going to be very different here, Ryan.'

'Yes. I think the magic we found at Christmas is still in this place – don't you, love?'

'Yes, it certainly is,' Janet agreed.

37

'Oh, Jan,' Peggy said, smiling as she heard the excitement in her daughter's voice. 'The house sounds wonderful – and your news is the best of all. Just take care of yourself, darling. If there is anything I can do, you only have to say.'

'If you could come up and stay a bit nearer the time,' Janet said a little tentatively. 'It is beautiful here but a bit out of the way – and if the baby came as quickly as Maggie did...'

'It is better to have someone to organise things,' Peggy said quickly. 'I shall make sure I come, love. Sheila's baby should be here at the end of August, so it will be all babies and knitting for the next few months.' She paused then, 'How do you feel?'

'Wonderful – and even better since I saw the house. I wasn't looking forward to it, Mum, but it's so warm and cosy – and Maggie has a pony to ride. It belongs to Angus – the man who made sure she didn't go to the loch on her own that day.'

'He sounds reliable and trustworthy,' Peggy said. 'I'm so glad you're settling in, Jan, and I think you will all be very happy up there.'

'Yes, I think we shall,' Janet told her. 'It was magical at Christmas, Mum, and some of that magic seems to have lingered on. Maggie is running about all over and she absolutely loves it.'

'It is all very exciting,' Peggy said. 'I'll have two new grandchildren next year and I'm looking forward to that!'

They chatted for a bit longer and then Janet rang off because Maggie was calling for her to come and look at something.

Peggy smiled as she saw Able standing at the end of the hall looking at her curiously.

'Everything all right, hon?'

'Yes, fine,' she said. 'Ryan was teasing her with that modern house – they've got a wonderful old lodge house and Maggie's been loaned a pony, so she's going to learn to ride.' She went and hugged him. 'But that's not the best news, Able – Janet is having another baby and she's asked if I'll go up and stay next September, just in case she delivers in a rush, as she did with Maggie. I wasn't there then...'

'And she shut you out afterwards. I remember,' he said and bent his head to kiss her. 'I can see you're happy about it, Peggy. I'm glad for Janet and Ryan and I pray everything goes well for them now. They've had a rough time for a while and it's time they were settled.'

'Janet thinks it's Scotland. She says it's magical all around that area and they love it. I shall enjoy staying with her for the birth – and now I've got Pearl, you'll be able to manage without me.'

'You'll go to your daughter because she's asked and will need you,' he said, 'but the twins and I never want to be without you, Peggy.'

'I know.' She looked at him seriously. 'Sandra's problems made me realise how very lucky we were,' she said. 'I know she's getting it sorted now, but she almost lost her mum and her dad isn't always the person she loves and wants him to be. We have to make the most of all we have, Able. I'm so glad we moved back here. The café earned us a lot of money, but time with those you love is worth far more.'

'If everyone understood that, the world would be a happier place,' Able said and kissed her softly. They heard a shuffling sound on the stairs and then giggling. Turning, he saw Freddie and Fay jostling each other. Freddie was looking pleased with the world, but Fay was scowling.

'Are we going skating soon, Mum?' she demanded in a plaintive tone. 'I haven't been since Aunty Janet left with Maggie.'

'And that is one day.' Peggy said. 'Your dad and I have been busy, Fay, but I'll take you tomorrow.'

'If you tell me which bus to catch, I'll go with Fay,' Freddie said. 'You don't have to come, Mum. We know you're busy.'

'I want to make sure the lessons are arranged properly and that Fay has all the stuff she needs for her skating,' Peggy said. 'I'll be opening the bed and breakfast next week, so I may let you two go on your own then, but I'll come with you tomorrow and make sure you both know exactly what to do and which buses to catch.'

Freddie nodded and took his sister by the arm. 'Come on, let's get something to eat and a cup of cocoa before we go to bed. We can read for a while then.'

'He's growing up fast,' Able said, watching his son lead his twin away firmly. 'Sometimes, I think he must be at least two years older than Fay.'

'Freddie is very sensible,' Peggy said and smiled at him lovingly. 'I think he gets his nature from you, Able. If Fay is impatient and selfish, she must get it from me.'

'You don't have a selfish bone in your body,' her husband responded warmly.

'I'd better see how they're getting on with their supper.'

'No, leave them to it,' Able murmured with a sparkle in his eyes. 'It will do them good to learn – and I'll clear up the mess.'

Peggy laughed because she knew that the result of Freddie and Fay getting supper would be a pile of used plates and spills on the pine table, but it was easy to clean and Able was right: her twins were learning to flutter their wings and she had to let them, because it would be good for them both in their future lives.

Smiling at her husband, she decided to pop next door to the pub. Rose was helping out behind the bar so Sheila didn't need her, but she would enjoy a few minutes' chat with some of her old customers and Able could manage the kids perfectly on his own – he might even enjoy a bit of time to himself. There was a programme about

American politics on the wireless that evening and he would listen to that; Able seldom spoke of his home, perhaps because he had no one close there any more, and, as he always told her, these days his home was her and the kids and the country he'd adopted when he came here during the war.

She smiled to herself. Apart from buying American goods when he could, Able didn't bother much with the land of his birth. They had a nice meal at Thanksgiving and he sometimes spoke of what was happening over there, but never with regret or nostalgia. Able was content to live in the country that had accepted him after the war but then, as he so often told her, he could be happy anywhere as long as he had her and the children.

Rose beamed at Peggy as she entered the bar. She was pulling a pint for one of the customers. The man wasn't someone Peggy knew, but there were a lot of new people in the lanes and most of them found their way to the Pig & Whistle for a drink now and then.

'I thought I'd pop in,' Peggy said, glancing round. 'You're busy at the moment – where is Sheila?'

'She was fetching some sausage rolls a customer wanted warmed up,' Rose said. She took her customer's money and moved closer to Peggy. 'I'm glad you came in – I wanted to tell you my news...'

Rose was looking happy and very beautiful, her red hair shining in the lights of the bar. Peggy's spine tingled and she was sure she knew what Rose was going to tell her, but she waited for her to speak.

'Tom and me – we're havin' another baby,' Rose said and the words bubbled out of her. 'It must have happened just after Christmas...' She gave a little giggle. 'I thought Jackie might be the last – but Tom is over the moon. He wants another girl, though I warned him it might be a boy.'

'That is fantastic news,' Peggy said and laughed. 'I think there must have been something in the air this Christmas – you, Sheila and Janet – you're all having babies around the same time...' She looked at Rose in wonder. 'It's a bit like in the war – Maureen, I and Ellie all had babies within a few months of each other.'

'A little bit of Christmas magic,' Rose said. 'I wanted to tell you and Maureen, Peggy, because when I was ill that time... well, if it hadn't been for you two and Tom's father, I might have died. I felt as if my life was over and I should never be happy again, but now I'm so happy.'

'Good.' Peggy smiled at her. 'Have you heard from Jack recently?'

'He's coming home next month for a couple of weeks holiday,' Rose told her. 'You'll see him then, Peggy. Jack thinks a lot of you, always has.'

Peggy nodded. There had been a time when she was going through a bad patch with Laurie when Jack had been good to her and she'd known he liked her, but then she'd met Able. Jack had gone off to foreign parts with the Army and married a widow, with whom she understood, he was very happy.

'Jack was a good friend in the war to all of us...he sorted that devil out who hurt poor Ellie and made us all feel a bit safer...' Peggy confirmed to Jack's daughter-in-law and went to serve one of her neighbours with a pint. She was soon hearing all about Mr Johnson from number five's troubles at work.

'I told the so-and-so – if he don't like me havin' a day orf work ter take me missus to the hospital, he can shove it.'

'Oh, Bert,' Peggy said. 'You've worked in that lumber yard for years – what else would you do?'

'I'd get a job down the docks. There's a new lumber yard set up and they're looking for a manager. I reckon I could earn twice what I get from old stingy Banks.'

Peggy smiled. She knew that Bert Johnson liked to grumble. His boss wouldn't sack him and he wouldn't leave the lumber yard where he'd worked for so many years, but he just enjoyed threatening to leave.

'Have a pint on me, Bert,' she said. 'You tell old stingy, I'm sure you'd do well as the manager of that new yard.'

She pulled him a pint and put the money in the till. It wasn't her pub now and she was scrupulous about paying for drinks she gave away, but that didn't stop her treating special customers now and then.

The door opened and Maureen and Gordon walked in; while Gordon found them a table, Maureen came straight up to the bar to where Peggy was standing. She blew on her hands, giving an exaggerated shiver.

'It's cold out,' Peggy said. 'Never mind you'll soon warm up in here, love.'

'Yes, it's lovely and warm in here,' Maureen replied, then, 'Did you hear about Harry Lauder dying? It was on the wireless. I liked him...'

'Yes, so did I,' Peggy said. 'He was a wonderful comedian...' The Scottish actor had been very famous, earning more than £2,500 a week at the height of his fame and a knighthood. 'It is sad...'

'Yes, it is,' Maureen agreed. 'Anyway, let's think of something happier – Able told us your wonderful news – I know Janet must be delighted. She was worried about trying again and that's only natural, but once a baby is on the way, well that's it.'

'Yes, I know,' Peggy said. 'I'll be offering a few prayers to keep them both safe, Maureen, but apparently her doctor thinks the baby has taken well this time.'

'Good.' Maureen ordered their drinks and insisted on paying for them even though Peggy tried to wave her money away. 'I'm going to leave you to get on for a while, Peggy love – but when you get a minute, come and sit with us.'

'Yes, all right, I shall.' Peggy said.

She turned to serve a couple of new customers with pints and then Sheila came through from the direction of the kitchen carrying a basket of delicious-smelling warm sausage rolls. She placed them on the counter and they were soon being dispensed on to plates with little pots of her home-made pickles.

'They do smell good – can I try one?'

Sheila nodded and Peggy helped herself.

'Scrumptious, Sheila. I wasn't hungry until I smelled those.' She gave her daughter-in-law a look of approval. 'How do you feel, love?'

'I'm fine, Peggy,' Sheila said. 'Have you heard Rose's news? Tom popped in to look at a job I want doing in the kitchen and he was full of it.'

'Yes, she told me.' Peggy laughed. 'Janet is pregnant too – a few weeks after you, Sheila. We shall have new babies all round.'

'Oh, that's lovely,' Sheila said and placed a hand to the middle of her back.

'Are you all right, love?' Peggy asked. 'I think we can manage in here if you'd like an early night.'

'Well, if you're sure.' Sheila looked at her fondly. 'I wouldn't mind putting my feet up – and now you're here, I know things will be all right.'

'That's what I'm here for, love.'

'Thanks, Peggy. It makes us all feel better now you're back – I'll swear there's more customers in here tonight than there have been for months. They all love you, Peggy.'

Feeling the sting of emotional tears, Peggy brushed them away. Her heart swelled with love and pride as she looked about her and saw all the smiling faces. This was her place, her people, and she loved being back. The café had been an adventure, but now she was home and it felt good.

MORE FROM ROSIE CLARKE

We hope you enjoyed reading *A Reunion at Mulberry Lane*. If you did, please leave a review.

If you'd like to gift a copy, this book is also available as an ebook, digital audio download and audiobook CD.

Sign up to Rosie Clarke's mailing list for news, competitions and updates on future books.

http://bit.ly/RosieClarkeNewsletter

Why not explore the *Welcome to Harpers Emporium* series, another bestselling series from Rosie Clarke!

ABOUT THE AUTHOR

Rosie Clarke is a #1 bestselling saga writer whose most recent books include *The Mulberry Lane* series. She has written over 100 novels under different pseudonyms and is a RNA Award winner. She lives in Cambridgeshire.

Visit Rosie Clarke's website: http://www.rosieclarke.co.uk

Follow Rosie on social media:

 twitter.com/AnneHerries

 bookbub.com/authors/rosie-clarke

 facebook.com/Rosie-clarke-119457351778432

PINL

ABOUT BOLDWOOD BOOKS

Boldwood Books is a fiction publishing company seeking out the best stories from around the world.

Find out more at www.boldwoodbooks.com

Sign up to the Book and Tonic newsletter for news, offers and competitions from Boldwood Books!

http://www.bit.ly/bookandtonic

We'd love to hear from you, follow us on social media:

 facebook.com/BookandTonic
twitter.com/BoldwoodBooks
instagram.com/BookandTonic

Newport Library and Information Service

Newport Community
Learning & Libraries

Lightning Source UK Ltd.
Milton Keynes UK
UKHW020716121220
375051UK00009B/314